ANNA SEV

BLACK BEAUTY

THE GRAPHIC NOVEL

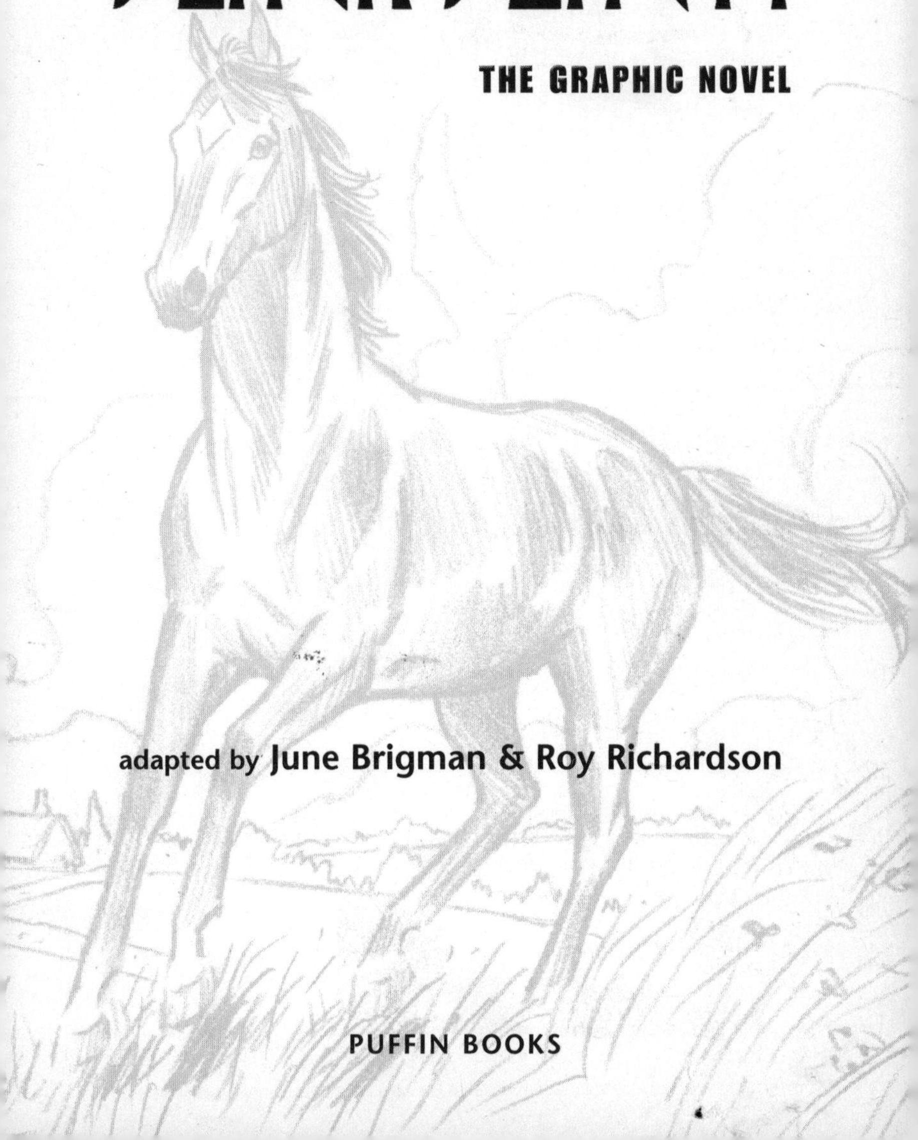

adapted by June Brigman & Roy Richardson

PUFFIN BOOKS

PUFFIN BOOKS
Published by the Penguin Group
Penguin Young Readers Group
345 Hudson Street, New York, NY 10014 U.S.A.
Penguin Group (Canada). 10 Alcorn Avenue, Toronto, Ontario, Canada M4V 3B2
(a division of Pearson Penguin Canada Inc.)
Penguin Books Ltd, 80 Strand, London WC2R 0RL, England
Penguin Ireland, 25 St. Stephen's Green, Dublin 2, Ireland
(a division of Penguin Books Ltd)
Penguin Group (Australia), 250 Camberwell Road, Camberwell, Victoria 3124,
Australia (a division of Pearson Australia Group Pty Ltd)
Penguin Books India Pvt Ltd, 11 Community Centre, Panchsheel Park,
New Delhi – 110 017, India
Penguin Group (NZ), Cnr Airborne and Rosedale Roads, Albany, Auckland 1310,
New Zealand (a division of Pearson New Zealand Ltd)
Penguin Books (South Africa) (Pty) Ltd, 24 Sturdee Avenue, Rosebank,
Johannesburg 2196, South Africa

Registered Offices: Penguin Books Ltd, 80 Strand, London WC2R 0RL, England

First Published by Puffin Books, a division of Penguin Young Readers Group, 2005

10 9 8 7

Copyright © 2005 Byron Preiss Visual Publications
All rights reserved

A Byron Preiss Book
Byron Preiss Visual Publications
24 West 25th Street, New York, NY 10010

Art assistants: Bob Berry, Al Milgrom and Keith Williams
Special thanks to Michael Kaluta for reference and inspiration.
Cover art by Bob Larkin
Lettering by J. Vita
Series Editor: Dwight Jon Zimmerman
Series Assistant Editor: April Isaacs
Interior Design by M. Postawa & Gilda Hannah
Cover Design by M. Postawa

Puffin Books ISBN 0-14-240408-X

Printed in the United States of America

BLACK BEAUTY

CHAPTER ONE: MY EARLY HOME

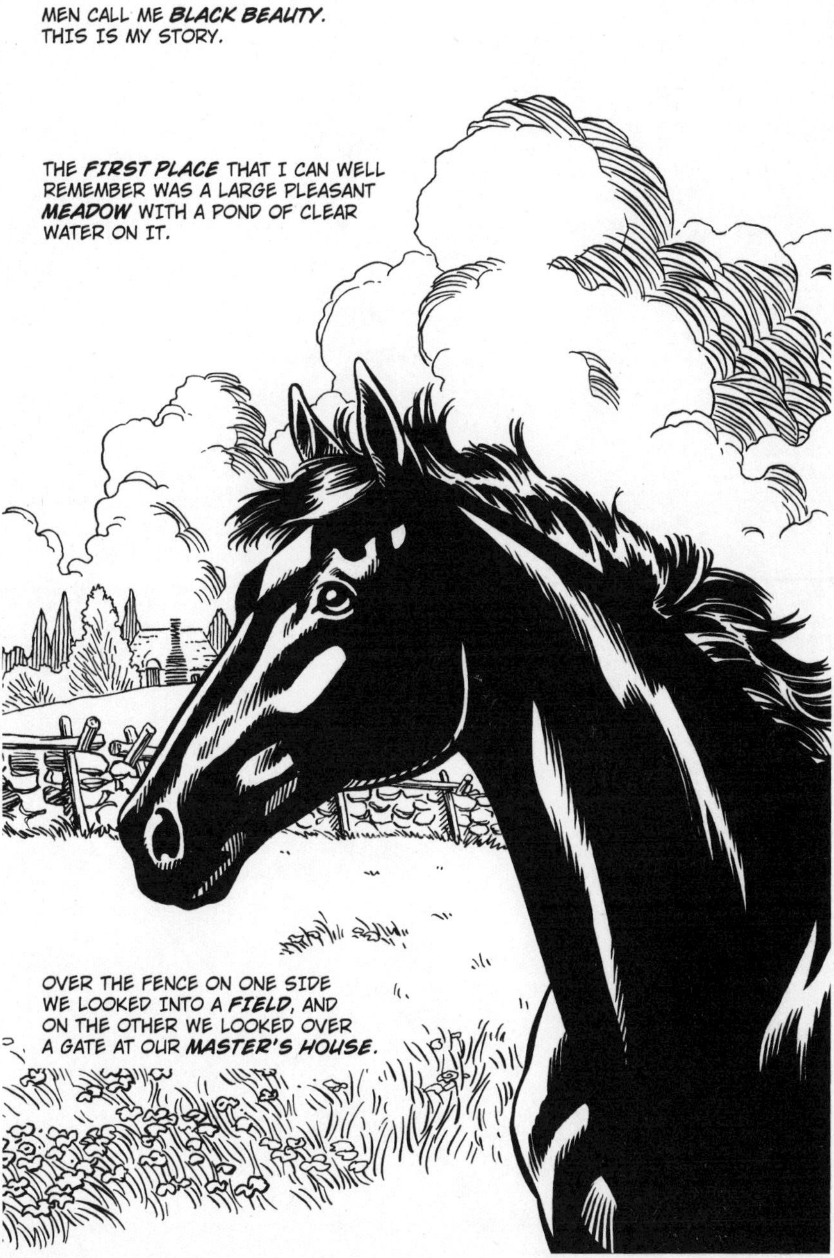
MEN CALL ME *BLACK BEAUTY*. THIS IS MY STORY.
THE *FIRST PLACE* THAT I CAN WELL REMEMBER WAS A LARGE PLEASANT *MEADOW* WITH A POND OF CLEAR WATER ON IT.
OVER THE FENCE ON ONE SIDE WE LOOKED INTO A *FIELD*, AND ON THE OTHER WE LOOKED OVER A GATE AT OUR *MASTER'S HOUSE*.

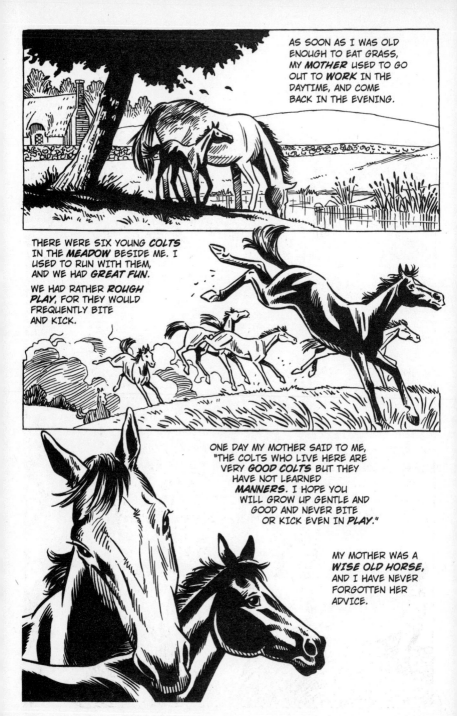

AS SOON AS I WAS OLD ENOUGH TO EAT GRASS, MY **MOTHER** USED TO GO OUT TO **WORK** IN THE DAYTIME, AND COME BACK IN THE EVENING.

THERE WERE SIX YOUNG **COLTS** IN THE **MEADOW** BESIDE ME. I USED TO RUN WITH THEM, AND WE HAD **GREAT FUN**.

WE HAD RATHER **ROUGH PLAY**, FOR THEY WOULD FREQUENTLY BITE AND KICK.

ONE DAY MY MOTHER SAID TO ME, "THE COLTS WHO LIVE HERE ARE VERY **GOOD COLTS** BUT THEY HAVE NOT LEARNED **MANNERS**. I HOPE YOU WILL GROW UP GENTLE AND GOOD AND NEVER BITE OR KICK EVEN IN **PLAY**."

MY MOTHER WAS A **WISE OLD HORSE**, AND I HAVE NEVER FORGOTTEN HER ADVICE.

6

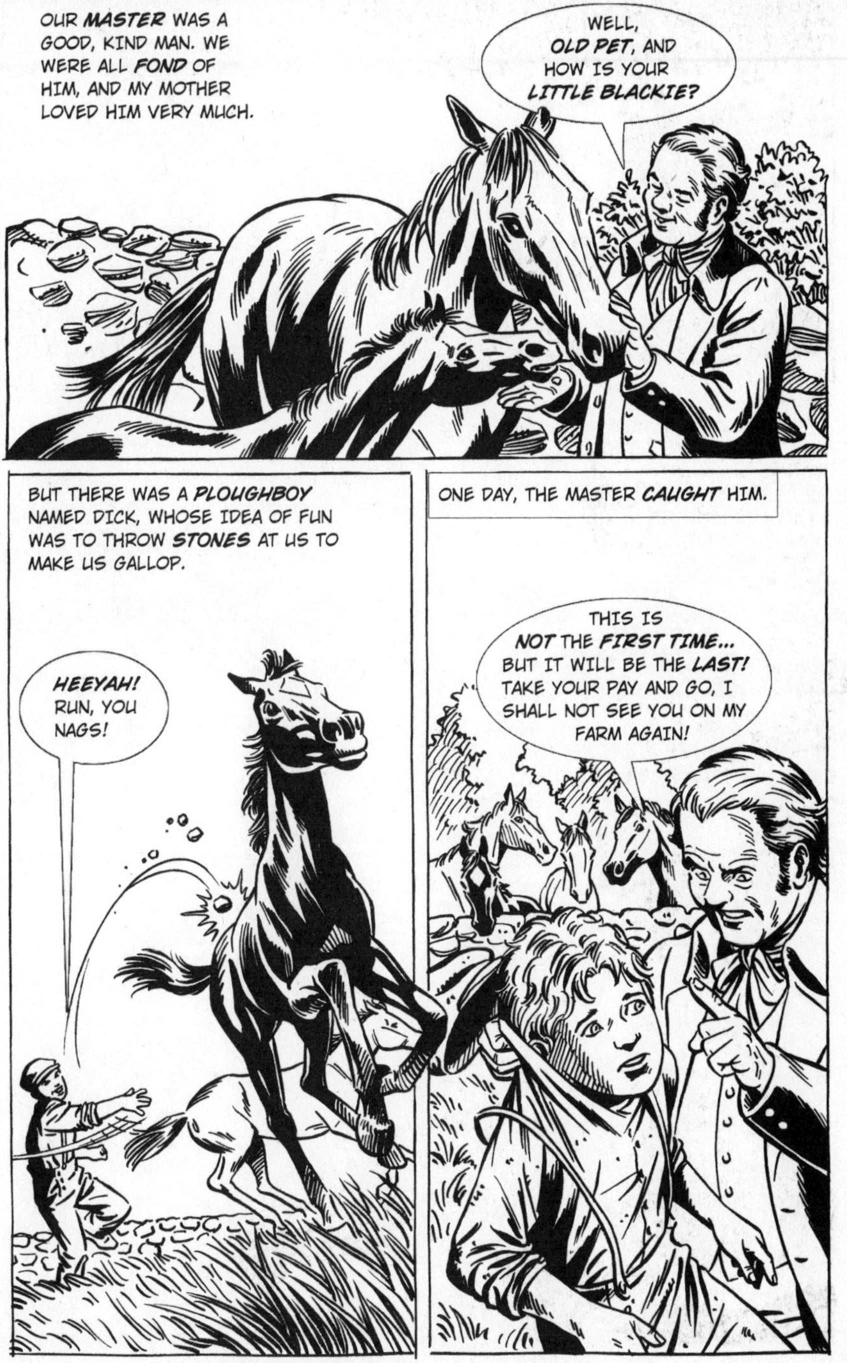
OUR MASTER WAS A GOOD, KIND MAN. WE WERE ALL FOND OF HIM, AND MY MOTHER LOVED HIM VERY MUCH.
WELL, OLD PET, AND HOW IS YOUR LITTLE BLACKIE?
BUT THERE WAS A PLOUGHBOY NAMED DICK, WHOSE IDEA OF FUN WAS TO THROW STONES AT US TO MAKE US GALLOP.
HEEYAH! RUN, YOU NAGS!
ONE DAY, THE MASTER CAUGHT HIM.
THIS IS NOT THE FIRST TIME... BUT IT WILL BE THE LAST! TAKE YOUR PAY AND GO, I SHALL NOT SEE YOU ON MY FARM AGAIN!

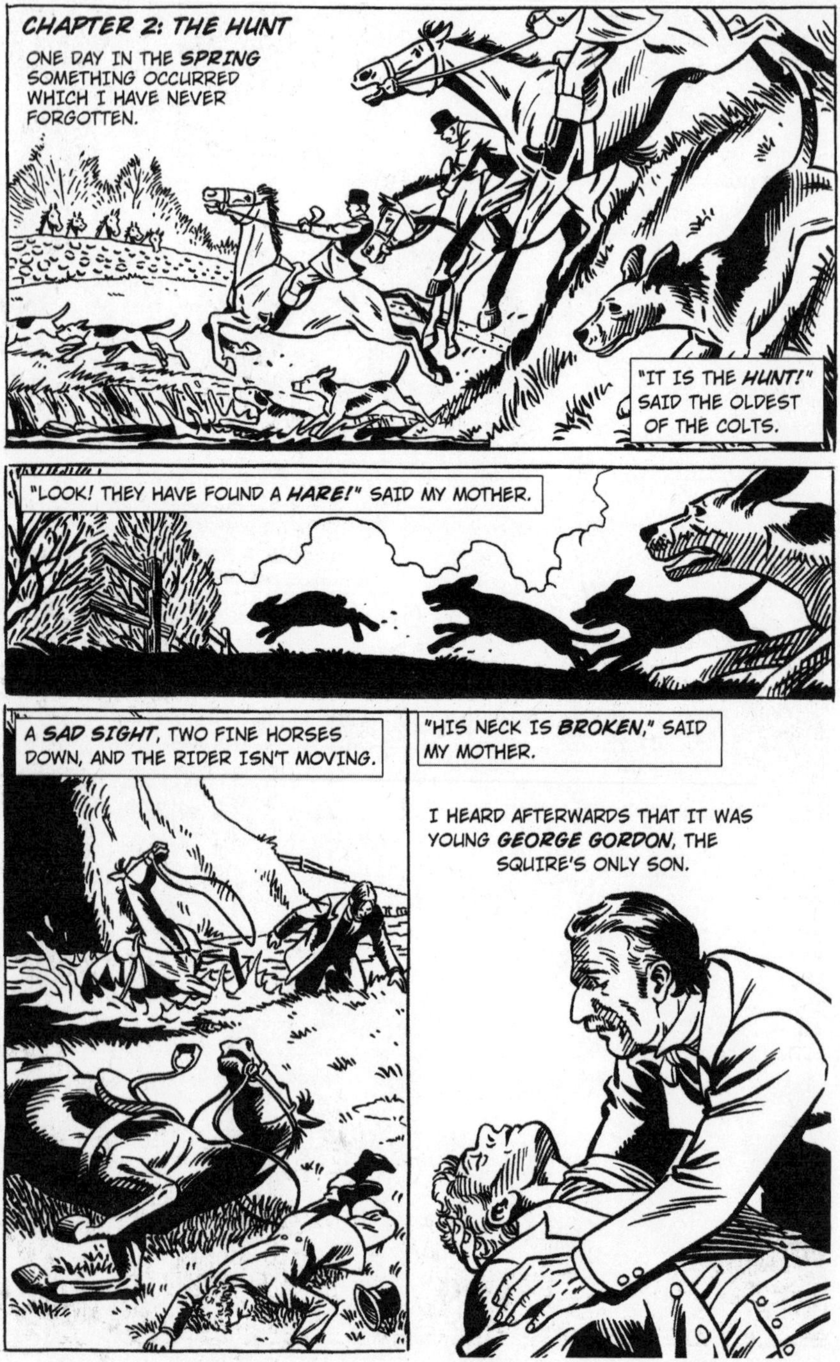
CHAPTER 2: THE HUNT
ONE DAY IN THE SPRING SOMETHING OCCURRED WHICH I HAVE NEVER FORGOTTEN.
"IT IS THE HUNT!" SAID THE OLDEST OF THE COLTS.
"LOOK! THEY HAVE FOUND A HARE!" SAID MY MOTHER.
A SAD SIGHT, TWO FINE HORSES DOWN, AND THE RIDER ISN'T MOVING.
"HIS NECK IS BROKEN," SAID MY MOTHER.
I HEARD AFTERWARDS THAT IT WAS YOUNG GEORGE GORDON, THE SQUIRE'S ONLY SON.

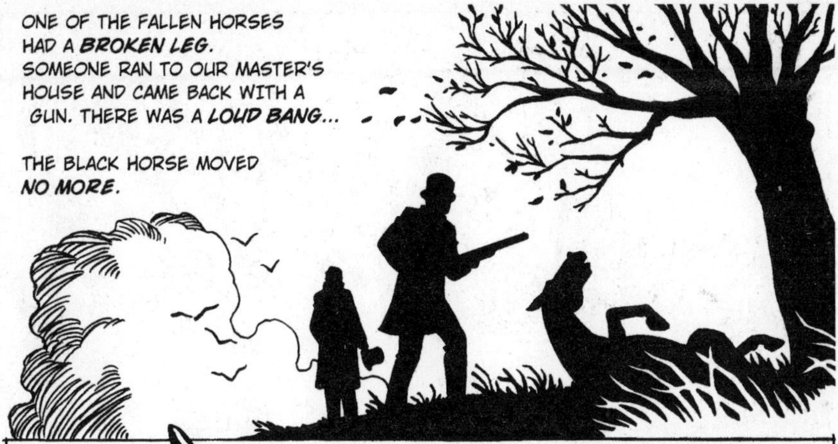
ONE OF THE FALLEN HORSES HAD A **BROKEN LEG.** SOMEONE RAN TO OUR MASTER'S HOUSE AND CAME BACK WITH A GUN. THERE WAS A **LOUD BANG...**
THE BLACK HORSE MOVED **NO MORE.**

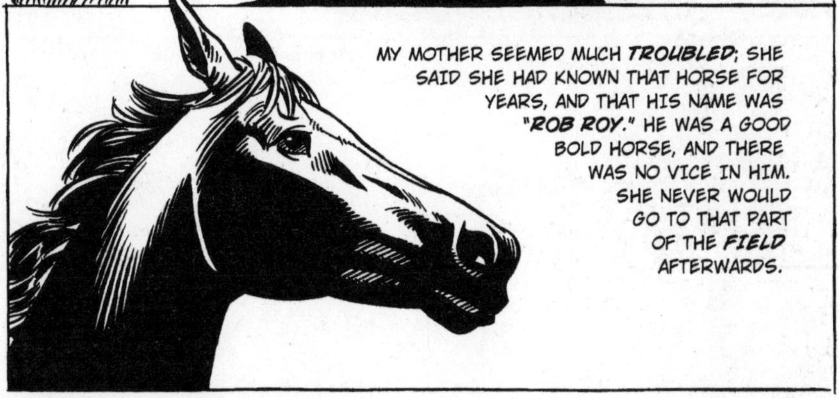
MY MOTHER SEEMED MUCH **TROUBLED**; SHE SAID SHE HAD KNOWN THAT HORSE FOR YEARS, AND THAT HIS NAME WAS "**ROB ROY.**" HE WAS A GOOD BOLD HORSE, AND THERE WAS NO VICE IN HIM. SHE NEVER WOULD GO TO THAT PART OF THE **FIELD** AFTERWARDS.

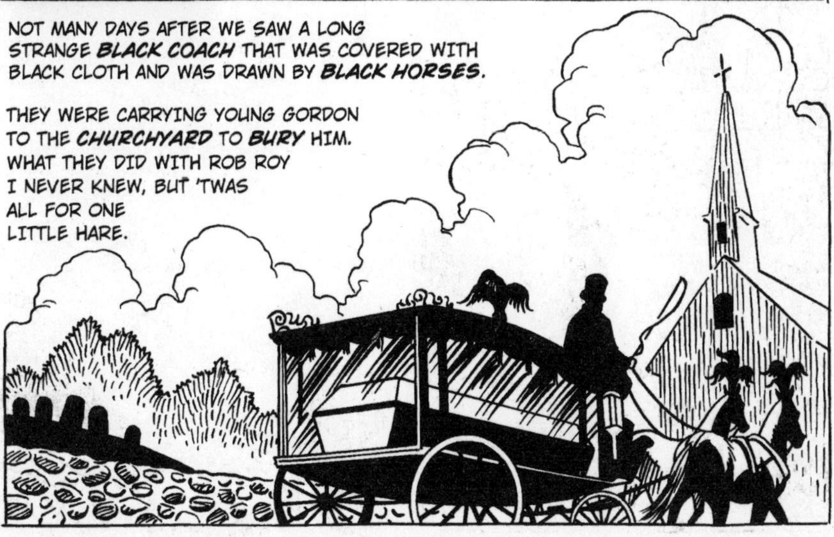
NOT MANY DAYS AFTER WE SAW A LONG STRANGE **BLACK COACH** THAT WAS COVERED WITH BLACK CLOTH AND WAS DRAWN BY **BLACK HORSES.**
THEY WERE CARRYING YOUNG GORDON TO THE **CHURCHYARD** TO **BURY** HIM. WHAT THEY DID WITH ROB ROY I NEVER KNEW, BUT 'TWAS ALL FOR ONE LITTLE HARE.

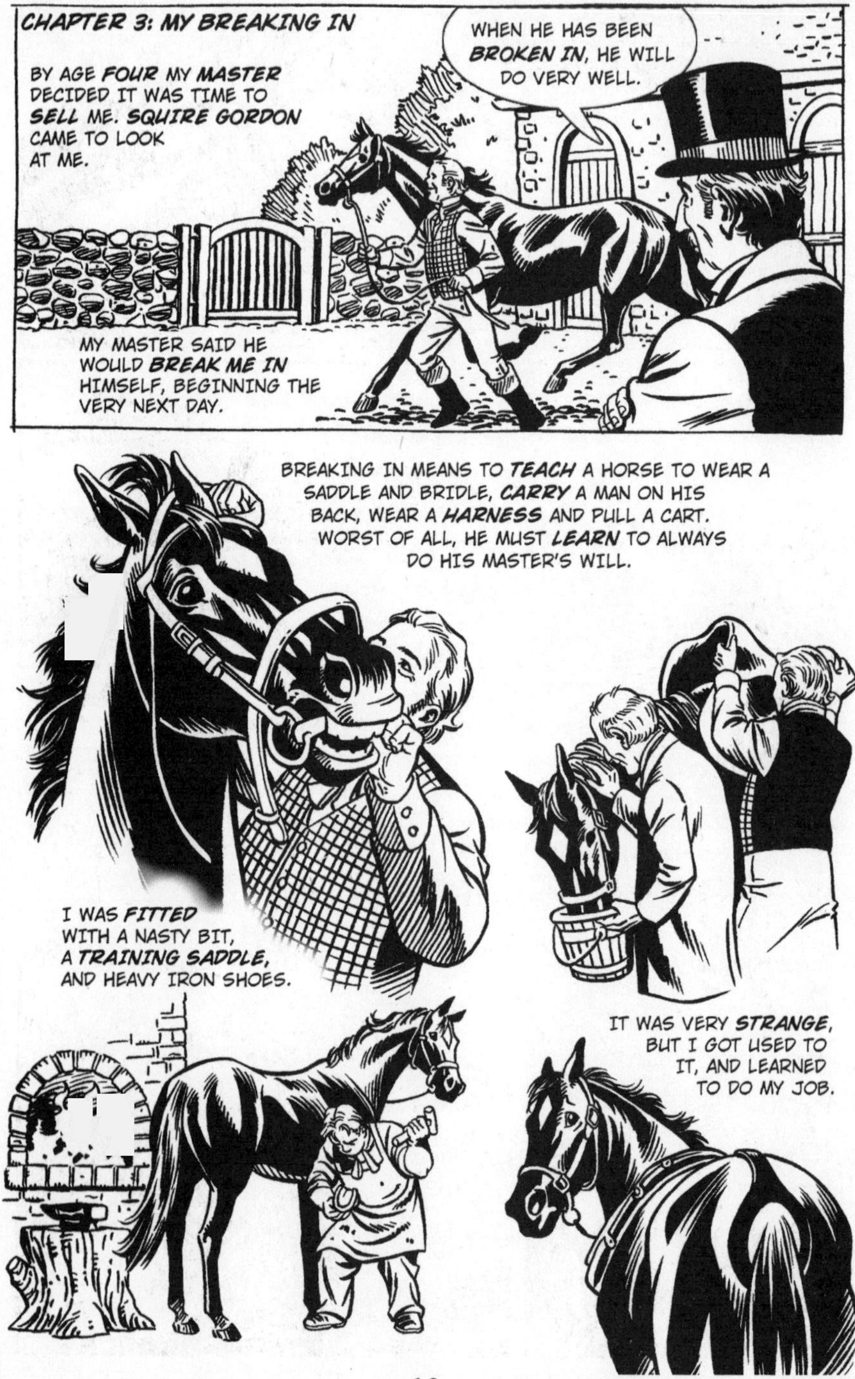
CHAPTER 3: MY BREAKING IN
BY AGE FOUR MY MASTER DECIDED IT WAS TIME TO SELL ME. SQUIRE GORDON CAME TO LOOK AT ME.
WHEN HE HAS BEEN BROKEN IN, HE WILL DO VERY WELL.
MY MASTER SAID HE WOULD BREAK ME IN HIMSELF, BEGINNING THE VERY NEXT DAY.
BREAKING IN MEANS TO TEACH A HORSE TO WEAR A SADDLE AND BRIDLE, CARRY A MAN ON HIS BACK, WEAR A HARNESS AND PULL A CART. WORST OF ALL, HE MUST LEARN TO ALWAYS DO HIS MASTER'S WILL.
I WAS FITTED WITH A NASTY BIT, A TRAINING SADDLE, AND HEAVY IRON SHOES.
IT WAS VERY STRANGE, BUT I GOT USED TO IT, AND LEARNED TO DO MY JOB.

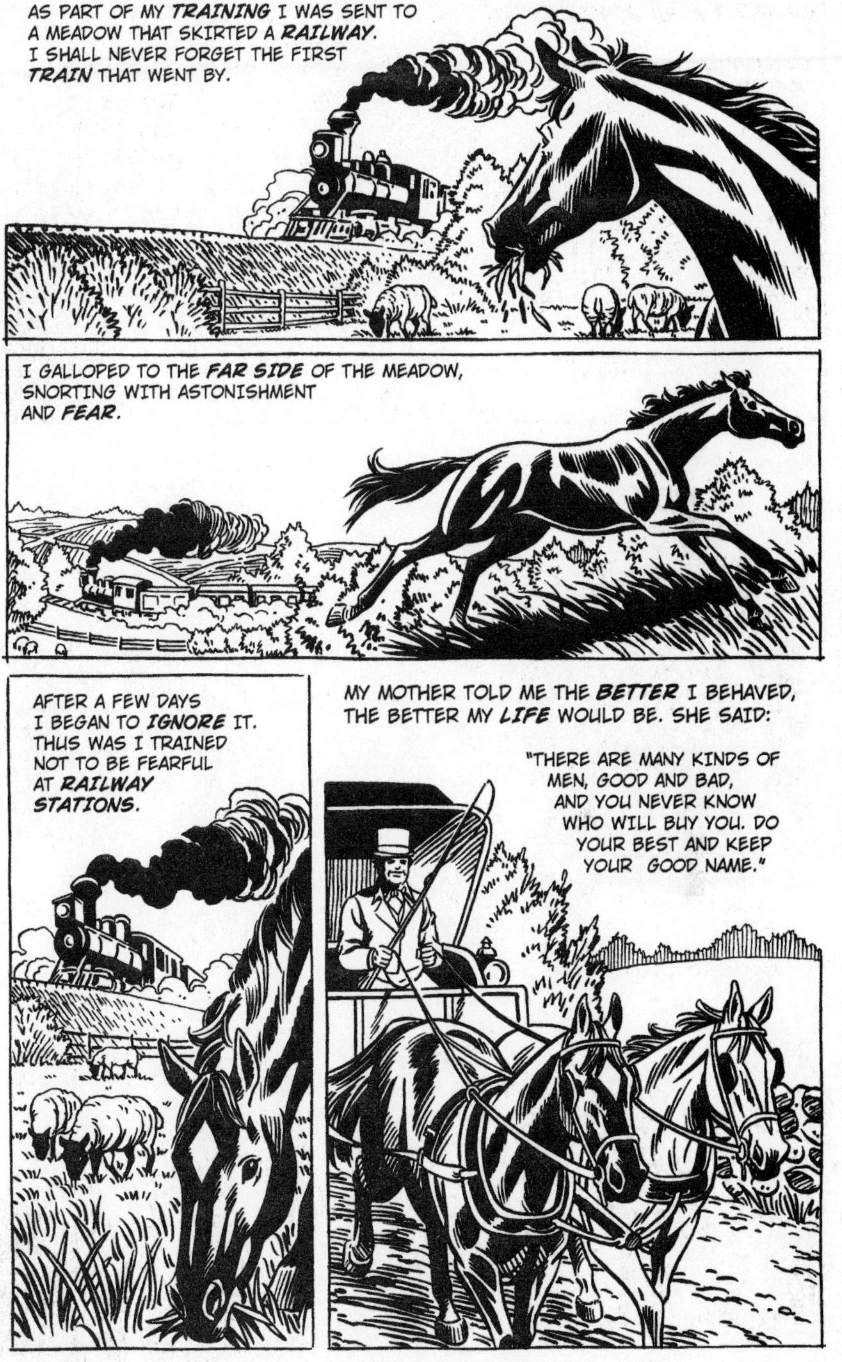
AS PART OF MY TRAINING I WAS SENT TO A MEADOW THAT SKIRTED A RAILWAY. I SHALL NEVER FORGET THE FIRST TRAIN THAT WENT BY.
I GALLOPED TO THE FAR SIDE OF THE MEADOW, SNORTING WITH ASTONISHMENT AND FEAR.
AFTER A FEW DAYS I BEGAN TO IGNORE IT. THUS WAS I TRAINED NOT TO BE FEARFUL AT RAILWAY STATIONS.
MY MOTHER TOLD ME THE BETTER I BEHAVED, THE BETTER MY LIFE WOULD BE. SHE SAID:
"THERE ARE MANY KINDS OF MEN, GOOD AND BAD, AND YOU NEVER KNOW WHO WILL BUY YOU. DO YOUR BEST AND KEEP YOUR GOOD NAME."

CHAPTER FOUR: BIRTWICK PARK

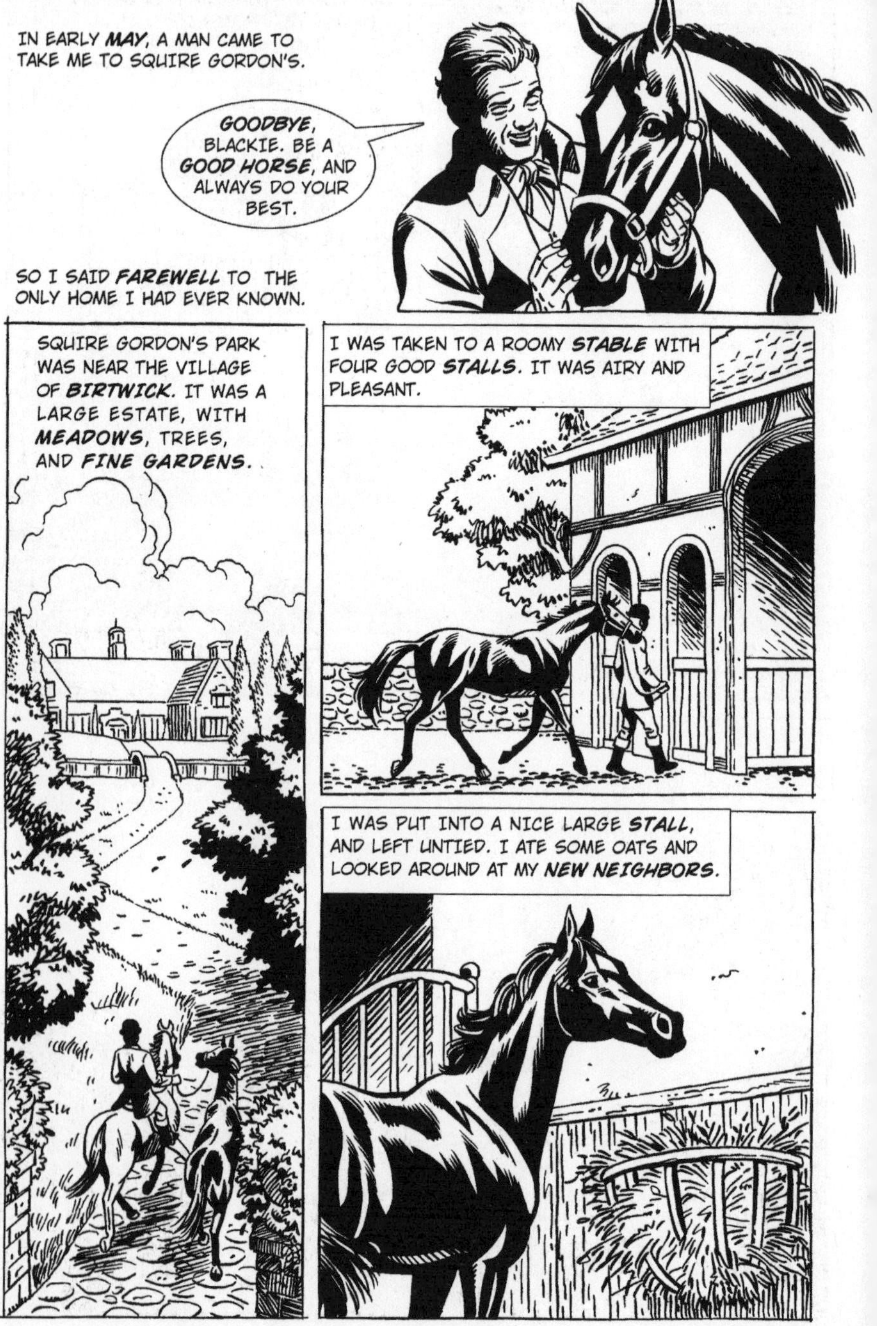
IN EARLY MAY, A MAN CAME TO TAKE ME TO SQUIRE GORDON'S.
GOODBYE, BLACKIE. BE A GOOD HORSE, AND ALWAYS DO YOUR BEST.
SO I SAID FAREWELL TO THE ONLY HOME I HAD EVER KNOWN.
SQUIRE GORDON'S PARK WAS NEAR THE VILLAGE OF BIRTWICK. IT WAS A LARGE ESTATE, WITH MEADOWS, TREES, AND FINE GARDENS.
I WAS TAKEN TO A ROOMY STABLE WITH FOUR GOOD STALLS. IT WAS AIRY AND PLEASANT.
I WAS PUT INTO A NICE LARGE STALL, AND LEFT UNTIED. I ATE SOME OATS AND LOOKED AROUND AT MY NEW NEIGHBORS.

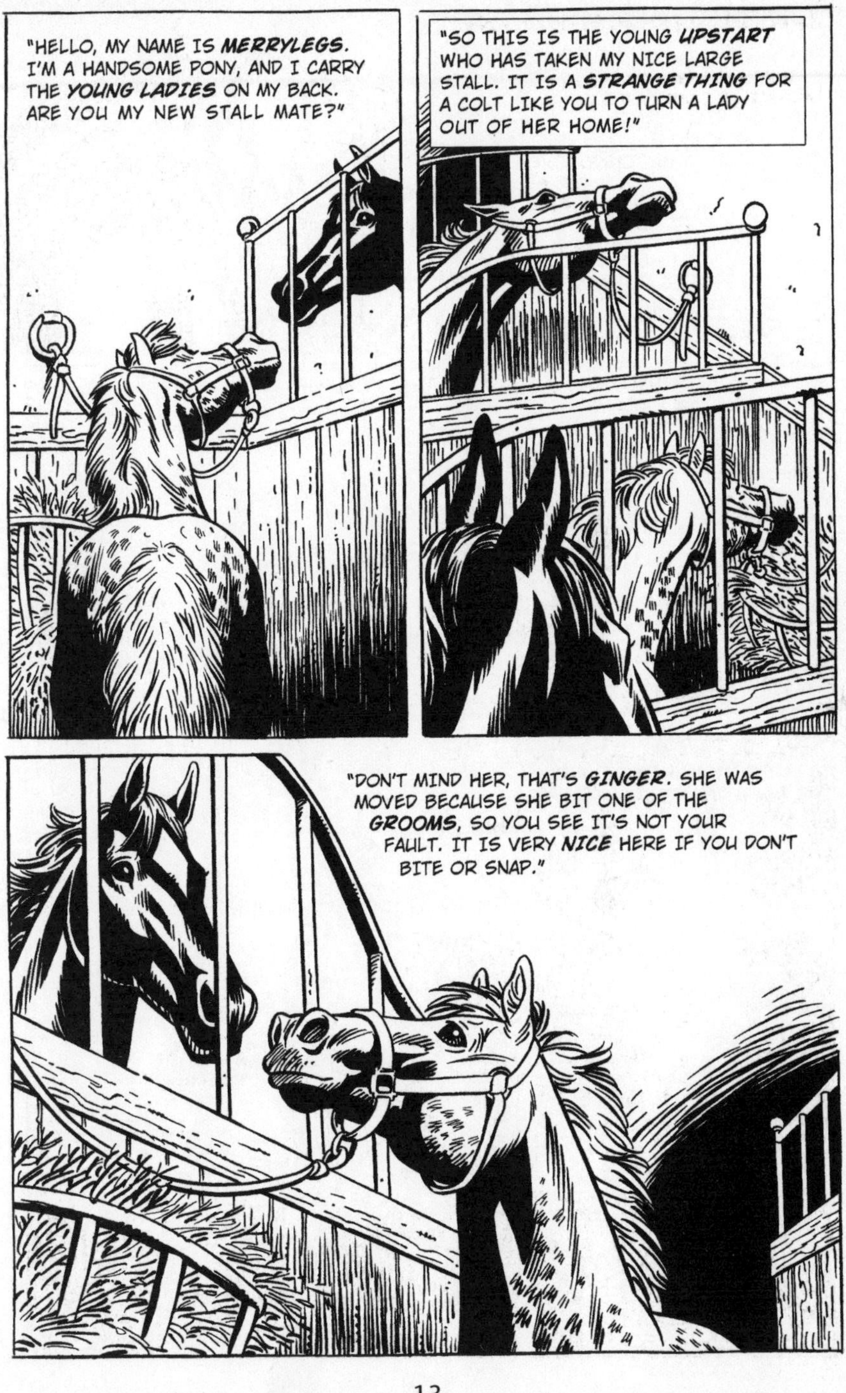
"HELLO, MY NAME IS MERRYLEGS. I'M A HANDSOME PONY, AND I CARRY THE YOUNG LADIES ON MY BACK. ARE YOU MY NEW STALL MATE?"
"SO THIS IS THE YOUNG UPSTART WHO HAS TAKEN MY NICE LARGE STALL. IT IS A STRANGE THING FOR A COLT LIKE YOU TO TURN A LADY OUT OF HER HOME!"
"DON'T MIND HER, THAT'S GINGER. SHE WAS MOVED BECAUSE SHE BIT ONE OF THE GROOMS, SO YOU SEE IT'S NOT YOUR FAULT. IT IS VERY NICE HERE IF YOU DON'T BITE OR SNAP."

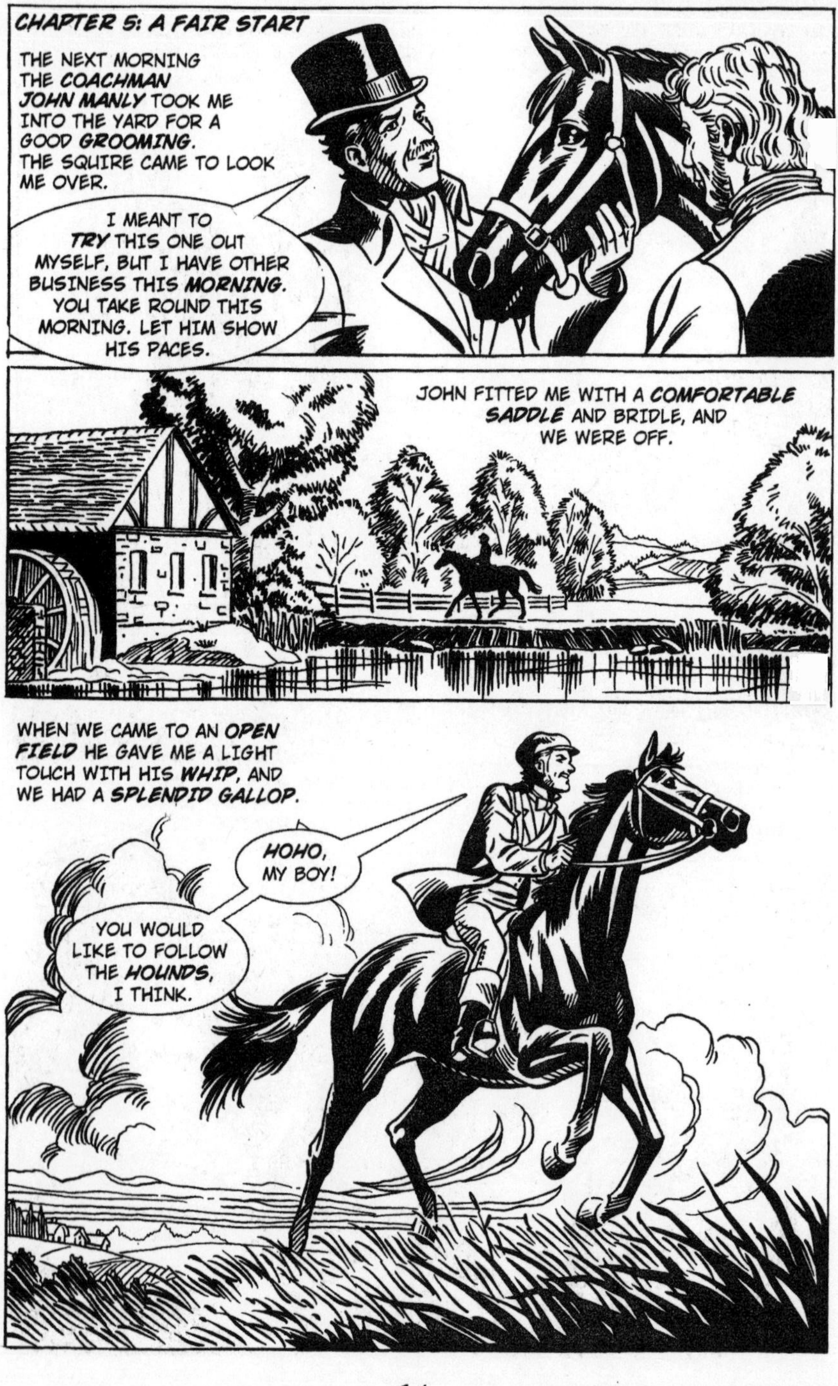
CHAPTER 5: A FAIR START
THE NEXT MORNING THE COACHMAN JOHN MANLY TOOK ME INTO THE YARD FOR A GOOD GROOMING. THE SQUIRE CAME TO LOOK ME OVER.
I MEANT TO TRY THIS ONE OUT MYSELF, BUT I HAVE OTHER BUSINESS THIS MORNING. YOU TAKE ROUND THIS MORNING. LET HIM SHOW HIS PACES.
JOHN FITTED ME WITH A COMFORTABLE SADDLE AND BRIDLE, AND WE WERE OFF.
WHEN WE CAME TO AN OPEN FIELD HE GAVE ME A LIGHT TOUCH WITH HIS WHIP, AND WE HAD A SPLENDID GALLOP.
HOHO, MY BOY!
YOU WOULD LIKE TO FOLLOW THE HOUNDS, I THINK.

AS WE CAME BACK, WE MET THE SQUIRE AND HIS *WIFE* WALKING.

WELL, JOHN, HOW DOES HE *GO*?

FIRST RATE, SIR. HE IS AS FLEET AS A DEER, AND HAS A *FINE SPIRIT*, TOO.

THAT'S WELL. I WILL TRY HIM MYSELF *TOMORROW*.

WE SET OFF EARLY THE *NEXT MORNING*. THE SQUIRE WAS A VERY *GOOD RIDER*, AND THOUGHTFUL FOR HIS HORSE, TOO.

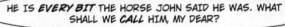

HE IS *EVERY BIT* THE HORSE JOHN SAID HE WAS. WHAT SHALL WE *CALL* HIM, MY DEAR?

FOR SUCH A FINE HORSE, I THINK ONLY *"BLACK BEAUTY"* WILL DO.

BLACK BEAUTY IT SHALL BE THEN!

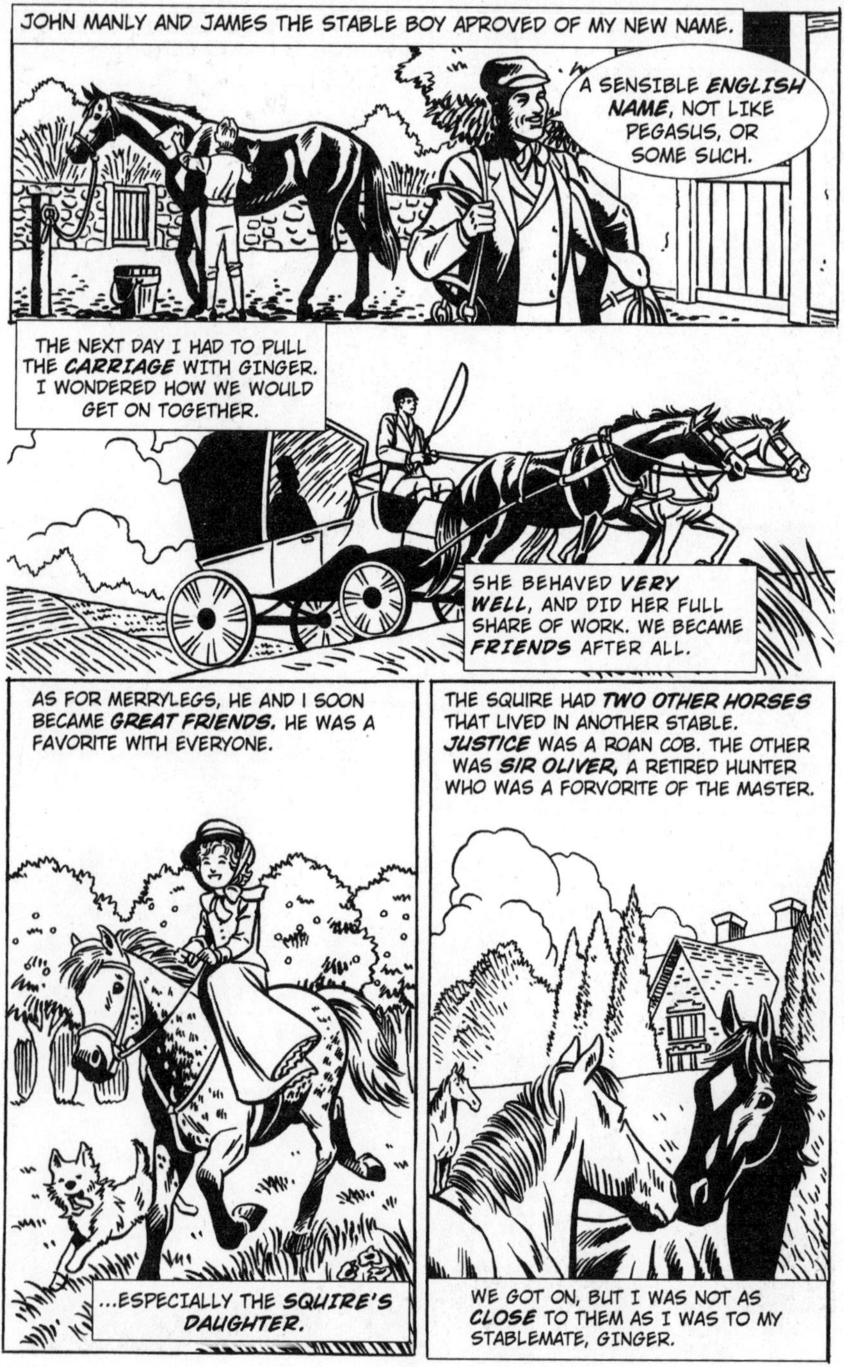

JOHN MANLY AND JAMES THE STABLE BOY APROVED OF MY NEW NAME.
A SENSIBLE ENGLISH NAME, NOT LIKE PEGASUS, OR SOME SUCH.
THE NEXT DAY I HAD TO PULL THE CARRIAGE WITH GINGER. I WONDERED HOW WE WOULD GET ON TOGETHER.
SHE BEHAVED VERY WELL, AND DID HER FULL SHARE OF WORK. WE BECAME FRIENDS AFTER ALL.
AS FOR MERRYLEGS, HE AND I SOON BECAME GREAT FRIENDS. HE WAS A FAVORITE WITH EVERYONE.
...ESPECIALLY THE SQUIRE'S DAUGHTER.
THE SQUIRE HAD TWO OTHER HORSES THAT LIVED IN ANOTHER STABLE. JUSTICE WAS A ROAN COB. THE OTHER WAS SIR OLIVER, A RETIRED HUNTER WHO WAS A FORVORITE OF THE MASTER.
WE GOT ON, BUT I WAS NOT AS CLOSE TO THEM AS I WAS TO MY STABLEMATE, GINGER.

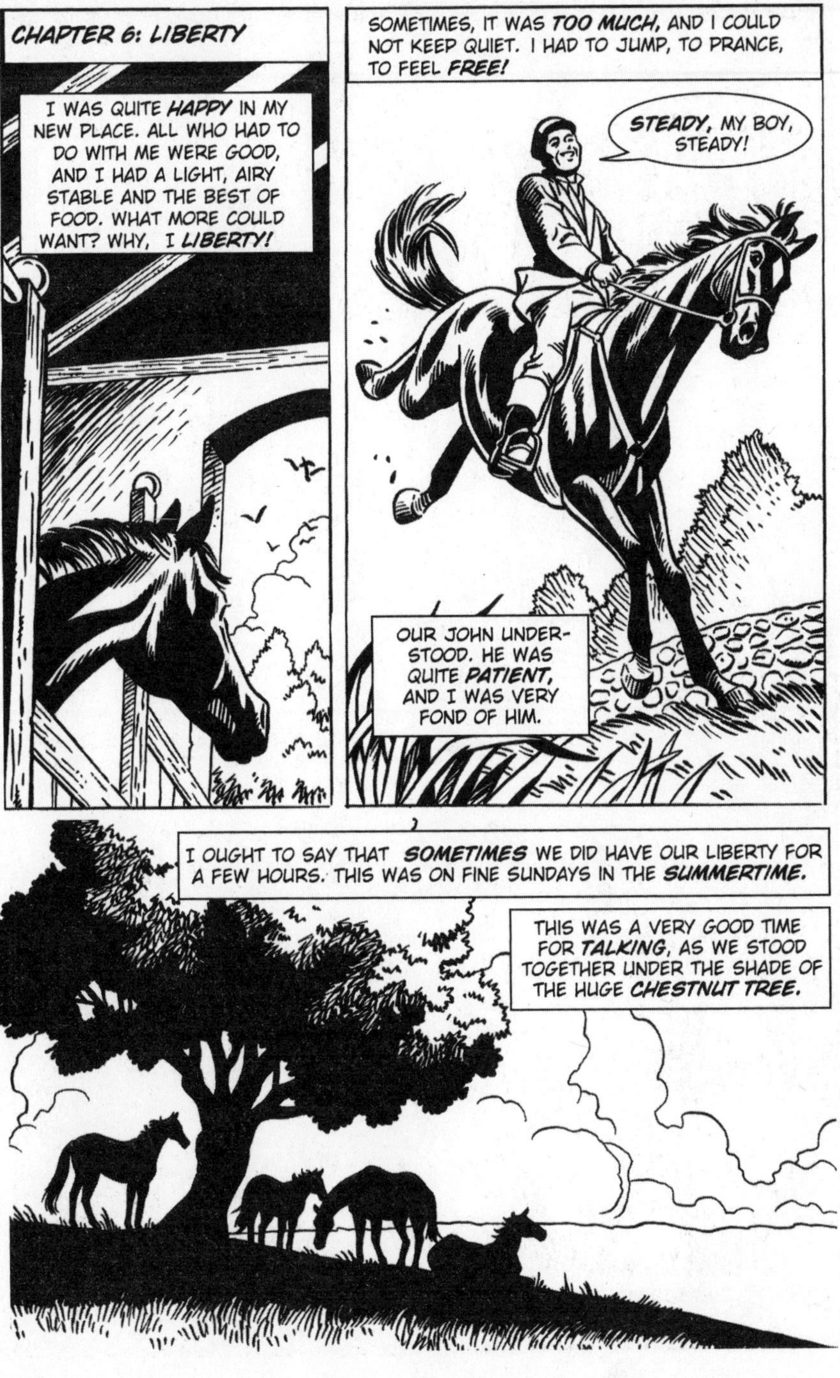

CHAPTER 6: LIBERTY
I WAS QUITE HAPPY IN MY NEW PLACE. ALL WHO HAD TO DO WITH ME WERE GOOD, AND I HAD A LIGHT, AIRY STABLE AND THE BEST OF FOOD. WHAT MORE COULD I WANT? WHY, LIBERTY!
SOMETIMES, IT WAS TOO MUCH, AND I COULD NOT KEEP QUIET. I HAD TO JUMP, TO PRANCE, TO FEEL FREE!
STEADY, MY BOY, STEADY!
OUR JOHN UNDERSTOOD. HE WAS QUITE PATIENT, AND I WAS VERY FOND OF HIM.
I OUGHT TO SAY THAT SOMETIMES WE DID HAVE OUR LIBERTY FOR A FEW HOURS. THIS WAS ON FINE SUNDAYS IN THE SUMMERTIME.
THIS WAS A VERY GOOD TIME FOR TALKING, AS WE STOOD TOGETHER UNDER THE SHADE OF THE HUGE CHESTNUT TREE.

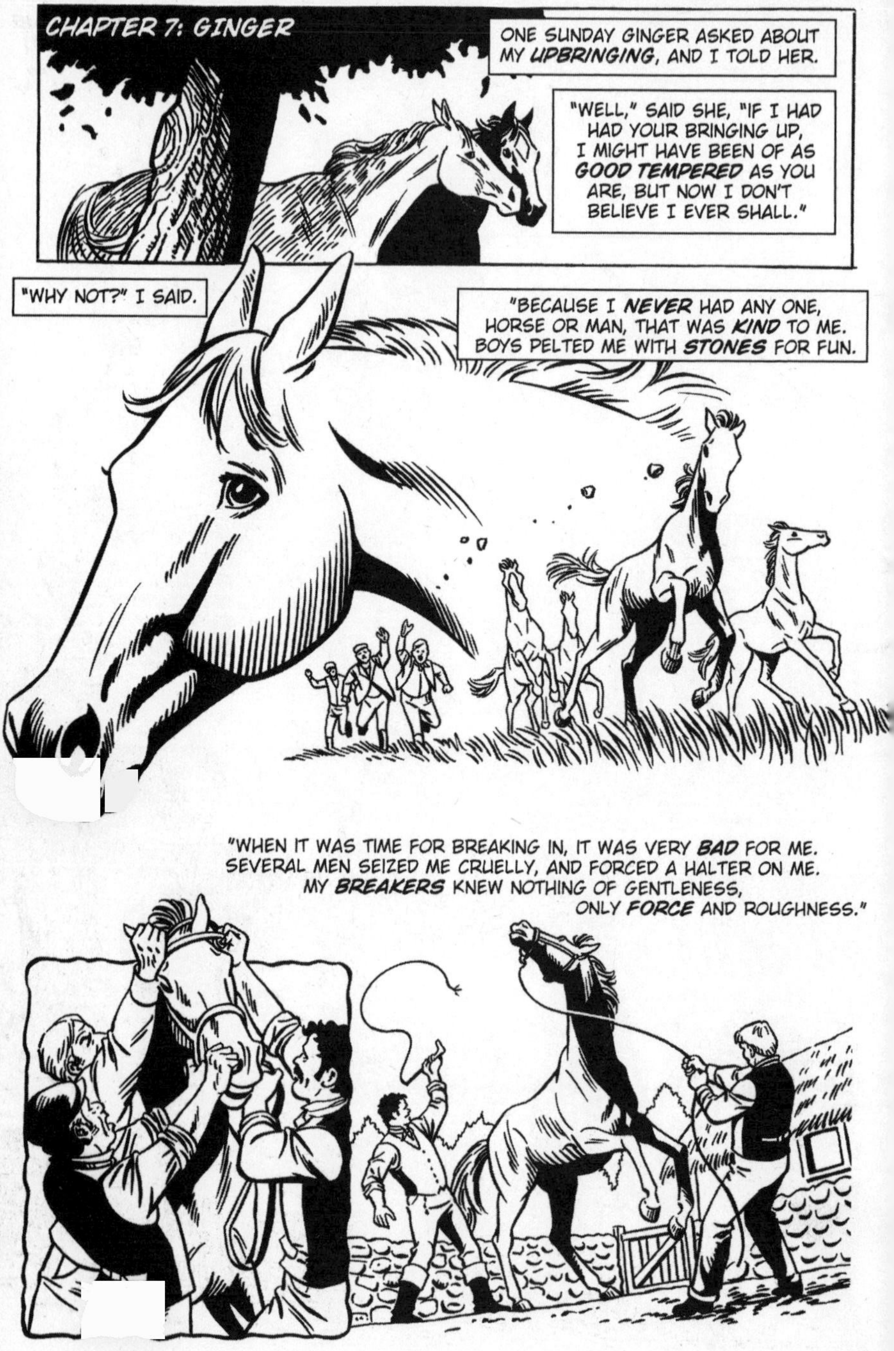
CHAPTER 7: GINGER
ONE SUNDAY GINGER ASKED ABOUT MY UPBRINGING, AND I TOLD HER.
"WELL," SAID SHE, "IF I HAD HAD YOUR BRINGING UP, I MIGHT HAVE BEEN OF AS GOOD TEMPERED AS YOU ARE, BUT NOW I DON'T BELIEVE I EVER SHALL."
"WHY NOT?" I SAID.
"BECAUSE I NEVER HAD ANY ONE, HORSE OR MAN, THAT WAS KIND TO ME. BOYS PELTED ME WITH STONES FOR FUN.
"WHEN IT WAS TIME FOR BREAKING IN, IT WAS VERY BAD FOR ME. SEVERAL MEN SEIZED ME CRUELLY, AND FORCED A HALTER ON ME. MY BREAKERS KNEW NOTHING OF GENTLENESS, ONLY FORCE AND ROUGHNESS."

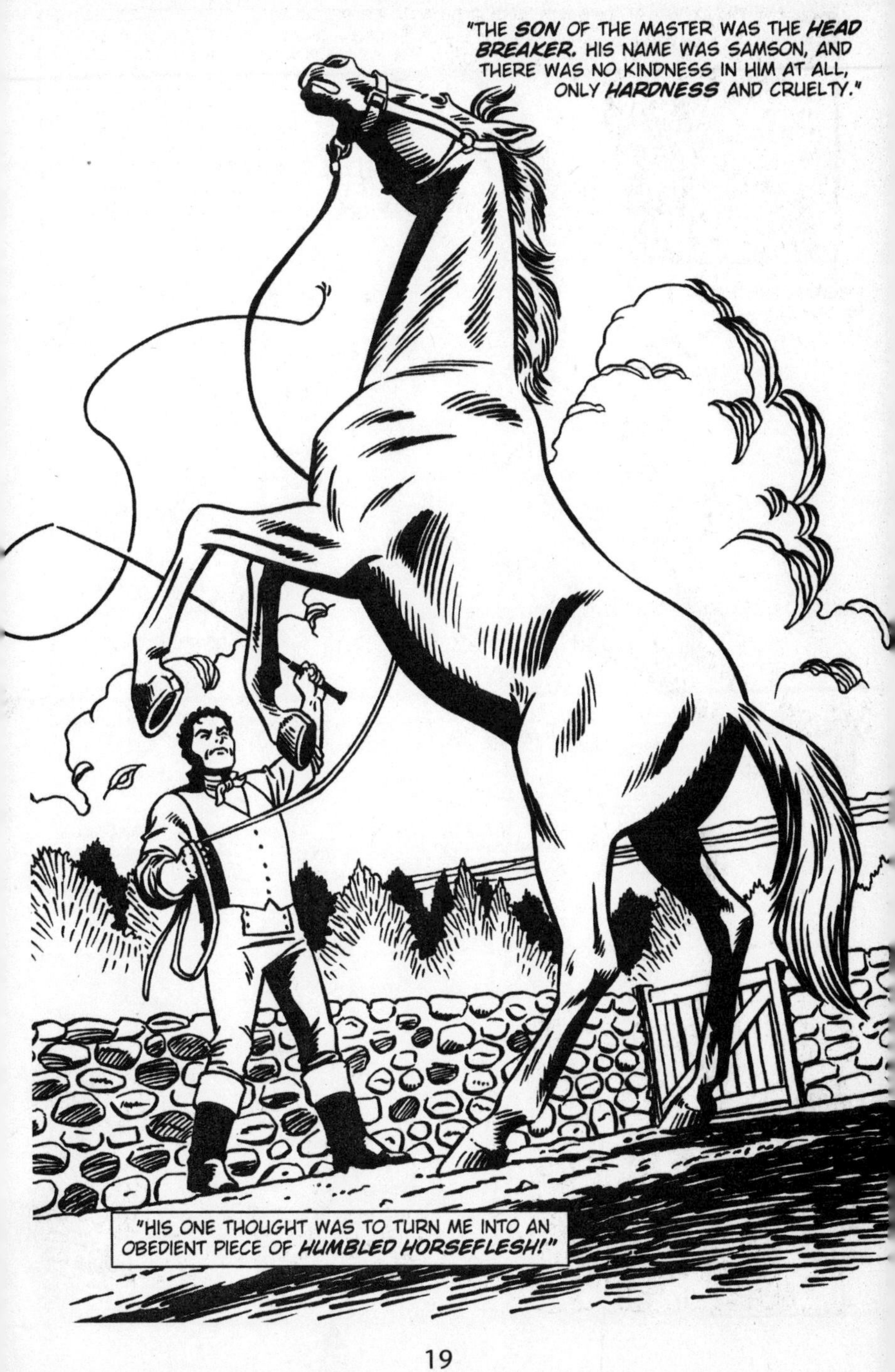
"THE SON OF THE MASTER WAS THE HEAD BREAKER. HIS NAME WAS SAMSON, AND THERE WAS NO KINDNESS IN HIM AT ALL, ONLY HARDNESS AND CRUELTY."
"HIS ONE THOUGHT WAS TO TURN ME INTO AN OBEDIENT PIECE OF HUMBLED HORSEFLESH!"

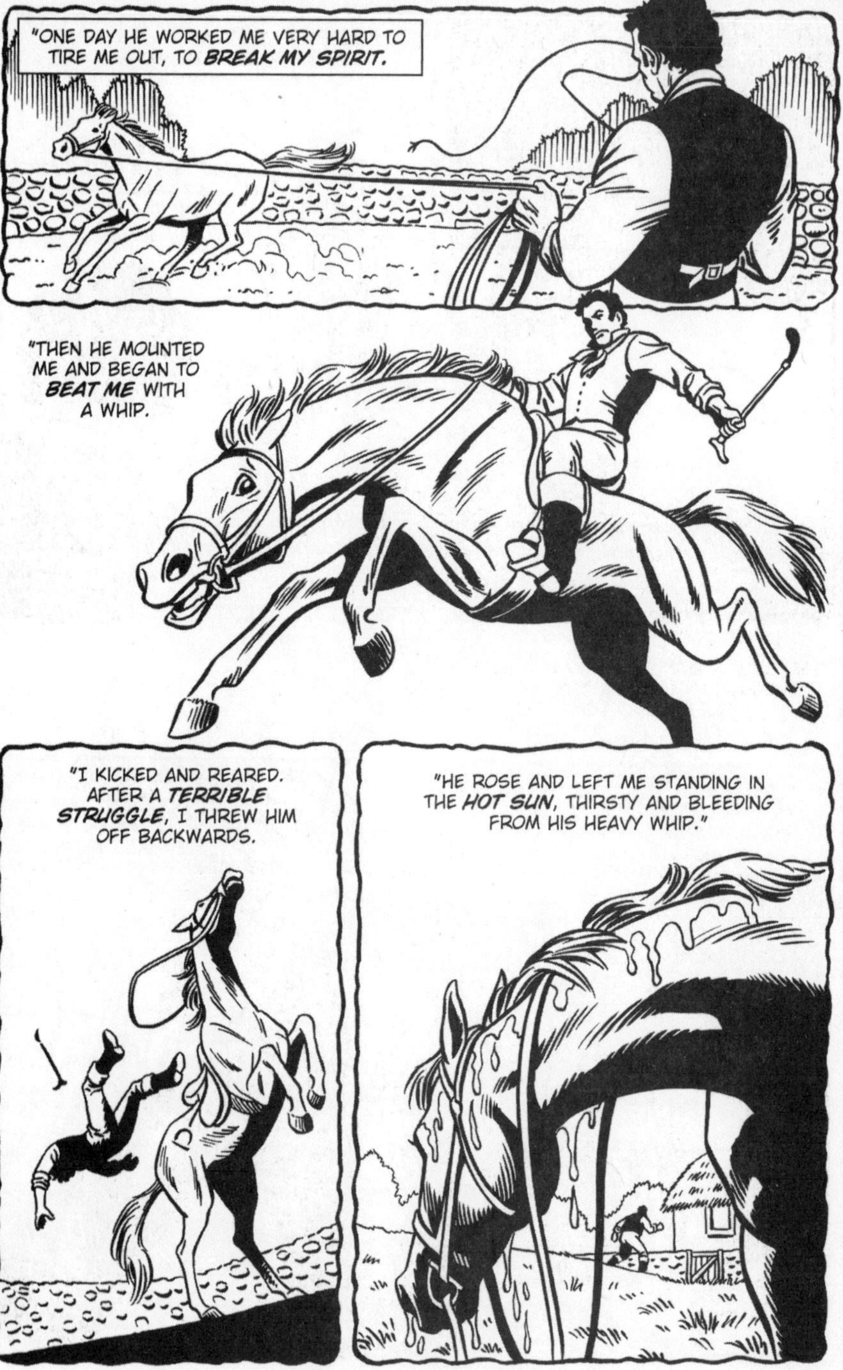
"ONE DAY HE WORKED ME VERY HARD TO TIRE ME OUT, TO BREAK MY SPIRIT.
"THEN HE MOUNTED ME AND BEGAN TO BEAT ME WITH A WHIP.
"I KICKED AND REARED. AFTER A TERRIBLE STRUGGLE, I THREW HIM OFF BACKWARDS.
"HE ROSE AND LEFT ME STANDING IN THE HOT SUN, THIRSTY AND BLEEDING FROM HIS HEAVY WHIP."

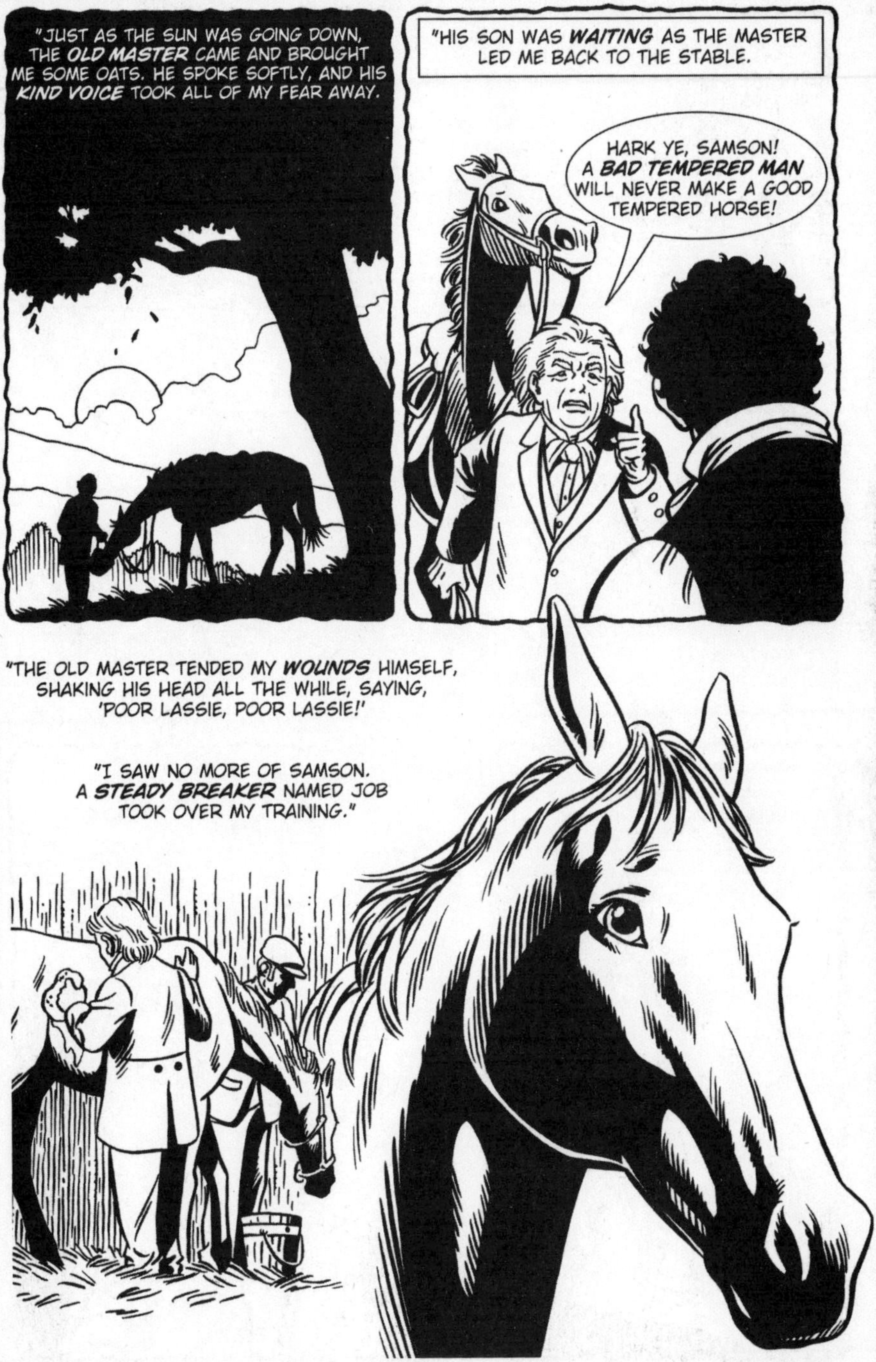
"JUST AS THE SUN WAS GOING DOWN, THE OLD MASTER CAME AND BROUGHT ME SOME OATS. HE SPOKE SOFTLY, AND HIS KIND VOICE TOOK ALL OF MY FEAR AWAY.
"HIS SON WAS WAITING AS THE MASTER LED ME BACK TO THE STABLE.
HARK YE, SAMSON! A BAD TEMPERED MAN WILL NEVER MAKE A GOOD TEMPERED HORSE!
"THE OLD MASTER TENDED MY WOUNDS HIMSELF, SHAKING HIS HEAD ALL THE WHILE, SAYING, 'POOR LASSIE, POOR LASSIE!'
"I SAW NO MORE OF SAMSON. A STEADY BREAKER NAMED JOB TOOK OVER MY TRAINING."

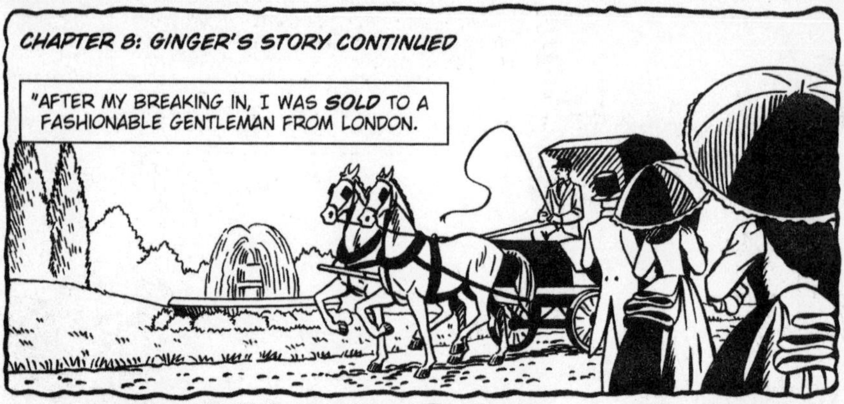
CHAPTER 8: GINGER'S STORY CONTINUED
"AFTER MY BREAKING IN, I WAS SOLD TO A FASHIONABLE GENTLEMAN FROM LONDON.

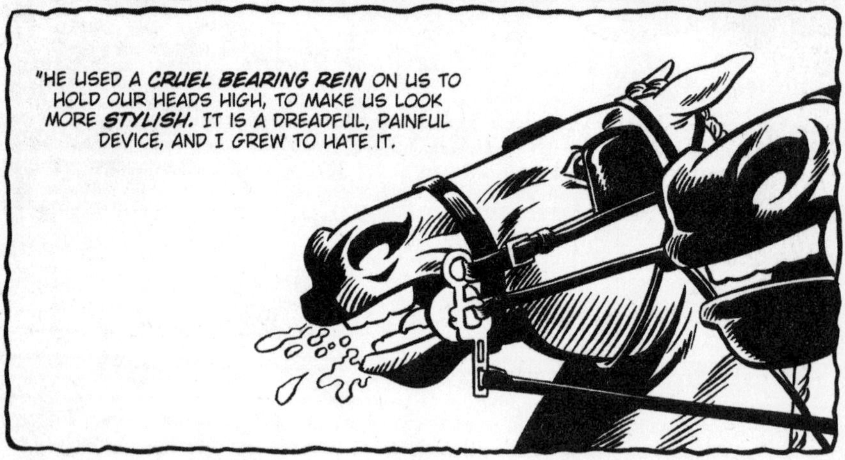
"HE USED A CRUEL BEARING REIN ON US TO HOLD OUR HEADS HIGH, TO MAKE US LOOK MORE STYLISH. IT IS A DREADFUL, PAINFUL DEVICE, AND I GREW TO HATE IT.

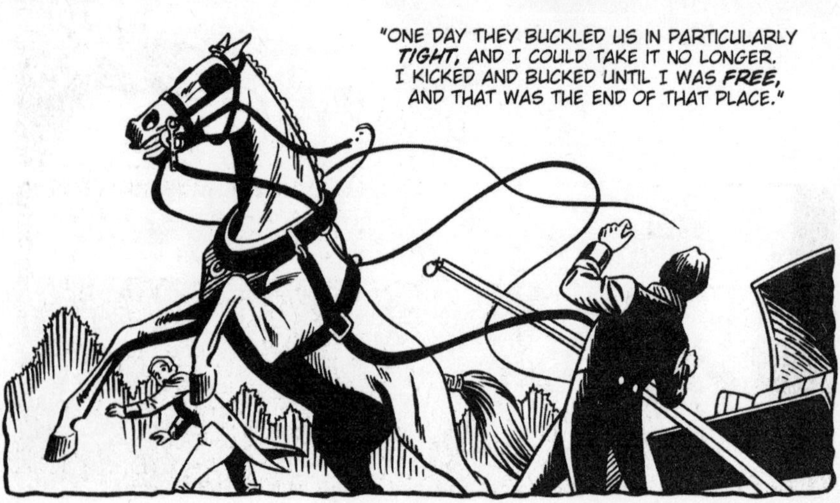
"ONE DAY THEY BUCKLED US IN PARTICULARLY TIGHT, AND I COULD TAKE IT NO LONGER. I KICKED AND BUCKED UNTIL I WAS FREE, AND THAT WAS THE END OF THAT PLACE."

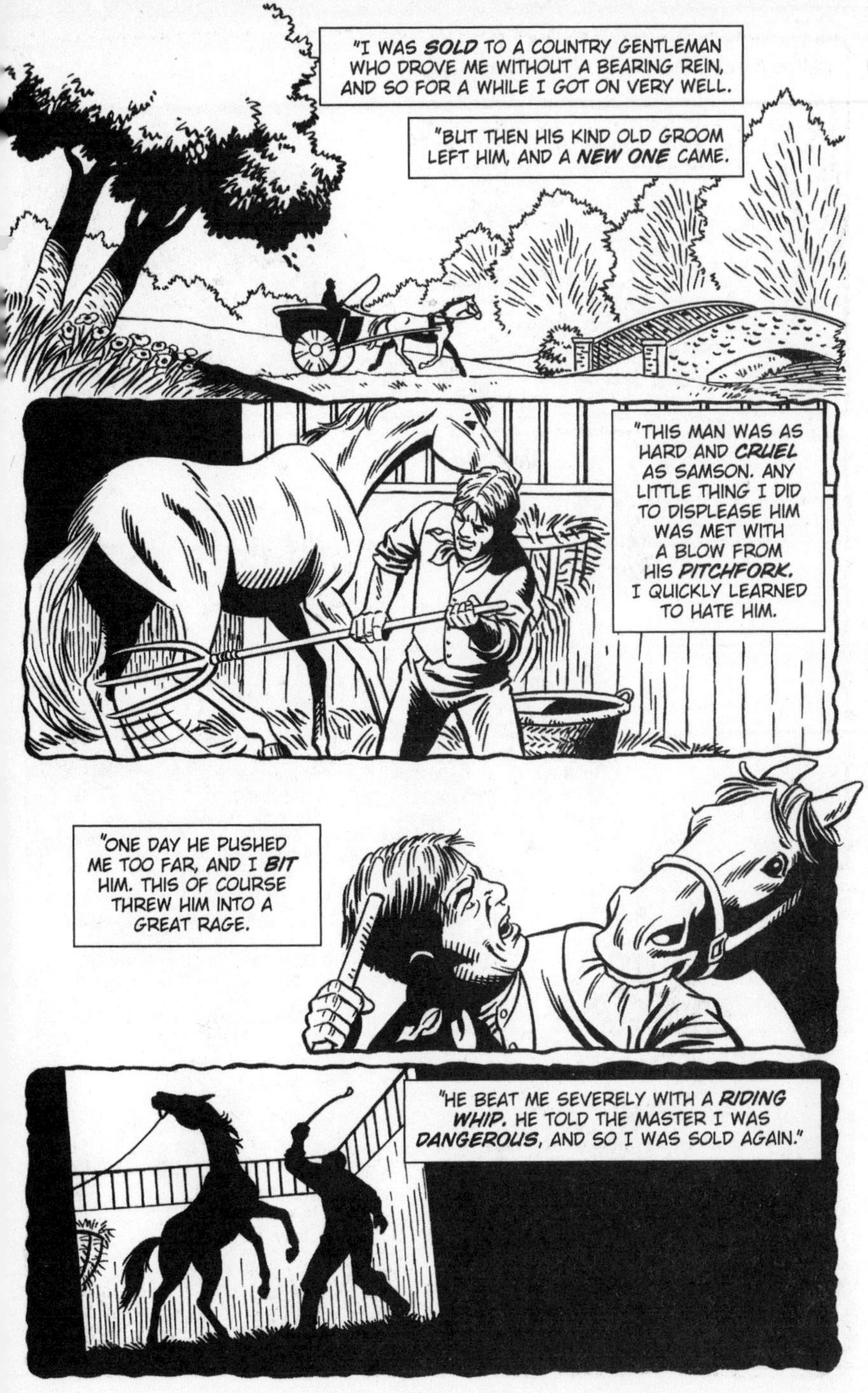
"I WAS SOLD TO A COUNTRY GENTLEMAN WHO DROVE ME WITHOUT A BEARING REIN, AND SO FOR A WHILE I GOT ON VERY WELL.
"BUT THEN HIS KIND OLD GROOM LEFT HIM, AND A NEW ONE CAME.
"THIS MAN WAS AS HARD AND CRUEL AS SAMSON. ANY LITTLE THING I DID TO DISPLEASE HIM WAS MET WITH A BLOW FROM HIS PITCHFORK. I QUICKLY LEARNED TO HATE HIM.
"ONE DAY HE PUSHED ME TOO FAR, AND I BIT HIM. THIS OF COURSE THREW HIM INTO A GREAT RAGE.
"HE BEAT ME SEVERELY WITH A RIDING WHIP. HE TOLD THE MASTER I WAS DANGEROUS, AND SO I WAS SOLD AGAIN."

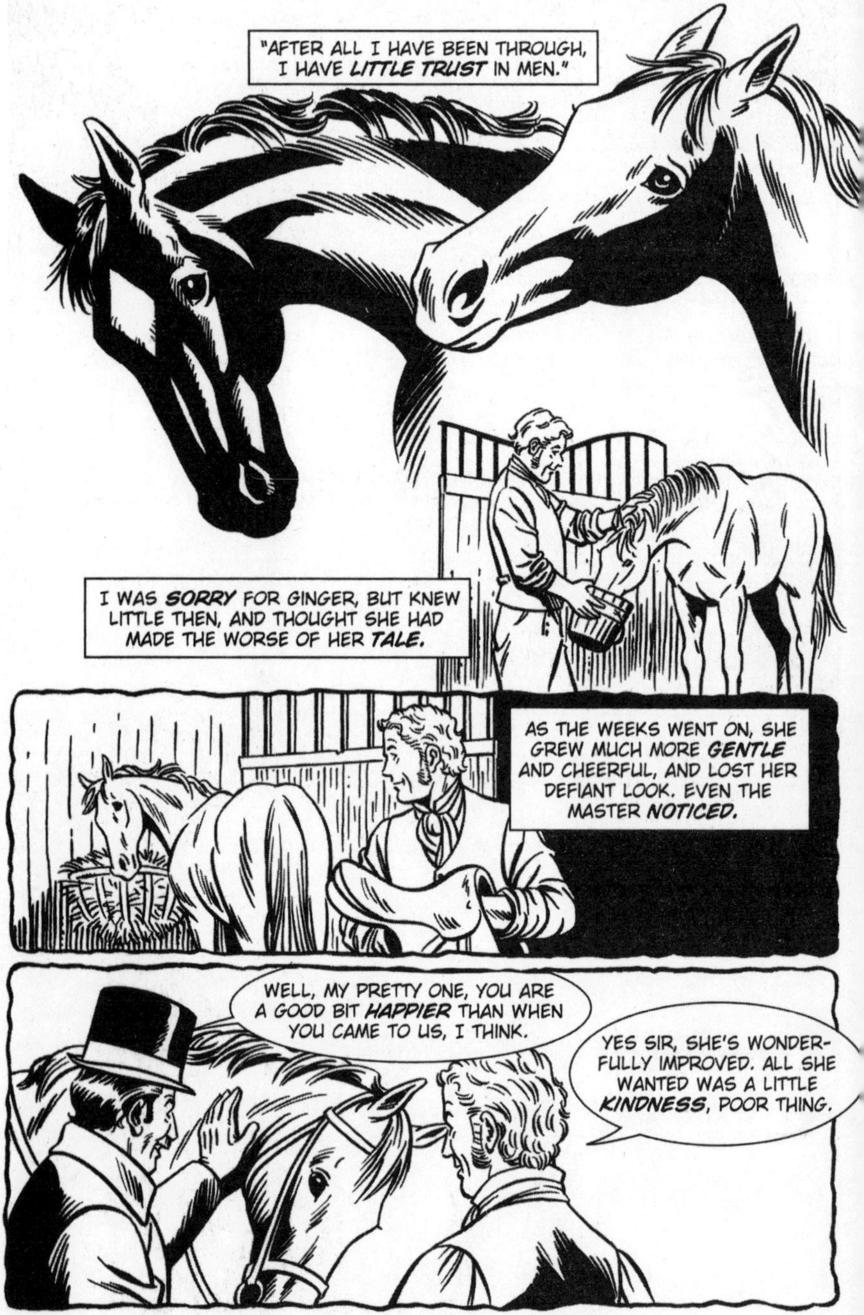
"AFTER ALL I HAVE BEEN THROUGH, I HAVE LITTLE TRUST IN MEN."
I WAS SORRY FOR GINGER, BUT KNEW LITTLE THEN, AND THOUGHT SHE HAD MADE THE WORSE OF HER TALE.
AS THE WEEKS WENT ON, SHE GREW MUCH MORE GENTLE AND CHEERFUL, AND LOST HER DEFIANT LOOK. EVEN THE MASTER NOTICED.
WELL, MY PRETTY ONE, YOU ARE A GOOD BIT HAPPIER THAN WHEN YOU CAME TO US, I THINK.
YES SIR, SHE'S WONDERFULLY IMPROVED. ALL SHE WANTED WAS A LITTLE KINDNESS, POOR THING.

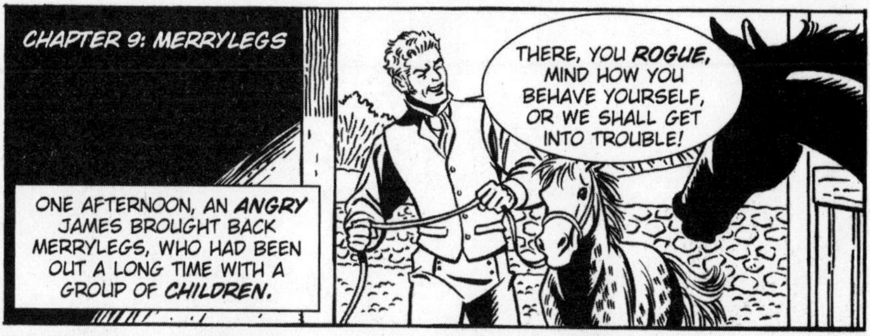
CHAPTER 9: MERRYLEGS
ONE AFTERNOON, AN ANGRY JAMES BROUGHT BACK MERRYLEGS, WHO HAD BEEN OUT A LONG TIME WITH A GROUP OF CHILDREN.
THERE, YOU ROGUE, MIND HOW YOU BEHAVE YOURSELF, OR WE SHALL GET INTO TROUBLE!

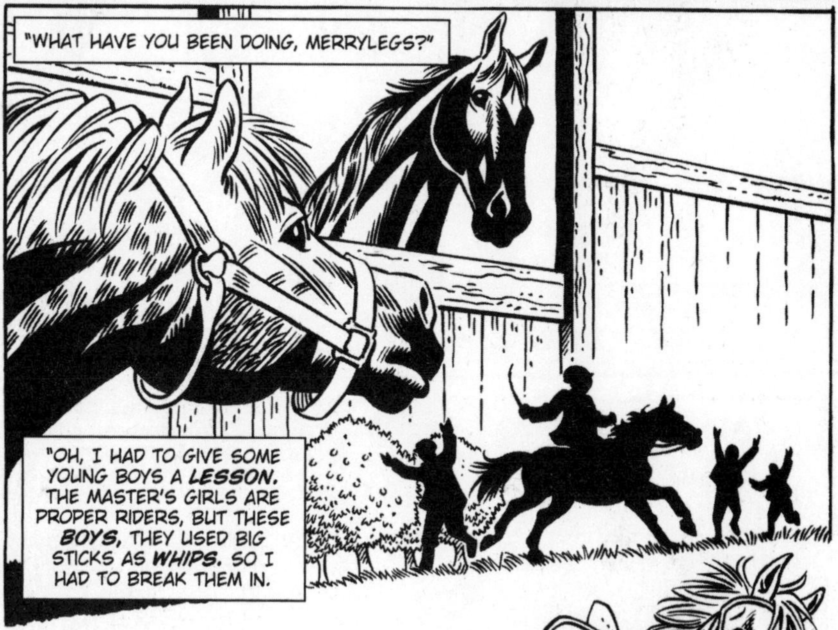
"WHAT HAVE YOU BEEN DOING, MERRYLEGS?"
"OH, I HAD TO GIVE SOME YOUNG BOYS A LESSON. THE MASTER'S GIRLS ARE PROPER RIDERS, BUT THESE BOYS, THEY USED BIG STICKS AS WHIPS. SO I HAD TO BREAK THEM IN.

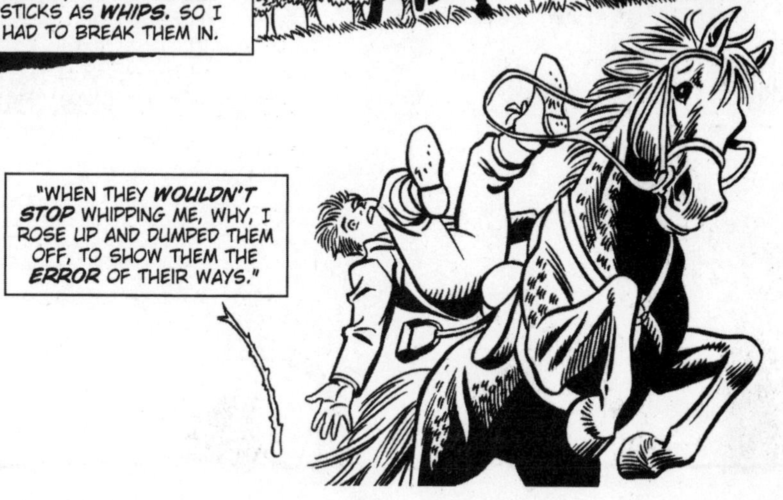
"WHEN THEY WOULDN'T STOP WHIPPING ME, WHY, I ROSE UP AND DUMPED THEM OFF, TO SHOW THEM THE ERROR OF THEIR WAYS."

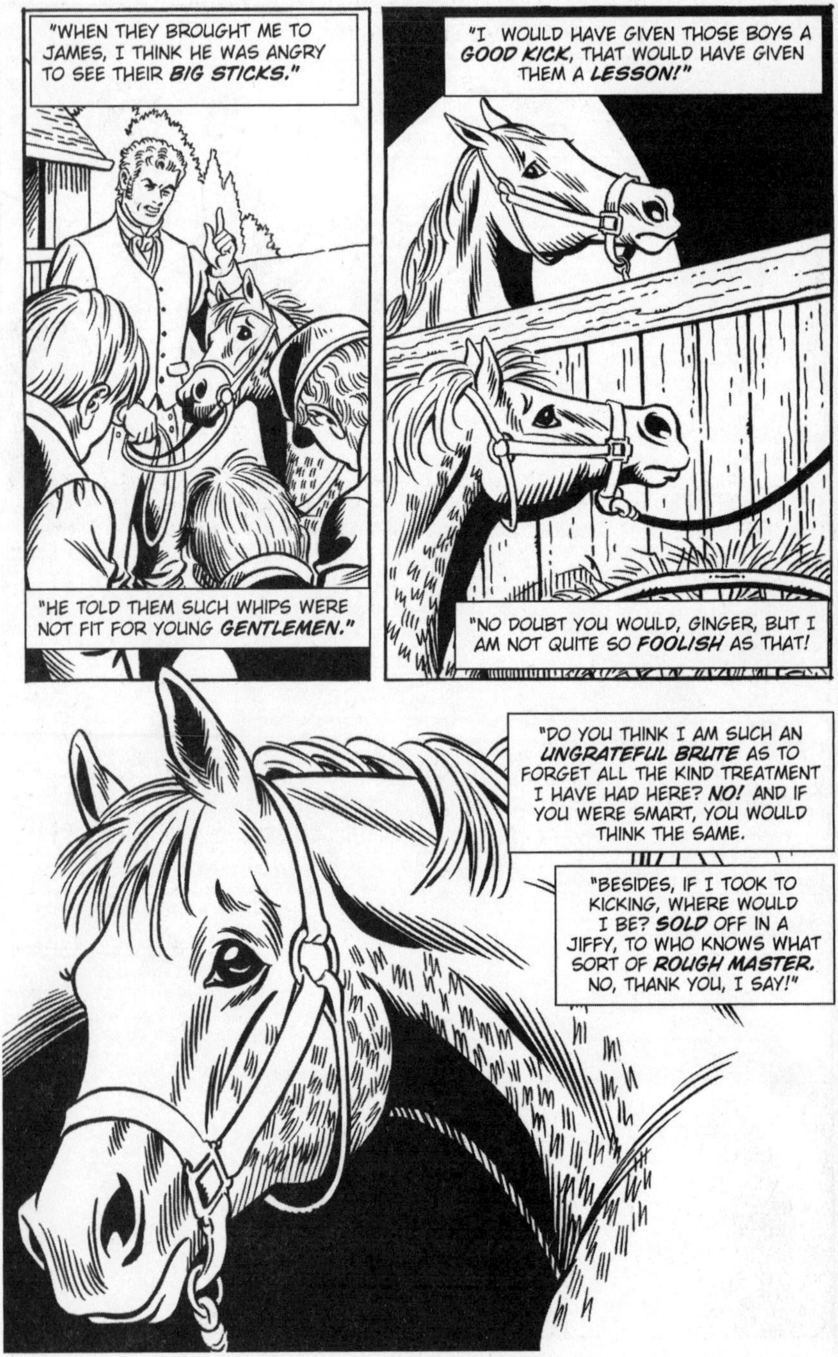
"WHEN THEY BROUGHT ME TO JAMES, I THINK HE WAS ANGRY TO SEE THEIR BIG STICKS."
"HE TOLD THEM SUCH WHIPS WERE NOT FIT FOR YOUNG GENTLEMEN."
"I WOULD HAVE GIVEN THOSE BOYS A GOOD KICK, THAT WOULD HAVE GIVEN THEM A LESSON!"
"NO DOUBT YOU WOULD, GINGER, BUT I AM NOT QUITE SO FOOLISH AS THAT!
"DO YOU THINK I AM SUCH AN UNGRATEFUL BRUTE AS TO FORGET ALL THE KIND TREATMENT I HAVE HAD HERE? NO! AND IF YOU WERE SMART, YOU WOULD THINK THE SAME.
"BESIDES, IF I TOOK TO KICKING, WHERE WOULD I BE? SOLD OFF IN A JIFFY, TO WHO KNOWS WHAT SORT OF ROUGH MASTER. NO, THANK YOU, I SAY!"

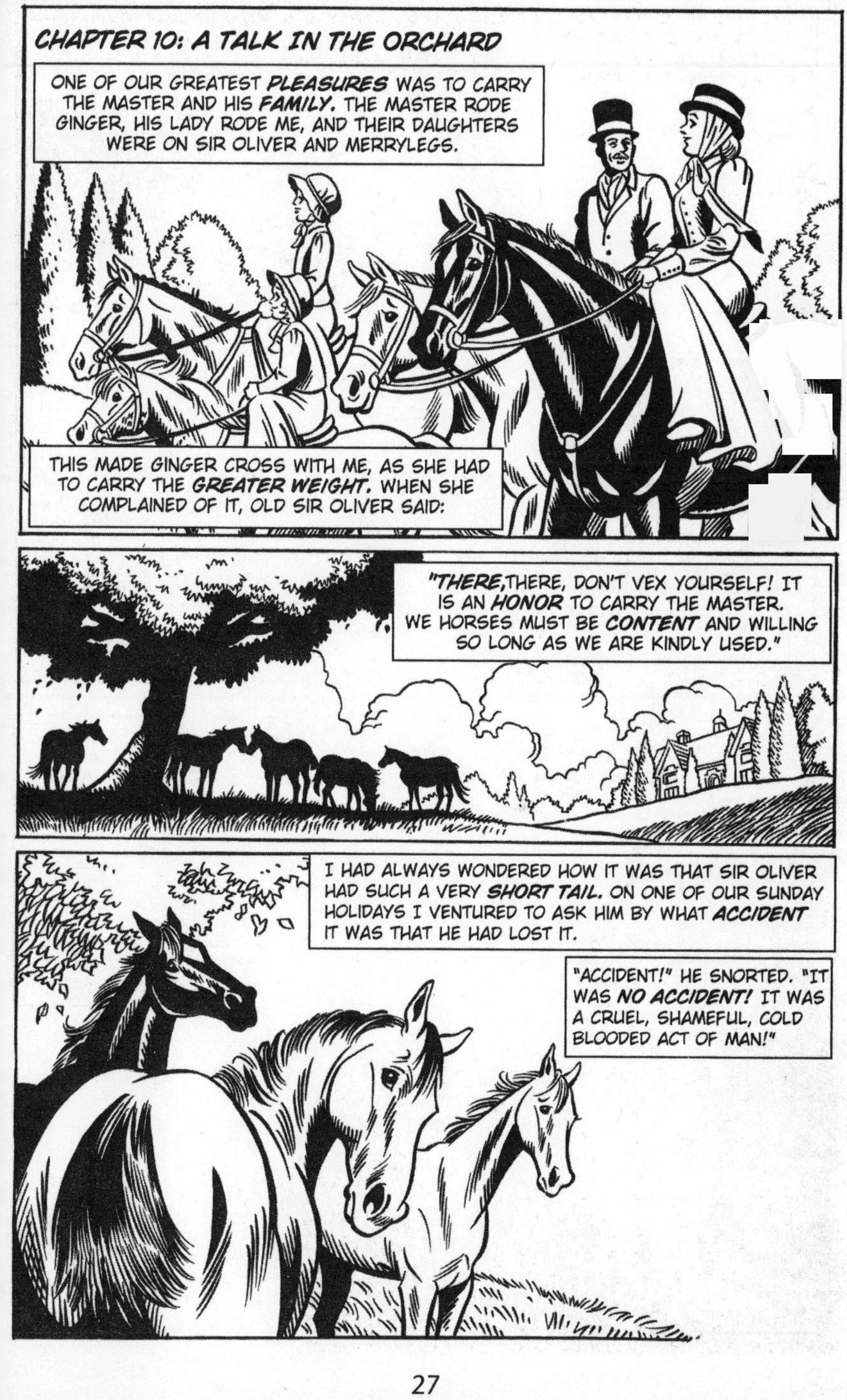
CHAPTER 10: A TALK IN THE ORCHARD
ONE OF OUR GREATEST PLEASURES WAS TO CARRY THE MASTER AND HIS FAMILY. THE MASTER RODE GINGER, HIS LADY RODE ME, AND THEIR DAUGHTERS WERE ON SIR OLIVER AND MERRYLEGS.
THIS MADE GINGER CROSS WITH ME, AS SHE HAD TO CARRY THE GREATER WEIGHT. WHEN SHE COMPLAINED OF IT, OLD SIR OLIVER SAID:
"THERE,THERE, DON'T VEX YOURSELF! IT IS AN HONOR TO CARRY THE MASTER. WE HORSES MUST BE CONTENT AND WILLING SO LONG AS WE ARE KINDLY USED."
I HAD ALWAYS WONDERED HOW IT WAS THAT SIR OLIVER HAD SUCH A VERY SHORT TAIL. ON ONE OF OUR SUNDAY HOLIDAYS I VENTURED TO ASK HIM BY WHAT ACCIDENT IT WAS THAT HE HAD LOST IT.
"ACCIDENT!" HE SNORTED. "IT WAS NO ACCIDENT! IT WAS A CRUEL, SHAMEFUL, COLD BLOODED ACT OF MAN!"

"WHEN I WAS YOUNG, I WAS TIED UP, AND THEY *CUT OFF* MY LONG BEAUTIFUL TAIL, BONE AND ALL, AND THREW IT AWAY! AND ALL FOR THE SAKE OF *FASHION!* MEN LIKE THE LOOK OF BUTCHERY!

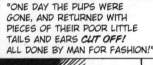

"THEY DO THE SAME TO THEIR PETS. I HAD A DEAR FRIEND ONCE, A *TERRIER* WHO HAD HER PUPS IN MY STALL.

"ONE DAY THE PUPS WERE GONE, AND RETURNED WITH PIECES OF THEIR POOR LITTLE TAILS AND EARS *CUT OFF!* ALL DONE BY MAN FOR FASHION!"

"WHY DON'T THEY CUT THEIR OWN *CHILDREN'S EARS* INTO POINTS TO MAKE THEM LOOK SHARP? WHAT RIGHT HAVE THEY TO TORMENT AND *DISFIGURE* GOD'S CREATURES?" ASKED SIR OLIVER INDIGNANTLY.

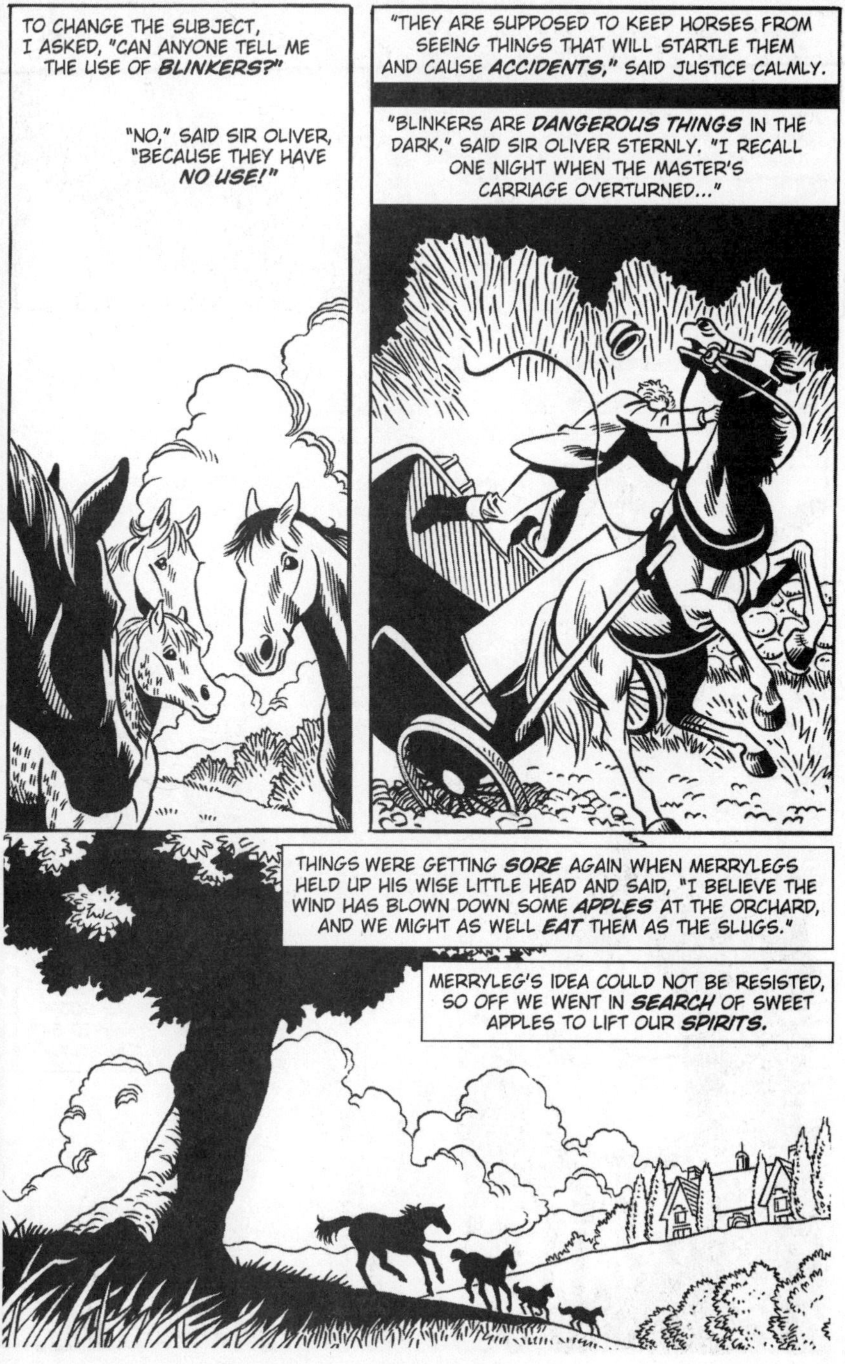
TO CHANGE THE SUBJECT, I ASKED, "CAN ANYONE TELL ME THE USE OF **BLINKERS?**"
"NO," SAID SIR OLIVER, "BECAUSE THEY HAVE **NO USE!**"
"THEY ARE SUPPOSED TO KEEP HORSES FROM SEEING THINGS THAT WILL STARTLE THEM AND CAUSE **ACCIDENTS,**" SAID JUSTICE CALMLY.
"BLINKERS ARE **DANGEROUS THINGS** IN THE DARK," SAID SIR OLIVER STERNLY. "I RECALL ONE NIGHT WHEN THE MASTER'S CARRIAGE OVERTURNED..."
THINGS WERE GETTING **SORE** AGAIN WHEN MERRYLEGS HELD UP HIS WISE LITTLE HEAD AND SAID, "I BELIEVE THE WIND HAS BLOWN DOWN SOME **APPLES** AT THE ORCHARD, AND WE MIGHT AS WELL **EAT** THEM AS THE SLUGS."
MERRYLEG'S IDEA COULD NOT BE RESISTED, SO OFF WE WENT IN **SEARCH** OF SWEET APPLES TO LIFT OUR **SPIRITS.**

CHAPTER 11: PLAIN SPEAKING

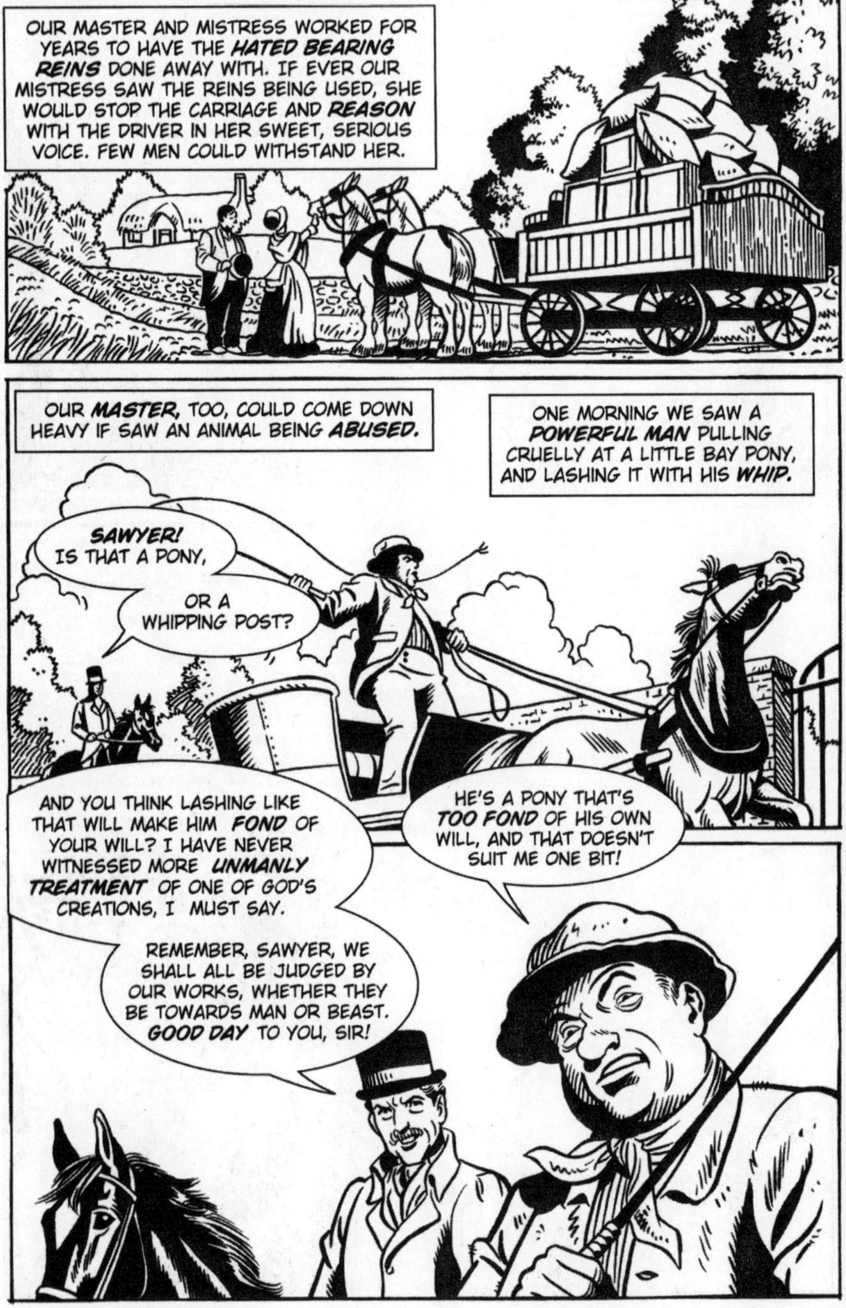
OUR MASTER AND MISTRESS WORKED FOR YEARS TO HAVE THE HATED BEARING REINS DONE AWAY WITH. IF EVER OUR MISTRESS SAW THE REINS BEING USED, SHE WOULD STOP THE CARRIAGE AND REASON WITH THE DRIVER IN HER SWEET, SERIOUS VOICE. FEW MEN COULD WITHSTAND HER.
OUR MASTER, TOO, COULD COME DOWN HEAVY IF SAW AN ANIMAL BEING ABUSED.
ONE MORNING WE SAW A POWERFUL MAN PULLING CRUELLY AT A LITTLE BAY PONY, AND LASHING IT WITH HIS WHIP.
SAWYER! IS THAT A PONY,
OR A WHIPPING POST?
HE'S A PONY THAT'S TOO FOND OF HIS OWN WILL, AND THAT DOESN'T SUIT ME ONE BIT!
AND YOU THINK LASHING LIKE THAT WILL MAKE HIM FOND OF YOUR WILL? I HAVE NEVER WITNESSED MORE UNMANLY TREATMENT OF ONE OF GOD'S CREATIONS, I MUST SAY.
REMEMBER, SAWYER, WE SHALL ALL BE JUDGED BY OUR WORKS, WHETHER THEY BE TOWARDS MAN OR BEAST. GOOD DAY TO YOU, SIR!

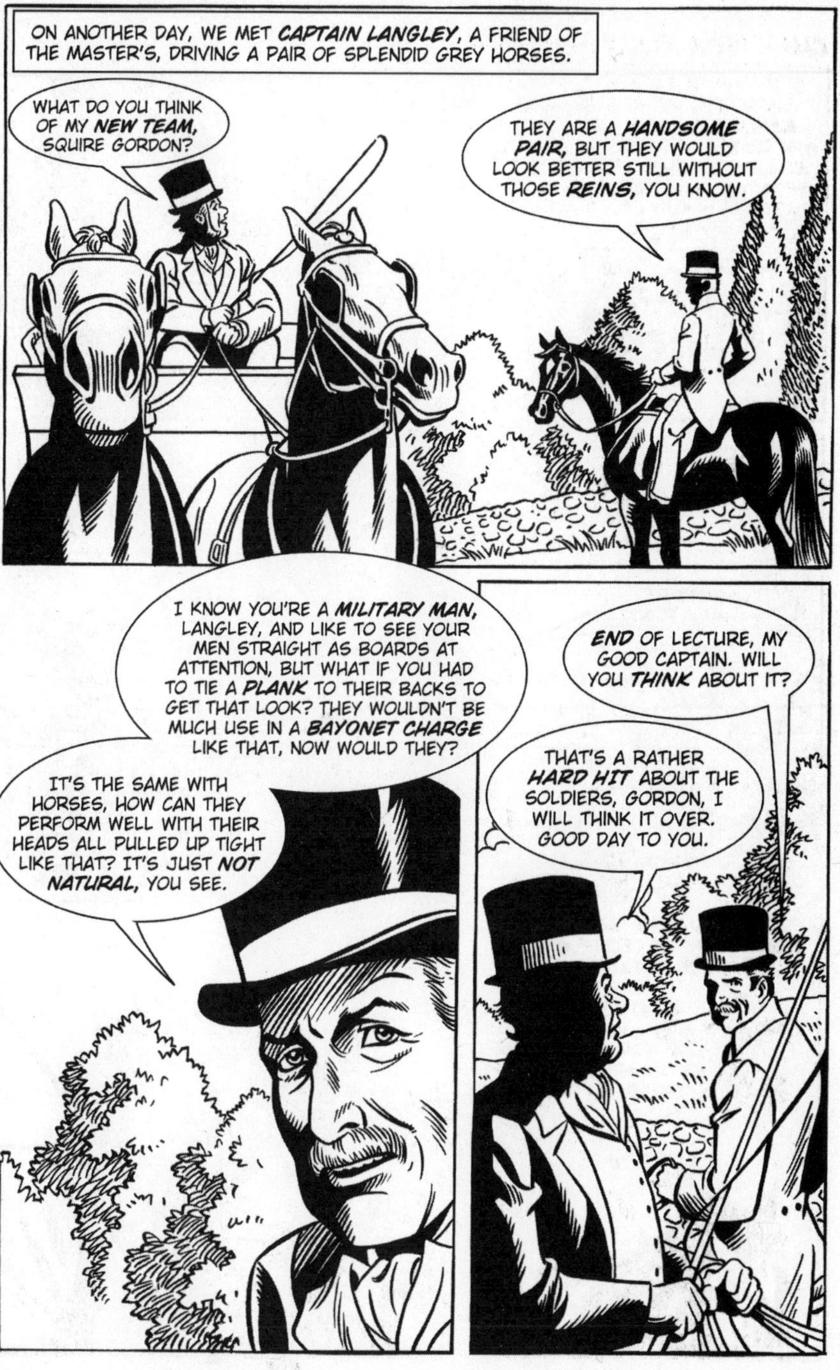

ON ANOTHER DAY, WE MET CAPTAIN LANGLEY, A FRIEND OF THE MASTER'S, DRIVING A PAIR OF SPLENDID GREY HORSES.
WHAT DO YOU THINK OF MY NEW TEAM, SQUIRE GORDON?
THEY ARE A HANDSOME PAIR, BUT THEY WOULD LOOK BETTER STILL WITHOUT THOSE REINS, YOU KNOW.
I KNOW YOU'RE A MILITARY MAN, LANGLEY, AND LIKE TO SEE YOUR MEN STRAIGHT AS BOARDS AT ATTENTION, BUT WHAT IF YOU HAD TO TIE A PLANK TO THEIR BACKS TO GET THAT LOOK? THEY WOULDN'T BE MUCH USE IN A BAYONET CHARGE LIKE THAT, NOW WOULD THEY?
IT'S THE SAME WITH HORSES, HOW CAN THEY PERFORM WELL WITH THEIR HEADS ALL PULLED UP TIGHT LIKE THAT? IT'S JUST NOT NATURAL, YOU SEE.
END OF LECTURE, MY GOOD CAPTAIN. WILL YOU THINK ABOUT IT?
THAT'S A RATHER HARD HIT ABOUT THE SOLDIERS, GORDON, I WILL THINK IT OVER. GOOD DAY TO YOU.

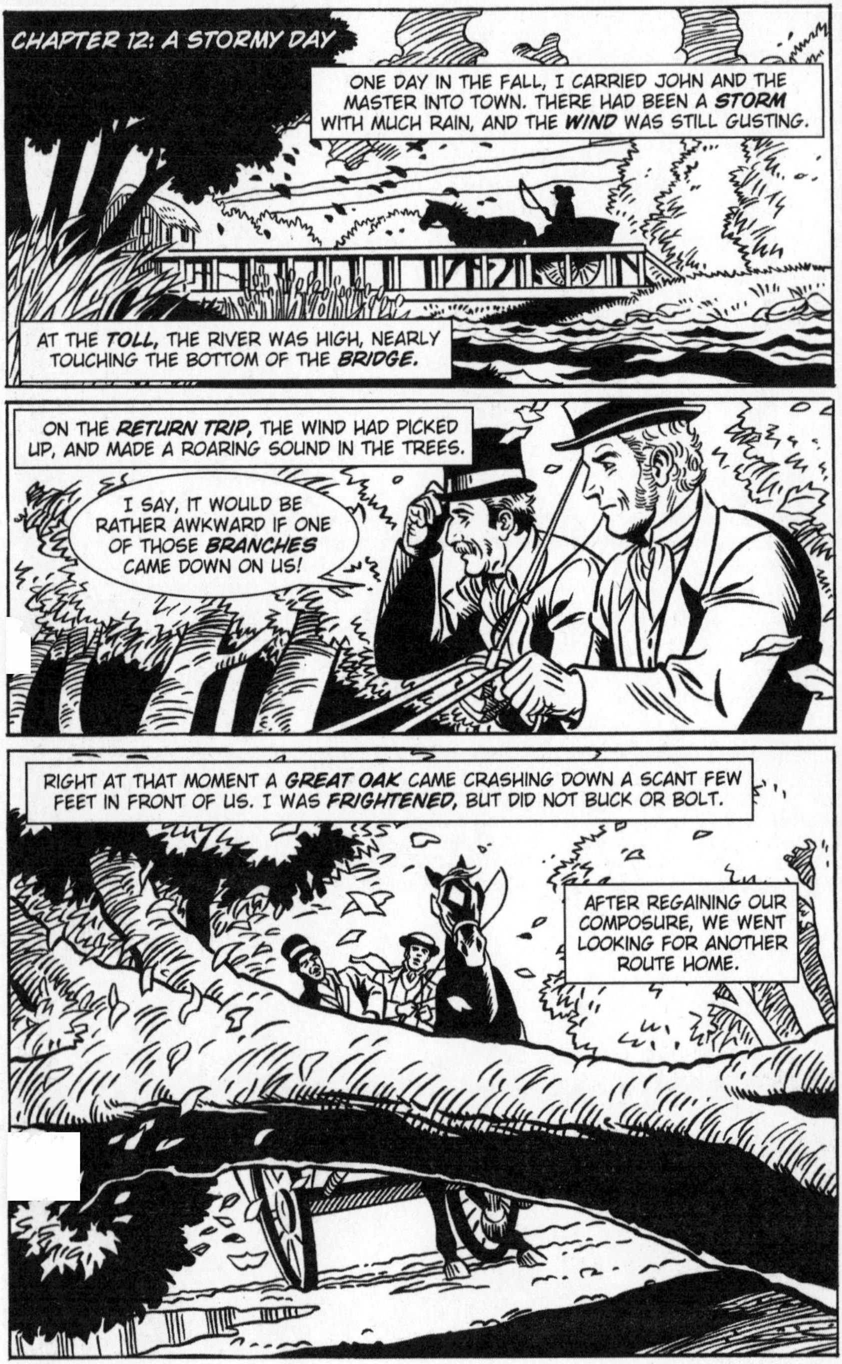
CHAPTER 12: A STORMY DAY
ONE DAY IN THE FALL, I CARRIED JOHN AND THE MASTER INTO TOWN. THERE HAD BEEN A STORM WITH MUCH RAIN, AND THE WIND WAS STILL GUSTING.
AT THE TOLL, THE RIVER WAS HIGH, NEARLY TOUCHING THE BOTTOM OF THE BRIDGE.
ON THE RETURN TRIP, THE WIND HAD PICKED UP, AND MADE A ROARING SOUND IN THE TREES.
I SAY, IT WOULD BE RATHER AWKWARD IF ONE OF THOSE BRANCHES CAME DOWN ON US!
RIGHT AT THAT MOMENT A GREAT OAK CAME CRASHING DOWN A SCANT FEW FEET IN FRONT OF US. I WAS FRIGHTENED, BUT DID NOT BUCK OR BOLT.
AFTER REGAINING OUR COMPOSURE, WE WENT LOOKING FOR ANOTHER ROUTE HOME.

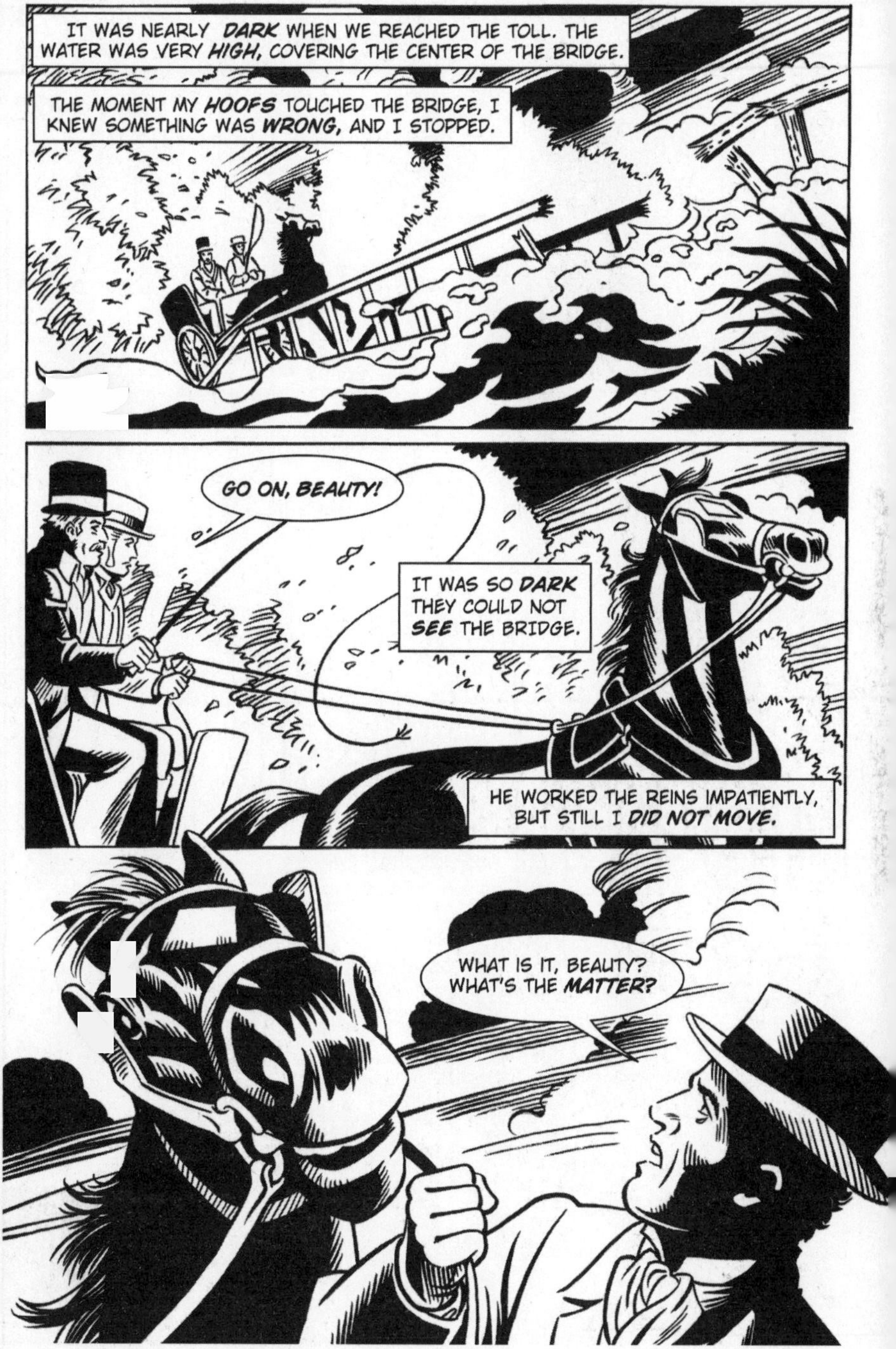
IT WAS NEARLY DARK WHEN WE REACHED THE TOLL. THE WATER WAS VERY HIGH, COVERING THE CENTER OF THE BRIDGE.
THE MOMENT MY HOOFS TOUCHED THE BRIDGE, I KNEW SOMETHING WAS WRONG, AND I STOPPED.
GO ON, BEAUTY!
IT WAS SO DARK THEY COULD NOT SEE THE BRIDGE.
HE WORKED THE REINS IMPATIENTLY, BUT STILL I DID NOT MOVE.
WHAT IS IT, BEAUTY? WHAT'S THE MATTER?

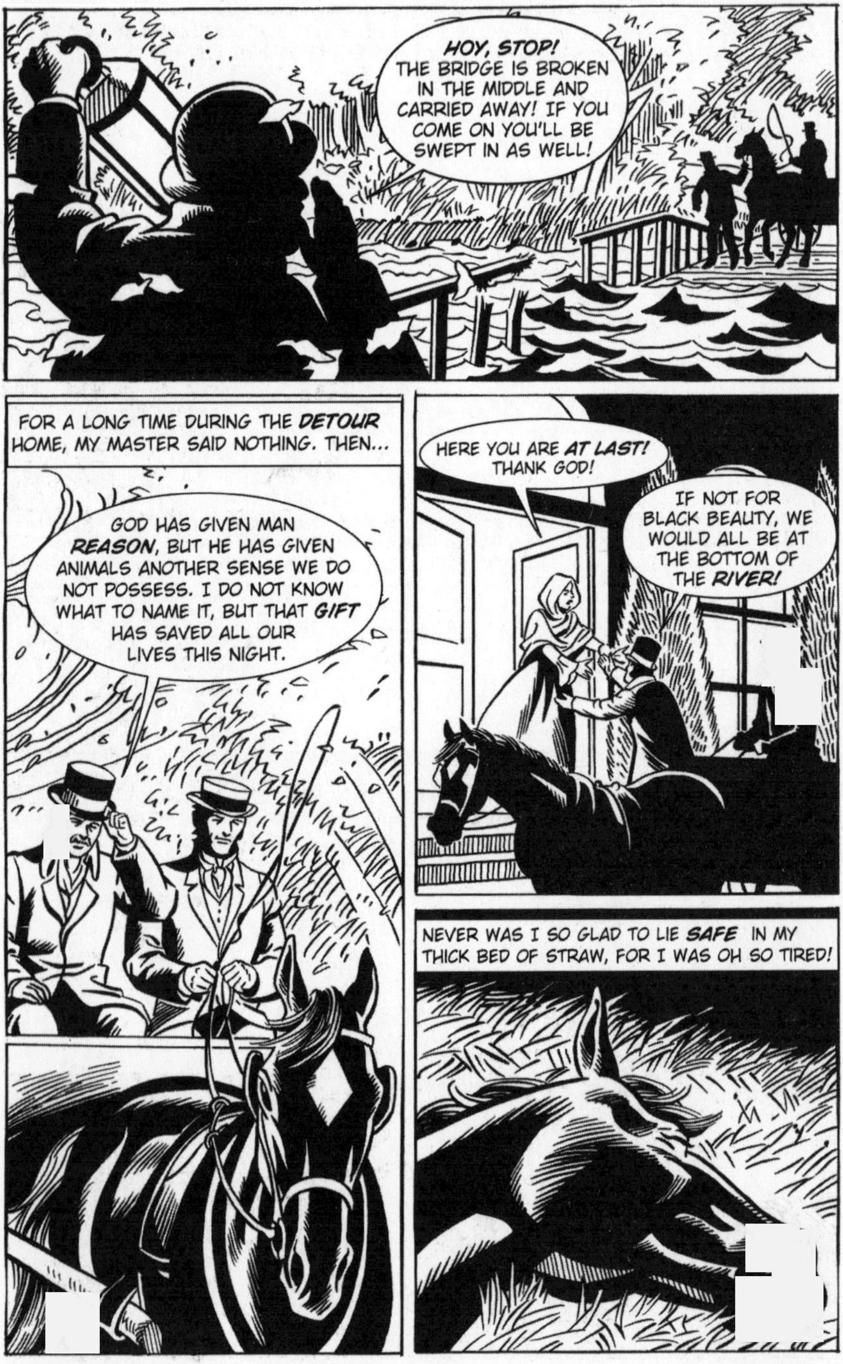
HOY, STOP! THE BRIDGE IS BROKEN IN THE MIDDLE AND CARRIED AWAY! IF YOU COME ON YOU'LL BE SWEPT IN AS WELL!
FOR A LONG TIME DURING THE DETOUR HOME, MY MASTER SAID NOTHING. THEN...
GOD HAS GIVEN MAN REASON, BUT HE HAS GIVEN ANIMALS ANOTHER SENSE WE DO NOT POSSESS. I DO NOT KNOW WHAT TO NAME IT, BUT THAT GIFT HAS SAVED ALL OUR LIVES THIS NIGHT.
HERE YOU ARE AT LAST! THANK GOD!
IF NOT FOR BLACK BEAUTY, WE WOULD ALL BE AT THE BOTTOM OF THE RIVER!
NEVER WAS I SO GLAD TO LIE SAFE IN MY THICK BED OF STRAW, FOR I WAS OH SO TIRED!

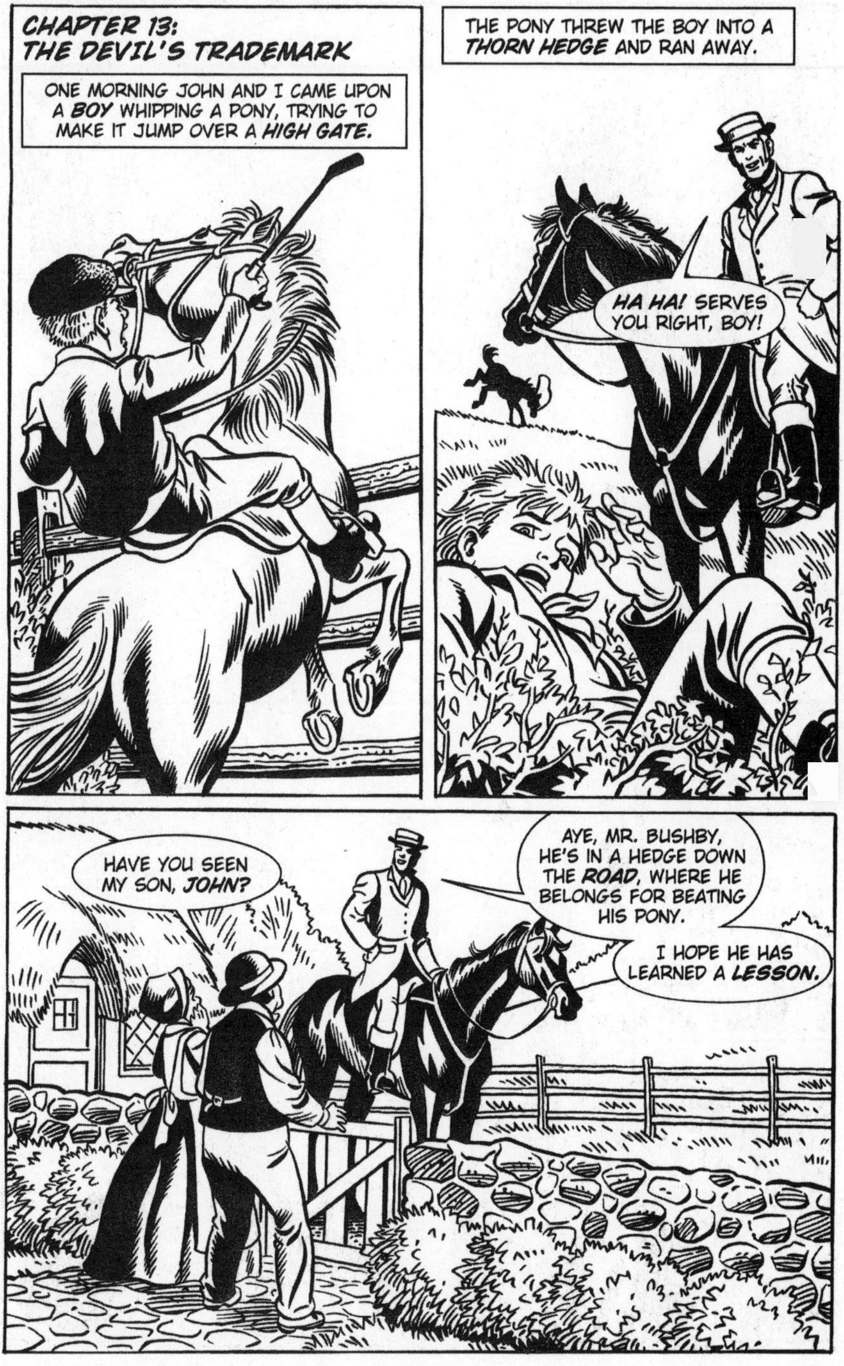
CHAPTER 13:
THE DEVIL'S TRADEMARK
ONE MORNING JOHN AND I CAME UPON A BOY WHIPPING A PONY, TRYING TO MAKE IT JUMP OVER A HIGH GATE.
THE PONY THREW THE BOY INTO A THORN HEDGE AND RAN AWAY.
HA HA! SERVES YOU RIGHT, BOY!
HAVE YOU SEEN MY SON, JOHN?
AYE, MR. BUSHBY, HE'S IN A HEDGE DOWN THE ROAD, WHERE HE BELONGS FOR BEATING HIS PONY.
I HOPE HE HAS LEARNED A LESSON.

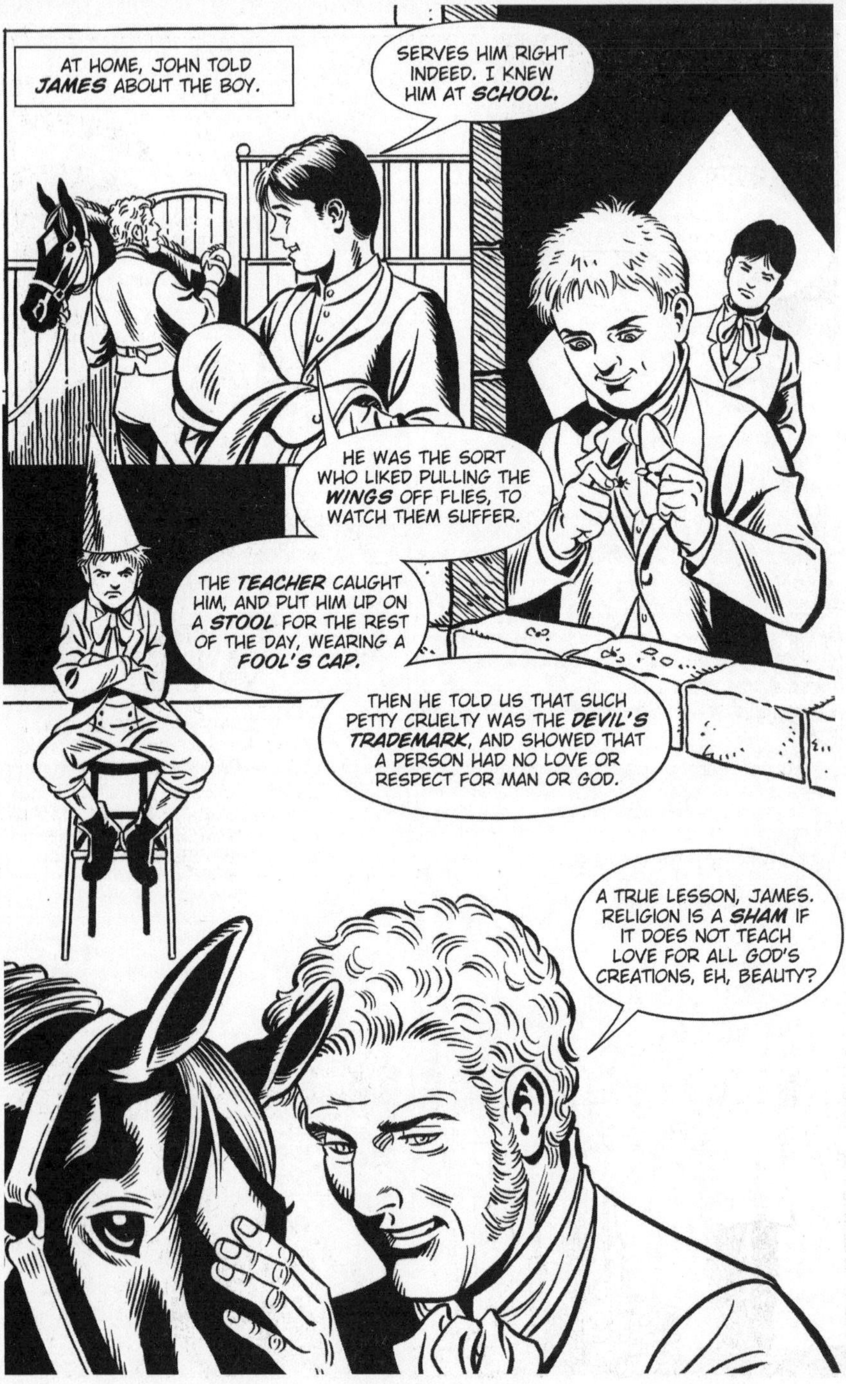
AT HOME, JOHN TOLD JAMES ABOUT THE BOY.
SERVES HIM RIGHT INDEED. I KNEW HIM AT SCHOOL.
HE WAS THE SORT WHO LIKED PULLING THE WINGS OFF FLIES, TO WATCH THEM SUFFER.
THE TEACHER CAUGHT HIM, AND PUT HIM UP ON A STOOL FOR THE REST OF THE DAY, WEARING A FOOL'S CAP.
THEN HE TOLD US THAT SUCH PETTY CRUELTY WAS THE DEVIL'S TRADEMARK, AND SHOWED THAT A PERSON HAD NO LOVE OR RESPECT FOR MAN OR GOD.
A TRUE LESSON, JAMES. RELIGION IS A SHAM IF IT DOES NOT TEACH LOVE FOR ALL GOD'S CREATIONS, EH, BEAUTY?

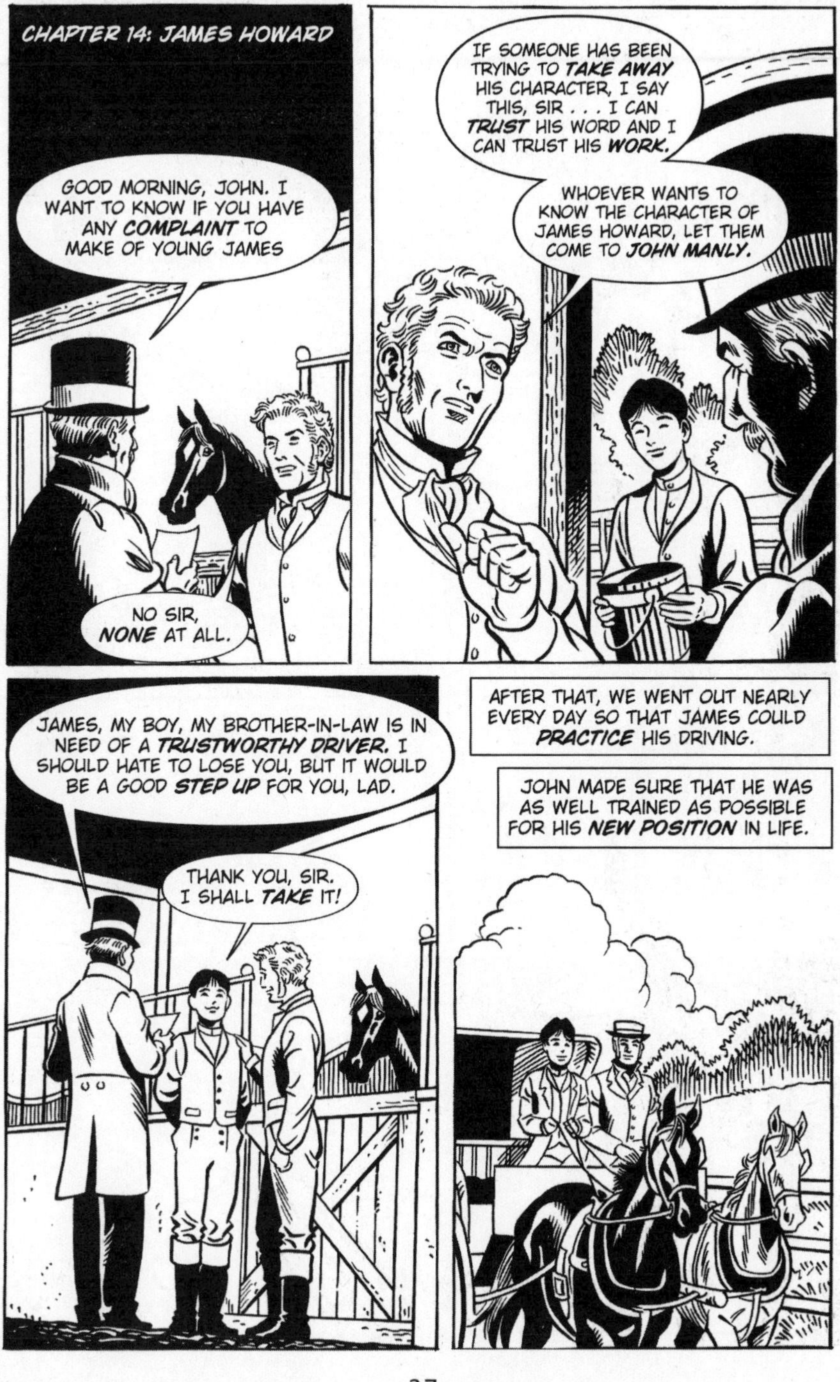

CHAPTER 14: JAMES HOWARD
GOOD MORNING, JOHN. I WANT TO KNOW IF YOU HAVE ANY COMPLAINT TO MAKE OF YOUNG JAMES
NO SIR, NONE AT ALL.
IF SOMEONE HAS BEEN TRYING TO TAKE AWAY HIS CHARACTER, I SAY THIS, SIR . . . I CAN TRUST HIS WORD AND I CAN TRUST HIS WORK.
WHOEVER WANTS TO KNOW THE CHARACTER OF JAMES HOWARD, LET THEM COME TO JOHN MANLY.
JAMES, MY BOY, MY BROTHER-IN-LAW IS IN NEED OF A TRUSTWORTHY DRIVER. I SHOULD HATE TO LOSE YOU, BUT IT WOULD BE A GOOD STEP UP FOR YOU, LAD.
THANK YOU, SIR. I SHALL TAKE IT!
AFTER THAT, WE WENT OUT NEARLY EVERY DAY SO THAT JAMES COULD PRACTICE HIS DRIVING.
JOHN MADE SURE THAT HE WAS AS WELL TRAINED AS POSSIBLE FOR HIS NEW POSITION IN LIFE.

CHAPTER 15: THE OLD OSTLER

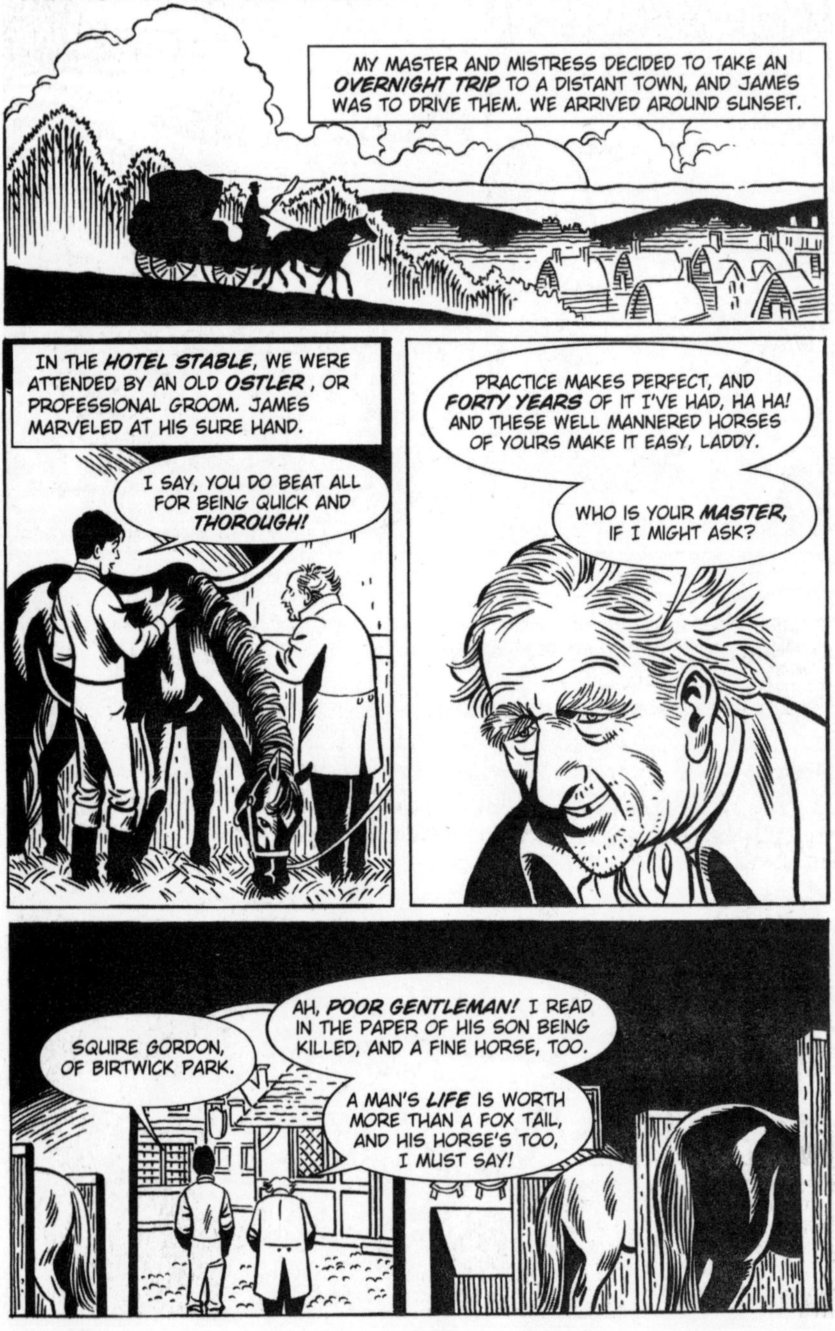

MY MASTER AND MISTRESS DECIDED TO TAKE AN OVERNIGHT TRIP TO A DISTANT TOWN, AND JAMES WAS TO DRIVE THEM. WE ARRIVED AROUND SUNSET.
IN THE HOTEL STABLE, WE WERE ATTENDED BY AN OLD OSTLER, OR PROFESSIONAL GROOM. JAMES MARVELED AT HIS SURE HAND.
I SAY, YOU DO BEAT ALL FOR BEING QUICK AND THOROUGH!
PRACTICE MAKES PERFECT, AND FORTY YEARS OF IT I'VE HAD, HA HA! AND THESE WELL MANNERED HORSES OF YOURS MAKE IT EASY, LADDY.
WHO IS YOUR MASTER, IF I MIGHT ASK?
SQUIRE GORDON, OF BIRTWICK PARK.
AH, POOR GENTLEMAN! I READ IN THE PAPER OF HIS SON BEING KILLED, AND A FINE HORSE, TOO.
A MAN'S LIFE IS WORTH MORE THAN A FOX TAIL, AND HIS HORSE'S TOO, I MUST SAY!

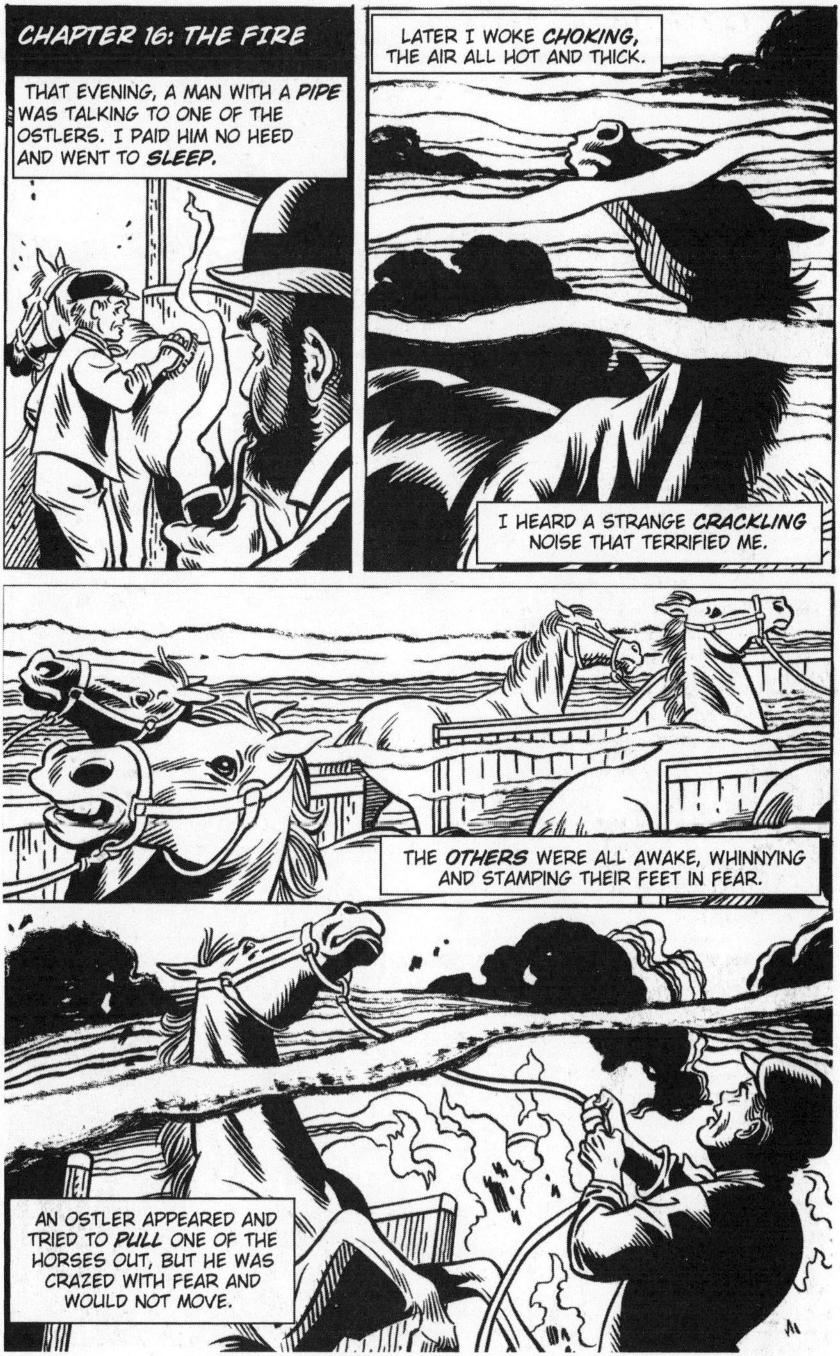
CHAPTER 16: THE FIRE
THAT EVENING, A MAN WITH A PIPE WAS TALKING TO ONE OF THE OSTLERS. I PAID HIM NO HEED AND WENT TO SLEEP.
LATER I WOKE CHOKING, THE AIR ALL HOT AND THICK.
I HEARD A STRANGE CRACKLING NOISE THAT TERRIFIED ME.
THE OTHERS WERE ALL AWAKE, WHINNYING AND STAMPING THEIR FEET IN FEAR.
AN OSTLER APPEARED AND TRIED TO PULL ONE OF THE HORSES OUT, BUT HE WAS CRAZED WITH FEAR AND WOULD NOT MOVE.

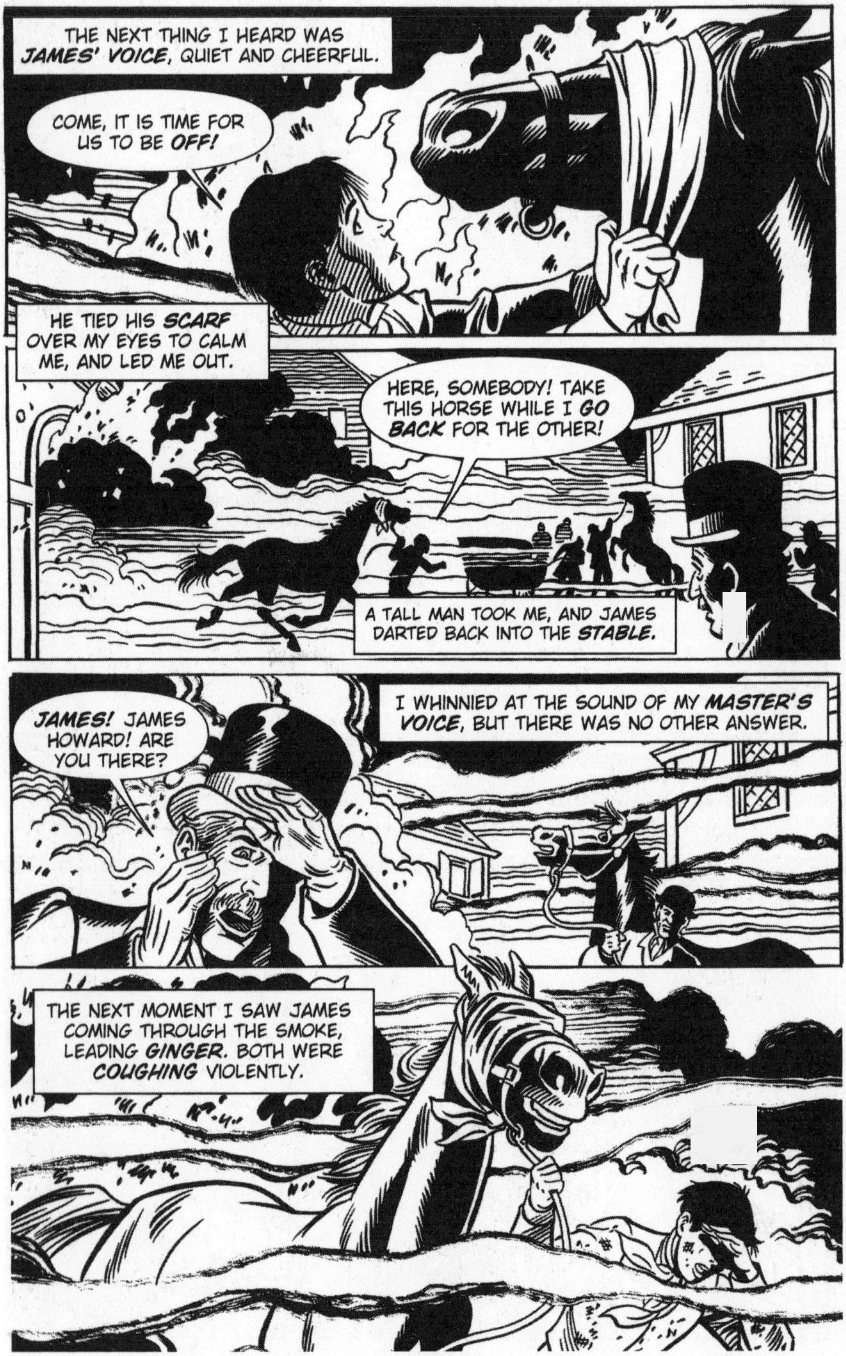
THE NEXT THING I HEARD WAS JAMES' VOICE, QUIET AND CHEERFUL.
COME, IT IS TIME FOR US TO BE OFF!
HE TIED HIS SCARF OVER MY EYES TO CALM ME, AND LED ME OUT.
HERE, SOMEBODY! TAKE THIS HORSE WHILE I GO BACK FOR THE OTHER!
A TALL MAN TOOK ME, AND JAMES DARTED BACK INTO THE STABLE.
JAMES! JAMES HOWARD! ARE YOU THERE?
I WHINNIED AT THE SOUND OF MY MASTER'S VOICE, BUT THERE WAS NO OTHER ANSWER.
THE NEXT MOMENT I SAW JAMES COMING THROUGH THE SMOKE, LEADING GINGER. BOTH WERE COUGHING VIOLENTLY.

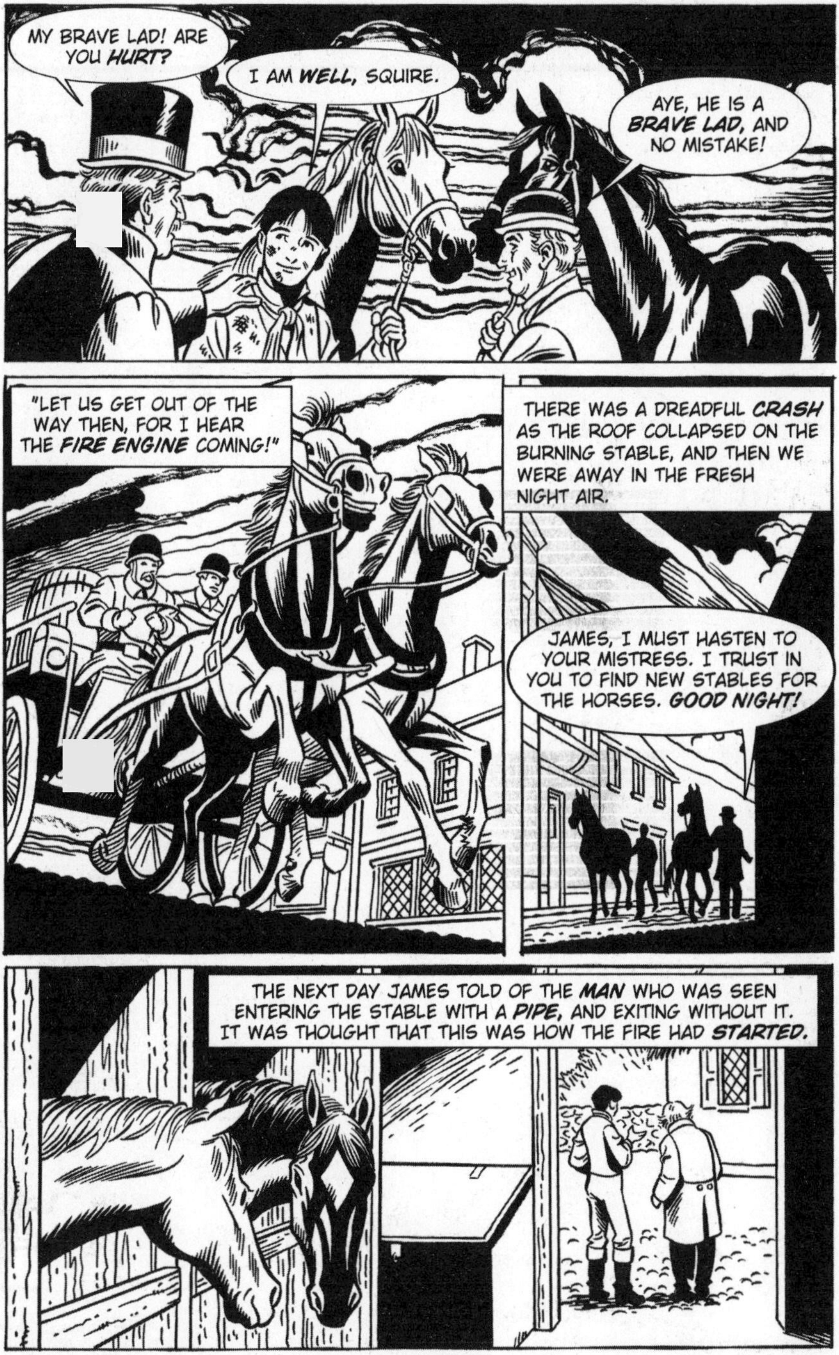
MY BRAVE LAD! ARE YOU HURT?
I AM WELL, SQUIRE.
AYE, HE IS A BRAVE LAD, AND NO MISTAKE!
"LET US GET OUT OF THE WAY THEN, FOR I HEAR THE FIRE ENGINE COMING!"
THERE WAS A DREADFUL CRASH AS THE ROOF COLLAPSED ON THE BURNING STABLE, AND THEN WE WERE AWAY IN THE FRESH NIGHT AIR.
JAMES, I MUST HASTEN TO YOUR MISTRESS. I TRUST IN YOU TO FIND NEW STABLES FOR THE HORSES. GOOD NIGHT!
THE NEXT DAY JAMES TOLD OF THE MAN WHO WAS SEEN ENTERING THE STABLE WITH A PIPE, AND EXITING WITHOUT IT. IT WAS THOUGHT THAT THIS WAS HOW THE FIRE HAD STARTED.

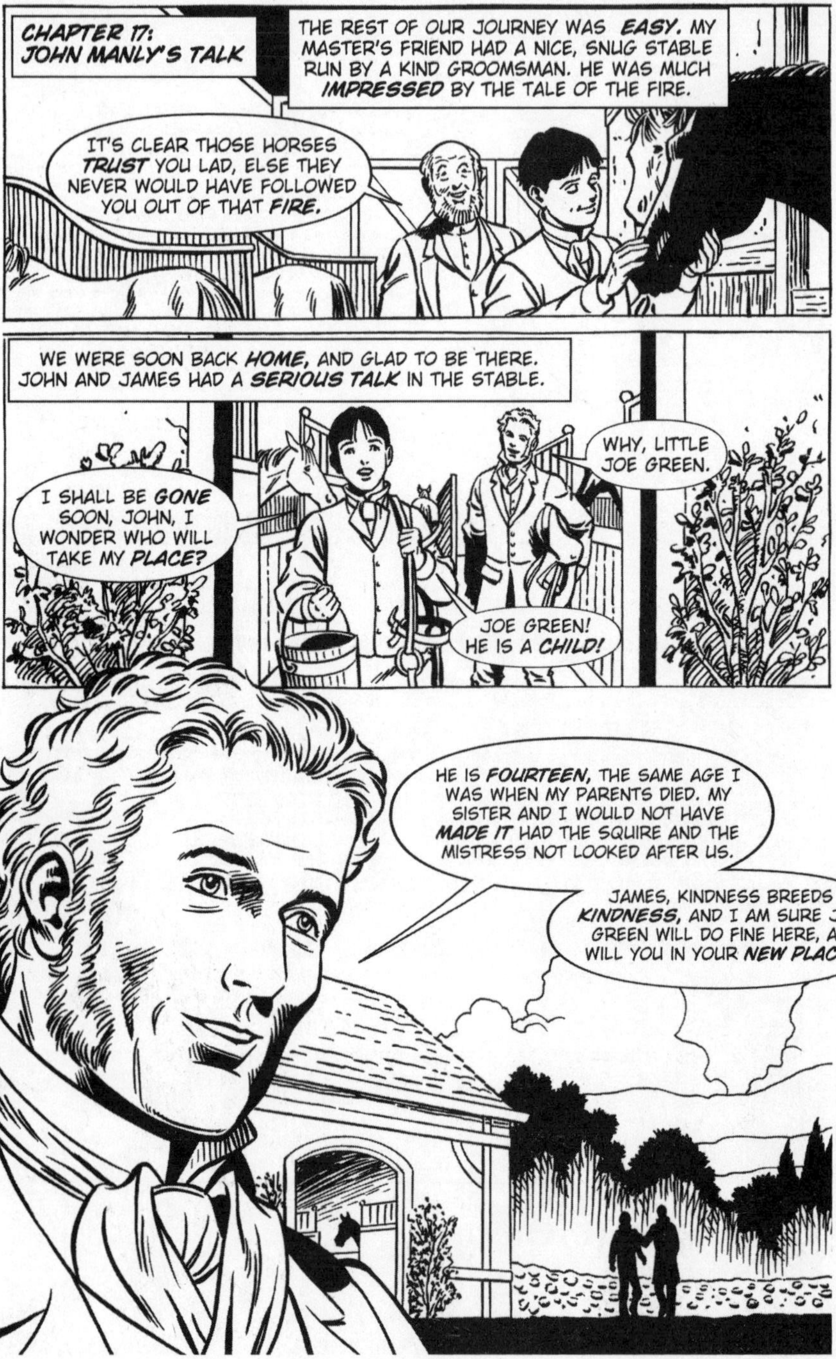

CHAPTER 17: JOHN MANLY'S TALK
THE REST OF OUR JOURNEY WAS EASY. MY MASTER'S FRIEND HAD A NICE, SNUG STABLE RUN BY A KIND GROOMSMAN. HE WAS MUCH IMPRESSED BY THE TALE OF THE FIRE.
IT'S CLEAR THOSE HORSES TRUST YOU LAD, ELSE THEY NEVER WOULD HAVE FOLLOWED YOU OUT OF THAT FIRE.
WE WERE SOON BACK HOME, AND GLAD TO BE THERE. JOHN AND JAMES HAD A SERIOUS TALK IN THE STABLE.
I SHALL BE GONE SOON, JOHN, I WONDER WHO WILL TAKE MY PLACE?
WHY, LITTLE JOE GREEN.
JOE GREEN! HE IS A CHILD!
HE IS FOURTEEN, THE SAME AGE I WAS WHEN MY PARENTS DIED. MY SISTER AND I WOULD NOT HAVE MADE IT HAD THE SQUIRE AND THE MISTRESS NOT LOOKED AFTER US.
JAMES, KINDNESS BREEDS KINDNESS, AND I AM SURE JOE GREEN WILL DO FINE HERE, AS WILL YOU IN YOUR NEW PLACE.

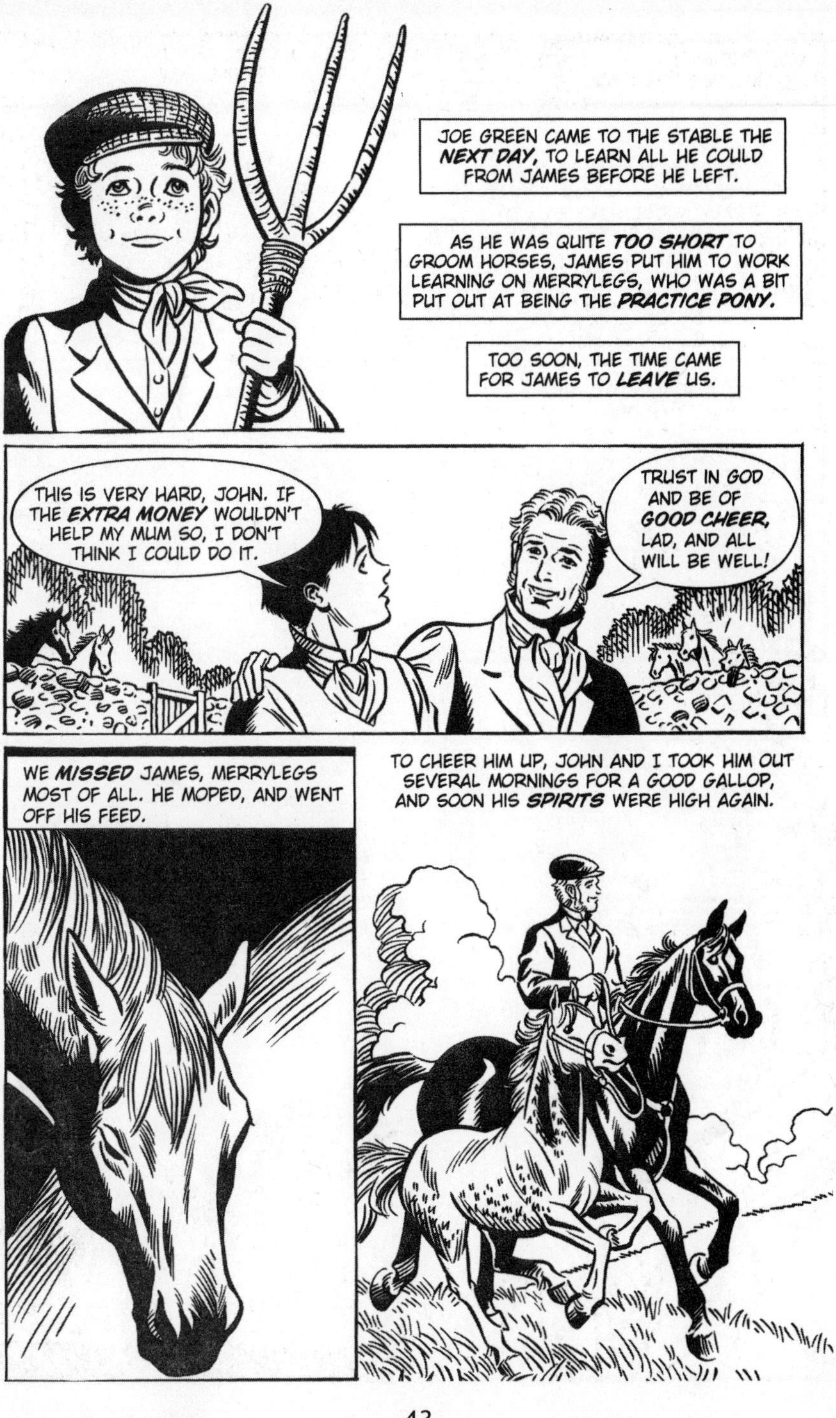
JOE GREEN CAME TO THE STABLE THE NEXT DAY, TO LEARN ALL HE COULD FROM JAMES BEFORE HE LEFT.
AS HE WAS QUITE TOO SHORT TO GROOM HORSES, JAMES PUT HIM TO WORK LEARNING ON MERRYLEGS, WHO WAS A BIT PUT OUT AT BEING THE PRACTICE PONY.
TOO SOON, THE TIME CAME FOR JAMES TO LEAVE US.
THIS IS VERY HARD, JOHN. IF THE EXTRA MONEY WOULDN'T HELP MY MUM SO, I DON'T THINK I COULD DO IT.
TRUST IN GOD AND BE OF GOOD CHEER, LAD, AND ALL WILL BE WELL!
WE MISSED JAMES, MERRYLEGS MOST OF ALL. HE MOPED, AND WENT OFF HIS FEED.
TO CHEER HIM UP, JOHN AND I TOOK HIM OUT SEVERAL MORNINGS FOR A GOOD GALLOP, AND SOON HIS SPIRITS WERE HIGH AGAIN.

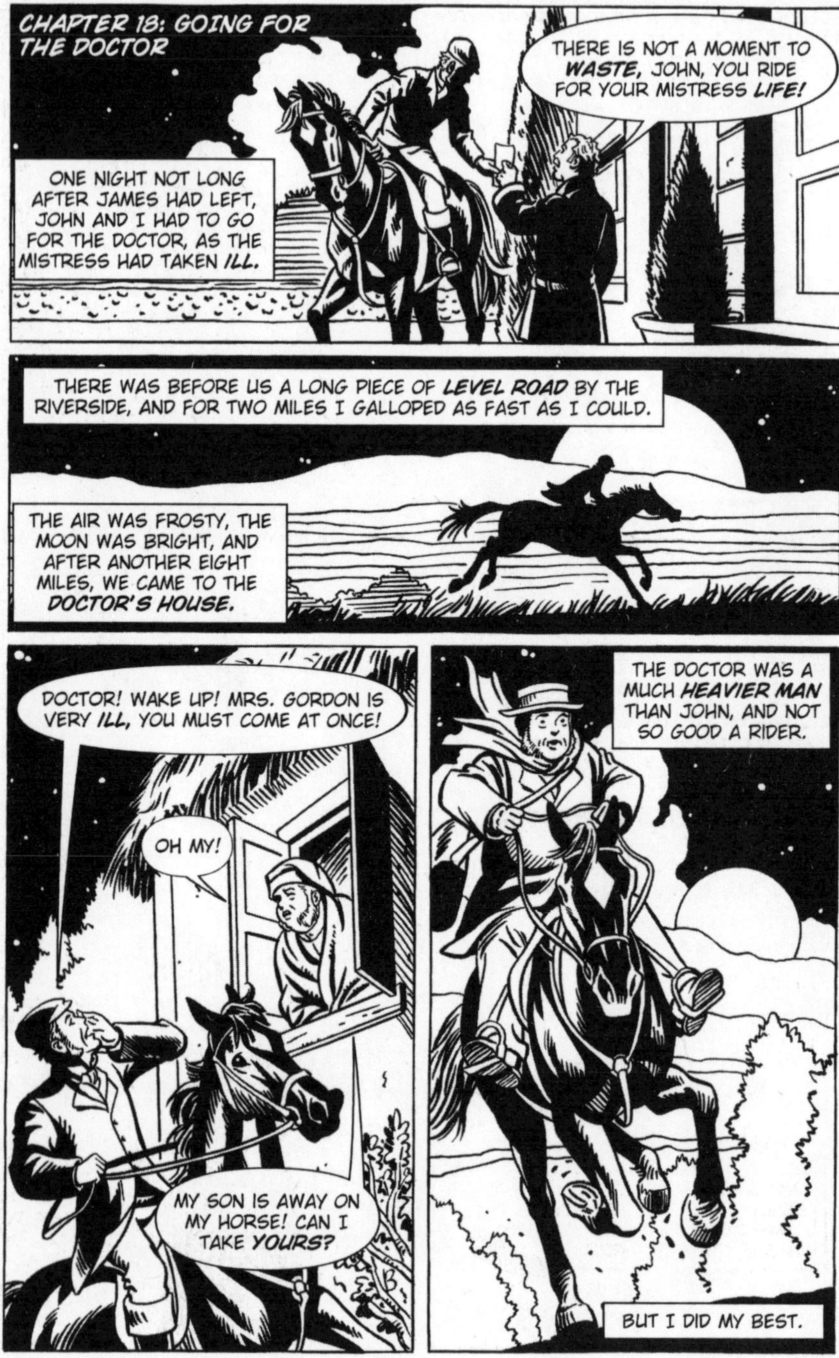
CHAPTER 18: GOING FOR THE DOCTOR
THERE IS NOT A MOMENT TO WASTE, JOHN, YOU RIDE FOR YOUR MISTRESS LIFE!
ONE NIGHT NOT LONG AFTER JAMES HAD LEFT, JOHN AND I HAD TO GO FOR THE DOCTOR, AS THE MISTRESS HAD TAKEN ILL.
THERE WAS BEFORE US A LONG PIECE OF LEVEL ROAD BY THE RIVERSIDE, AND FOR TWO MILES I GALLOPED AS FAST AS I COULD.
THE AIR WAS FROSTY, THE MOON WAS BRIGHT, AND AFTER ANOTHER EIGHT MILES, WE CAME TO THE DOCTOR'S HOUSE.
DOCTOR! WAKE UP! MRS. GORDON IS VERY ILL, YOU MUST COME AT ONCE!
OH MY!
MY SON IS AWAY ON MY HORSE! CAN I TAKE YOURS?
THE DOCTOR WAS A MUCH HEAVIER MAN THAN JOHN, AND NOT SO GOOD A RIDER.
BUT I DID MY BEST.

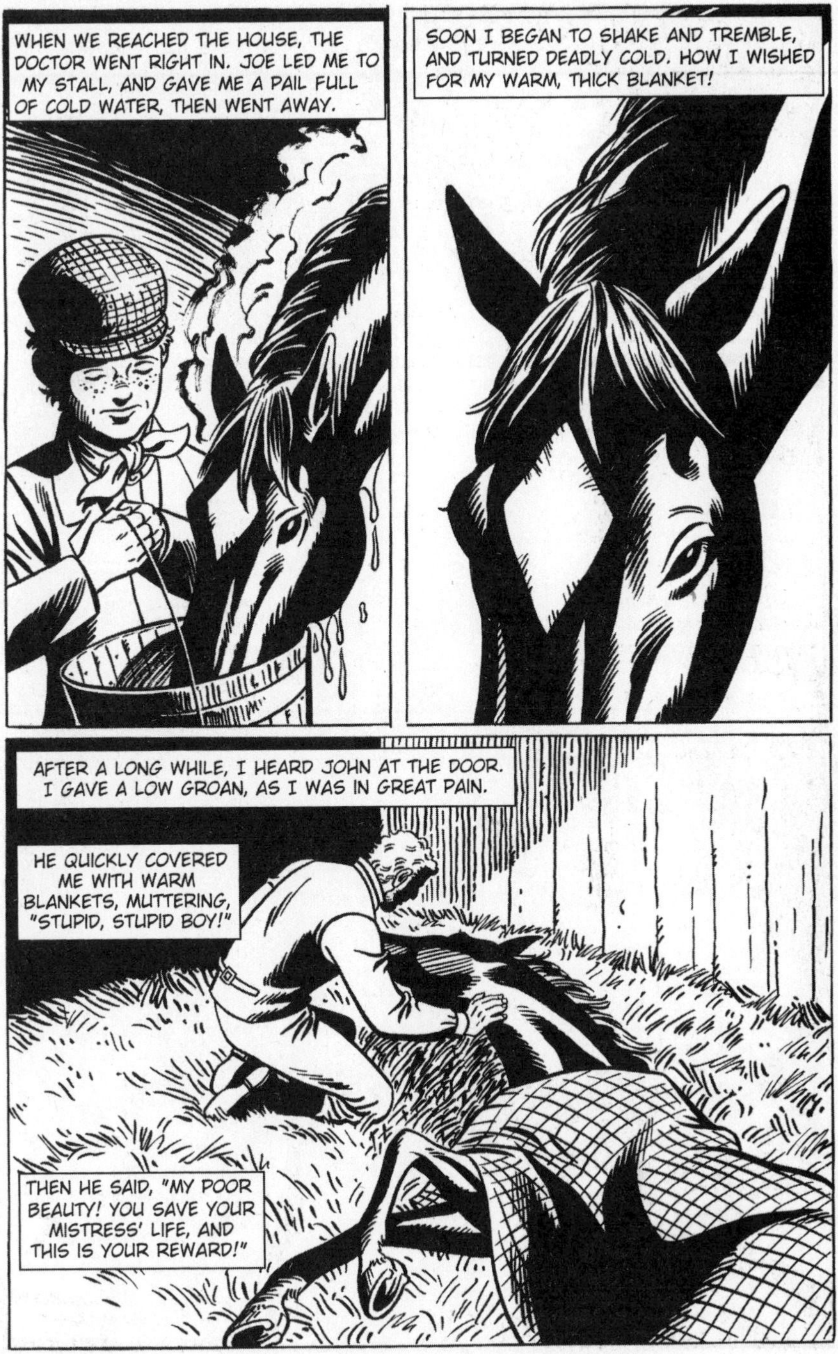
WHEN WE REACHED THE HOUSE, THE DOCTOR WENT RIGHT IN. JOE LED ME TO MY STALL, AND GAVE ME A PAIL FULL OF COLD WATER, THEN WENT AWAY.
SOON I BEGAN TO SHAKE AND TREMBLE, AND TURNED DEADLY COLD. HOW I WISHED FOR MY WARM, THICK BLANKET!
AFTER A LONG WHILE, I HEARD JOHN AT THE DOOR. I GAVE A LOW GROAN, AS I WAS IN GREAT PAIN.
HE QUICKLY COVERED ME WITH WARM BLANKETS, MUTTERING, "STUPID, STUPID BOY!"
THEN HE SAID, "MY POOR BEAUTY! YOU SAVE YOUR MISTRESS' LIFE, AND THIS IS YOUR REWARD!"

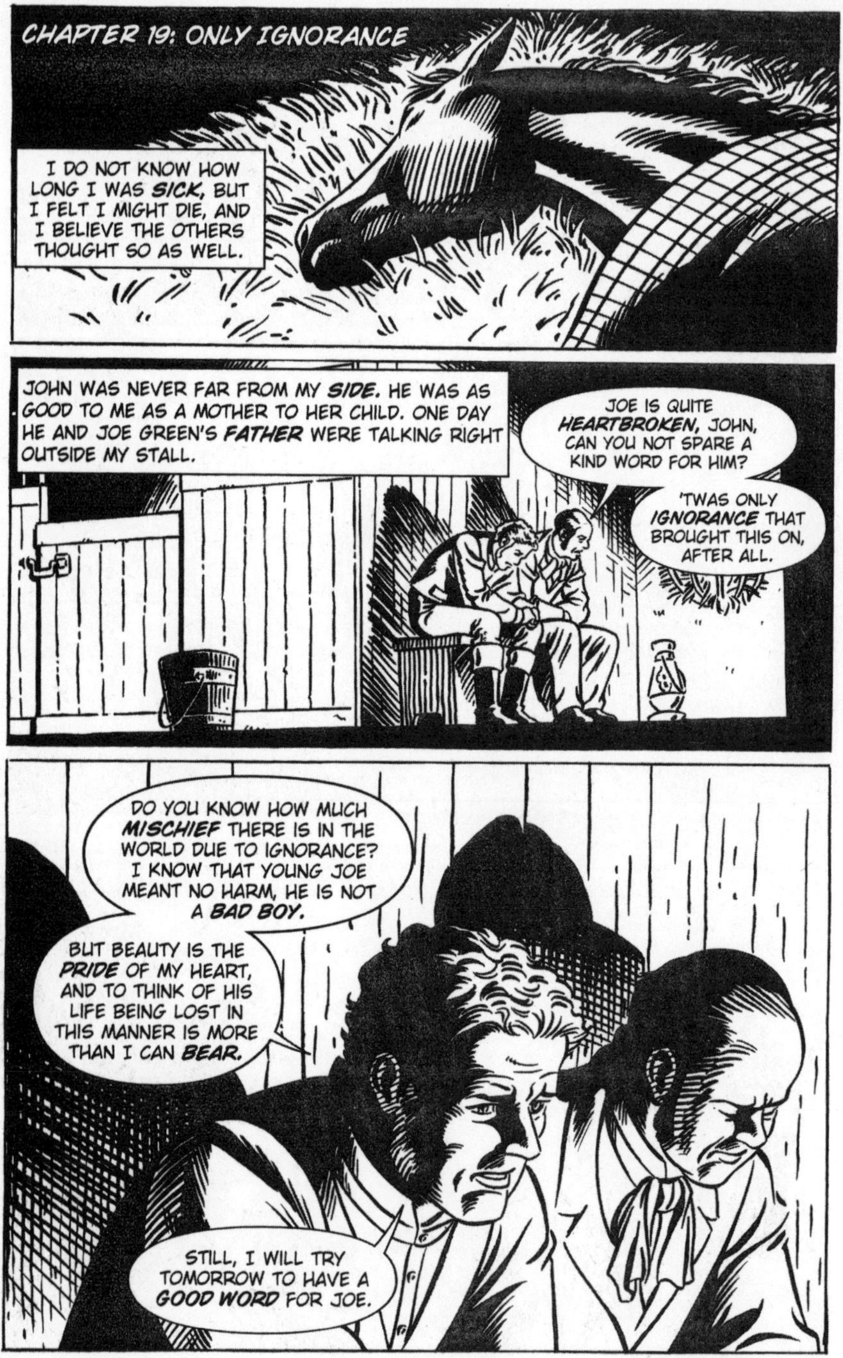
CHAPTER 19: ONLY IGNORANCE
I DO NOT KNOW HOW LONG I WAS SICK, BUT I FELT I MIGHT DIE, AND I BELIEVE THE OTHERS THOUGHT SO AS WELL.
JOHN WAS NEVER FAR FROM MY SIDE. HE WAS AS GOOD TO ME AS A MOTHER TO HER CHILD. ONE DAY HE AND JOE GREEN'S FATHER WERE TALKING RIGHT OUTSIDE MY STALL.
JOE IS QUITE HEARTBROKEN, JOHN, CAN YOU NOT SPARE A KIND WORD FOR HIM?
'TWAS ONLY IGNORANCE THAT BROUGHT THIS ON, AFTER ALL.
DO YOU KNOW HOW MUCH MISCHIEF THERE IS IN THE WORLD DUE TO IGNORANCE? I KNOW THAT YOUNG JOE MEANT NO HARM, HE IS NOT A BAD BOY.
BUT BEAUTY IS THE PRIDE OF MY HEART, AND TO THINK OF HIS LIFE BEING LOST IN THIS MANNER IS MORE THAN I CAN BEAR.
STILL, I WILL TRY TOMORROW TO HAVE A GOOD WORD FOR JOE.

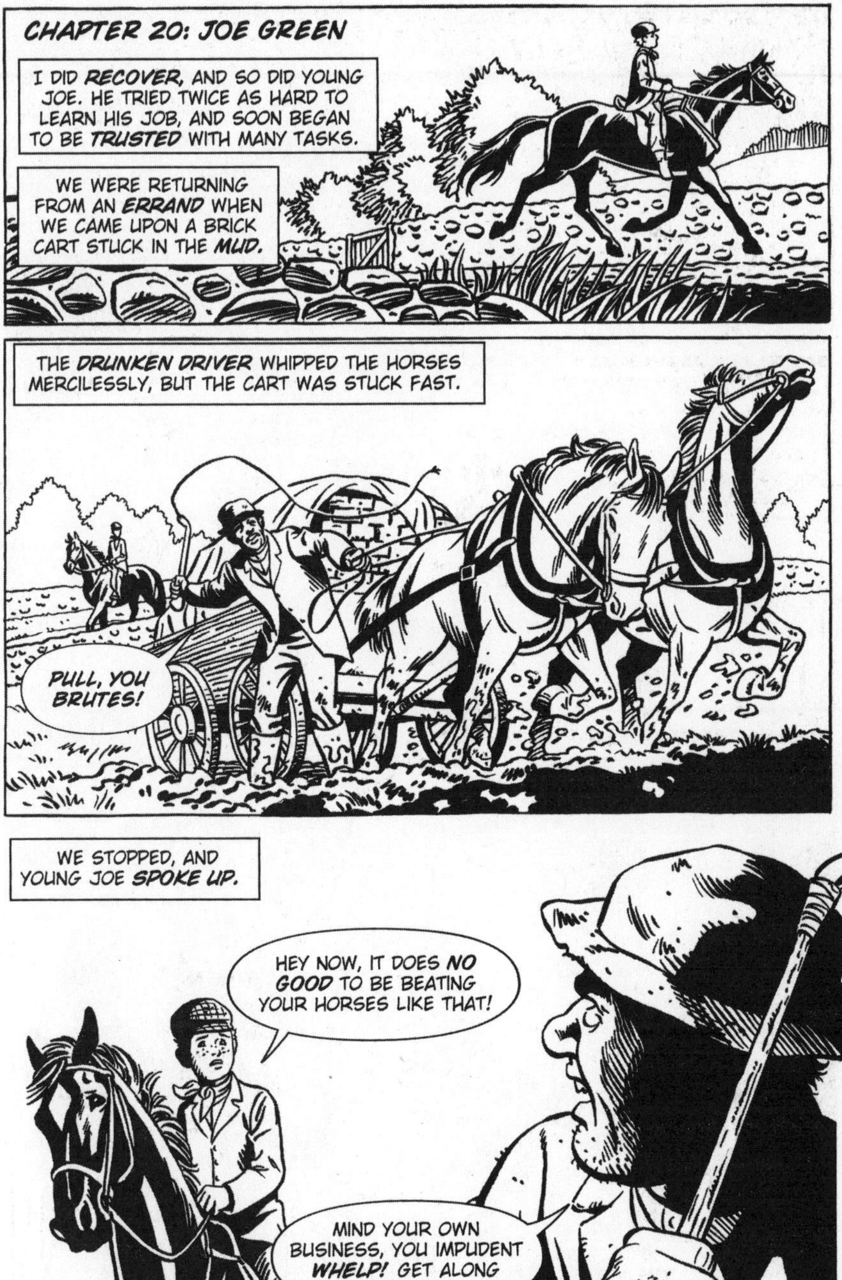
CHAPTER 20: JOE GREEN
I DID RECOVER, AND SO DID YOUNG JOE. HE TRIED TWICE AS HARD TO LEARN HIS JOB, AND SOON BEGAN TO BE TRUSTED WITH MANY TASKS.
WE WERE RETURNING FROM AN ERRAND WHEN WE CAME UPON A BRICK CART STUCK IN THE MUD.
THE DRUNKEN DRIVER WHIPPED THE HORSES MERCILESSLY, BUT THE CART WAS STUCK FAST.
PULL, YOU BRUTES!
WE STOPPED, AND YOUNG JOE SPOKE UP.
HEY NOW, IT DOES NO GOOD TO BE BEATING YOUR HORSES LIKE THAT!
MIND YOUR OWN BUSINESS, YOU IMPUDENT WHELP! GET ALONG WITH YOU!

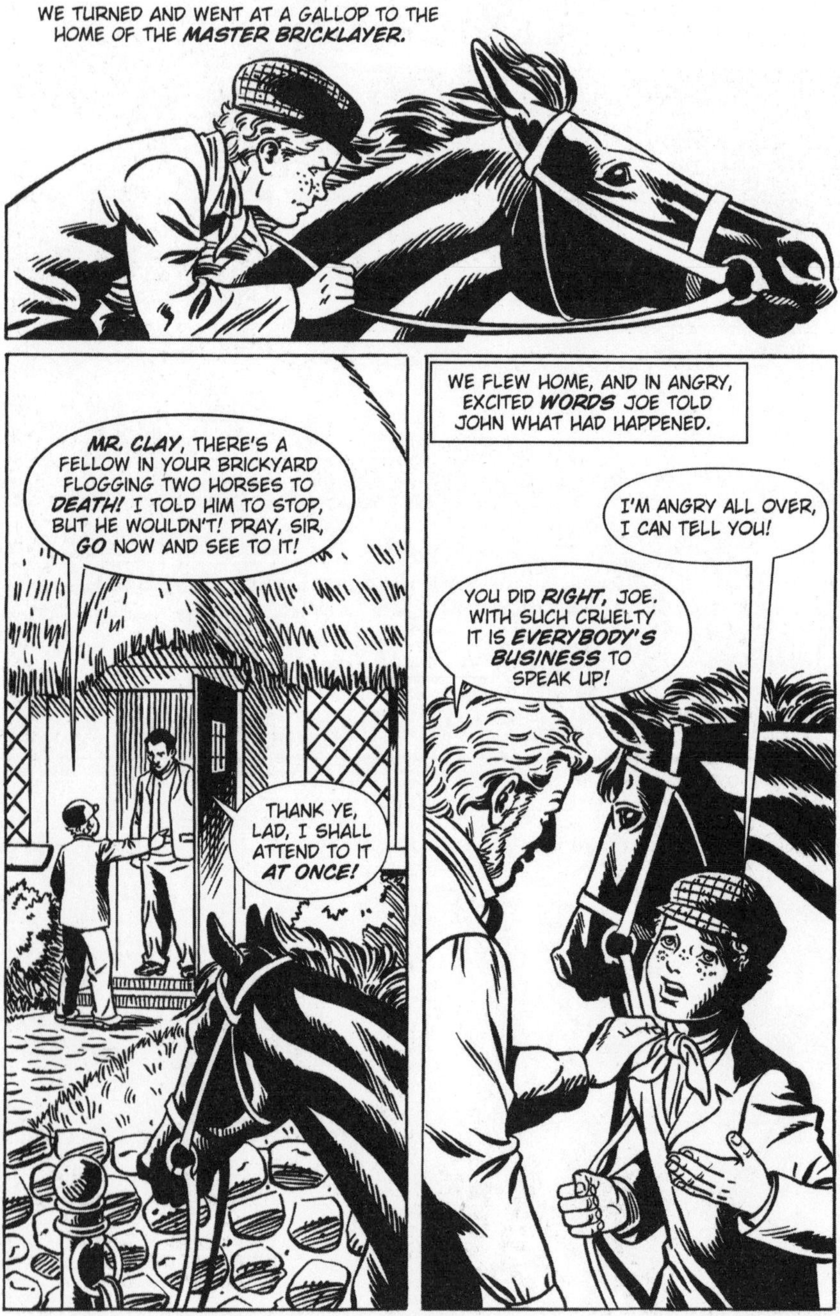
WE TURNED AND WENT AT A GALLOP TO THE HOME OF THE MASTER BRICKLAYER.
MR. CLAY, THERE'S A FELLOW IN YOUR BRICKYARD FLOGGING TWO HORSES TO DEATH! I TOLD HIM TO STOP, BUT HE WOULDN'T! PRAY, SIR, GO NOW AND SEE TO IT!
THANK YE, LAD, I SHALL ATTEND TO IT AT ONCE!
WE FLEW HOME, AND IN ANGRY, EXCITED WORDS JOE TOLD JOHN WHAT HAD HAPPENED.
I'M ANGRY ALL OVER, I CAN TELL YOU!
YOU DID RIGHT, JOE. WITH SUCH CRUELTY IT IS EVERYBODY'S BUSINESS TO SPEAK UP!

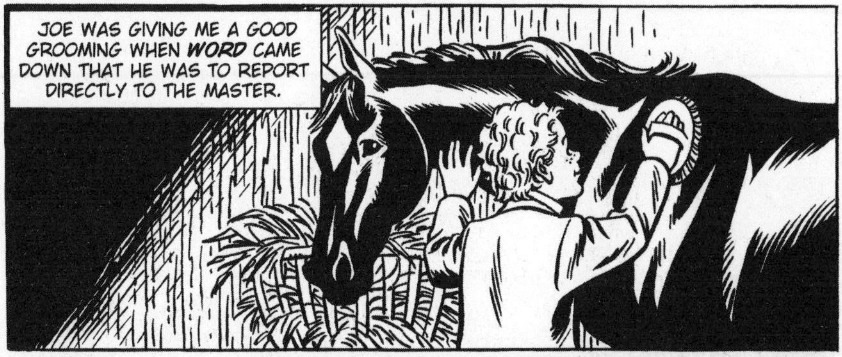
JOE WAS GIVING ME A GOOD GROOMING WHEN ***WORD*** CAME DOWN THAT HE WAS TO REPORT DIRECTLY TO THE MASTER.

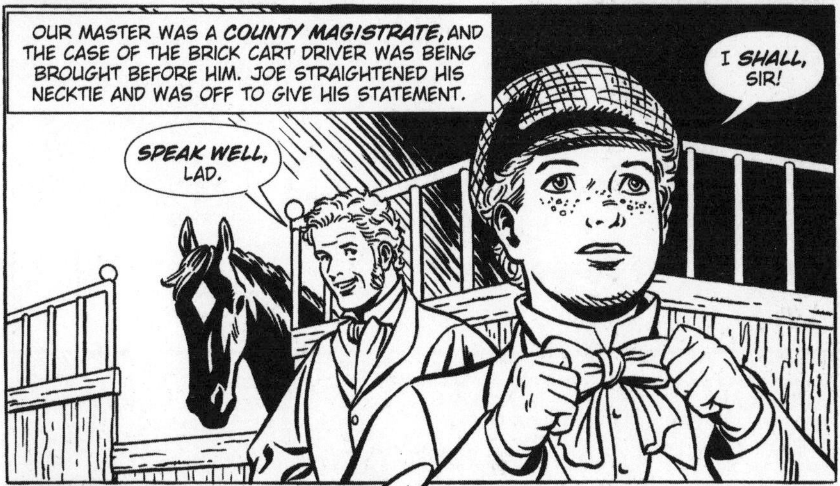
OUR MASTER WAS A ***COUNTY MAGISTRATE,*** AND THE CASE OF THE BRICK CART DRIVER WAS BEING BROUGHT BEFORE HIM. JOE STRAIGHTENED HIS NECKTIE AND WAS OFF TO GIVE HIS STATEMENT.
SPEAK WELL, LAD.
I ***SHALL,*** SIR!

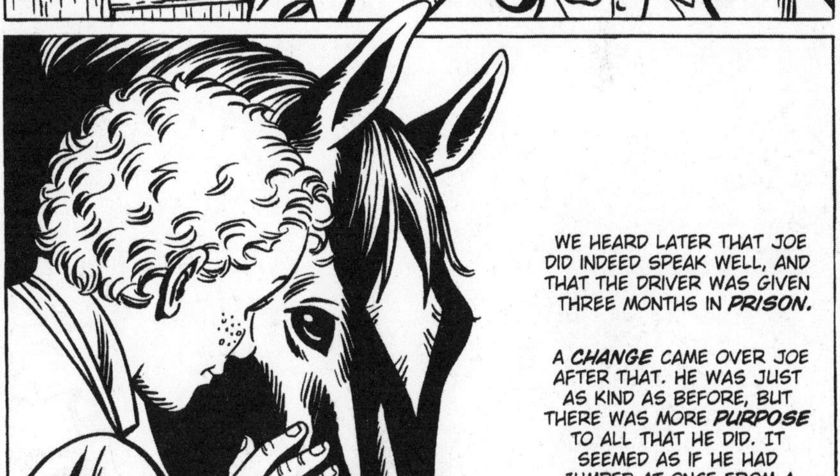
WE HEARD LATER THAT JOE DID INDEED SPEAK WELL, AND THAT THE DRIVER WAS GIVEN THREE MONTHS IN ***PRISON.***
A ***CHANGE*** CAME OVER JOE AFTER THAT. HE WAS JUST AS KIND AS BEFORE, BUT THERE WAS MORE ***PURPOSE*** TO ALL THAT HE DID. IT SEEMED AS IF HE HAD JUMPED AT ONCE FROM A BOY INTO A ***MAN.***

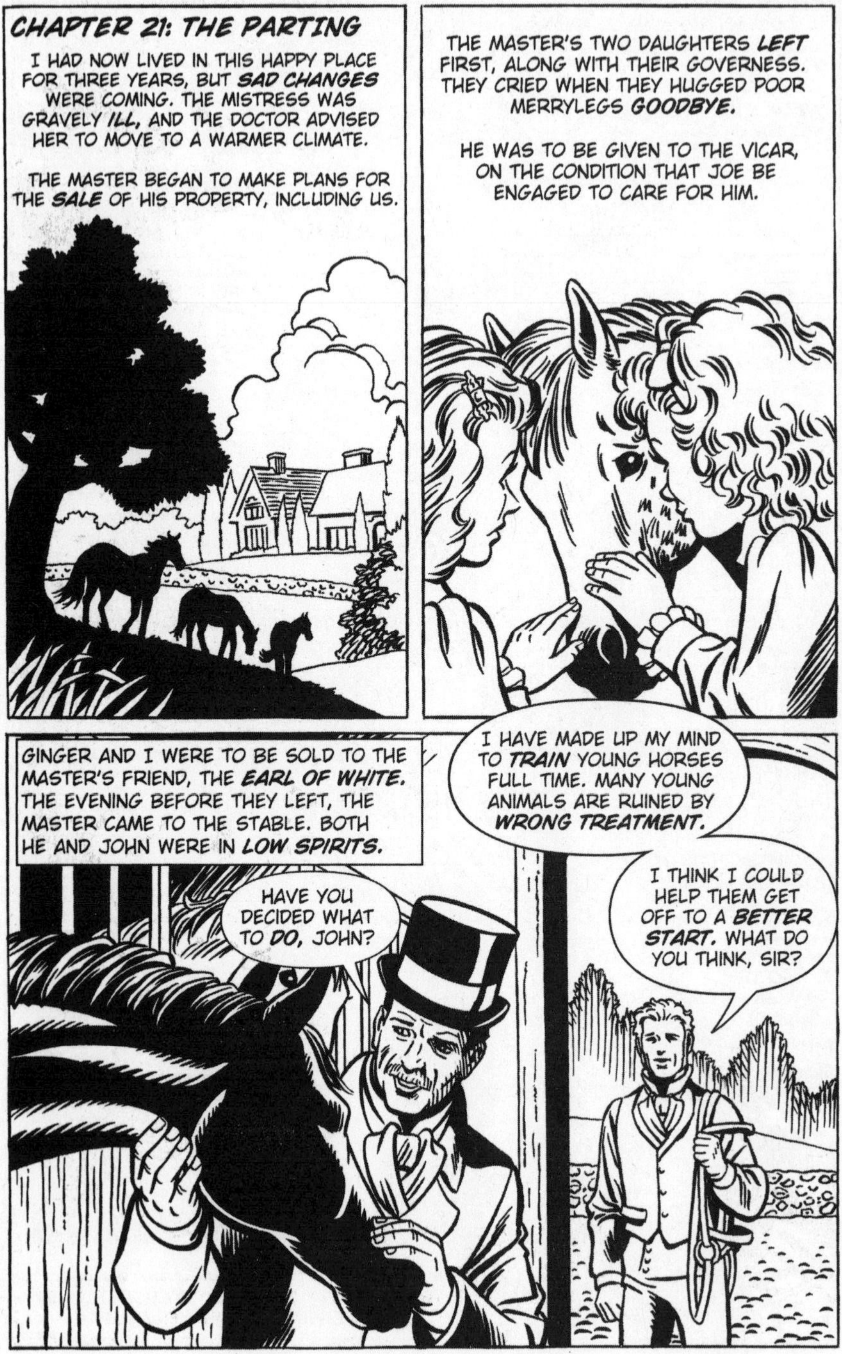
CHAPTER 21: THE PARTING
I HAD NOW LIVED IN THIS HAPPY PLACE FOR THREE YEARS, BUT SAD CHANGES WERE COMING. THE MISTRESS WAS GRAVELY ILL, AND THE DOCTOR ADVISED HER TO MOVE TO A WARMER CLIMATE.
THE MASTER BEGAN TO MAKE PLANS FOR THE SALE OF HIS PROPERTY, INCLUDING US.
THE MASTER'S TWO DAUGHTERS LEFT FIRST, ALONG WITH THEIR GOVERNESS. THEY CRIED WHEN THEY HUGGED POOR MERRYLEGS GOODBYE.
HE WAS TO BE GIVEN TO THE VICAR, ON THE CONDITION THAT JOE BE ENGAGED TO CARE FOR HIM.
GINGER AND I WERE TO BE SOLD TO THE MASTER'S FRIEND, THE EARL OF WHITE. THE EVENING BEFORE THEY LEFT, THE MASTER CAME TO THE STABLE. BOTH HE AND JOHN WERE IN LOW SPIRITS.
HAVE YOU DECIDED WHAT TO DO, JOHN?
I HAVE MADE UP MY MIND TO TRAIN YOUNG HORSES FULL TIME. MANY YOUNG ANIMALS ARE RUINED BY WRONG TREATMENT.
I THINK I COULD HELP THEM GET OFF TO A BETTER START. WHAT DO YOU THINK, SIR?

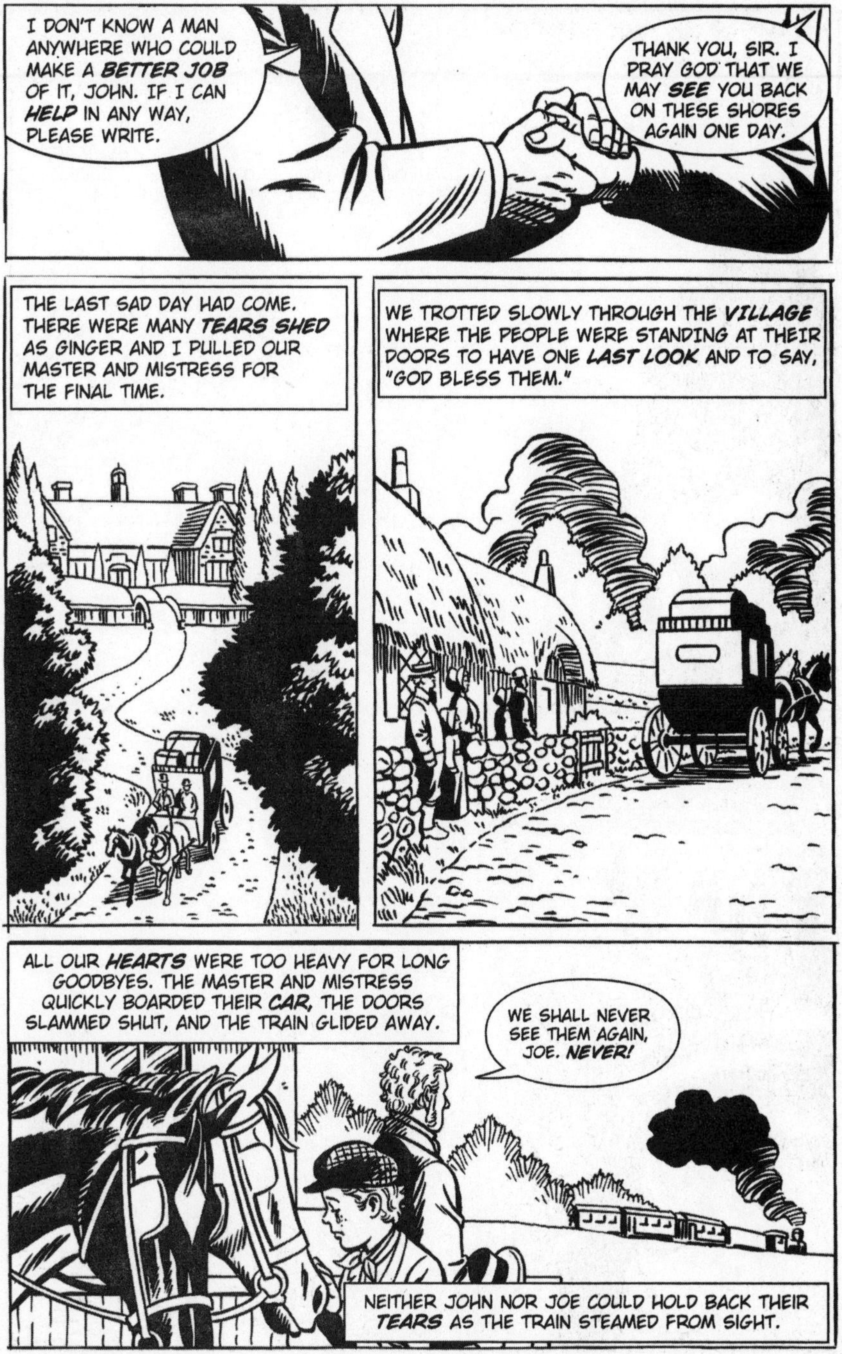
I DON'T KNOW A MAN ANYWHERE WHO COULD MAKE A **BETTER JOB** OF IT, JOHN. IF I CAN **HELP** IN ANY WAY, PLEASE WRITE.
THANK YOU, SIR. I PRAY GOD THAT WE MAY **SEE** YOU BACK ON THESE SHORES AGAIN ONE DAY.
THE LAST SAD DAY HAD COME. THERE WERE MANY **TEARS SHED** AS GINGER AND I PULLED OUR MASTER AND MISTRESS FOR THE FINAL TIME.
WE TROTTED SLOWLY THROUGH THE **VILLAGE** WHERE THE PEOPLE WERE STANDING AT THEIR DOORS TO HAVE ONE **LAST LOOK** AND TO SAY, "GOD BLESS THEM."
ALL OUR **HEARTS** WERE TOO HEAVY FOR LONG GOODBYES. THE MASTER AND MISTRESS QUICKLY BOARDED THEIR **CAR,** THE DOORS SLAMMED SHUT, AND THE TRAIN GLIDED AWAY.
WE SHALL NEVER SEE THEM AGAIN, JOE. **NEVER!**
NEITHER JOHN NOR JOE COULD HOLD BACK THEIR **TEARS** AS THE TRAIN STEAMED FROM SIGHT.

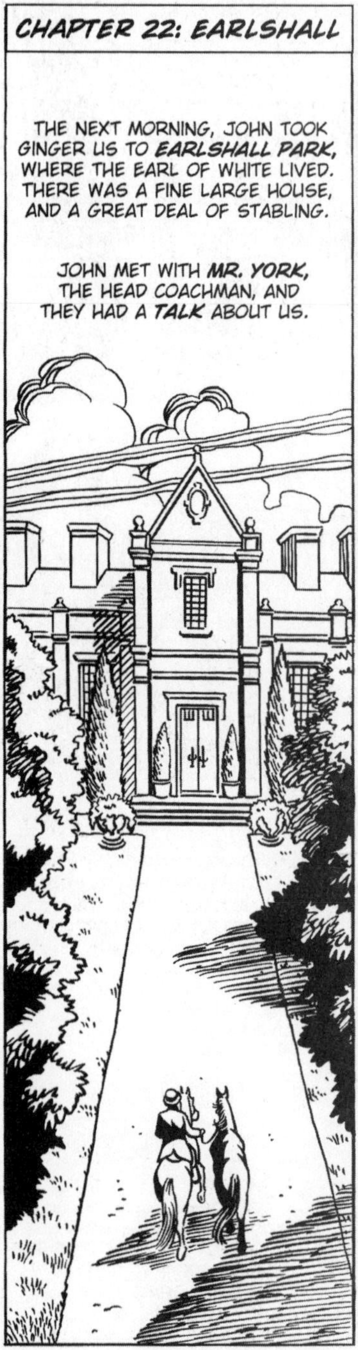
CHAPTER 22: EARLSHALL
THE NEXT MORNING, JOHN TOOK GINGER US TO EARLSHALL PARK, WHERE THE EARL OF WHITE LIVED. THERE WAS A FINE LARGE HOUSE, AND A GREAT DEAL OF STABLING.
JOHN MET WITH MR. YORK, THE HEAD COACHMAN, AND THEY HAD A TALK ABOUT US.

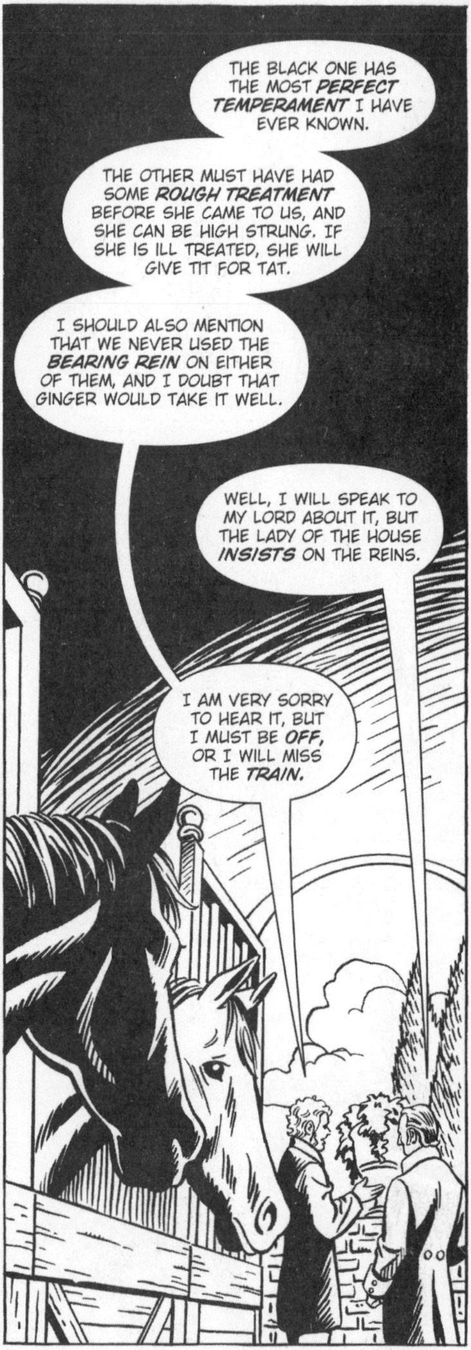
THE BLACK ONE HAS THE MOST PERFECT TEMPERAMENT I HAVE EVER KNOWN.
THE OTHER MUST HAVE HAD SOME ROUGH TREATMENT BEFORE SHE CAME TO US, AND SHE CAN BE HIGH STRUNG. IF SHE IS ILL TREATED, SHE WILL GIVE TIT FOR TAT.
I SHOULD ALSO MENTION THAT WE NEVER USED THE BEARING REIN ON EITHER OF THEM, AND I DOUBT THAT GINGER WOULD TAKE IT WELL.
WELL, I WILL SPEAK TO MY LORD ABOUT IT, BUT THE LADY OF THE HOUSE INSISTS ON THE REINS.
I AM VERY SORRY TO HEAR IT, BUT I MUST BE OFF, OR I WILL MISS THE TRAIN.

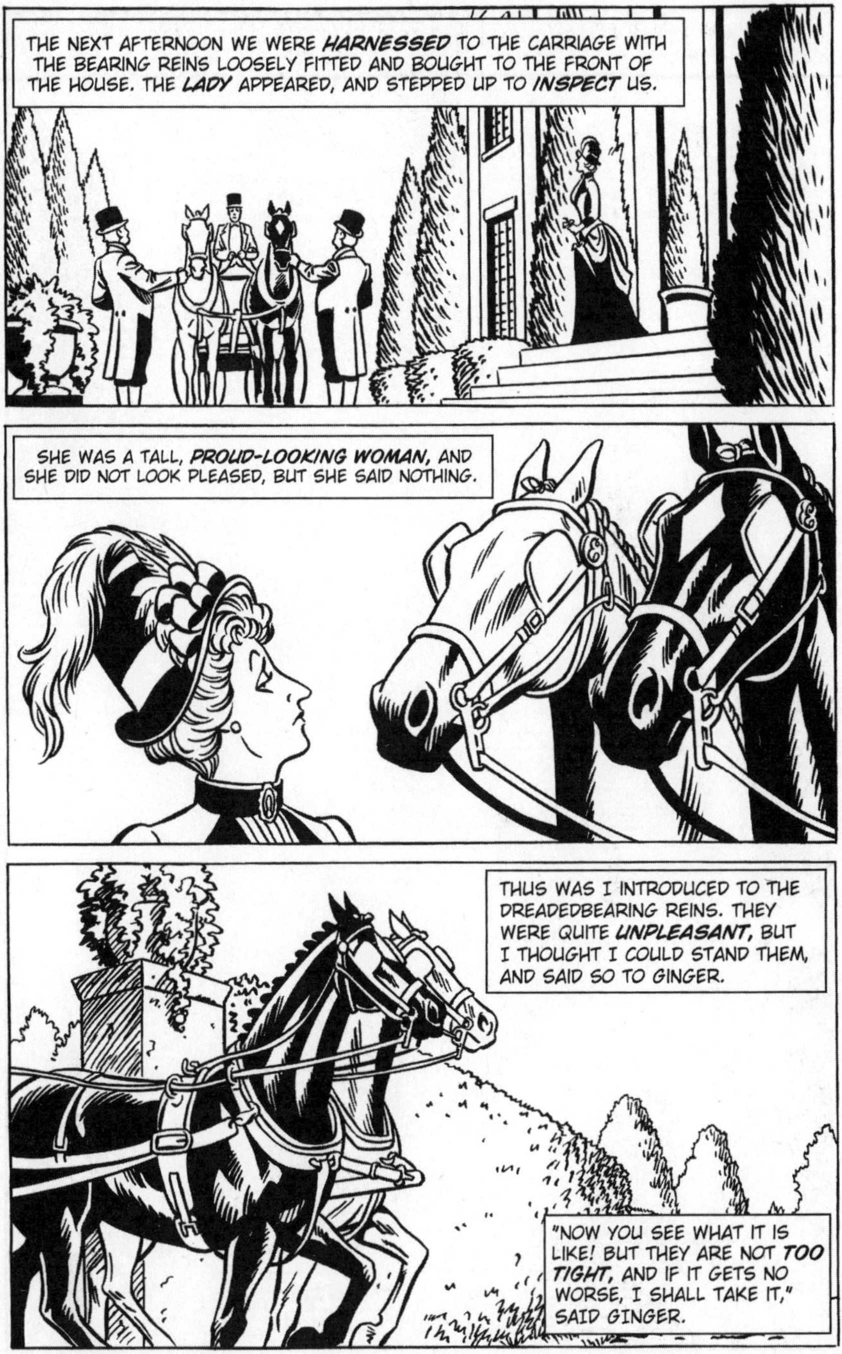
THE NEXT AFTERNOON WE WERE HARNESSED TO THE CARRIAGE WITH THE BEARING REINS LOOSELY FITTED AND BOUGHT TO THE FRONT OF THE HOUSE. THE LADY APPEARED, AND STEPPED UP TO INSPECT US.
SHE WAS A TALL, PROUD-LOOKING WOMAN, AND SHE DID NOT LOOK PLEASED, BUT SHE SAID NOTHING.
THUS WAS I INTRODUCED TO THE DREADEDBEARING REINS. THEY WERE QUITE UNPLEASANT, BUT I THOUGHT I COULD STAND THEM, AND SAID SO TO GINGER.
"NOW YOU SEE WHAT IT IS LIKE! BUT THEY ARE NOT TOO TIGHT, AND IF IT GETS NO WORSE, I SHALL TAKE IT," SAID GINGER.

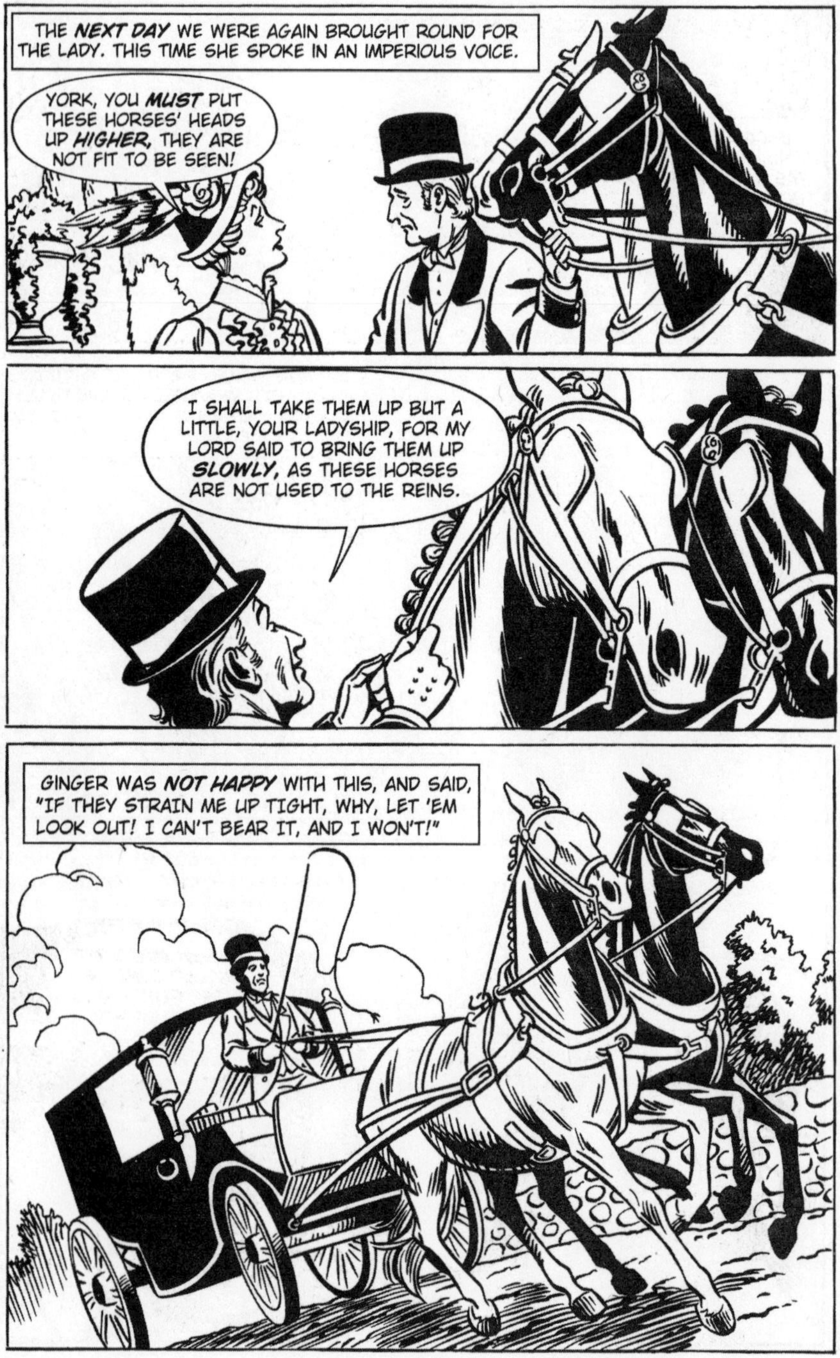
THE NEXT DAY WE WERE AGAIN BROUGHT ROUND FOR THE LADY. THIS TIME SHE SPOKE IN AN IMPERIOUS VOICE.
YORK, YOU MUST PUT THESE HORSES' HEADS UP HIGHER, THEY ARE NOT FIT TO BE SEEN!
I SHALL TAKE THEM UP BUT A LITTLE, YOUR LADYSHIP, FOR MY LORD SAID TO BRING THEM UP SLOWLY, AS THESE HORSES ARE NOT USED TO THE REINS.
GINGER WAS NOT HAPPY WITH THIS, AND SAID, "IF THEY STRAIN ME UP TIGHT, WHY, LET 'EM LOOK OUT! I CAN'T BEAR IT, AND I WON'T!"

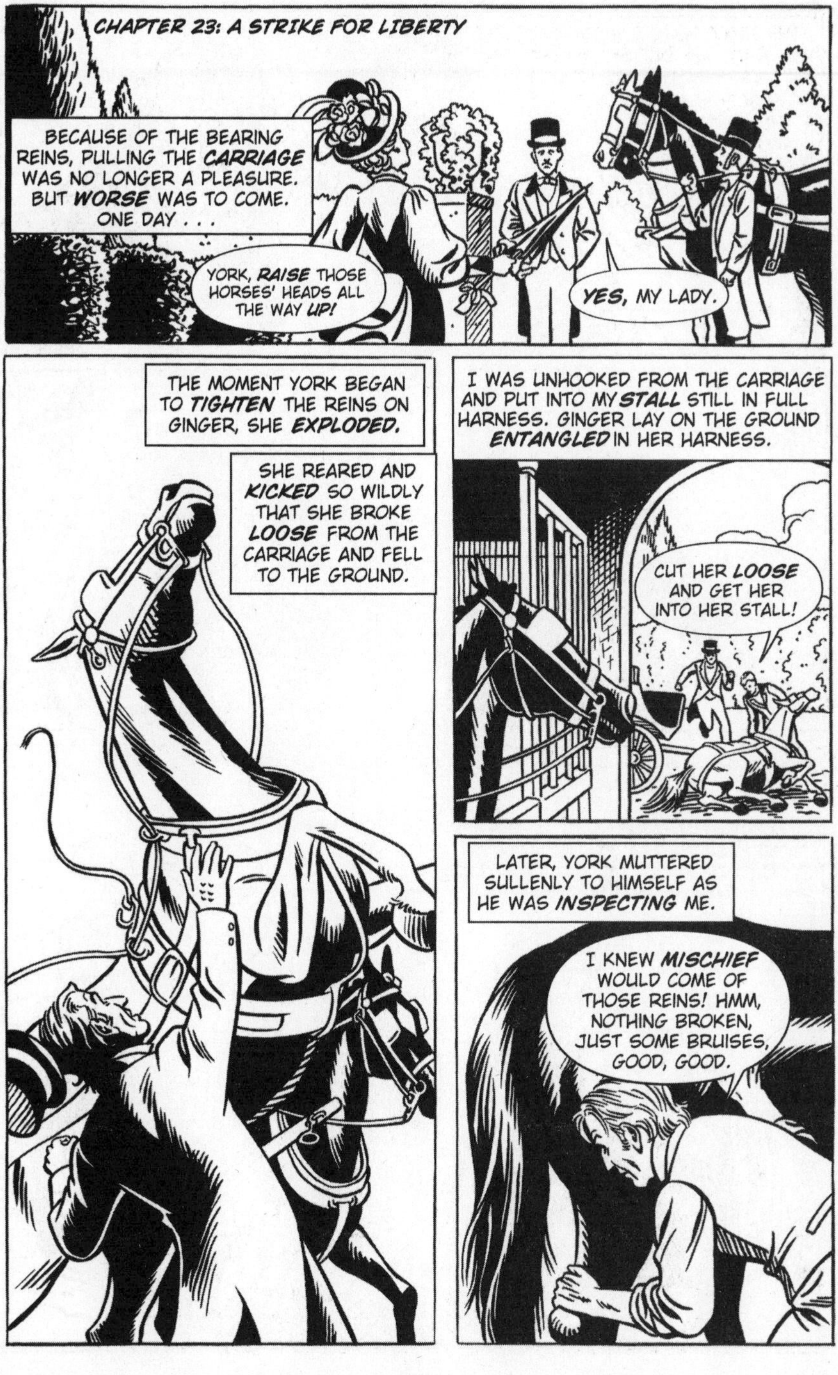
CHAPTER 23: A STRIKE FOR LIBERTY
BECAUSE OF THE BEARING REINS, PULLING THE CARRIAGE WAS NO LONGER A PLEASURE. BUT WORSE WAS TO COME. ONE DAY . . .
YORK, RAISE THOSE HORSES' HEADS ALL THE WAY UP!
YES, MY LADY.
THE MOMENT YORK BEGAN TO TIGHTEN THE REINS ON GINGER, SHE EXPLODED.
SHE REARED AND KICKED SO WILDLY THAT SHE BROKE LOOSE FROM THE CARRIAGE AND FELL TO THE GROUND.
I WAS UNHOOKED FROM THE CARRIAGE AND PUT INTO MY STALL STILL IN FULL HARNESS. GINGER LAY ON THE GROUND ENTANGLED IN HER HARNESS.
CUT HER LOOSE AND GET HER INTO HER STALL!
LATER, YORK MUTTERED SULLENLY TO HIMSELF AS HE WAS INSPECTING ME.
I KNEW MISCHIEF WOULD COME OF THOSE REINS! HMM, NOTHING BROKEN, JUST SOME BRUISES, GOOD, GOOD.

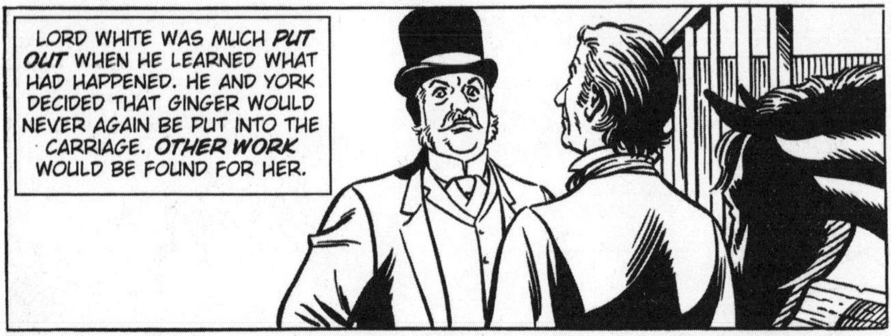
LORD WHITE WAS MUCH PUT OUT WHEN HE LEARNED WHAT HAD HAPPENED. HE AND YORK DECIDED THAT GINGER WOULD NEVER AGAIN BE PUT INTO THE CARRIAGE. OTHER WORK WOULD BE FOUND FOR HER.

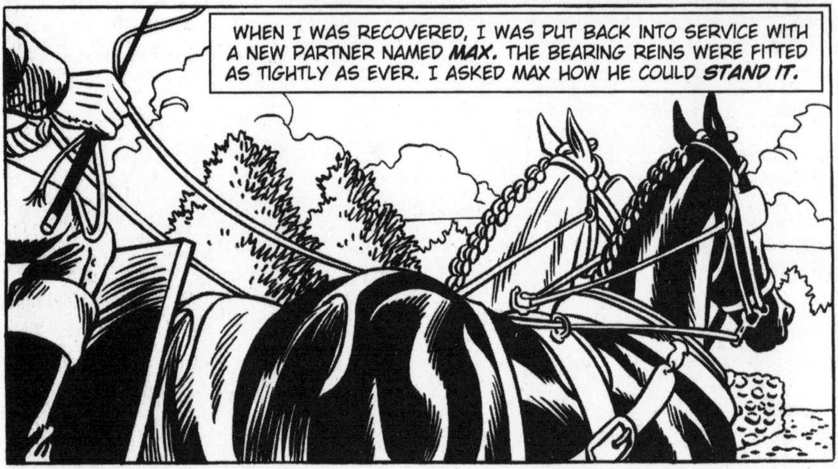
WHEN I WAS RECOVERED, I WAS PUT BACK INTO SERVICE WITH A NEW PARTNER NAMED MAX. THE BEARING REINS WERE FITTED AS TIGHTLY AS EVER. I ASKED MAX HOW HE COULD STAND IT.

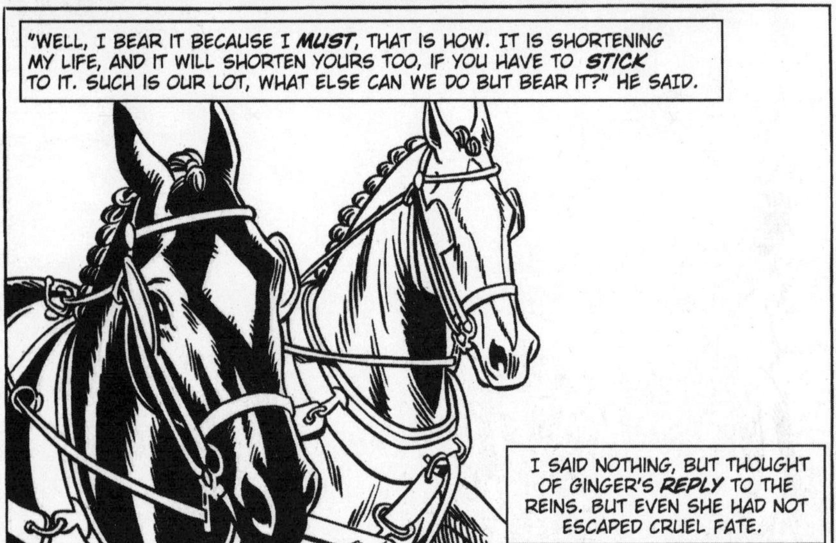
"WELL, I BEAR IT BECAUSE I MUST, THAT IS HOW. IT IS SHORTENING MY LIFE, AND IT WILL SHORTEN YOURS TOO, IF YOU HAVE TO STICK TO IT. SUCH IS OUR LOT, WHAT ELSE CAN WE DO BUT BEAR IT?" HE SAID.
I SAID NOTHING, BUT THOUGHT OF GINGER'S REPLY TO THE REINS. BUT EVEN SHE HAD NOT ESCAPED CRUEL FATE.

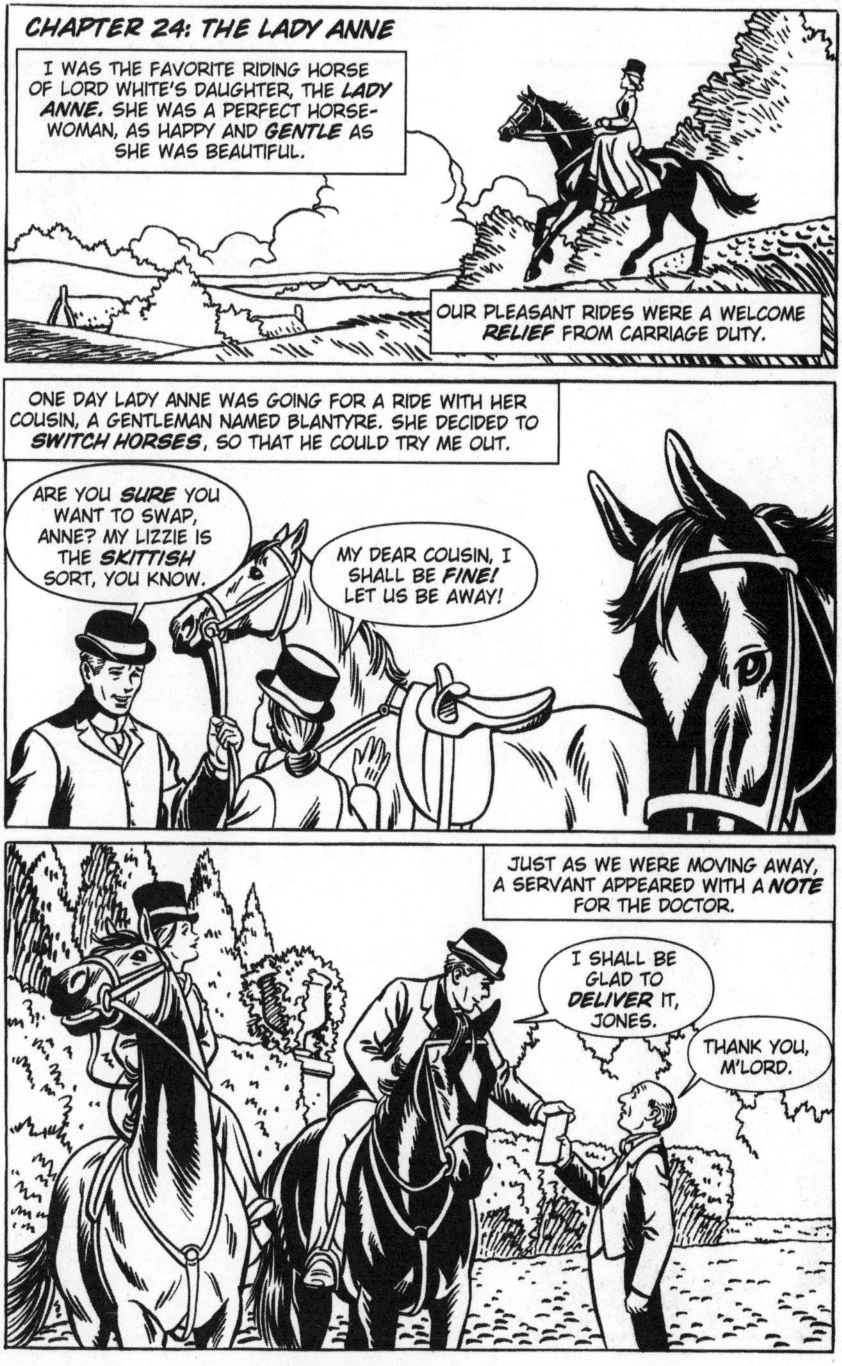
CHAPTER 24: THE LADY ANNE
I WAS THE FAVORITE RIDING HORSE OF LORD WHITE'S DAUGHTER, THE LADY ANNE. SHE WAS A PERFECT HORSE-WOMAN, AS HAPPY AND GENTLE AS SHE WAS BEAUTIFUL.
OUR PLEASANT RIDES WERE A WELCOME RELIEF FROM CARRIAGE DUTY.
ONE DAY LADY ANNE WAS GOING FOR A RIDE WITH HER COUSIN, A GENTLEMAN NAMED BLANTYRE. SHE DECIDED TO SWITCH HORSES, SO THAT HE COULD TRY ME OUT.
ARE YOU SURE YOU WANT TO SWAP, ANNE? MY LIZZIE IS THE SKITTISH SORT, YOU KNOW.
MY DEAR COUSIN, I SHALL BE FINE! LET US BE AWAY!
JUST AS WE WERE MOVING AWAY, A SERVANT APPEARED WITH A NOTE FOR THE DOCTOR.
I SHALL BE GLAD TO DELIVER IT, JONES.
THANK YOU, M'LORD.

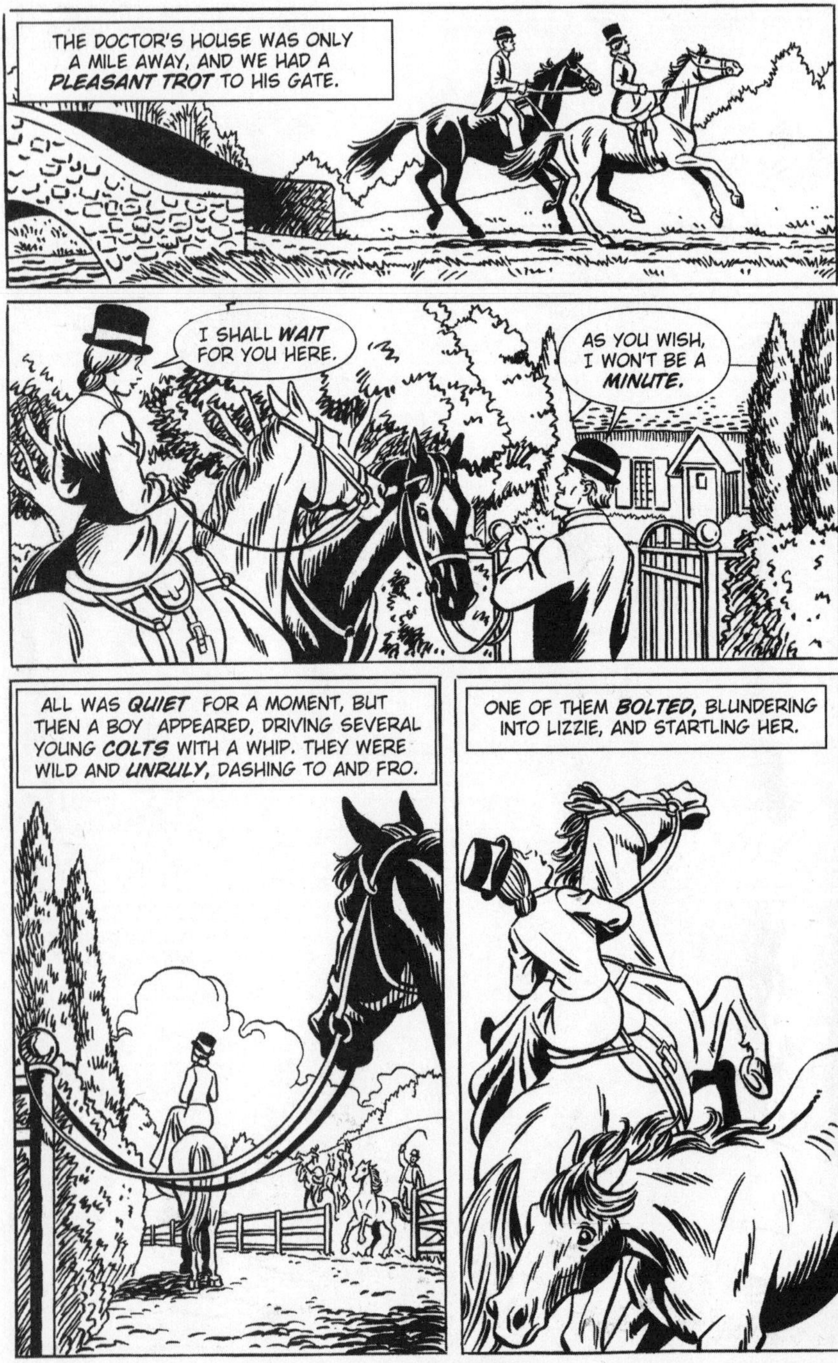
THE DOCTOR'S HOUSE WAS ONLY A MILE AWAY, AND WE HAD A PLEASANT TROT TO HIS GATE.
I SHALL WAIT FOR YOU HERE.
AS YOU WISH, I WON'T BE A MINUTE.
ALL WAS QUIET FOR A MOMENT, BUT THEN A BOY APPEARED, DRIVING SEVERAL YOUNG COLTS WITH A WHIP. THEY WERE WILD AND UNRULY, DASHING TO AND FRO.
ONE OF THEM BOLTED, BLUNDERING INTO LIZZIE, AND STARTLING HER.

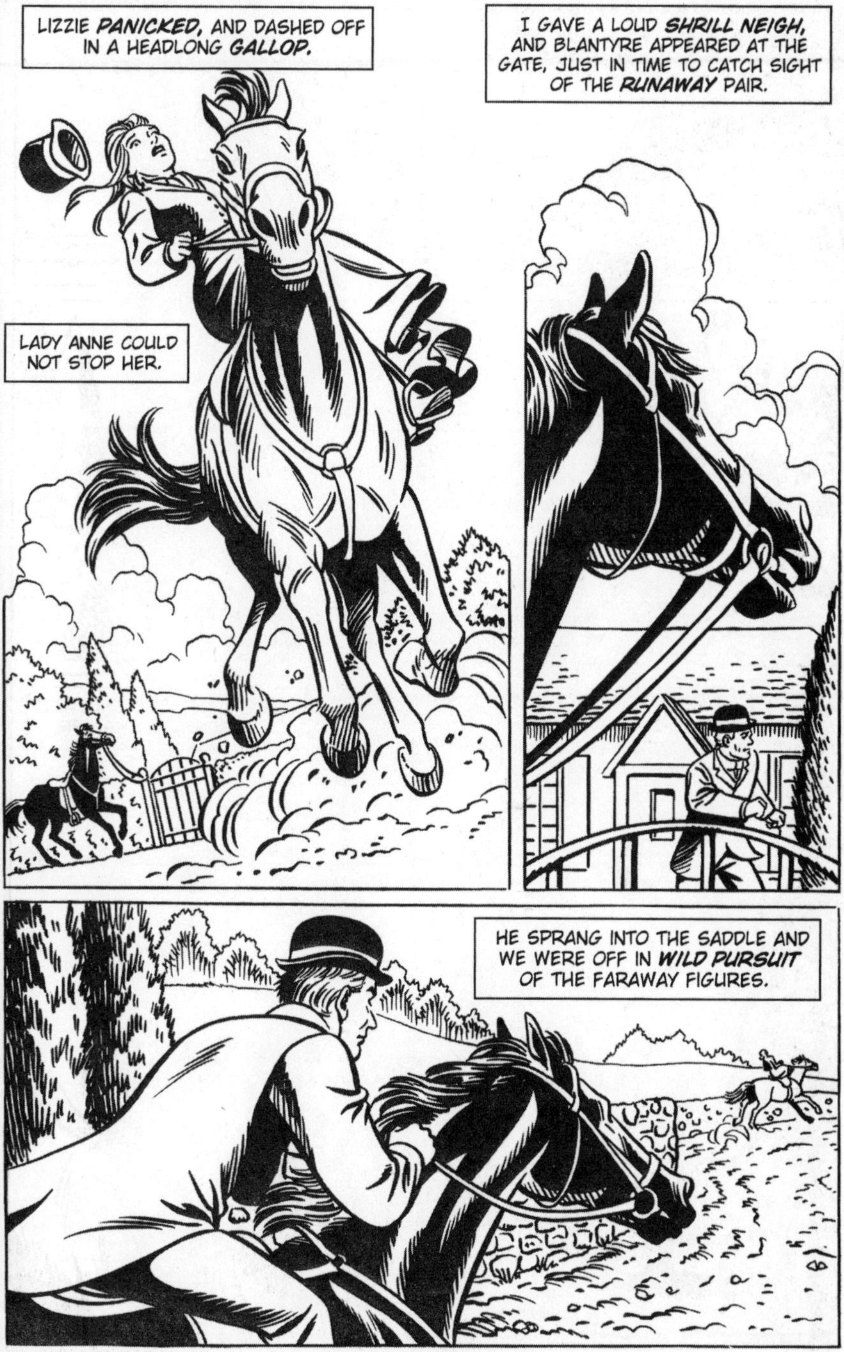

LIZZIE PANICKED, AND DASHED OFF IN A HEADLONG GALLOP.
LADY ANNE COULD NOT STOP HER.
I GAVE A LOUD SHRILL NEIGH, AND BLANTYRE APPEARED AT THE GATE, JUST IN TIME TO CATCH SIGHT OF THE RUNAWAY PAIR.
HE SPRANG INTO THE SADDLE AND WE WERE OFF IN WILD PURSUIT OF THE FARAWAY FIGURES.

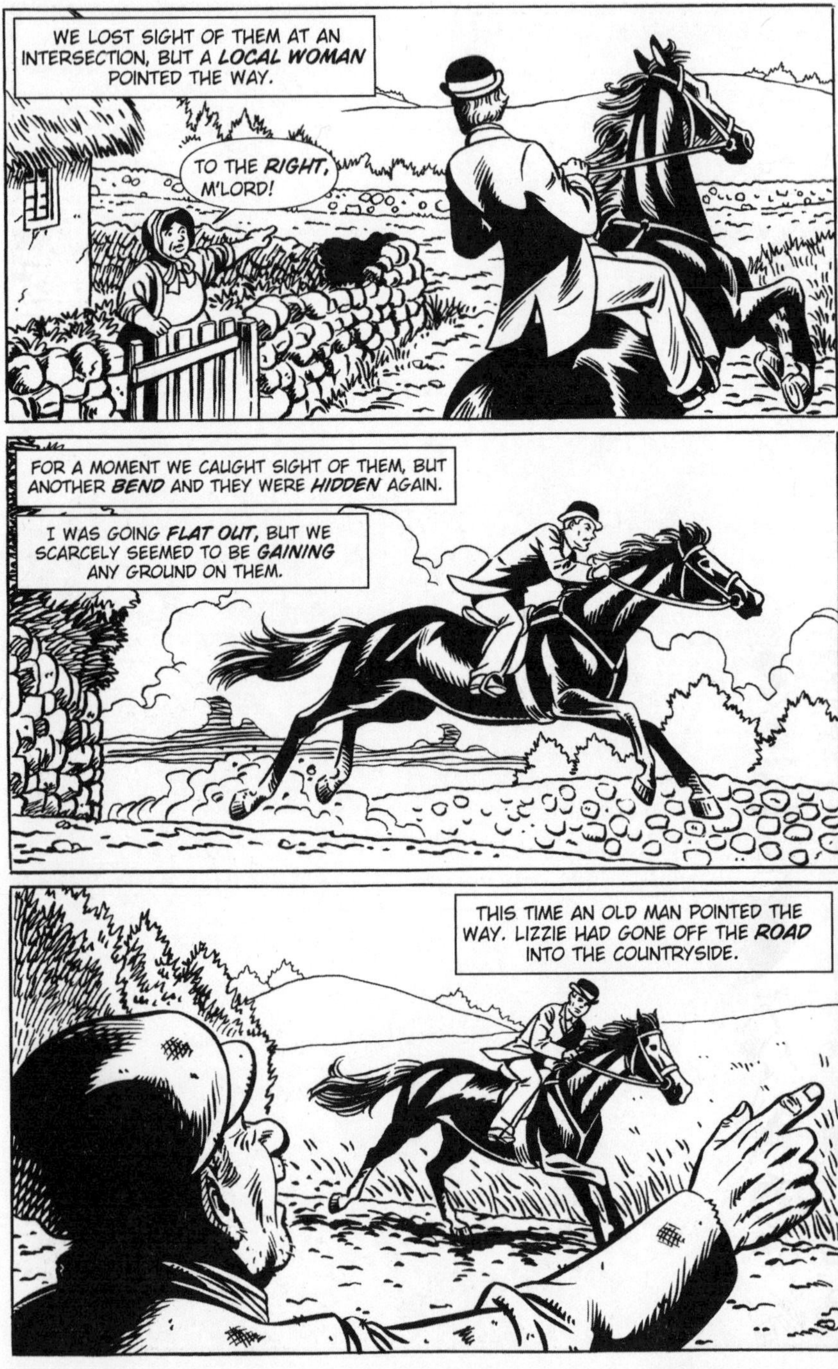
WE LOST SIGHT OF THEM AT AN INTERSECTION, BUT A LOCAL WOMAN POINTED THE WAY.
TO THE RIGHT, M'LORD!
FOR A MOMENT WE CAUGHT SIGHT OF THEM, BUT ANOTHER BEND AND THEY WERE HIDDEN AGAIN.
I WAS GOING FLAT OUT, BUT WE SCARCELY SEEMED TO BE GAINING ANY GROUND ON THEM.
THIS TIME AN OLD MAN POINTED THE WAY. LIZZIE HAD GONE OFF THE ROAD INTO THE COUNTRYSIDE.

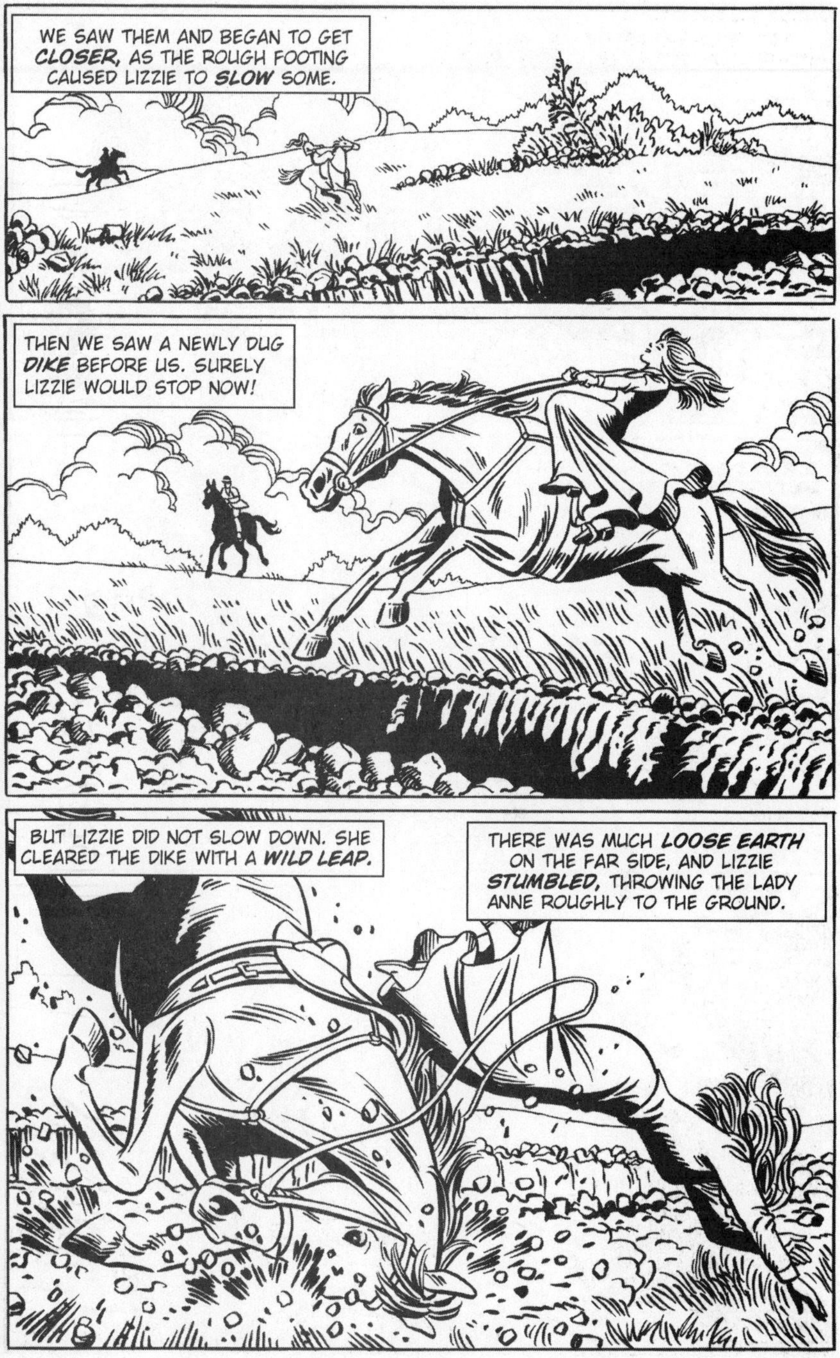
WE SAW THEM AND BEGAN TO GET CLOSER, AS THE ROUGH FOOTING CAUSED LIZZIE TO SLOW SOME.
THEN WE SAW A NEWLY DUG DIKE BEFORE US. SURELY LIZZIE WOULD STOP NOW!
BUT LIZZIE DID NOT SLOW DOWN. SHE CLEARED THE DIKE WITH A WILD LEAP.
THERE WAS MUCH LOOSE EARTH ON THE FAR SIDE, AND LIZZIE STUMBLED, THROWING THE LADY ANNE ROUGHLY TO THE GROUND.

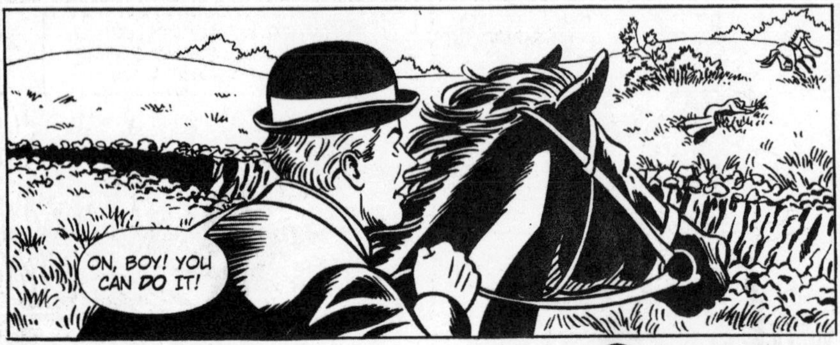
ON, BOY! YOU CAN DO IT!

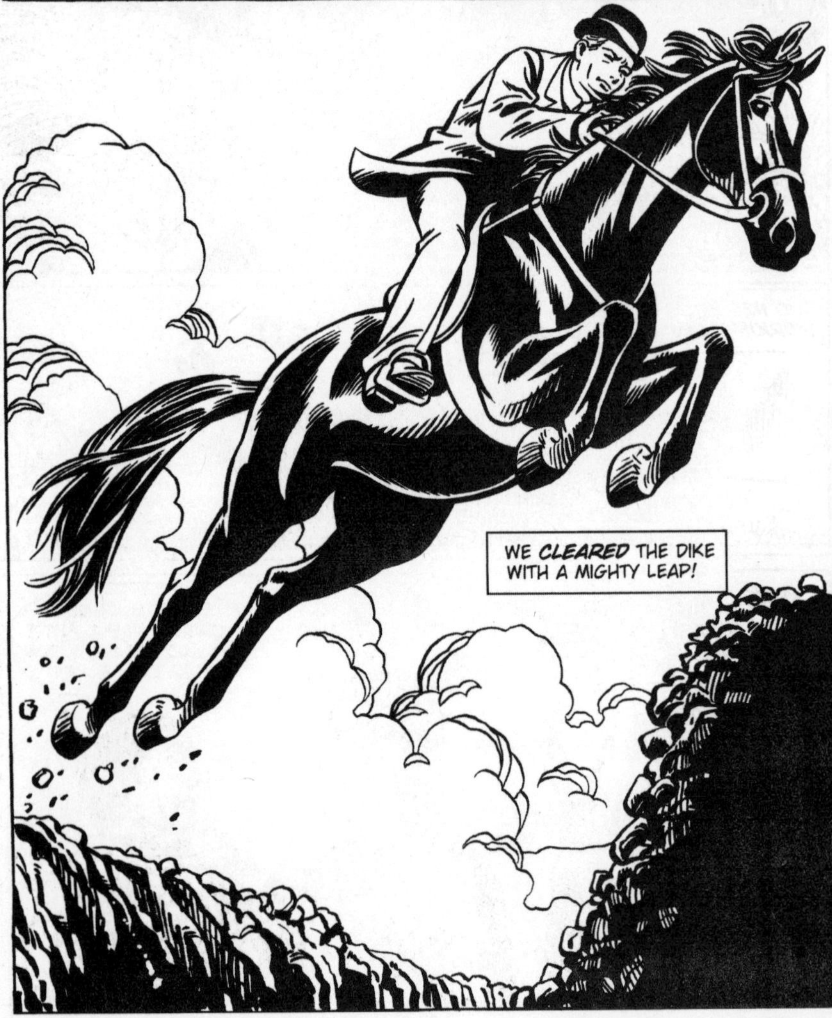
WE CLEARED THE DIKE WITH A MIGHTY LEAP!

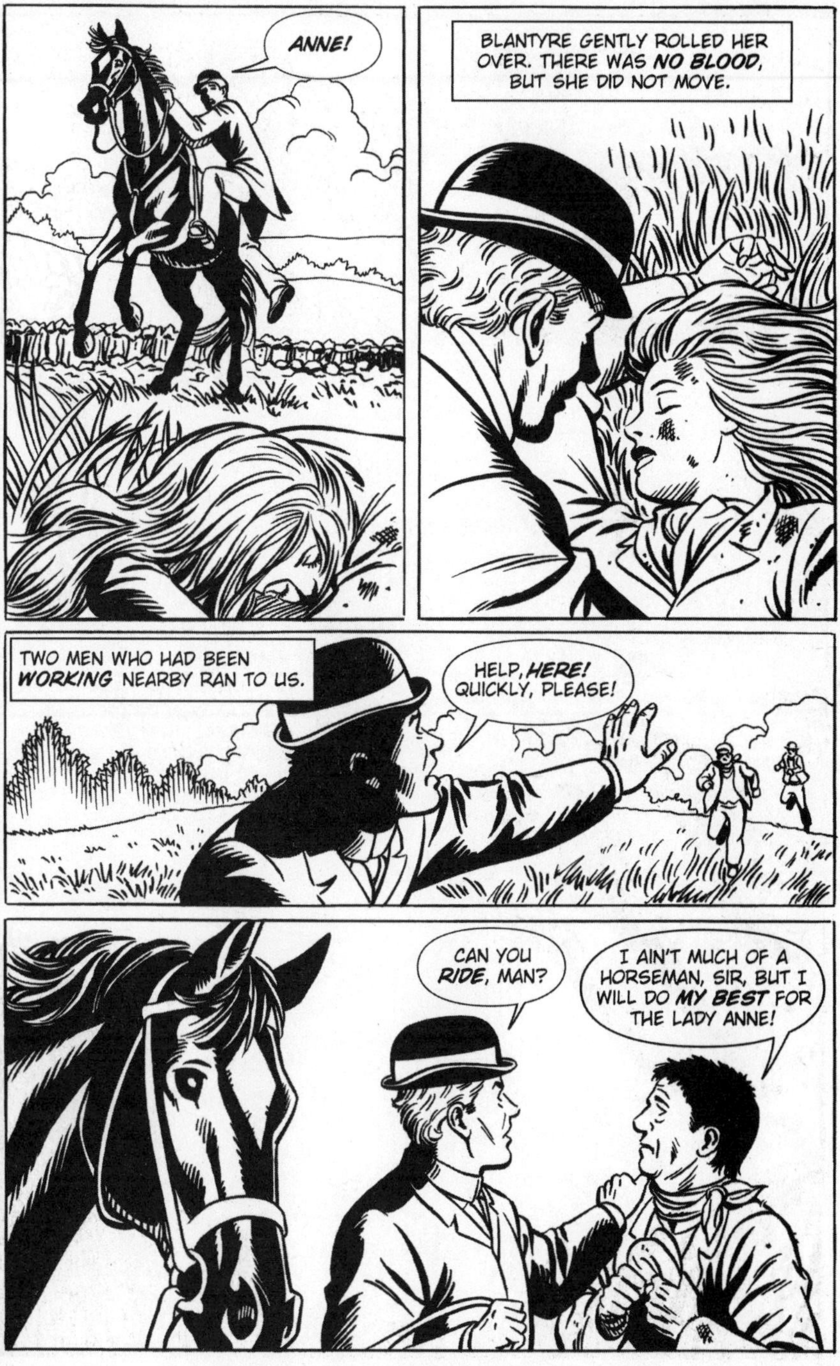
ANNE!
BLANTYRE GENTLY ROLLED HER OVER. THERE WAS NO BLOOD, BUT SHE DID NOT MOVE.
TWO MEN WHO HAD BEEN WORKING NEARBY RAN TO US.
HELP, HERE! QUICKLY, PLEASE!
CAN YOU RIDE, MAN?
I AIN'T MUCH OF A HORSEMAN, SIR, BUT I WILL DO MY BEST FOR THE LADY ANNE!

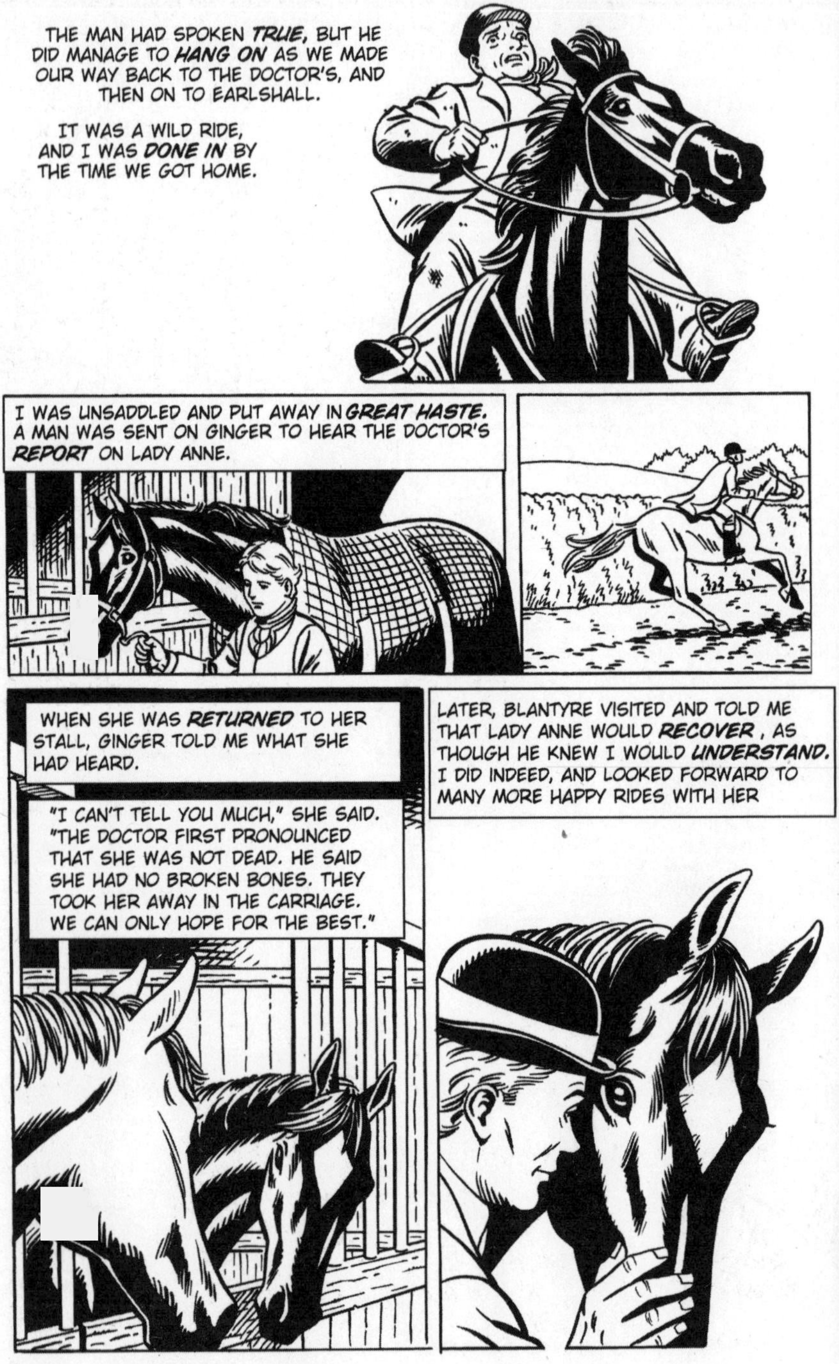
THE MAN HAD SPOKEN TRUE, BUT HE DID MANAGE TO HANG ON AS WE MADE OUR WAY BACK TO THE DOCTOR'S, AND THEN ON TO EARLSHALL.
IT WAS A WILD RIDE, AND I WAS DONE IN BY THE TIME WE GOT HOME.
I WAS UNSADDLED AND PUT AWAY IN GREAT HASTE. A MAN WAS SENT ON GINGER TO HEAR THE DOCTOR'S REPORT ON LADY ANNE.
WHEN SHE WAS RETURNED TO HER STALL, GINGER TOLD ME WHAT SHE HAD HEARD.
"I CAN'T TELL YOU MUCH," SHE SAID. "THE DOCTOR FIRST PRONOUNCED THAT SHE WAS NOT DEAD. HE SAID SHE HAD NO BROKEN BONES. THEY TOOK HER AWAY IN THE CARRIAGE. WE CAN ONLY HOPE FOR THE BEST."
LATER, BLANTYRE VISITED AND TOLD ME THAT LADY ANNE WOULD RECOVER , AS THOUGH HE KNEW I WOULD UNDERSTAND. I DID INDEED, AND LOOKED FORWARD TO MANY MORE HAPPY RIDES WITH HER

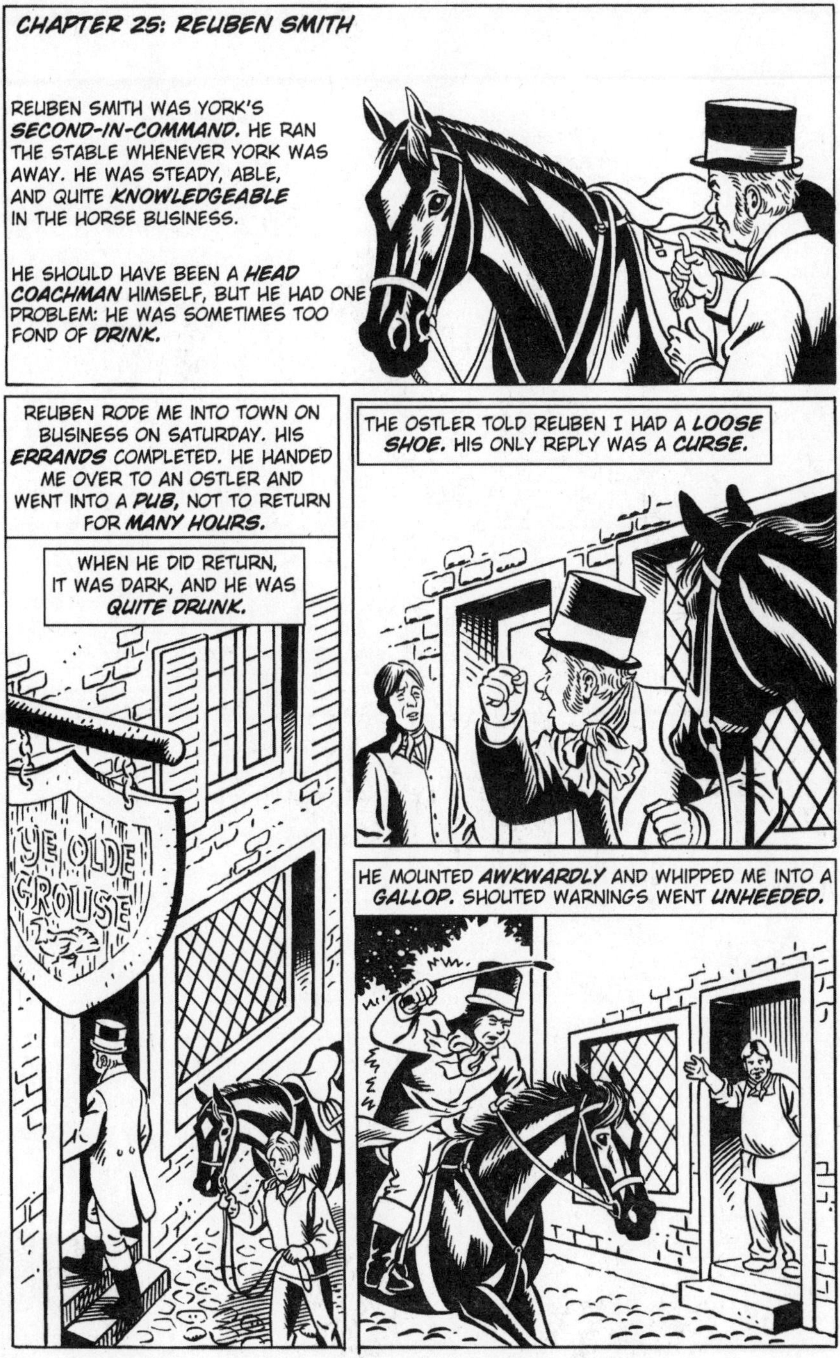
CHAPTER 25: REUBEN SMITH
REUBEN SMITH WAS YORK'S SECOND-IN-COMMAND. HE RAN THE STABLE WHENEVER YORK WAS AWAY. HE WAS STEADY, ABLE, AND QUITE KNOWLEDGEABLE IN THE HORSE BUSINESS.
HE SHOULD HAVE BEEN A HEAD COACHMAN HIMSELF, BUT HE HAD ONE PROBLEM: HE WAS SOMETIMES TOO FOND OF DRINK.
REUBEN RODE ME INTO TOWN ON BUSINESS ON SATURDAY. HIS ERRANDS COMPLETED. HE HANDED ME OVER TO AN OSTLER AND WENT INTO A PUB, NOT TO RETURN FOR MANY HOURS.
WHEN HE DID RETURN, IT WAS DARK, AND HE WAS QUITE DRUNK.
YE OLDE GROUSE
THE OSTLER TOLD REUBEN I HAD A LOOSE SHOE. HIS ONLY REPLY WAS A CURSE.
HE MOUNTED AWKWARDLY AND WHIPPED ME INTO A GALLOP. SHOUTED WARNINGS WENT UNHEEDED.

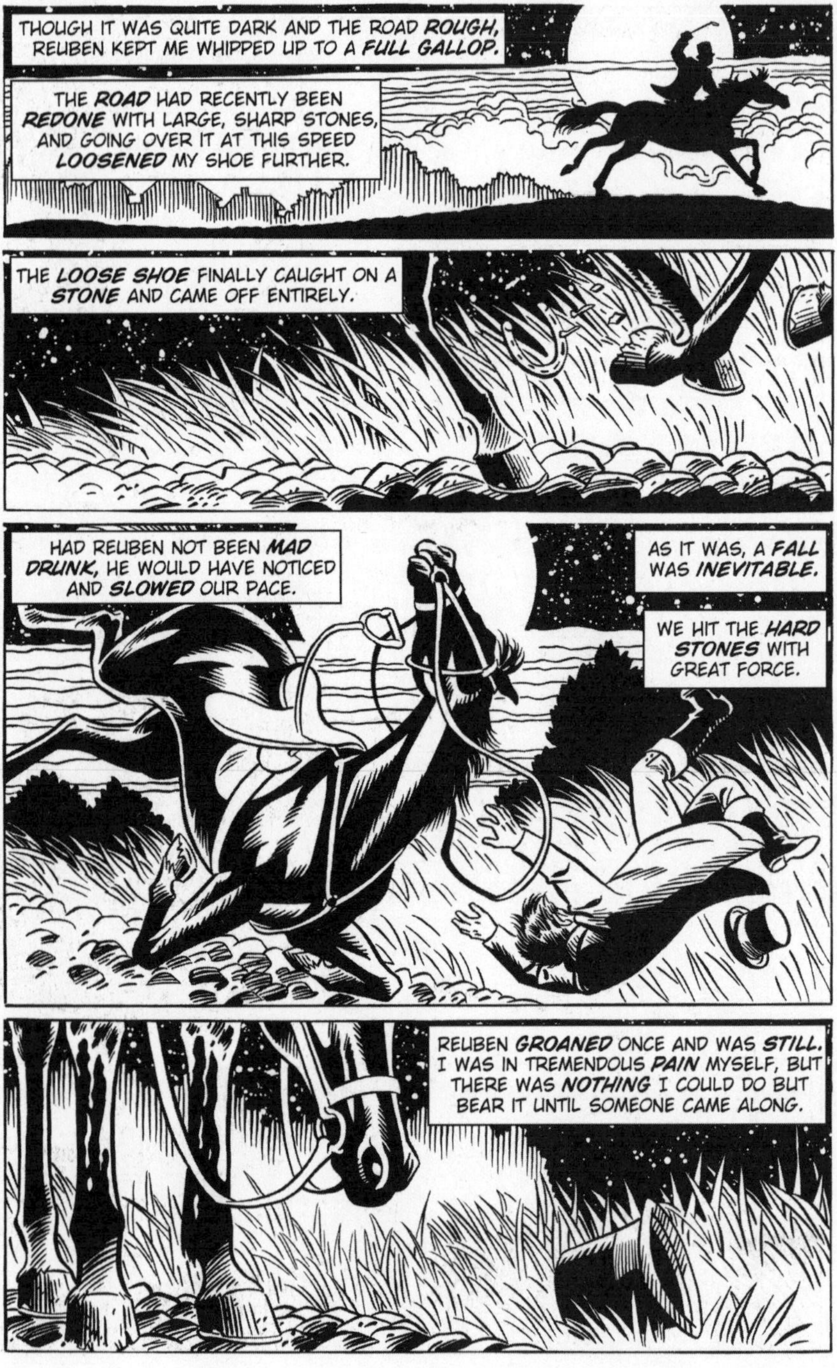
THOUGH IT WAS QUITE DARK AND THE ROAD ROUGH, REUBEN KEPT ME WHIPPED UP TO A FULL GALLOP.
THE ROAD HAD RECENTLY BEEN REDONE WITH LARGE, SHARP STONES, AND GOING OVER IT AT THIS SPEED LOOSENED MY SHOE FURTHER.
THE LOOSE SHOE FINALLY CAUGHT ON A STONE AND CAME OFF ENTIRELY.
HAD REUBEN NOT BEEN MAD DRUNK, HE WOULD HAVE NOTICED AND SLOWED OUR PACE.
AS IT WAS, A FALL WAS INEVITABLE.
WE HIT THE HARD STONES WITH GREAT FORCE.
REUBEN GROANED ONCE AND WAS STILL. I WAS IN TREMENDOUS PAIN MYSELF, BUT THERE WAS NOTHING I COULD DO BUT BEAR IT UNTIL SOMEONE CAME ALONG.

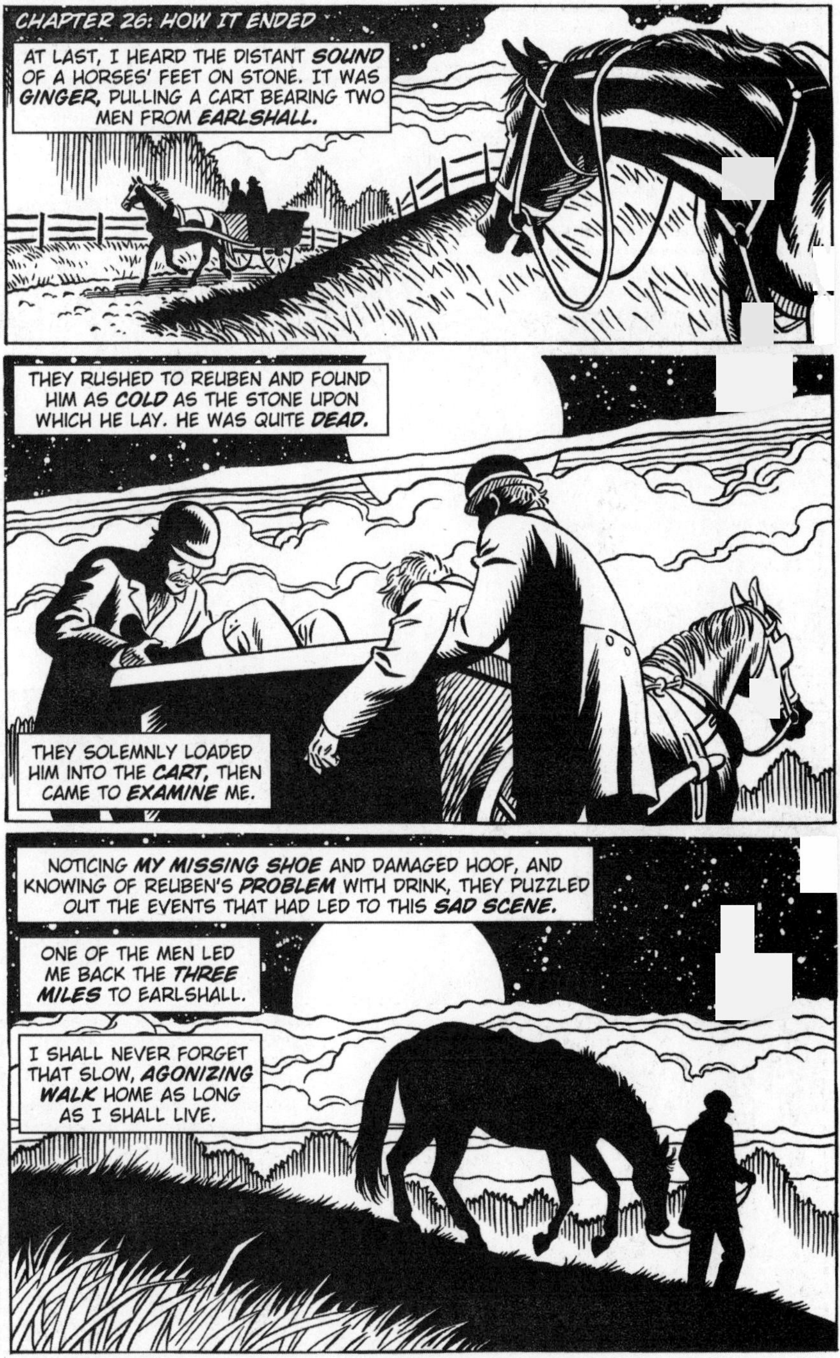
CHAPTER 26: HOW IT ENDED
AT LAST, I HEARD THE DISTANT SOUND OF A HORSES' FEET ON STONE. IT WAS GINGER, PULLING A CART BEARING TWO MEN FROM EARLSHALL.
THEY RUSHED TO REUBEN AND FOUND HIM AS COLD AS THE STONE UPON WHICH HE LAY. HE WAS QUITE DEAD.
THEY SOLEMNLY LOADED HIM INTO THE CART, THEN CAME TO EXAMINE ME.
NOTICING MY MISSING SHOE AND DAMAGED HOOF, AND KNOWING OF REUBEN'S PROBLEM WITH DRINK, THEY PUZZLED OUT THE EVENTS THAT HAD LED TO THIS SAD SCENE.
ONE OF THE MEN LED ME BACK THE THREE MILES TO EARLSHALL.
I SHALL NEVER FORGET THAT SLOW, AGONIZING WALK HOME AS LONG AS I SHALL LIVE.

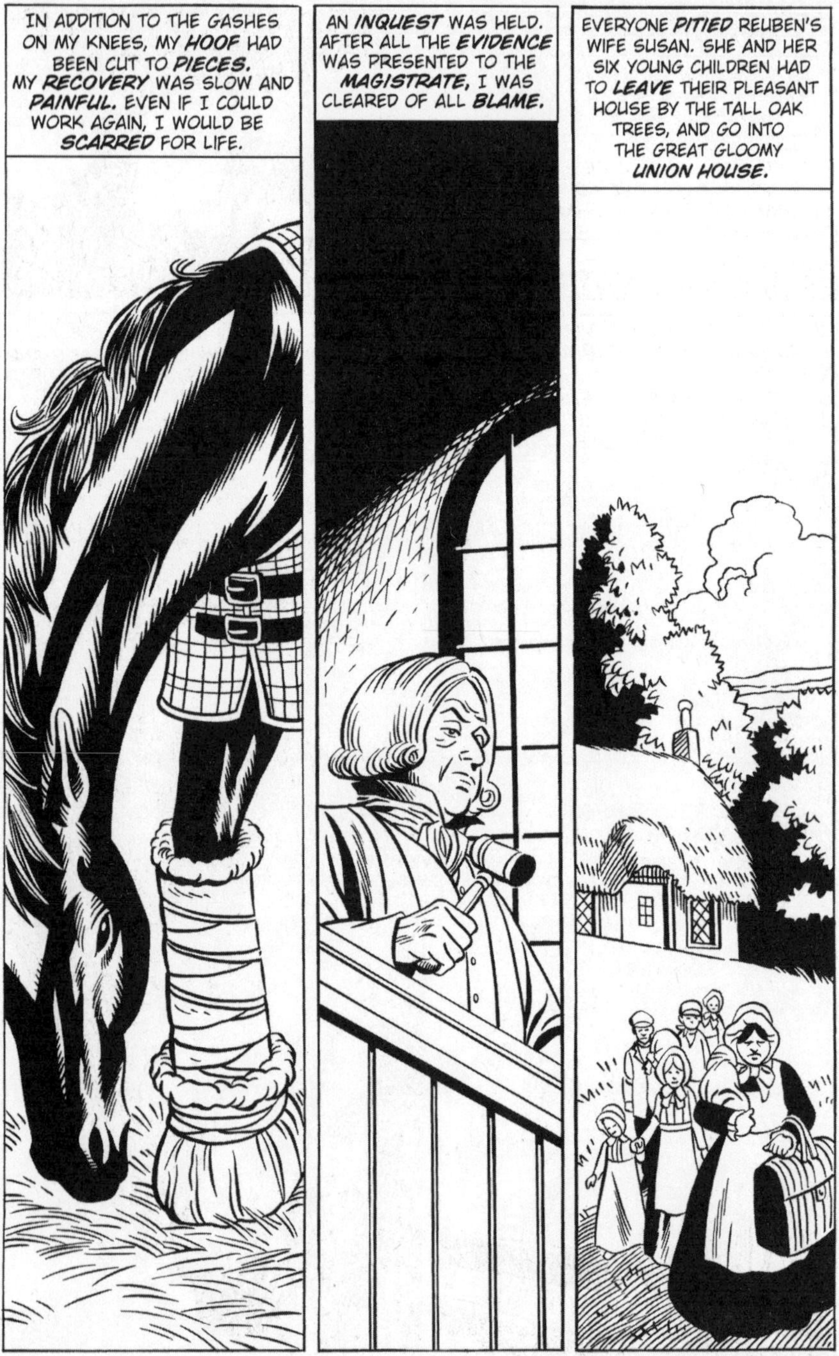
IN ADDITION TO THE GASHES ON MY KNEES, MY HOOF HAD BEEN CUT TO PIECES. MY RECOVERY WAS SLOW AND PAINFUL. EVEN IF I COULD WORK AGAIN, I WOULD BE SCARRED FOR LIFE.
AN INQUEST WAS HELD. AFTER ALL THE EVIDENCE WAS PRESENTED TO THE MAGISTRATE, I WAS CLEARED OF ALL BLAME.
EVERYONE PITIED REUBEN'S WIFE SUSAN. SHE AND HER SIX YOUNG CHILDREN HAD TO LEAVE THEIR PLEASANT HOUSE BY THE TALL OAK TREES, AND GO INTO THE GREAT GLOOMY UNION HOUSE.

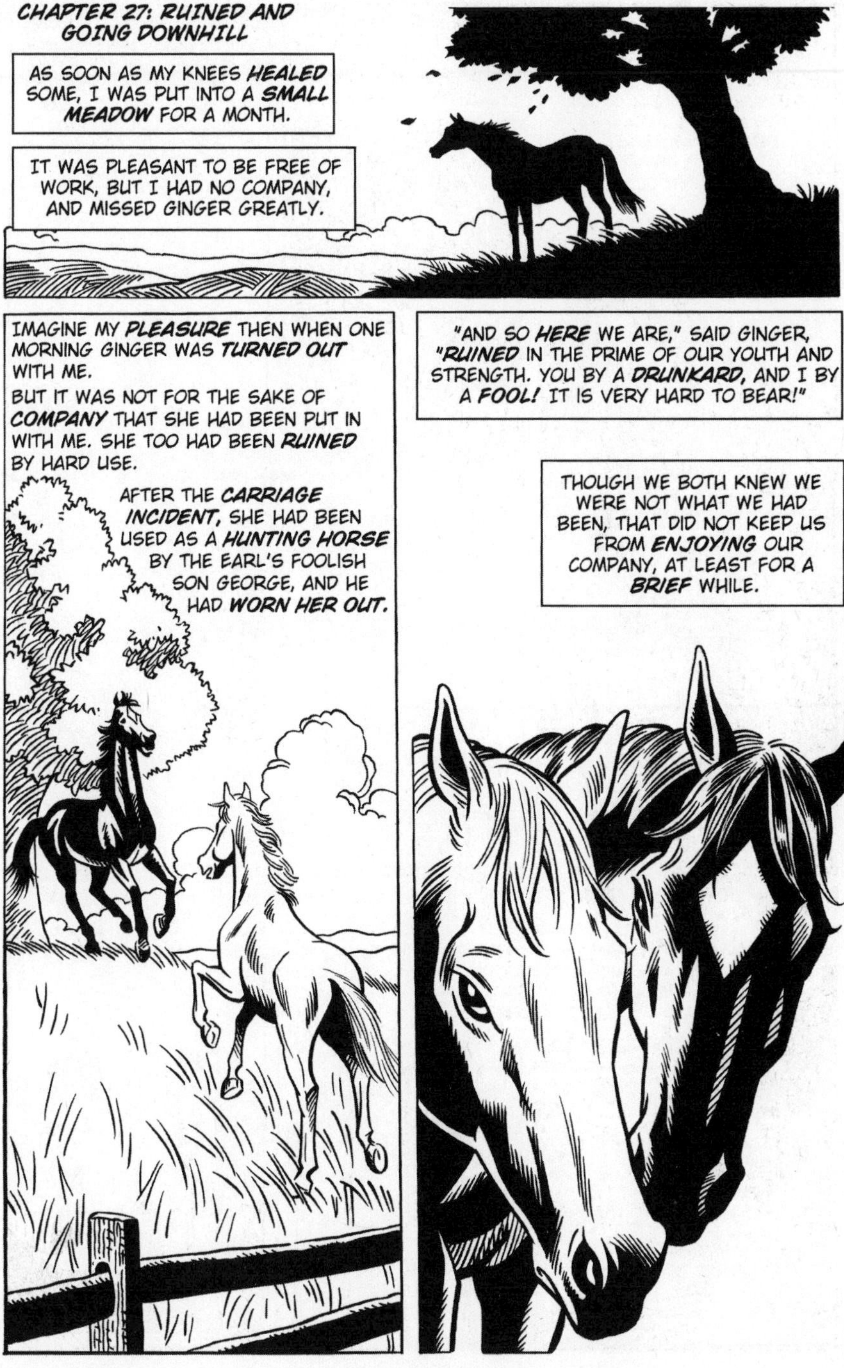
CHAPTER 27: RUINED AND GOING DOWNHILL
AS SOON AS MY KNEES HEALED SOME, I WAS PUT INTO A SMALL MEADOW FOR A MONTH.
IT WAS PLEASANT TO BE FREE OF WORK, BUT I HAD NO COMPANY, AND MISSED GINGER GREATLY.
IMAGINE MY PLEASURE THEN WHEN ONE MORNING GINGER WAS TURNED OUT WITH ME.
BUT IT WAS NOT FOR THE SAKE OF COMPANY THAT SHE HAD BEEN PUT IN WITH ME. SHE TOO HAD BEEN RUINED BY HARD USE.
AFTER THE CARRIAGE INCIDENT, SHE HAD BEEN USED AS A HUNTING HORSE BY THE EARL'S FOOLISH SON GEORGE, AND HE HAD WORN HER OUT.
"AND SO HERE WE ARE," SAID GINGER, "RUINED IN THE PRIME OF OUR YOUTH AND STRENGTH. YOU BY A DRUNKARD, AND I BY A FOOL! IT IS VERY HARD TO BEAR!"
THOUGH WE BOTH KNEW WE WERE NOT WHAT WE HAD BEEN, THAT DID NOT KEEP US FROM ENJOYING OUR COMPANY, AT LEAST FOR A BRIEF WHILE.

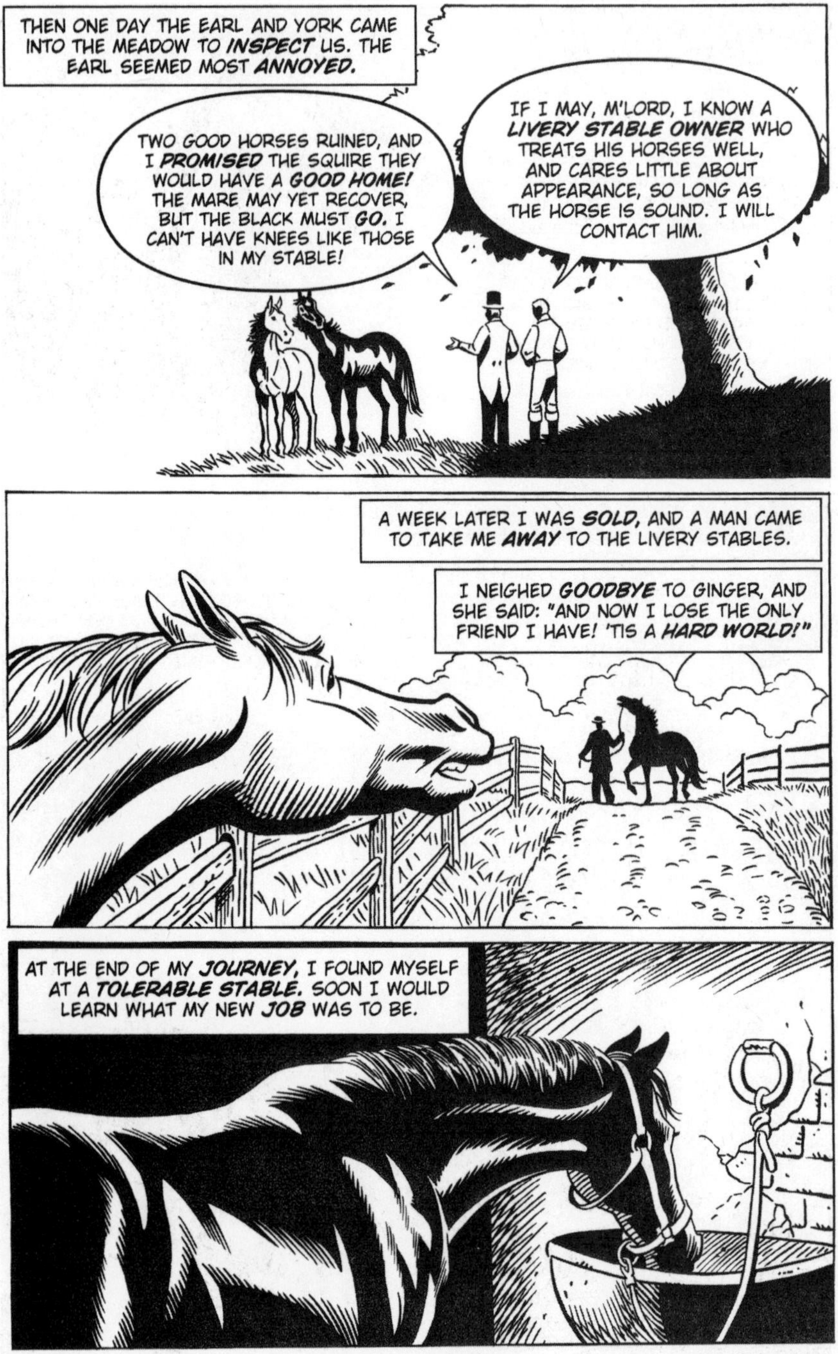
THEN ONE DAY THE EARL AND YORK CAME INTO THE MEADOW TO INSPECT US. THE EARL SEEMED MOST ANNOYED.
TWO GOOD HORSES RUINED, AND I PROMISED THE SQUIRE THEY WOULD HAVE A GOOD HOME! THE MARE MAY YET RECOVER, BUT THE BLACK MUST GO. I CAN'T HAVE KNEES LIKE THOSE IN MY STABLE!
IF I MAY, M'LORD, I KNOW A LIVERY STABLE OWNER WHO TREATS HIS HORSES WELL, AND CARES LITTLE ABOUT APPEARANCE, SO LONG AS THE HORSE IS SOUND. I WILL CONTACT HIM.
A WEEK LATER I WAS SOLD, AND A MAN CAME TO TAKE ME AWAY TO THE LIVERY STABLES.
I NEIGHED GOODBYE TO GINGER, AND SHE SAID: "AND NOW I LOSE THE ONLY FRIEND I HAVE! 'TIS A HARD WORLD!"
AT THE END OF MY JOURNEY, I FOUND MYSELF AT A TOLERABLE STABLE. SOON I WOULD LEARN WHAT MY NEW JOB WAS TO BE.

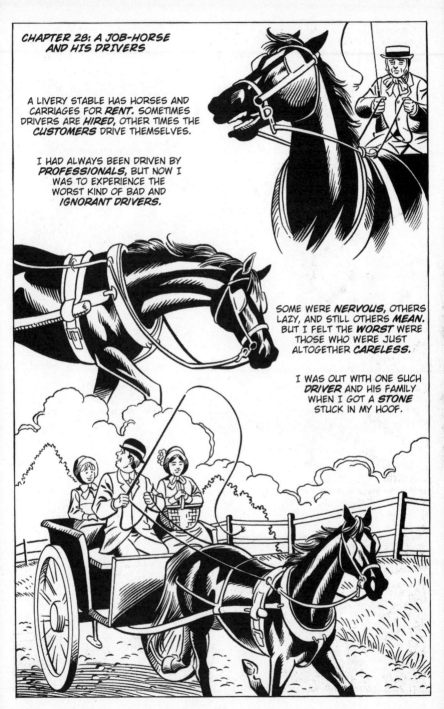

CHAPTER 28: A JOB-HORSE AND HIS DRIVERS

A LIVERY STABLE HAS HORSES AND CARRIAGES FOR *RENT.* SOMETIMES DRIVERS ARE *HIRED,* OTHER TIMES THE *CUSTOMERS* DRIVE THEMSELVES.

I HAD ALWAYS BEEN DRIVEN BY *PROFESSIONALS,* BUT NOW I WAS TO EXPERIENCE THE WORST KIND OF BAD AND *IGNORANT DRIVERS.*

SOME WERE *NERVOUS,* OTHERS LAZY, AND STILL OTHERS *MEAN.* BUT I FELT THE *WORST* WERE THOSE WHO WERE JUST ALTOGETHER *CARELESS.*

I WAS OUT WITH ONE SUCH *DRIVER* AND HIS FAMILY WHEN I GOT A *STONE* STUCK IN MY HOOF.

71

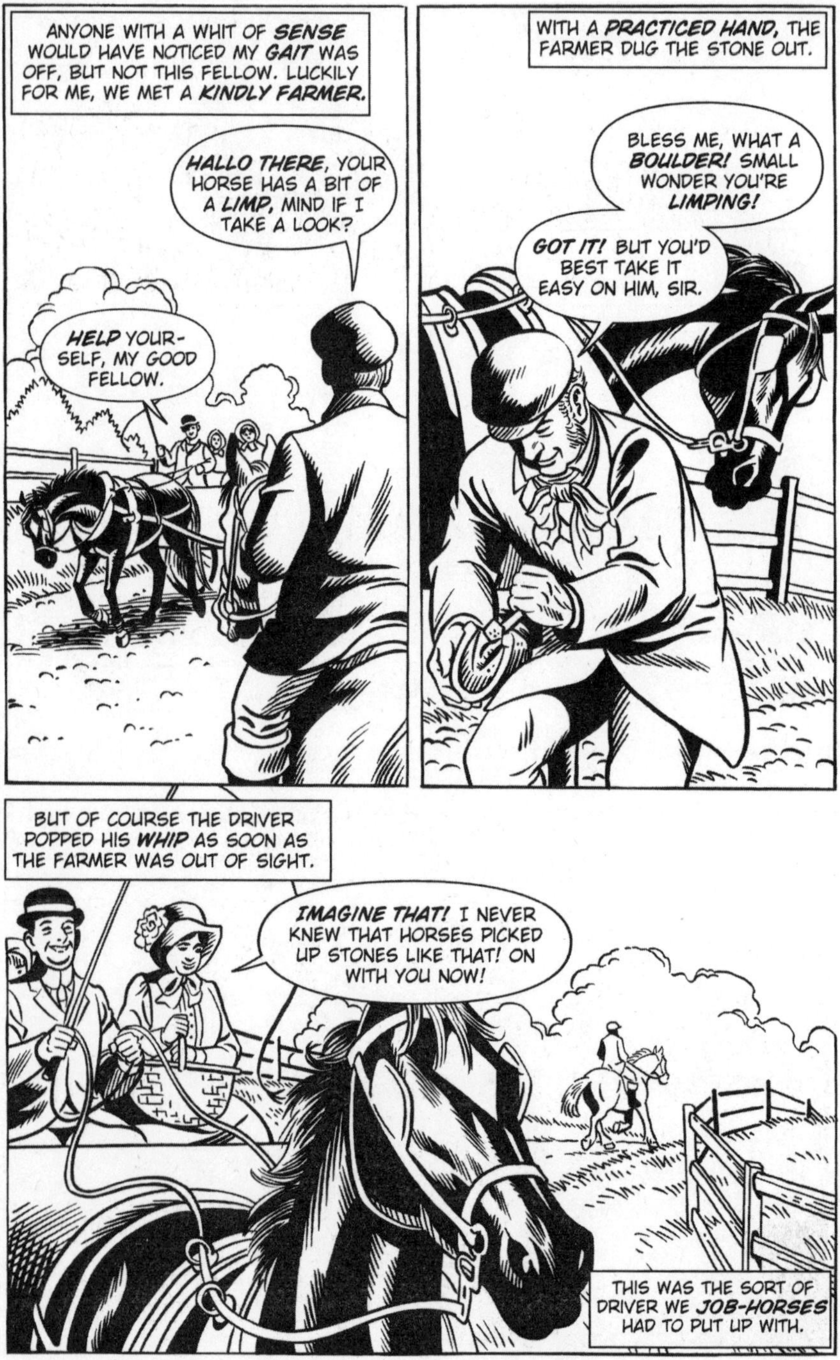
ANYONE WITH A WHIT OF SENSE WOULD HAVE NOTICED MY GAIT WAS OFF, BUT NOT THIS FELLOW. LUCKILY FOR ME, WE MET A KINDLY FARMER.
HALLO THERE, YOUR HORSE HAS A BIT OF A LIMP, MIND IF I TAKE A LOOK?
HELP YOURSELF, MY GOOD FELLOW.
WITH A PRACTICED HAND, THE FARMER DUG THE STONE OUT.
BLESS ME, WHAT A BOULDER! SMALL WONDER YOU'RE LIMPING!
GOT IT! BUT YOU'D BEST TAKE IT EASY ON HIM, SIR.
BUT OF COURSE THE DRIVER POPPED HIS WHIP AS SOON AS THE FARMER WAS OUT OF SIGHT.
IMAGINE THAT! I NEVER KNEW THAT HORSES PICKED UP STONES LIKE THAT! ON WITH YOU NOW!
THIS WAS THE SORT OF DRIVER WE JOB-HORSES HAD TO PUT UP WITH.

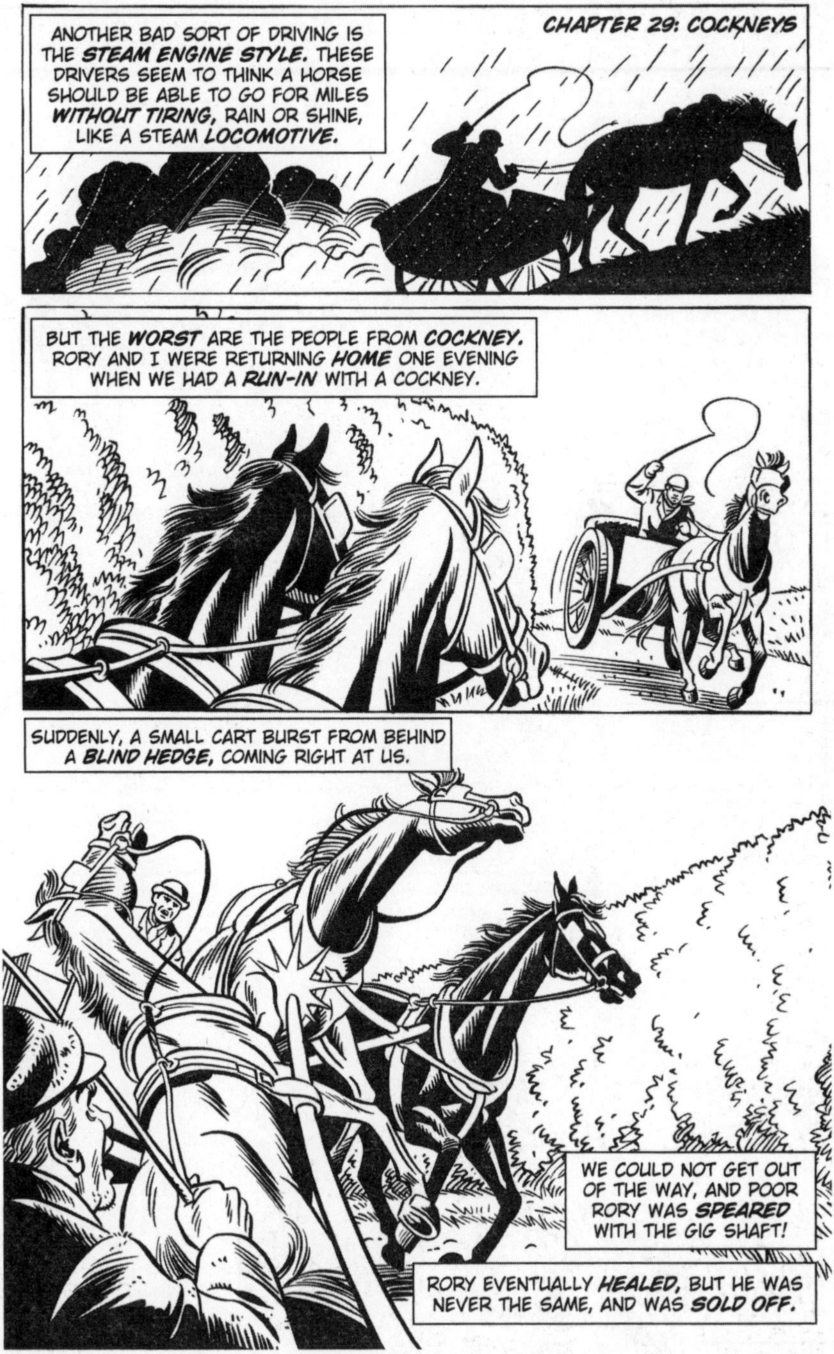
CHAPTER 29: COCKNEYS
ANOTHER BAD SORT OF DRIVING IS THE STEAM ENGINE STYLE. THESE DRIVERS SEEM TO THINK A HORSE SHOULD BE ABLE TO GO FOR MILES WITHOUT TIRING, RAIN OR SHINE, LIKE A STEAM LOCOMOTIVE.
BUT THE WORST ARE THE PEOPLE FROM COCKNEY. RORY AND I WERE RETURNING HOME ONE EVENING WHEN WE HAD A RUN-IN WITH A COCKNEY.
SUDDENLY, A SMALL CART BURST FROM BEHIND A BLIND HEDGE, COMING RIGHT AT US.
WE COULD NOT GET OUT OF THE WAY, AND POOR RORY WAS SPEARED WITH THE GIG SHAFT!
RORY EVENTUALLY HEALED, BUT HE WAS NEVER THE SAME, AND WAS SOLD OFF.

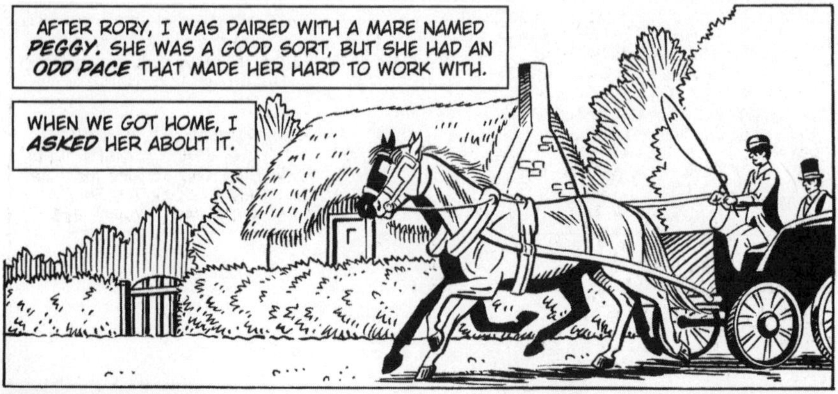
AFTER RORY, I WAS PAIRED WITH A MARE NAMED PEGGY. SHE WAS A GOOD SORT, BUT SHE HAD AN ODD PACE THAT MADE HER HARD TO WORK WITH.
WHEN WE GOT HOME, I ASKED HER ABOUT IT.

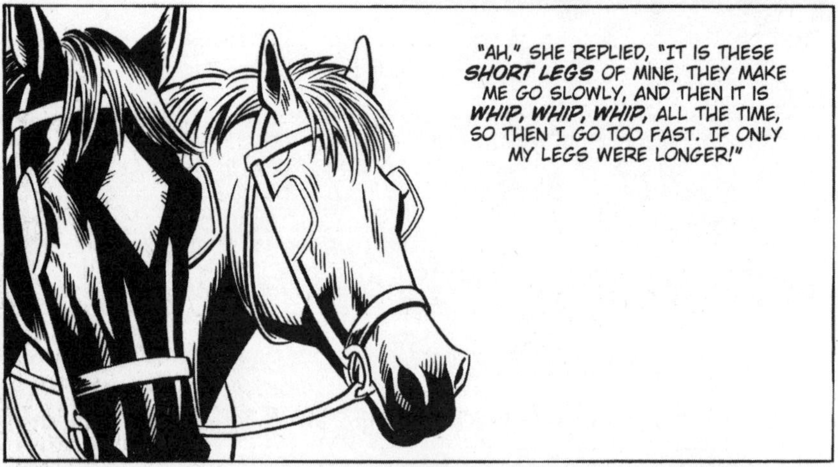
"AH," SHE REPLIED, "IT IS THESE SHORT LEGS OF MINE, THEY MAKE ME GO SLOWLY, AND THEN IT IS WHIP, WHIP, WHIP, ALL THE TIME, SO THEN I GO TOO FAST. IF ONLY MY LEGS WERE LONGER!"

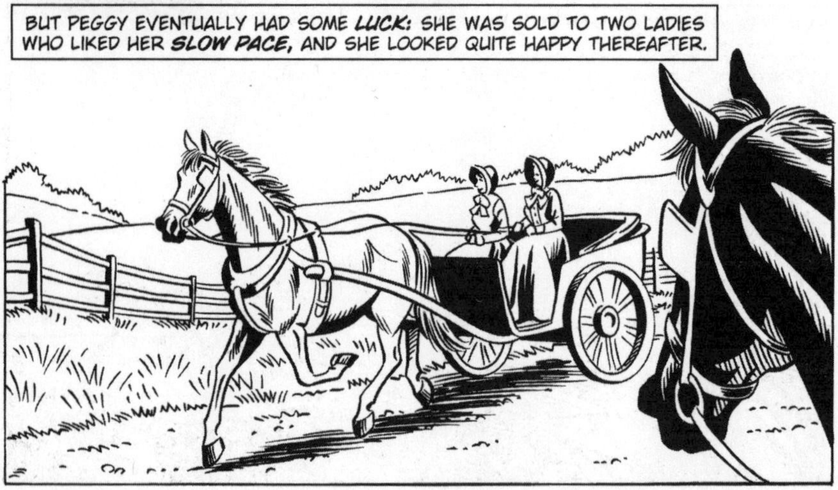
BUT PEGGY EVENTUALLY HAD SOME LUCK: SHE WAS SOLD TO TWO LADIES WHO LIKED HER SLOW PACE, AND SHE LOOKED QUITE HAPPY THEREAFTER.

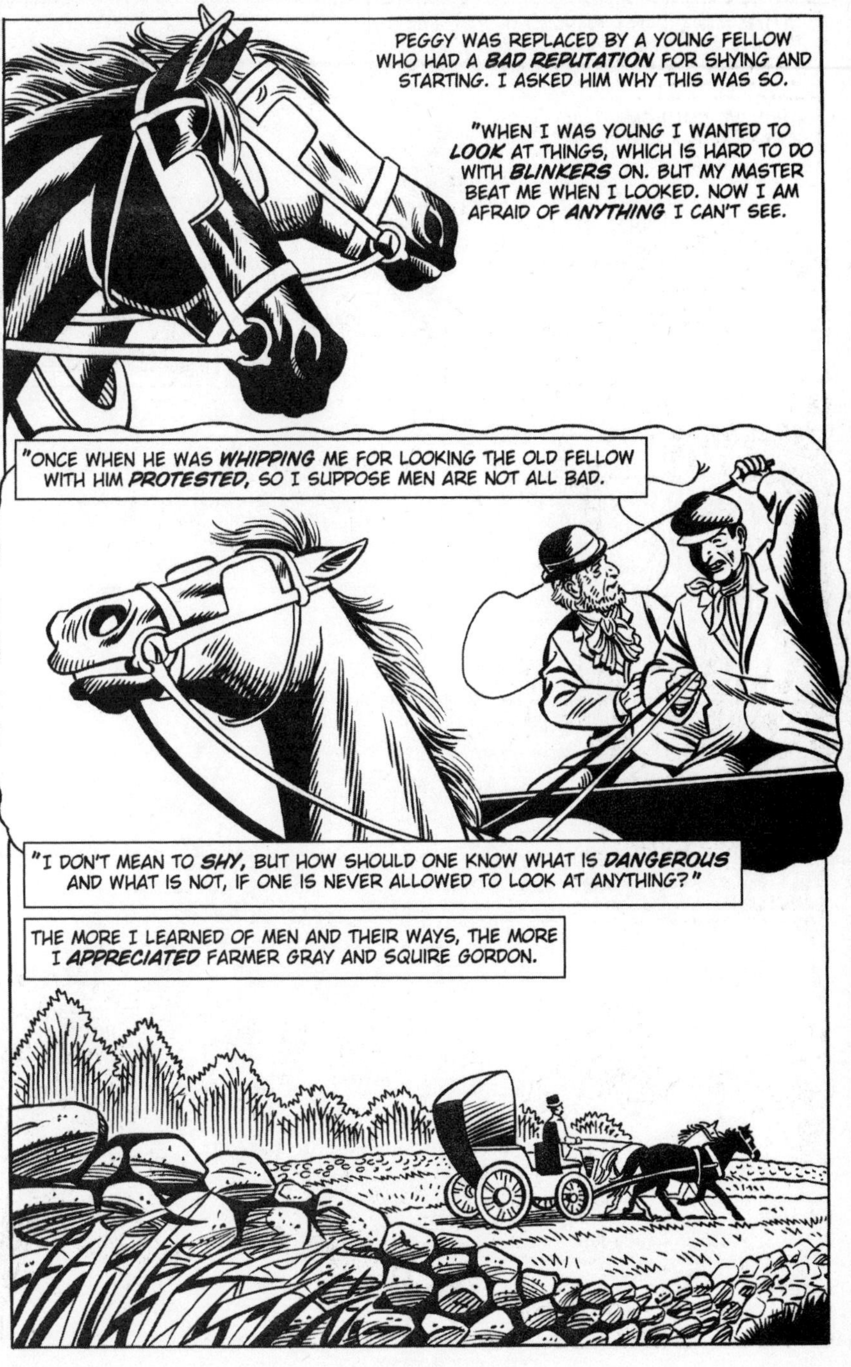
PEGGY WAS REPLACED BY A YOUNG FELLOW WHO HAD A BAD REPUTATION FOR SHYING AND STARTING. I ASKED HIM WHY THIS WAS SO.
"WHEN I WAS YOUNG I WANTED TO LOOK AT THINGS, WHICH IS HARD TO DO WITH BLINKERS ON. BUT MY MASTER BEAT ME WHEN I LOOKED. NOW I AM AFRAID OF ANYTHING I CAN'T SEE.
"ONCE WHEN HE WAS WHIPPING ME FOR LOOKING THE OLD FELLOW WITH HIM PROTESTED, SO I SUPPOSE MEN ARE NOT ALL BAD.
"I DON'T MEAN TO SHY, BUT HOW SHOULD ONE KNOW WHAT IS DANGEROUS AND WHAT IS NOT, IF ONE IS NEVER ALLOWED TO LOOK AT ANYTHING?"
THE MORE I LEARNED OF MEN AND THEIR WAYS, THE MORE I APPRECIATED FARMER GRAY AND SQUIRE GORDON.

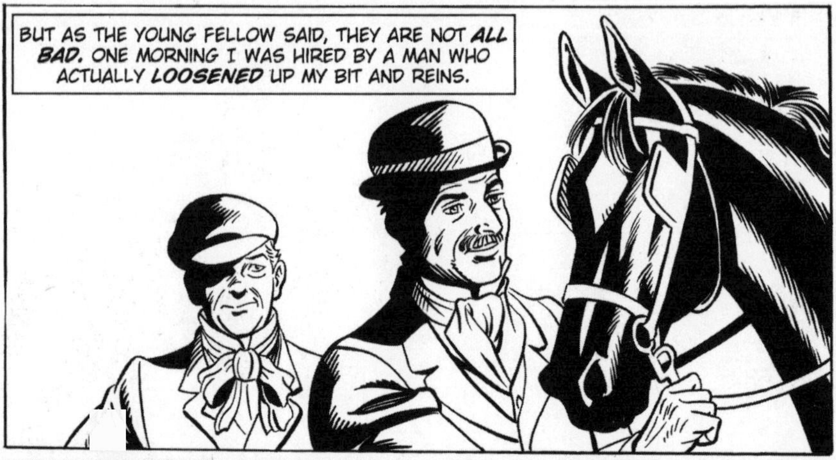
BUT AS THE YOUNG FELLOW SAID, THEY ARE NOT ALL BAD. ONE MORNING I WAS HIRED BY A MAN WHO ACTUALLY LOOSENED UP MY BIT AND REINS.

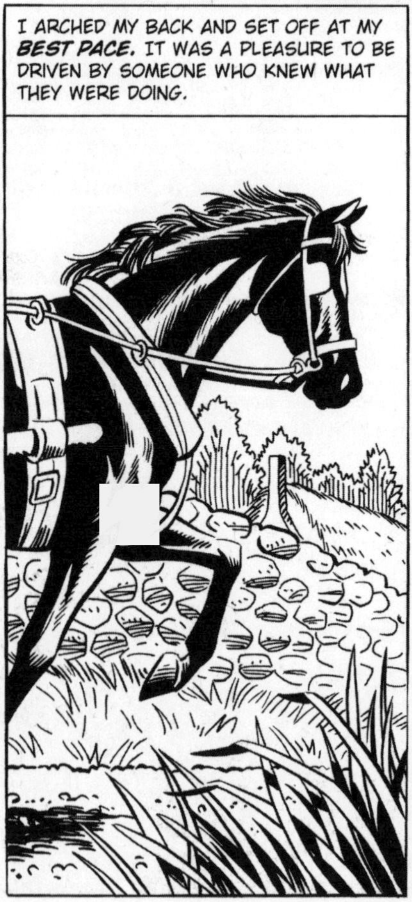
I ARCHED MY BACK AND SET OFF AT MY BEST PACE. IT WAS A PLEASURE TO BE DRIVEN BY SOMEONE WHO KNEW WHAT THEY WERE DOING.

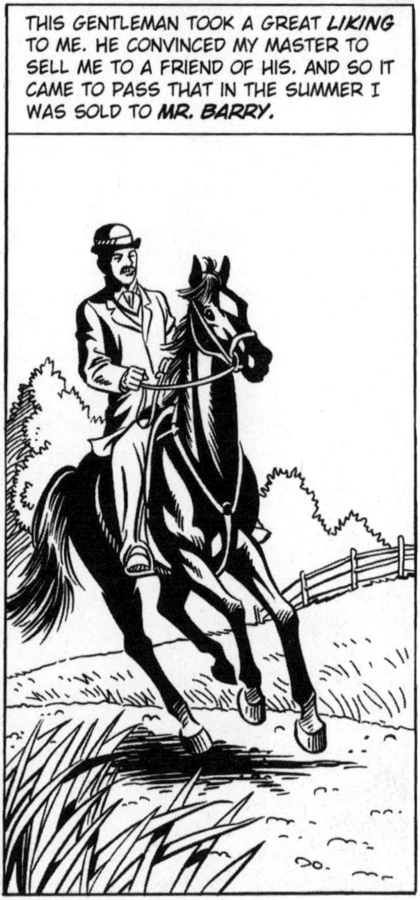
THIS GENTLEMAN TOOK A GREAT LIKING TO ME. HE CONVINCED MY MASTER TO SELL ME TO A FRIEND OF HIS. AND SO IT CAME TO PASS THAT IN THE SUMMER I WAS SOLD TO MR. BARRY.

CHAPTER 30: A THIEF

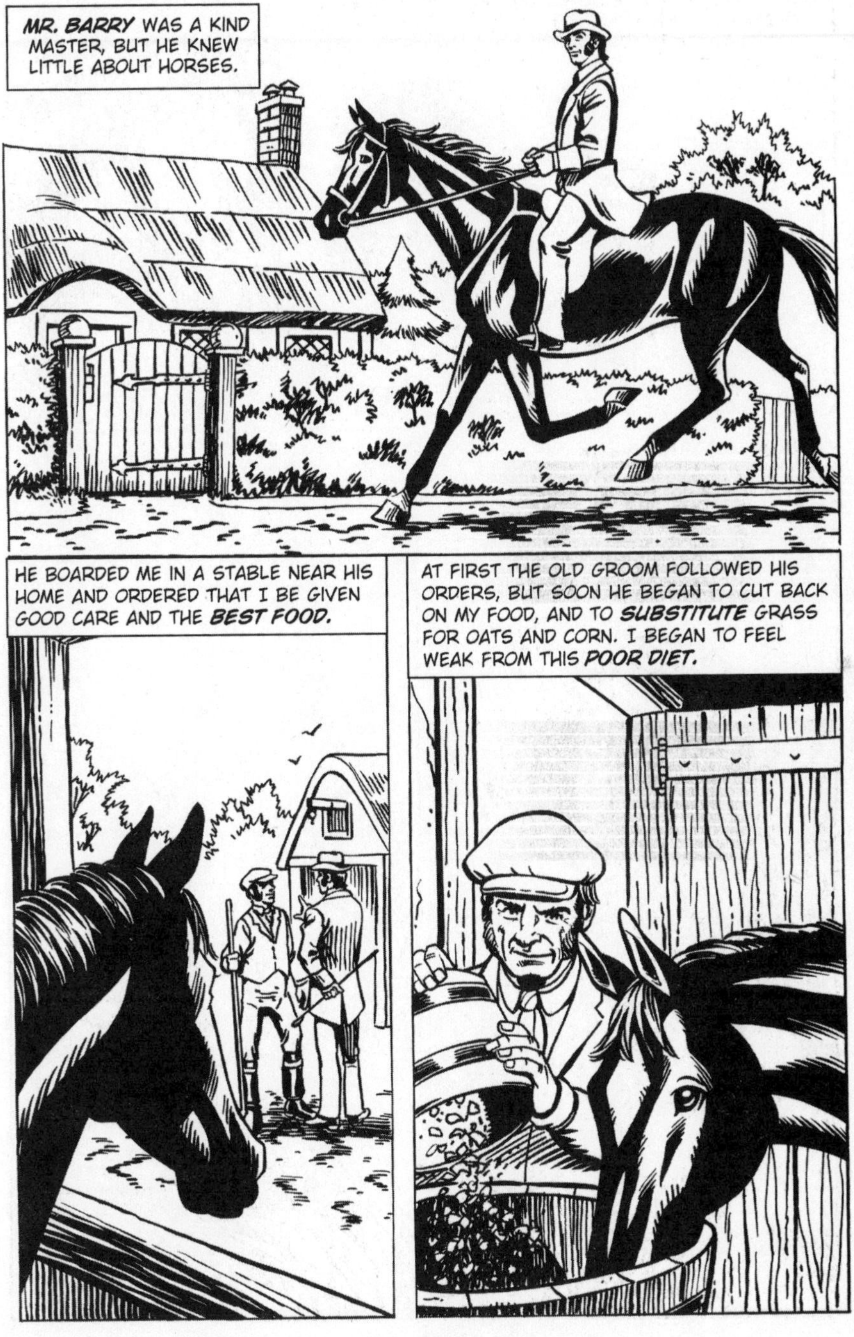
MR. BARRY WAS A KIND MASTER, BUT HE KNEW LITTLE ABOUT HORSES.
HE BOARDED ME IN A STABLE NEAR HIS HOME AND ORDERED THAT I BE GIVEN GOOD CARE AND THE BEST FOOD.
AT FIRST THE OLD GROOM FOLLOWED HIS ORDERS, BUT SOON HE BEGAN TO CUT BACK ON MY FOOD, AND TO SUBSTITUTE GRASS FOR OATS AND CORN. I BEGAN TO FEEL WEAK FROM THIS POOR DIET.

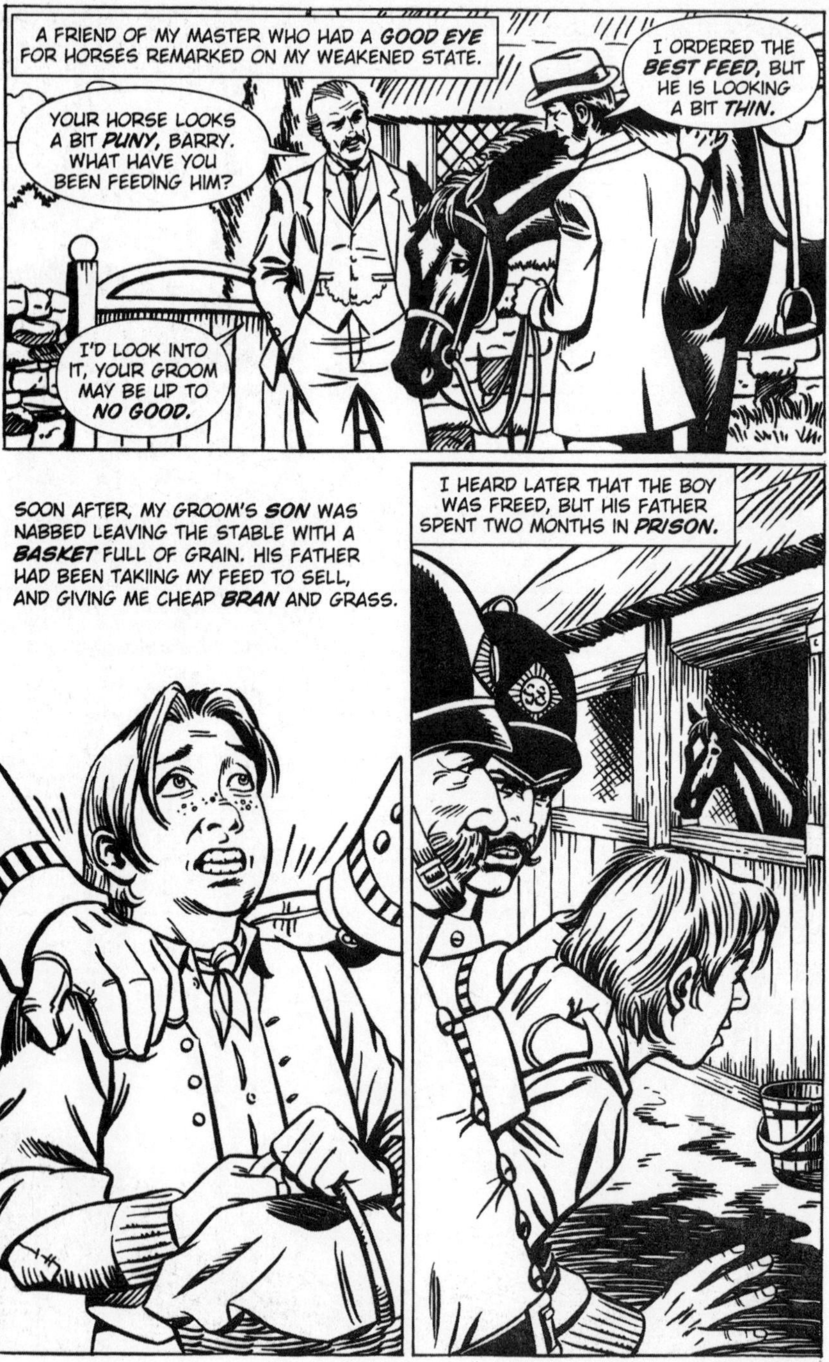
A FRIEND OF MY MASTER WHO HAD A GOOD EYE FOR HORSES REMARKED ON MY WEAKENED STATE.
YOUR HORSE LOOKS A BIT PUNY, BARRY. WHAT HAVE YOU BEEN FEEDING HIM?
I ORDERED THE BEST FEED, BUT HE IS LOOKING A BIT THIN.
I'D LOOK INTO IT, YOUR GROOM MAY BE UP TO NO GOOD.
SOON AFTER, MY GROOM'S SON WAS NABBED LEAVING THE STABLE WITH A BASKET FULL OF GRAIN. HIS FATHER HAD BEEN TAKIING MY FEED TO SELL, AND GIVING ME CHEAP BRAN AND GRASS.
I HEARD LATER THAT THE BOY WAS FREED, BUT HIS FATHER SPENT TWO MONTHS IN PRISON.

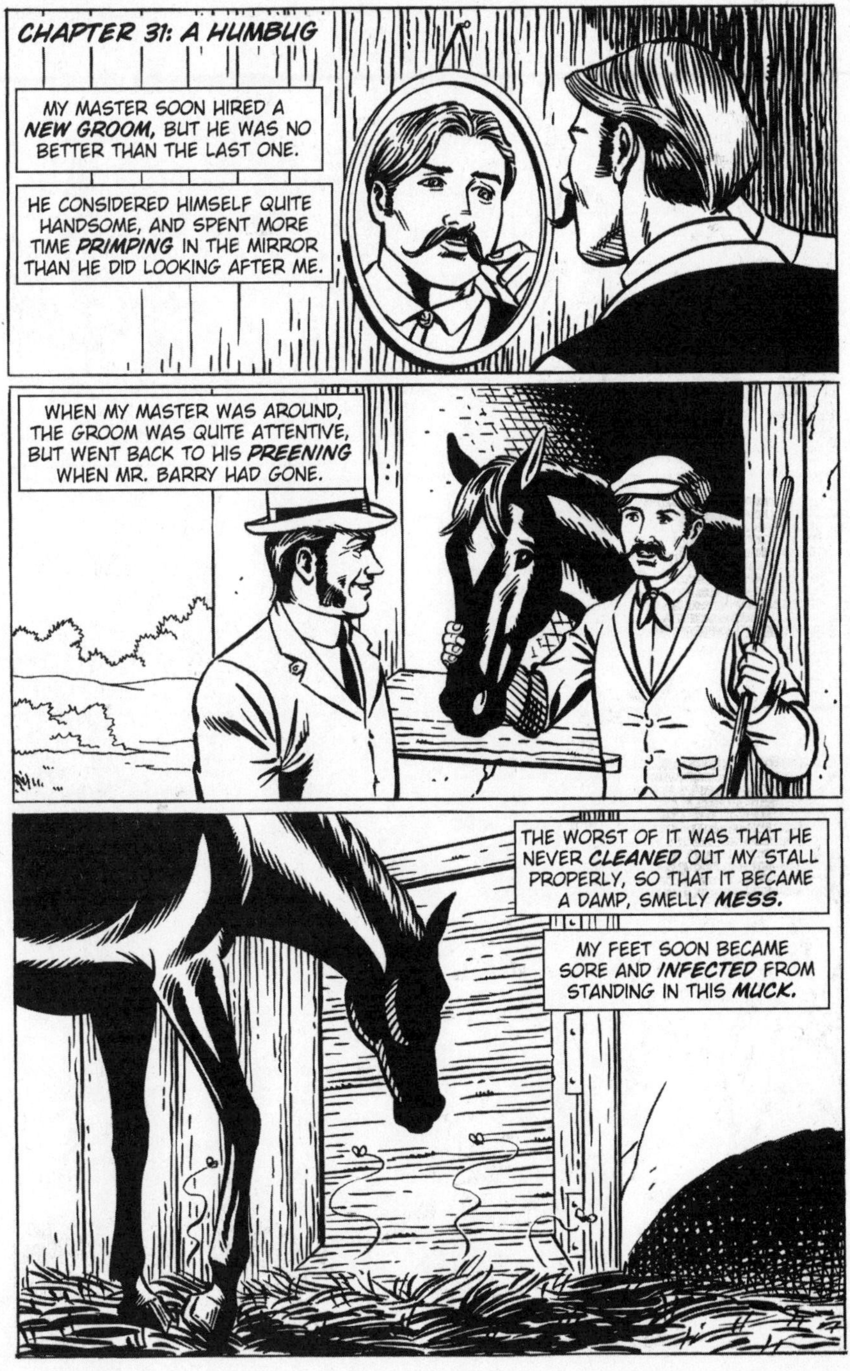

CHAPTER 31: A HUMBUG
MY MASTER SOON HIRED A NEW GROOM, BUT HE WAS NO BETTER THAN THE LAST ONE.
HE CONSIDERED HIMSELF QUITE HANDSOME, AND SPENT MORE TIME PRIMPING IN THE MIRROR THAN HE DID LOOKING AFTER ME.
WHEN MY MASTER WAS AROUND, THE GROOM WAS QUITE ATTENTIVE, BUT WENT BACK TO HIS PREENING WHEN MR. BARRY HAD GONE.
THE WORST OF IT WAS THAT HE NEVER CLEANED OUT MY STALL PROPERLY, SO THAT IT BECAME A DAMP, SMELLY MESS.
MY FEET SOON BECAME SORE AND INFECTED FROM STANDING IN THIS MUCK.

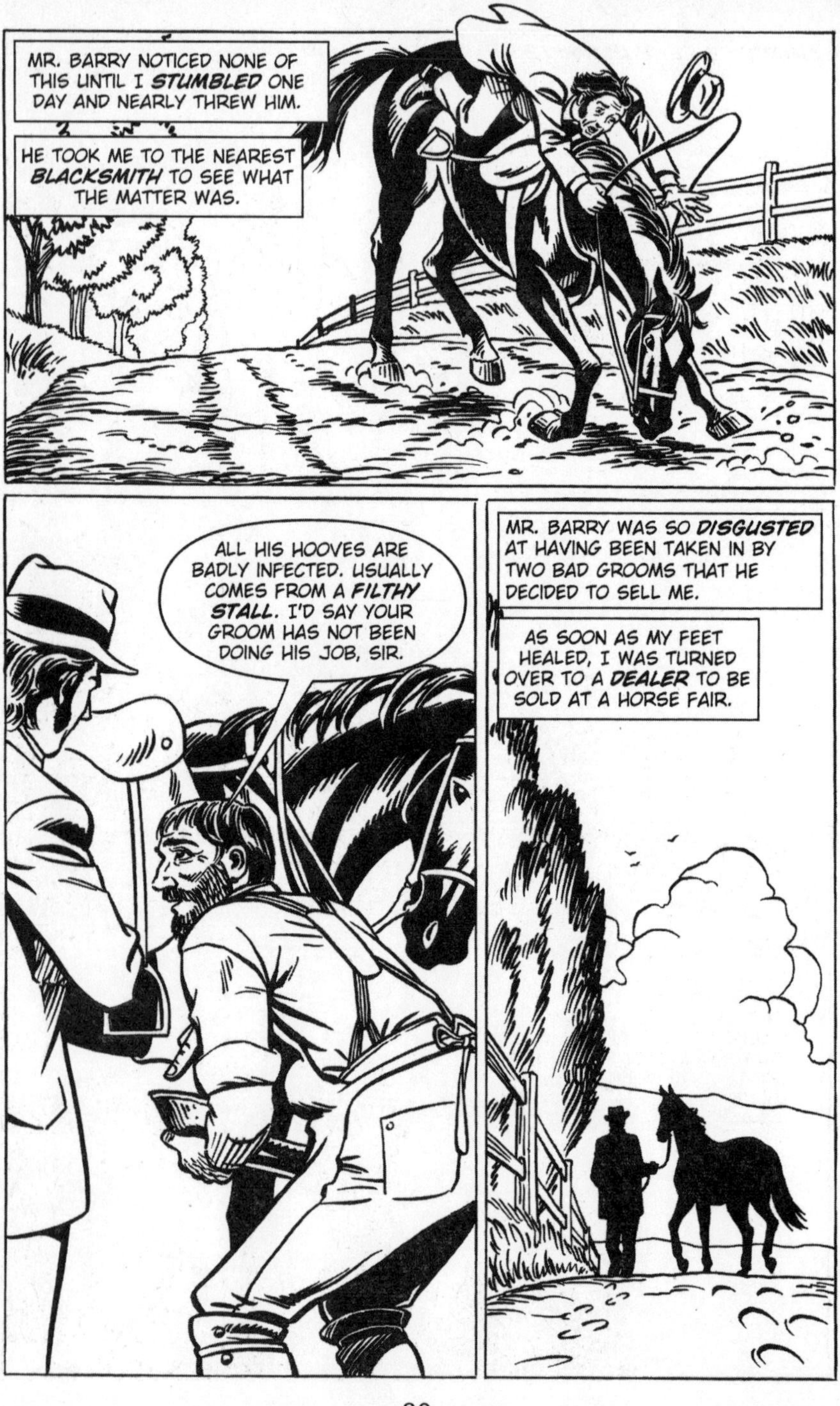
MR. BARRY NOTICED NONE OF THIS UNTIL I STUMBLED ONE DAY AND NEARLY THREW HIM.
HE TOOK ME TO THE NEAREST BLACKSMITH TO SEE WHAT THE MATTER WAS.
ALL HIS HOOVES ARE BADLY INFECTED. USUALLY COMES FROM A FILTHY STALL. I'D SAY YOUR GROOM HAS NOT BEEN DOING HIS JOB, SIR.
MR. BARRY WAS SO DISGUSTED AT HAVING BEEN TAKEN IN BY TWO BAD GROOMS THAT HE DECIDED TO SELL ME.
AS SOON AS MY FEET HEALED, I WAS TURNED OVER TO A DEALER TO BE SOLD AT A HORSE FAIR.

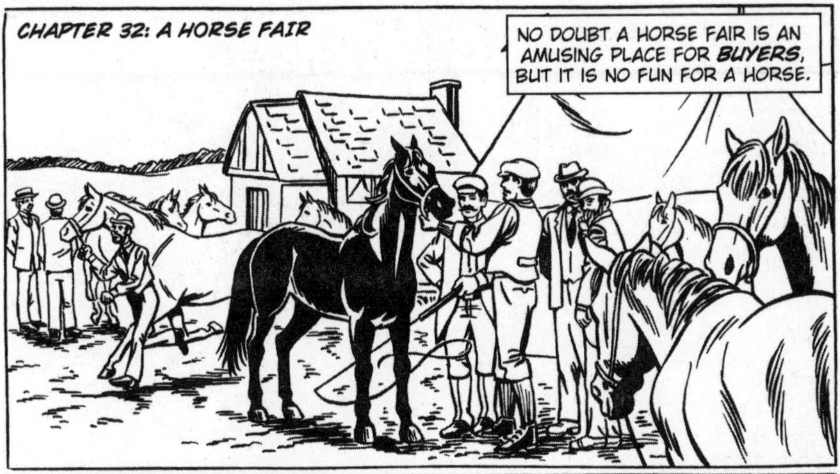
CHAPTER 32: A HORSE FAIR
NO DOUBT A HORSE FAIR IS AN AMUSING PLACE FOR BUYERS, BUT IT IS NO FUN FOR A HORSE.

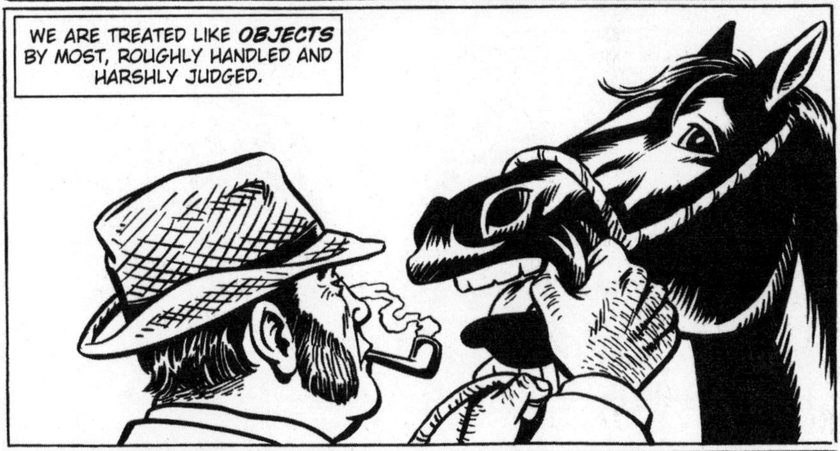
WE ARE TREATED LIKE OBJECTS BY MOST, ROUGHLY HANDLED AND HARSHLY JUDGED.

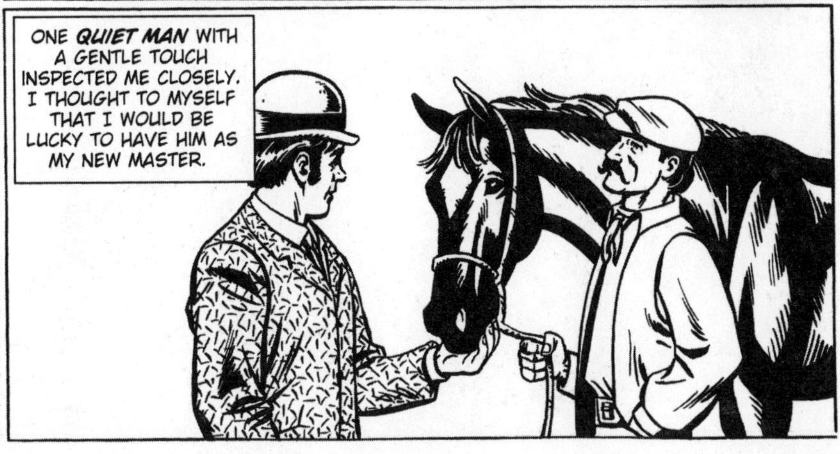
ONE QUIET MAN WITH A GENTLE TOUCH INSPECTED ME CLOSELY. I THOUGHT TO MYSELF THAT I WOULD BE LUCKY TO HAVE HIM AS MY NEW MASTER.

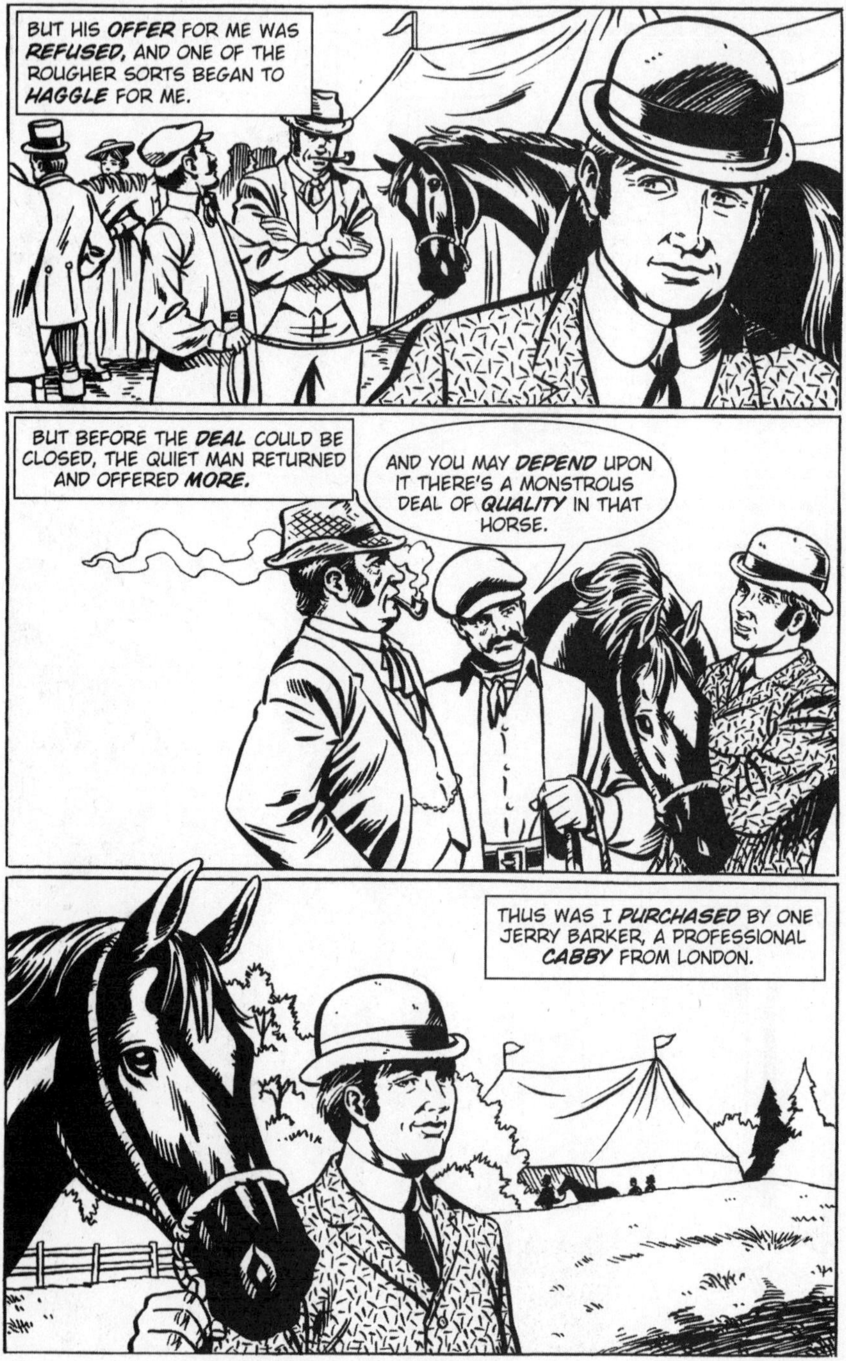
BUT HIS OFFER FOR ME WAS REFUSED, AND ONE OF THE ROUGHER SORTS BEGAN TO HAGGLE FOR ME.
BUT BEFORE THE DEAL COULD BE CLOSED, THE QUIET MAN RETURNED AND OFFERED MORE.
AND YOU MAY DEPEND UPON IT THERE'S A MONSTROUS DEAL OF QUALITY IN THAT HORSE.
THUS WAS I PURCHASED BY ONE JERRY BARKER, A PROFESSIONAL CABBY FROM LONDON.

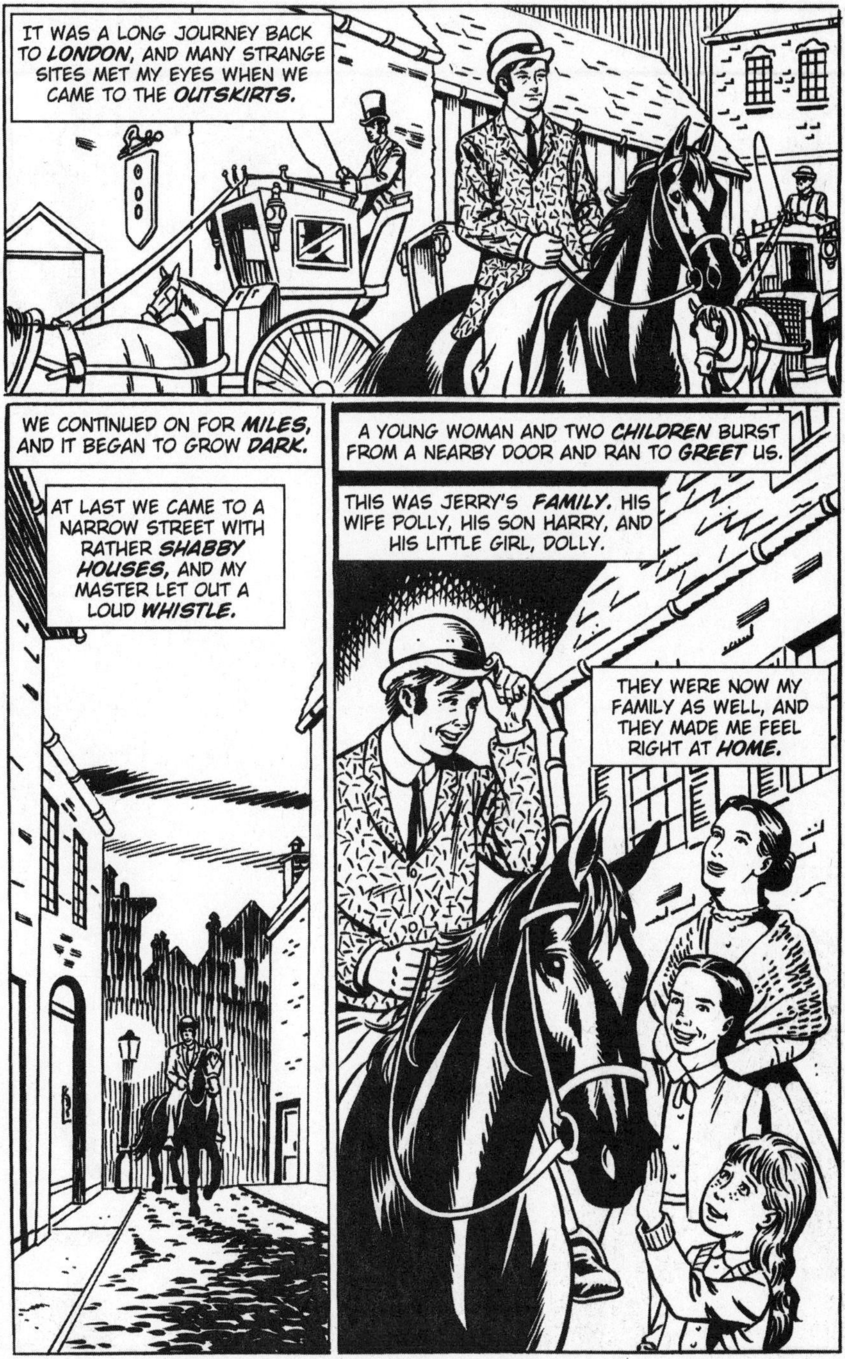
IT WAS A LONG JOURNEY BACK TO LONDON, AND MANY STRANGE SITES MET MY EYES WHEN WE CAME TO THE OUTSKIRTS.
WE CONTINUED ON FOR MILES, AND IT BEGAN TO GROW DARK.
AT LAST WE CAME TO A NARROW STREET WITH RATHER SHABBY HOUSES, AND MY MASTER LET OUT A LOUD WHISTLE.
A YOUNG WOMAN AND TWO CHILDREN BURST FROM A NEARBY DOOR AND RAN TO GREET US.
THIS WAS JERRY'S FAMILY. HIS WIFE POLLY, HIS SON HARRY, AND HIS LITTLE GIRL, DOLLY.
THEY WERE NOW MY FAMILY AS WELL, AND THEY MADE ME FEEL RIGHT AT HOME.

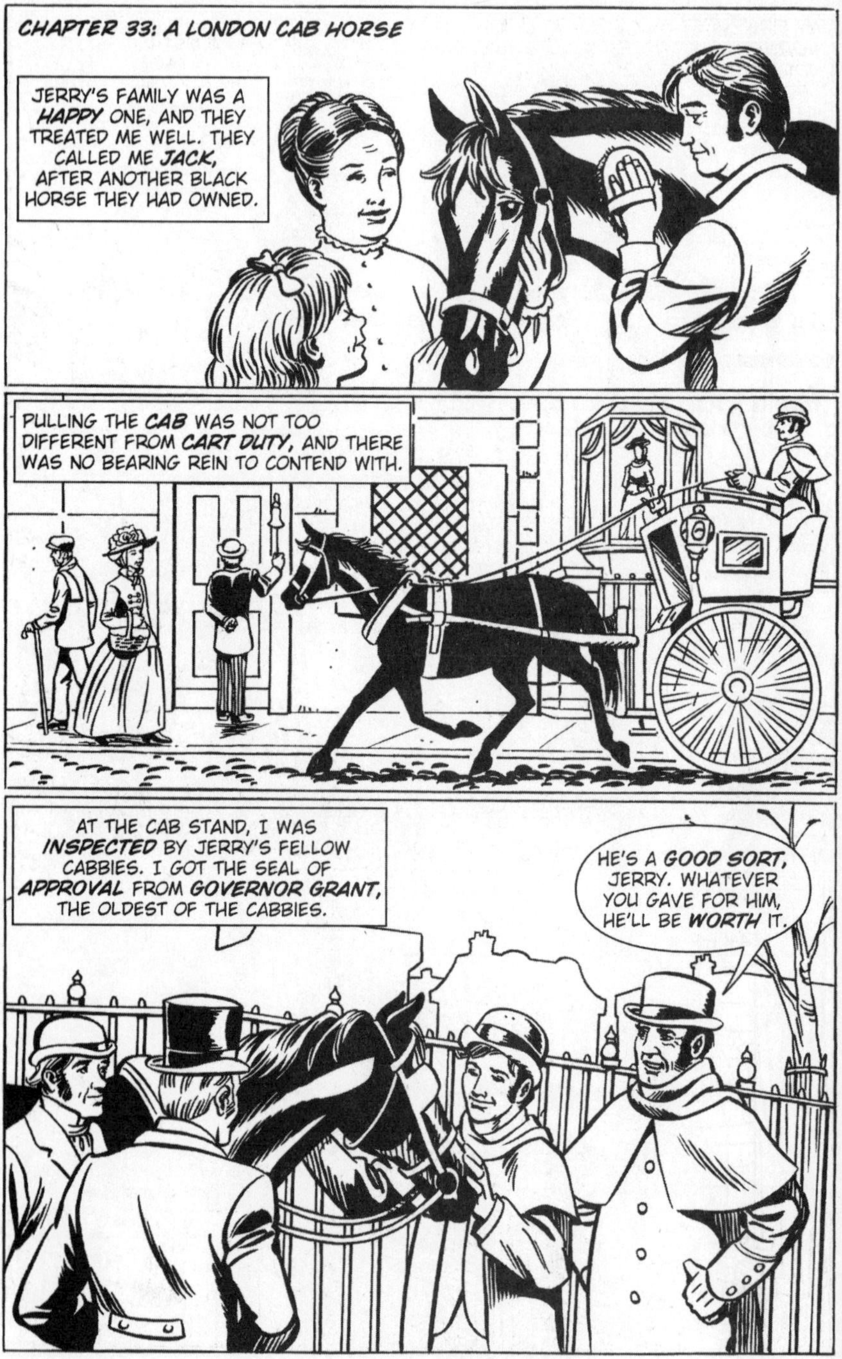
CHAPTER 33: A LONDON CAB HORSE
JERRY'S FAMILY WAS A HAPPY ONE, AND THEY TREATED ME WELL. THEY CALLED ME JACK, AFTER ANOTHER BLACK HORSE THEY HAD OWNED.
PULLING THE CAB WAS NOT TOO DIFFERENT FROM CART DUTY, AND THERE WAS NO BEARING REIN TO CONTEND WITH.
AT THE CAB STAND, I WAS INSPECTED BY JERRY'S FELLOW CABBIES. I GOT THE SEAL OF APPROVAL FROM GOVERNOR GRANT, THE OLDEST OF THE CABBIES.
HE'S A GOOD SORT, JERRY. WHATEVER YOU GAVE FOR HIM, HE'LL BE WORTH IT.

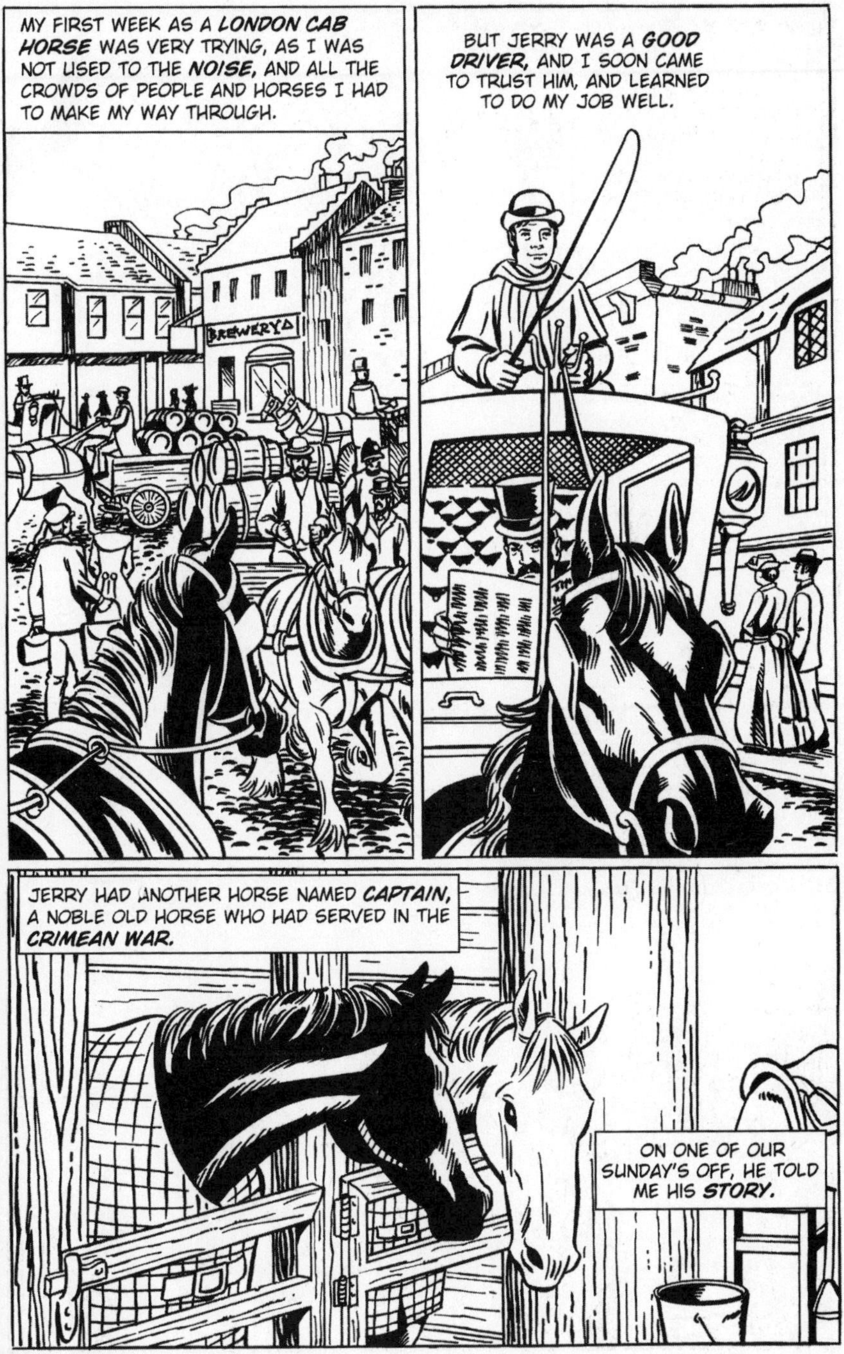
MY FIRST WEEK AS A LONDON CAB HORSE WAS VERY TRYING, AS I WAS NOT USED TO THE NOISE, AND ALL THE CROWDS OF PEOPLE AND HORSES I HAD TO MAKE MY WAY THROUGH.
BREWERY
BUT JERRY WAS A GOOD DRIVER, AND I SOON CAME TO TRUST HIM, AND LEARNED TO DO MY JOB WELL.
JERRY HAD ANOTHER HORSE NAMED CAPTAIN, A NOBLE OLD HORSE WHO HAD SERVED IN THE CRIMEAN WAR.
ON ONE OF OUR SUNDAY'S OFF, HE TOLD ME HIS STORY.

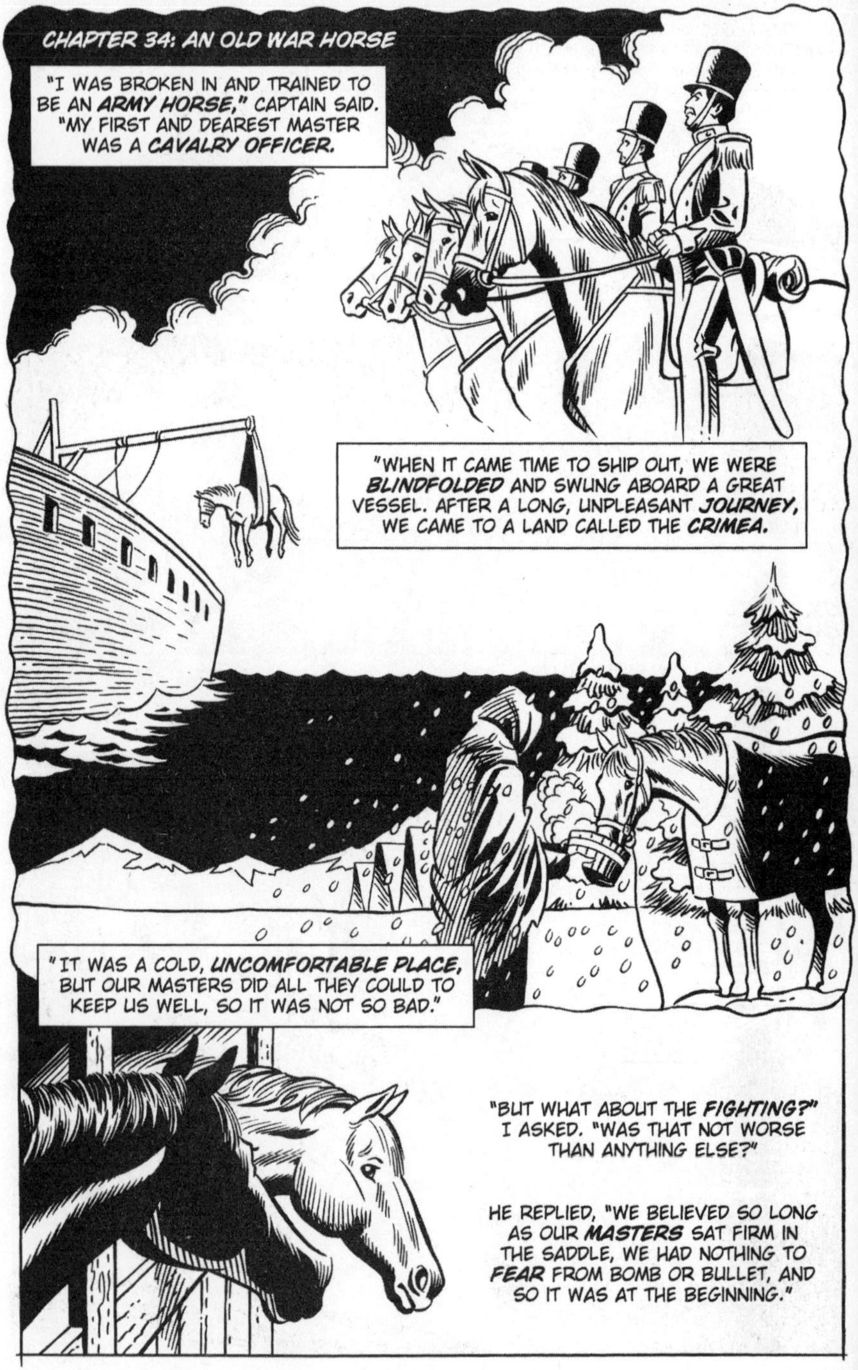
CHAPTER 34: AN OLD WAR HORSE
"I WAS BROKEN IN AND TRAINED TO BE AN ARMY HORSE," CAPTAIN SAID. "MY FIRST AND DEAREST MASTER WAS A CAVALRY OFFICER.
"WHEN IT CAME TIME TO SHIP OUT, WE WERE BLINDFOLDED AND SWUNG ABOARD A GREAT VESSEL. AFTER A LONG, UNPLEASANT JOURNEY, WE CAME TO A LAND CALLED THE CRIMEA.
"IT WAS A COLD, UNCOMFORTABLE PLACE, BUT OUR MASTERS DID ALL THEY COULD TO KEEP US WELL, SO IT WAS NOT SO BAD."
"BUT WHAT ABOUT THE FIGHTING?" I ASKED. "WAS THAT NOT WORSE THAN ANYTHING ELSE?"
HE REPLIED, "WE BELIEVED SO LONG AS OUR MASTERS SAT FIRM IN THE SADDLE, WE HAD NOTHING TO FEAR FROM BOMB OR BULLET, AND SO IT WAS AT THE BEGINNING."

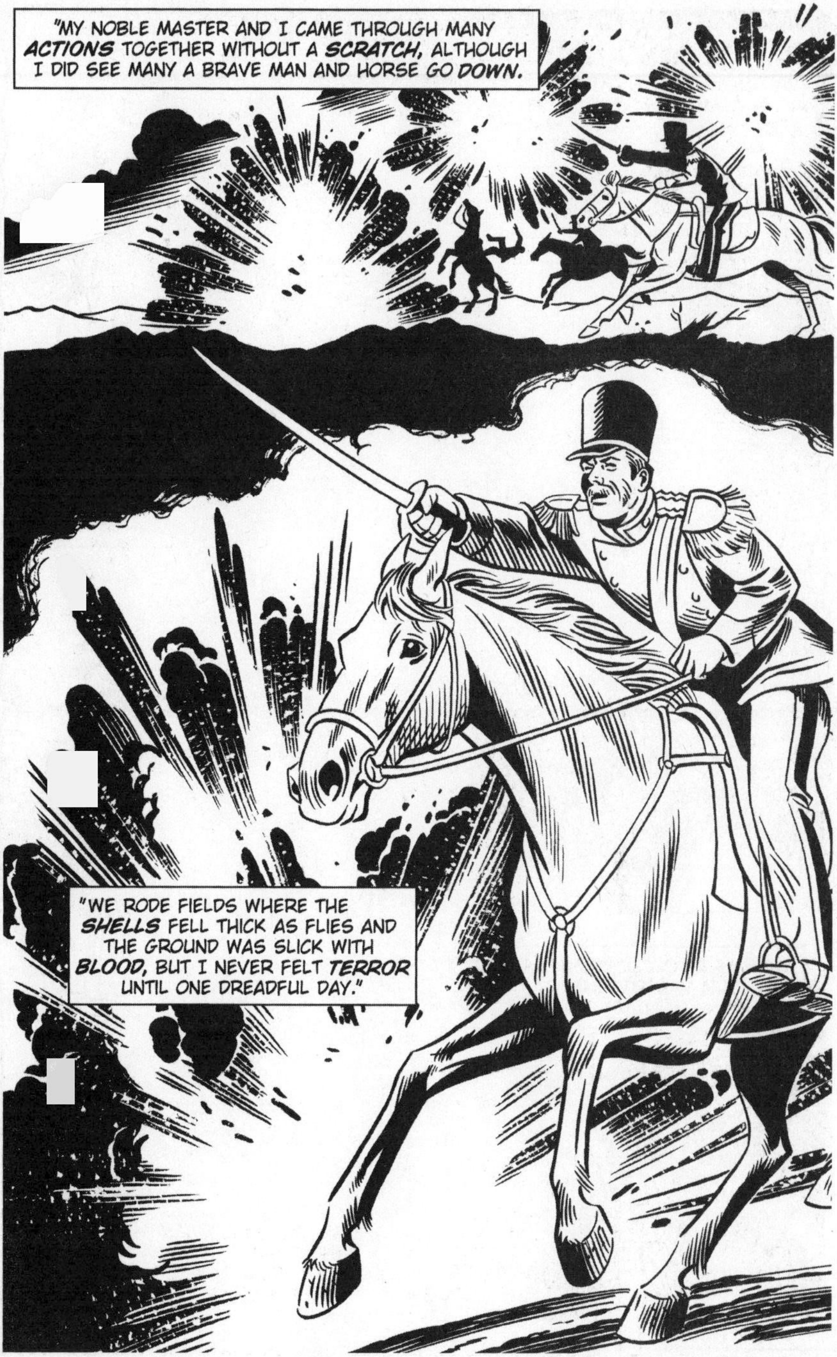
"MY NOBLE MASTER AND I CAME THROUGH MANY ACTIONS TOGETHER WITHOUT A SCRATCH, ALTHOUGH I DID SEE MANY A BRAVE MAN AND HORSE GO DOWN.
"WE RODE FIELDS WHERE THE SHELLS FELL THICK AS FLIES AND THE GROUND WAS SLICK WITH BLOOD, BUT I NEVER FELT TERROR UNTIL ONE DREADFUL DAY."

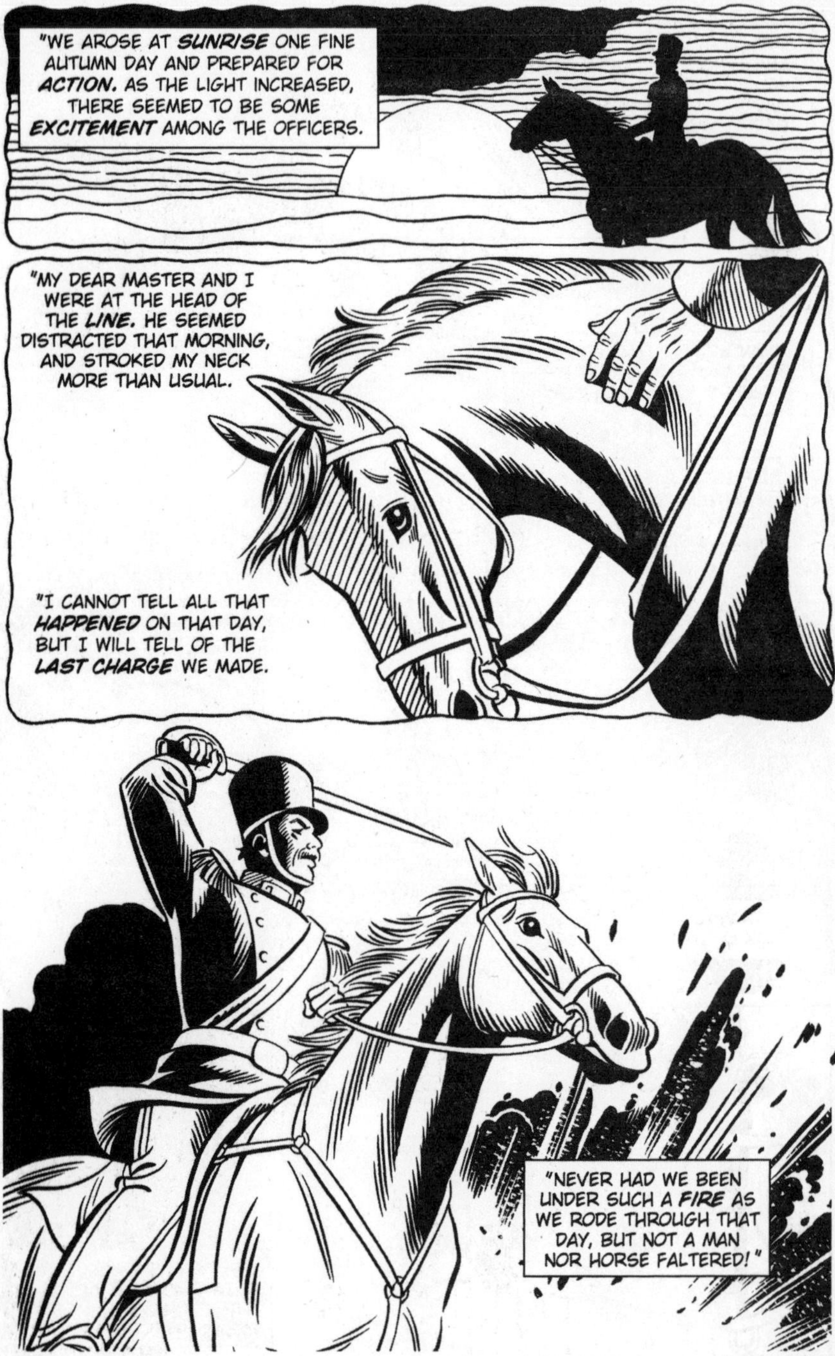
"WE AROSE AT SUNRISE ONE FINE AUTUMN DAY AND PREPARED FOR ACTION. AS THE LIGHT INCREASED, THERE SEEMED TO BE SOME EXCITEMENT AMONG THE OFFICERS.
"MY DEAR MASTER AND I WERE AT THE HEAD OF THE LINE. HE SEEMED DISTRACTED THAT MORNING, AND STROKED MY NECK MORE THAN USUAL.
"I CANNOT TELL ALL THAT HAPPENED ON THAT DAY, BUT I WILL TELL OF THE LAST CHARGE WE MADE.
"NEVER HAD WE BEEN UNDER SUCH A FIRE AS WE RODE THROUGH THAT DAY, BUT NOT A MAN NOR HORSE FALTERED!"

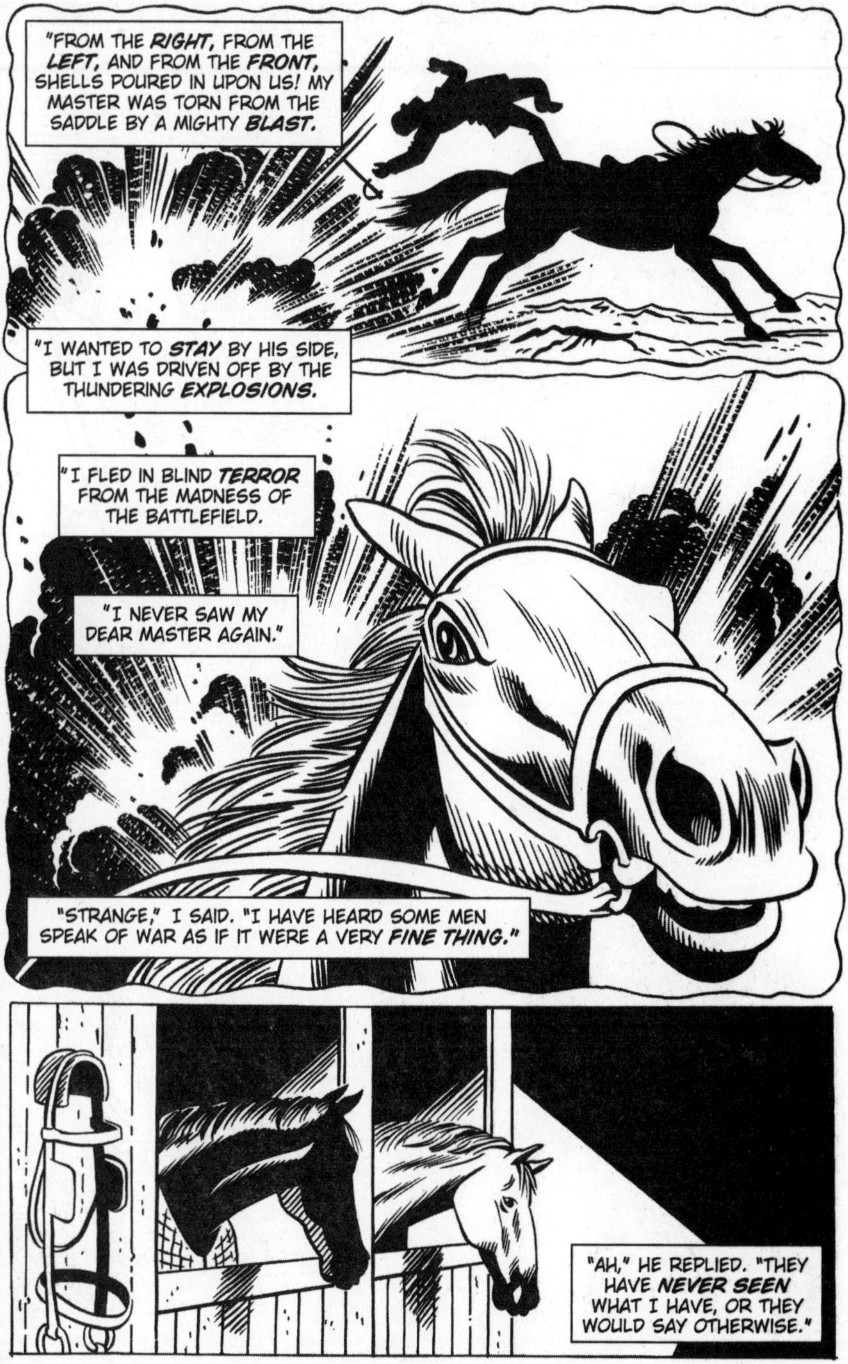
"FROM THE RIGHT, FROM THE LEFT, AND FROM THE FRONT, SHELLS POURED IN UPON US! MY MASTER WAS TORN FROM THE SADDLE BY A MIGHTY BLAST.
"I WANTED TO STAY BY HIS SIDE, BUT I WAS DRIVEN OFF BY THE THUNDERING EXPLOSIONS.
"I FLED IN BLIND TERROR FROM THE MADNESS OF THE BATTLEFIELD.
"I NEVER SAW MY DEAR MASTER AGAIN."
"STRANGE," I SAID. "I HAVE HEARD SOME MEN SPEAK OF WAR AS IF IT WERE A VERY FINE THING."
"AH," HE REPLIED. "THEY HAVE NEVER SEEN WHAT I HAVE, OR THEY WOULD SAY OTHERWISE."

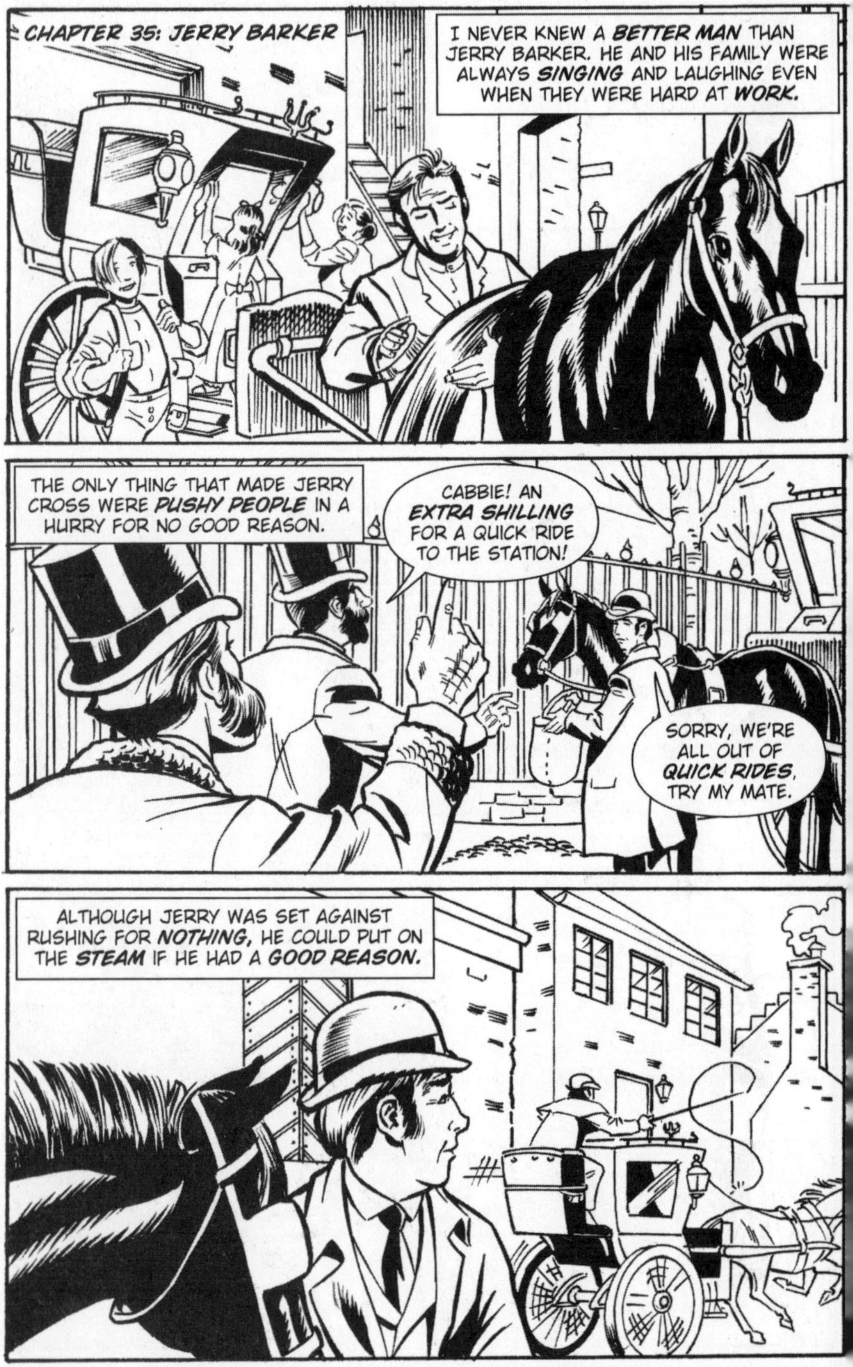

CHAPTER 35: JERRY BARKER
I NEVER KNEW A BETTER MAN THAN JERRY BARKER. HE AND HIS FAMILY WERE ALWAYS SINGING AND LAUGHING EVEN WHEN THEY WERE HARD AT WORK.
THE ONLY THING THAT MADE JERRY CROSS WERE PUSHY PEOPLE IN A HURRY FOR NO GOOD REASON.
CABBIE! AN EXTRA SHILLING FOR A QUICK RIDE TO THE STATION!
SORRY, WE'RE ALL OUT OF QUICK RIDES, TRY MY MATE.
ALTHOUGH JERRY WAS SET AGAINST RUSHING FOR NOTHING, HE COULD PUT ON THE STEAM IF HE HAD A GOOD REASON.

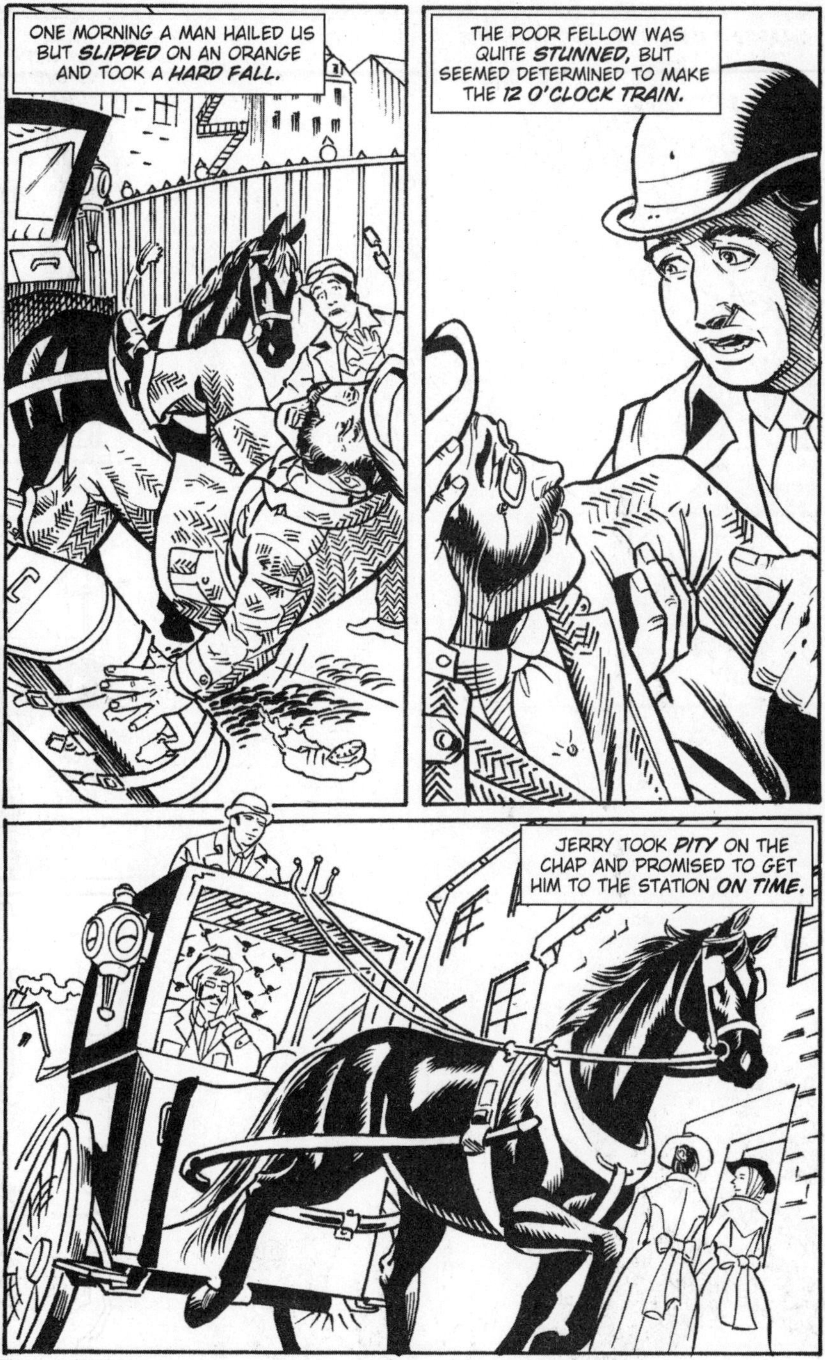
ONE MORNING A MAN HAILED US BUT SLIPPED ON AN ORANGE AND TOOK A HARD FALL.
THE POOR FELLOW WAS QUITE STUNNED, BUT SEEMED DETERMINED TO MAKE THE 12 O'CLOCK TRAIN.
JERRY TOOK PITY ON THE CHAP AND PROMISED TO GET HIM TO THE STATION ON TIME.

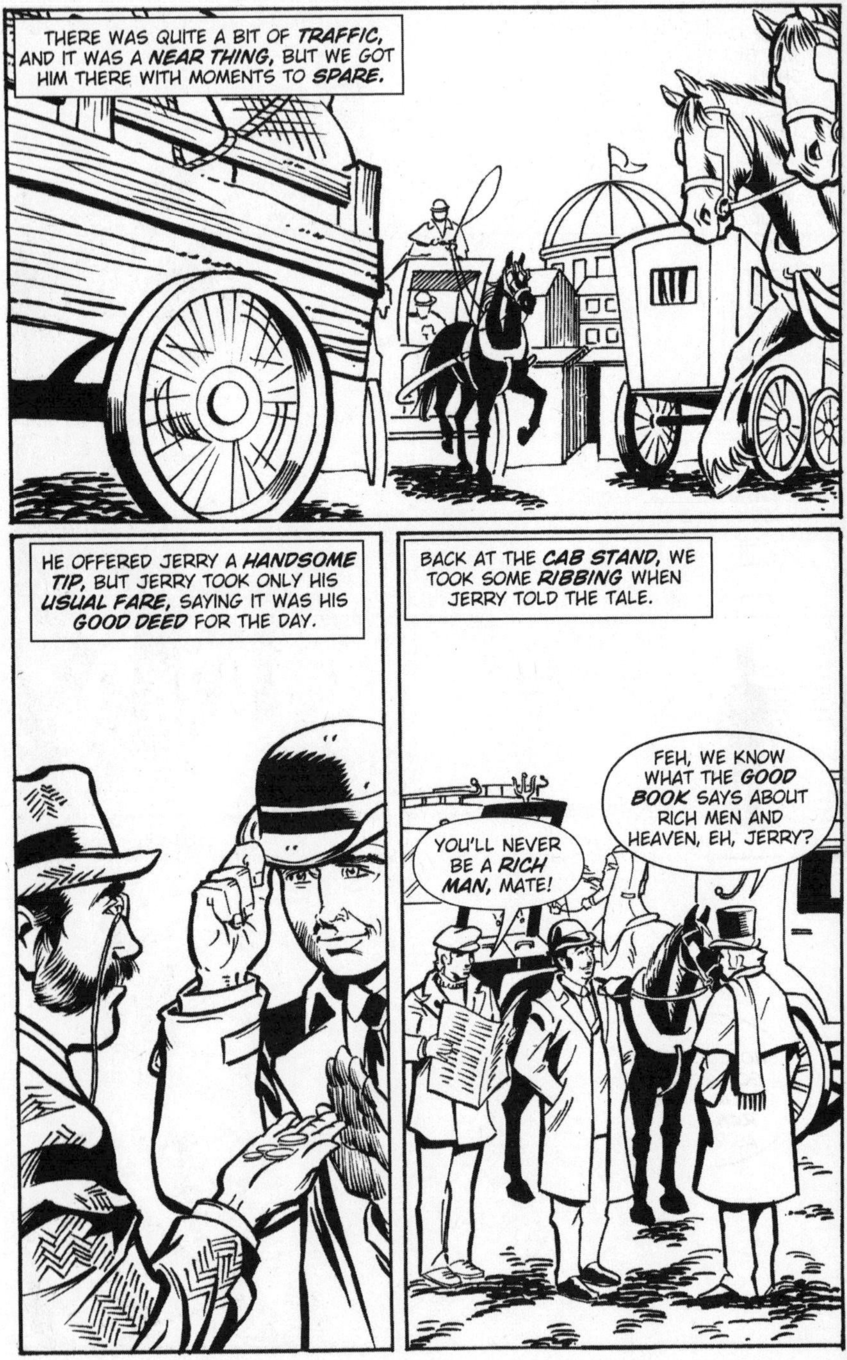

THERE WAS QUITE A BIT OF *TRAFFIC,* AND IT WAS A *NEAR THING,* BUT WE GOT HIM THERE WITH MOMENTS TO *SPARE.*
HE OFFERED JERRY A *HANDSOME TIP,* BUT JERRY TOOK ONLY HIS *USUAL FARE,* SAYING IT WAS HIS *GOOD DEED* FOR THE DAY.
BACK AT THE *CAB STAND,* WE TOOK SOME *RIBBING* WHEN JERRY TOLD THE TALE.
YOU'LL NEVER BE A *RICH MAN,* MATE!
FEH, WE KNOW WHAT THE *GOOD BOOK* SAYS ABOUT RICH MEN AND HEAVEN, EH, JERRY?

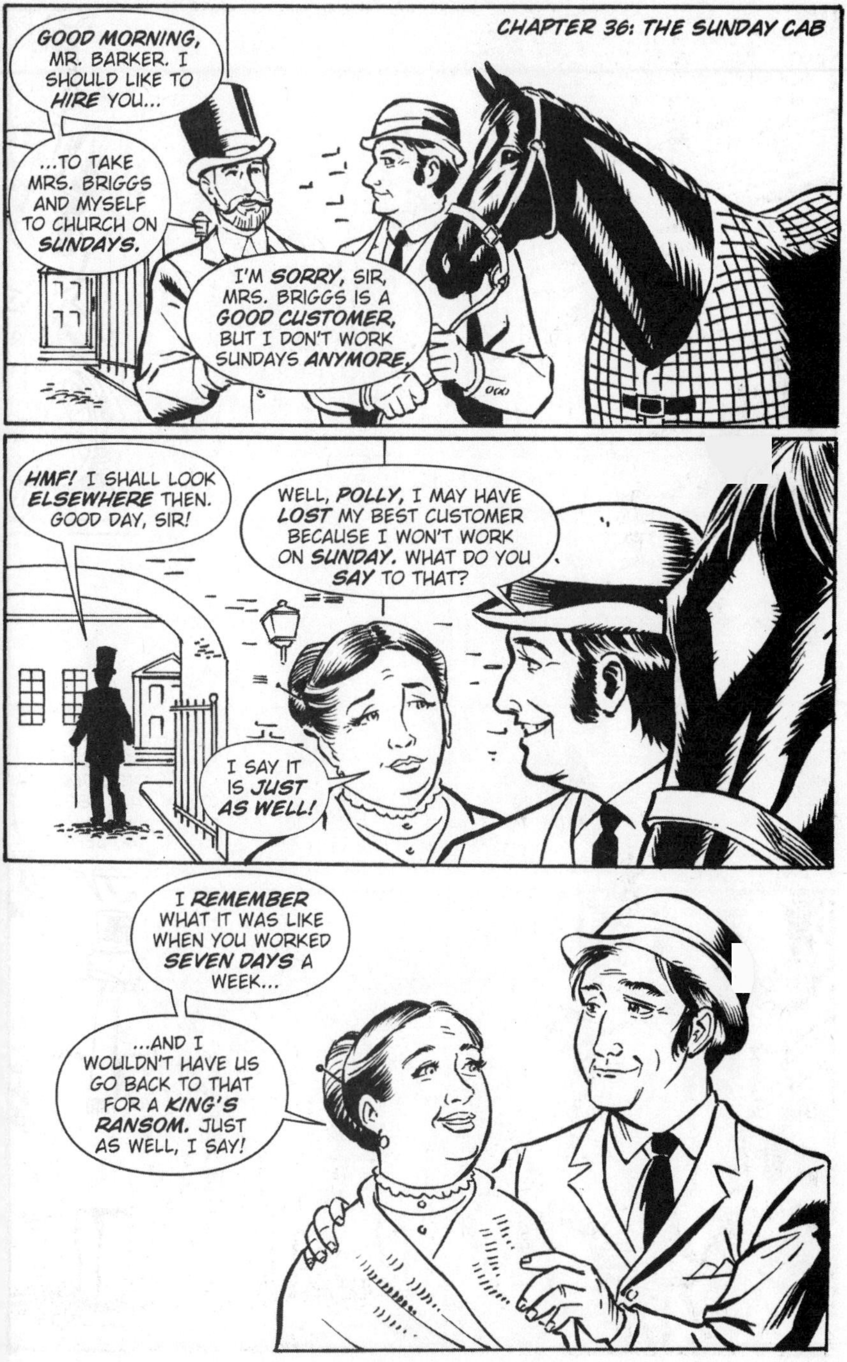
CHAPTER 36: THE SUNDAY CAB
GOOD MORNING, MR. BARKER. I SHOULD LIKE TO HIRE YOU...
...TO TAKE MRS. BRIGGS AND MYSELF TO CHURCH ON SUNDAYS.
I'M SORRY, SIR, MRS. BRIGGS IS A GOOD CUSTOMER, BUT I DON'T WORK SUNDAYS ANYMORE.
HMF! I SHALL LOOK ELSEWHERE THEN. GOOD DAY, SIR!
WELL, POLLY, I MAY HAVE LOST MY BEST CUSTOMER BECAUSE I WON'T WORK ON SUNDAY. WHAT DO YOU SAY TO THAT?
I SAY IT IS JUST AS WELL!
I REMEMBER WHAT IT WAS LIKE WHEN YOU WORKED SEVEN DAYS A WEEK...
...AND I WOULDN'T HAVE US GO BACK TO THAT FOR A KING'S RANSOM. JUST AS WELL, I SAY!

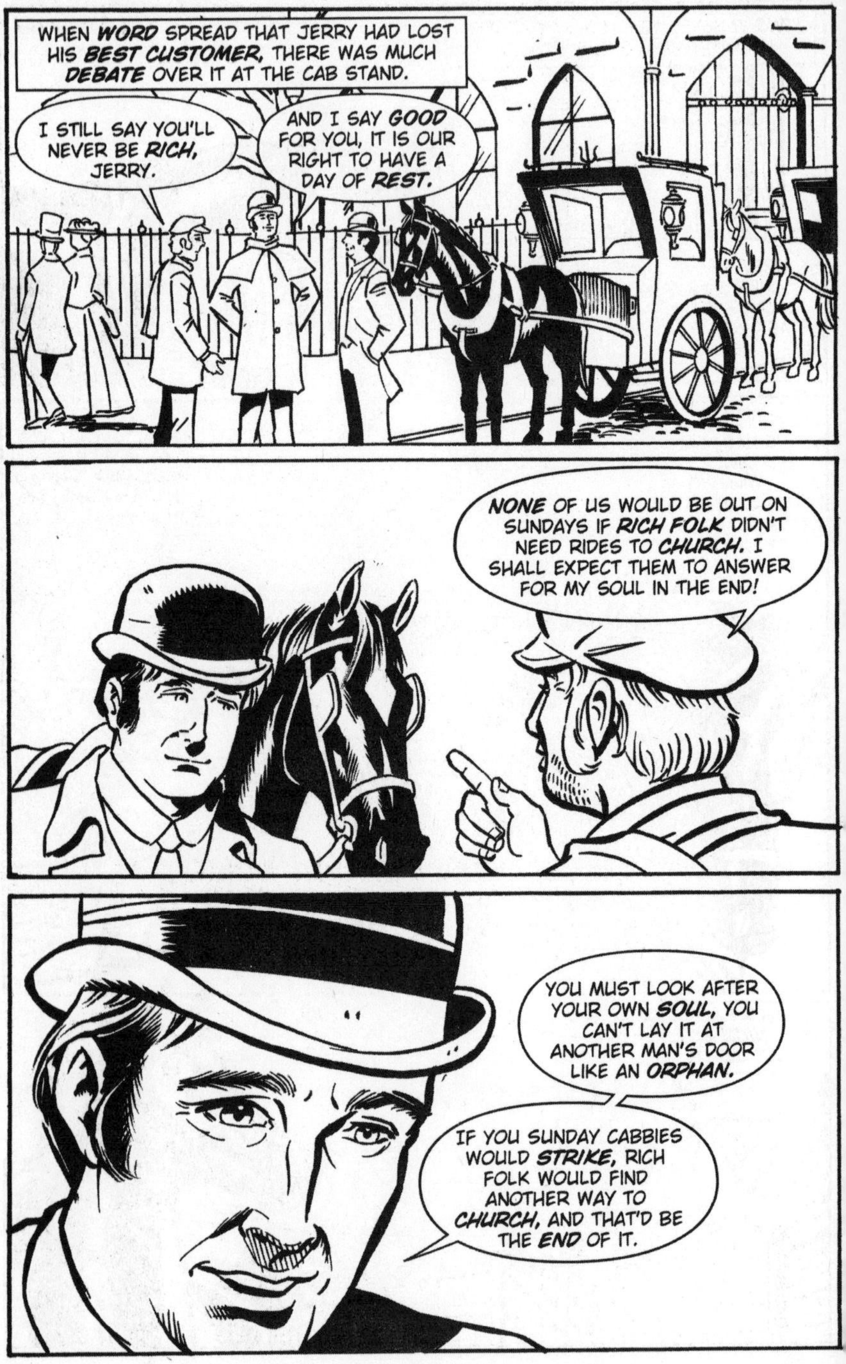
WHEN WORD SPREAD THAT JERRY HAD LOST HIS BEST CUSTOMER, THERE WAS MUCH DEBATE OVER IT AT THE CAB STAND.
I STILL SAY YOU'LL NEVER BE RICH, JERRY.
AND I SAY GOOD FOR YOU, IT IS OUR RIGHT TO HAVE A DAY OF REST.
NONE OF US WOULD BE OUT ON SUNDAYS IF RICH FOLK DIDN'T NEED RIDES TO CHURCH. I SHALL EXPECT THEM TO ANSWER FOR MY SOUL IN THE END!
YOU MUST LOOK AFTER YOUR OWN SOUL, YOU CAN'T LAY IT AT ANOTHER MAN'S DOOR LIKE AN ORPHAN.
IF YOU SUNDAY CABBIES WOULD STRIKE, RICH FOLK WOULD FIND ANOTHER WAY TO CHURCH, AND THAT'D BE THE END OF IT.

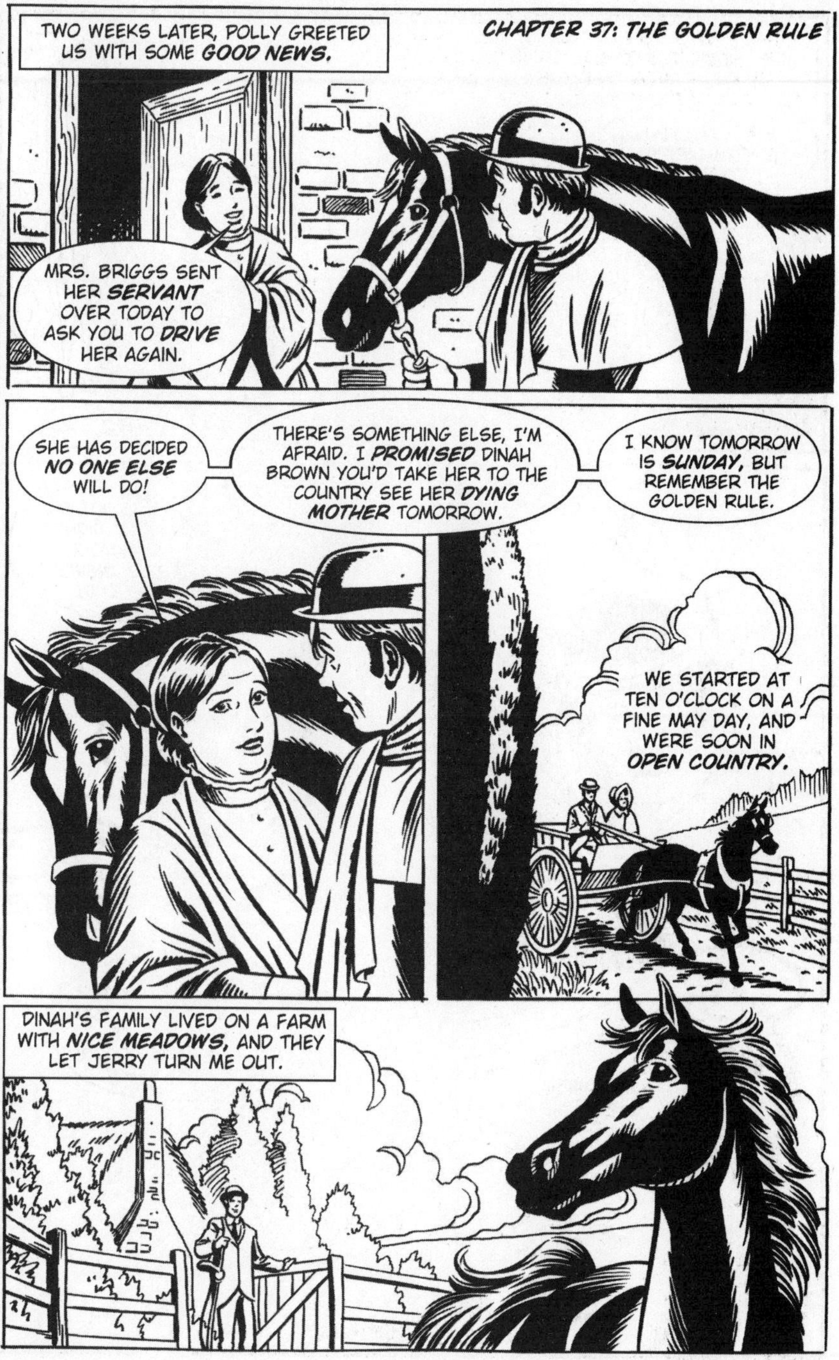
TWO WEEKS LATER, POLLY GREETED US WITH SOME GOOD NEWS.
CHAPTER 37: THE GOLDEN RULE
MRS. BRIGGS SENT HER SERVANT OVER TODAY TO ASK YOU TO DRIVE HER AGAIN.
SHE HAS DECIDED NO ONE ELSE WILL DO!
THERE'S SOMETHING ELSE, I'M AFRAID. I PROMISED DINAH BROWN YOU'D TAKE HER TO THE COUNTRY SEE HER DYING MOTHER TOMORROW.
I KNOW TOMORROW IS SUNDAY, BUT REMEMBER THE GOLDEN RULE.
WE STARTED AT TEN O'CLOCK ON A FINE MAY DAY, AND WERE SOON IN OPEN COUNTRY.
DINAH'S FAMILY LIVED ON A FARM WITH NICE MEADOWS, AND THEY LET JERRY TURN ME OUT.

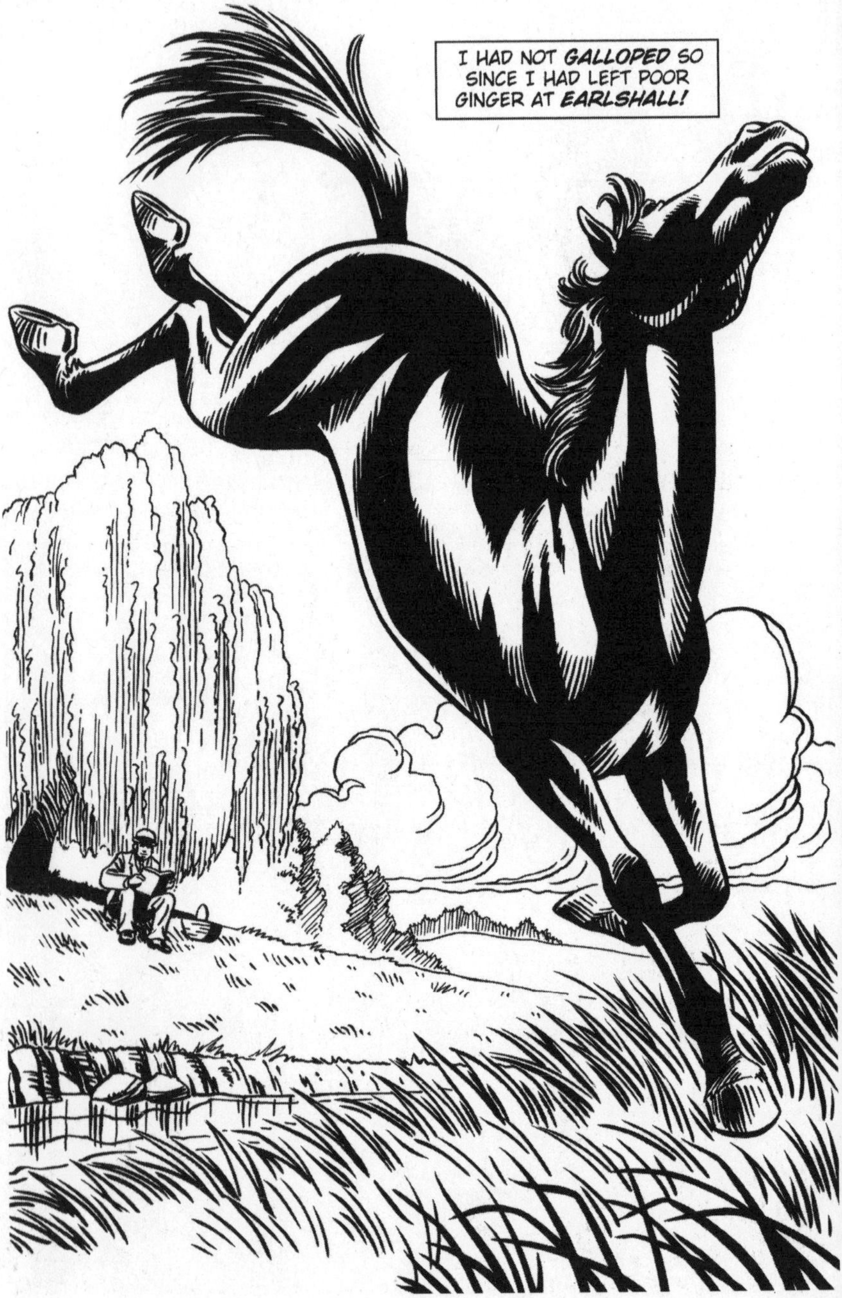
I HAD NOT GALLOPED SO SINCE I HAD LEFT POOR GINGER AT EARLSHALL!

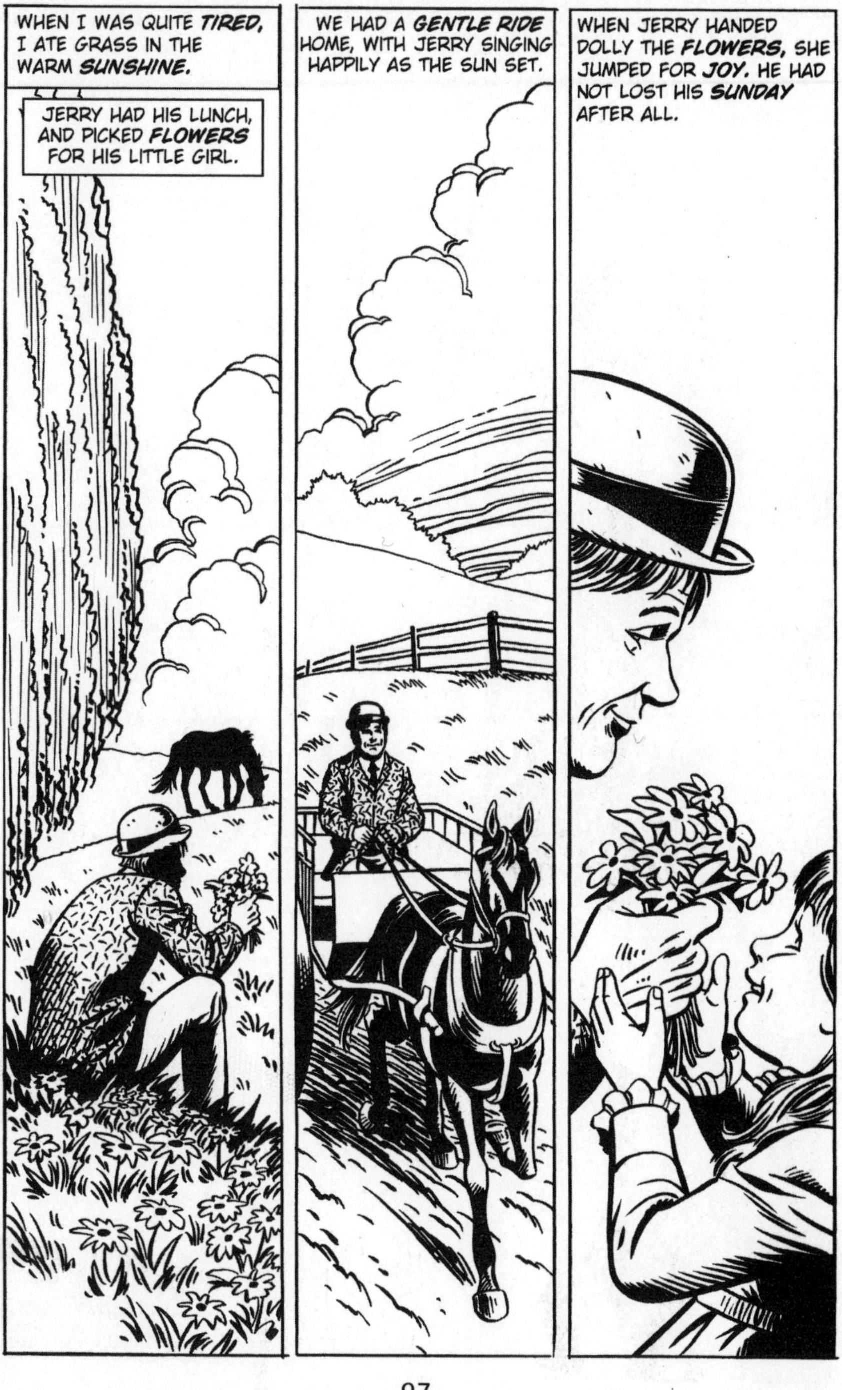
WHEN I WAS QUITE TIRED, I ATE GRASS IN THE WARM SUNSHINE.
JERRY HAD HIS LUNCH, AND PICKED FLOWERS FOR HIS LITTLE GIRL.
WE HAD A GENTLE RIDE HOME, WITH JERRY SINGING HAPPILY AS THE SUN SET.
WHEN JERRY HANDED DOLLY THE FLOWERS, SHE JUMPED FOR JOY. HE HAD NOT LOST HIS SUNDAY AFTER ALL.

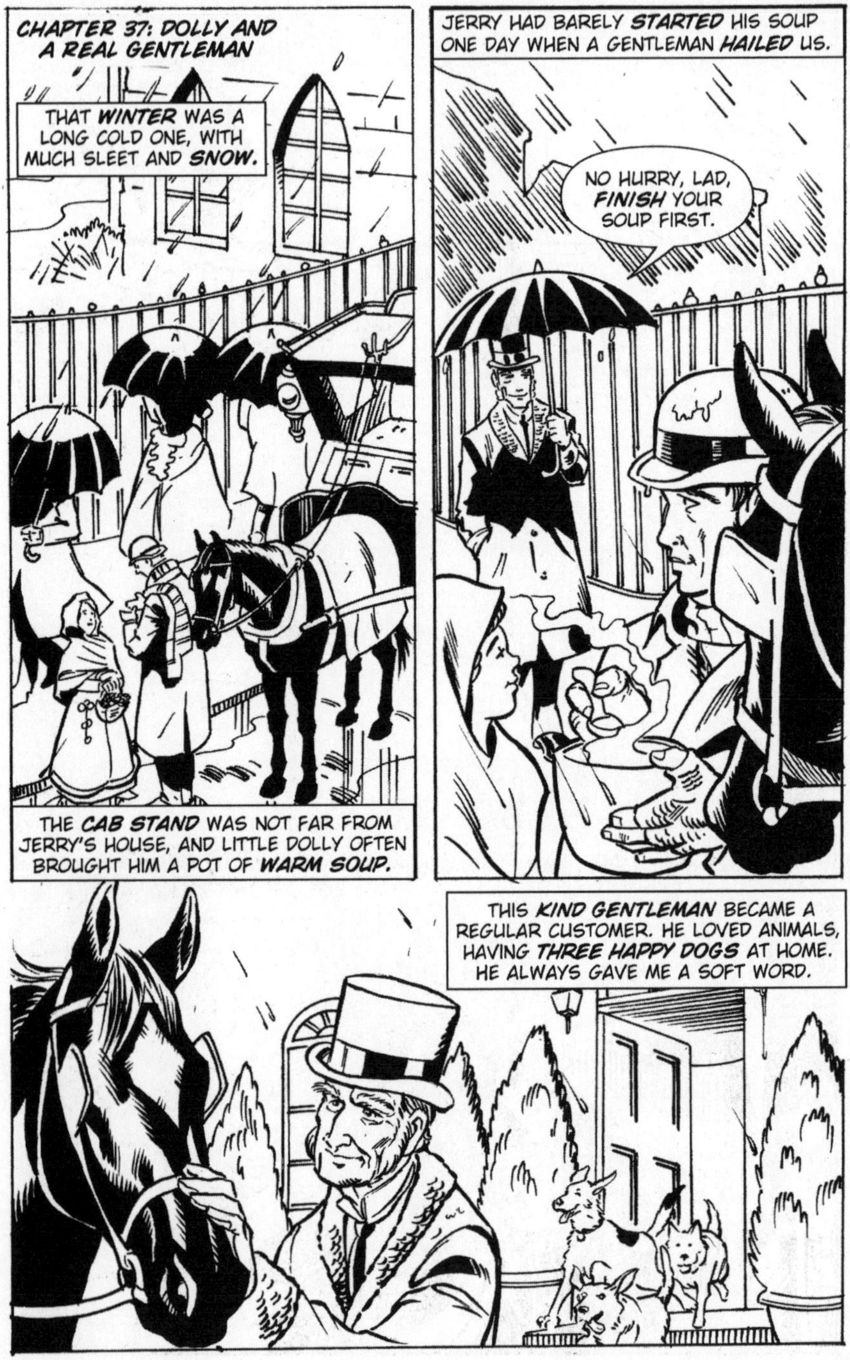
CHAPTER 37: DOLLY AND A REAL GENTLEMAN
THAT WINTER WAS A LONG COLD ONE, WITH MUCH SLEET AND SNOW.
THE CAB STAND WAS NOT FAR FROM JERRY'S HOUSE, AND LITTLE DOLLY OFTEN BROUGHT HIM A POT OF WARM SOUP.
JERRY HAD BARELY STARTED HIS SOUP ONE DAY WHEN A GENTLEMAN HAILED US.
NO HURRY, LAD, FINISH YOUR SOUP FIRST.
THIS KIND GENTLEMAN BECAME A REGULAR CUSTOMER. HE LOVED ANIMALS, HAVING THREE HAPPY DOGS AT HOME. HE ALWAYS GAVE ME A SOFT WORD.

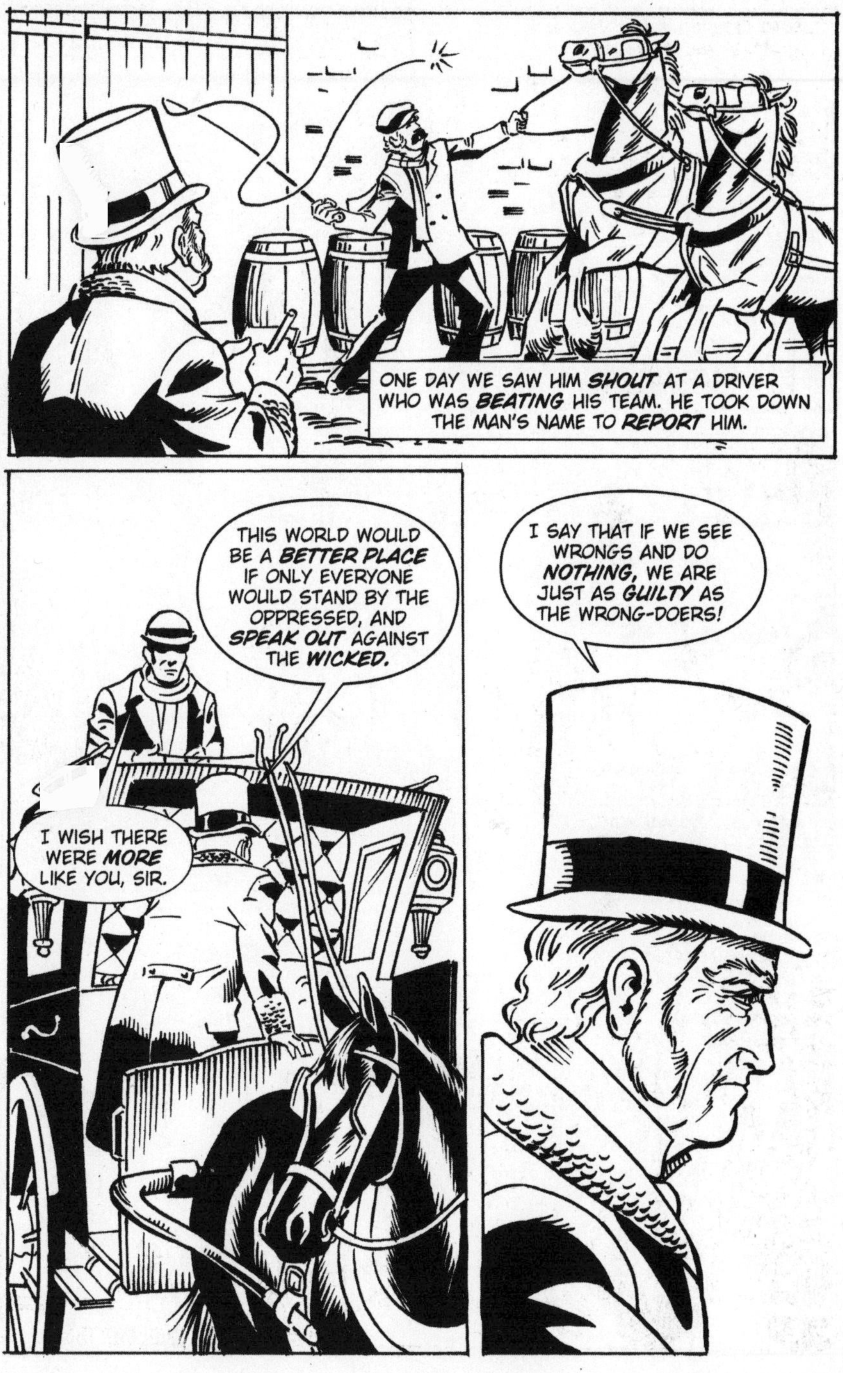
ONE DAY WE SAW HIM SHOUT AT A DRIVER WHO WAS BEATING HIS TEAM. HE TOOK DOWN THE MAN'S NAME TO REPORT HIM.
THIS WORLD WOULD BE A BETTER PLACE IF ONLY EVERYONE WOULD STAND BY THE OPPRESSED, AND SPEAK OUT AGAINST THE WICKED.
I SAY THAT IF WE SEE WRONGS AND DO NOTHING, WE ARE JUST AS GUILTY AS THE WRONG-DOERS!
I WISH THERE WERE MORE LIKE YOU, SIR.

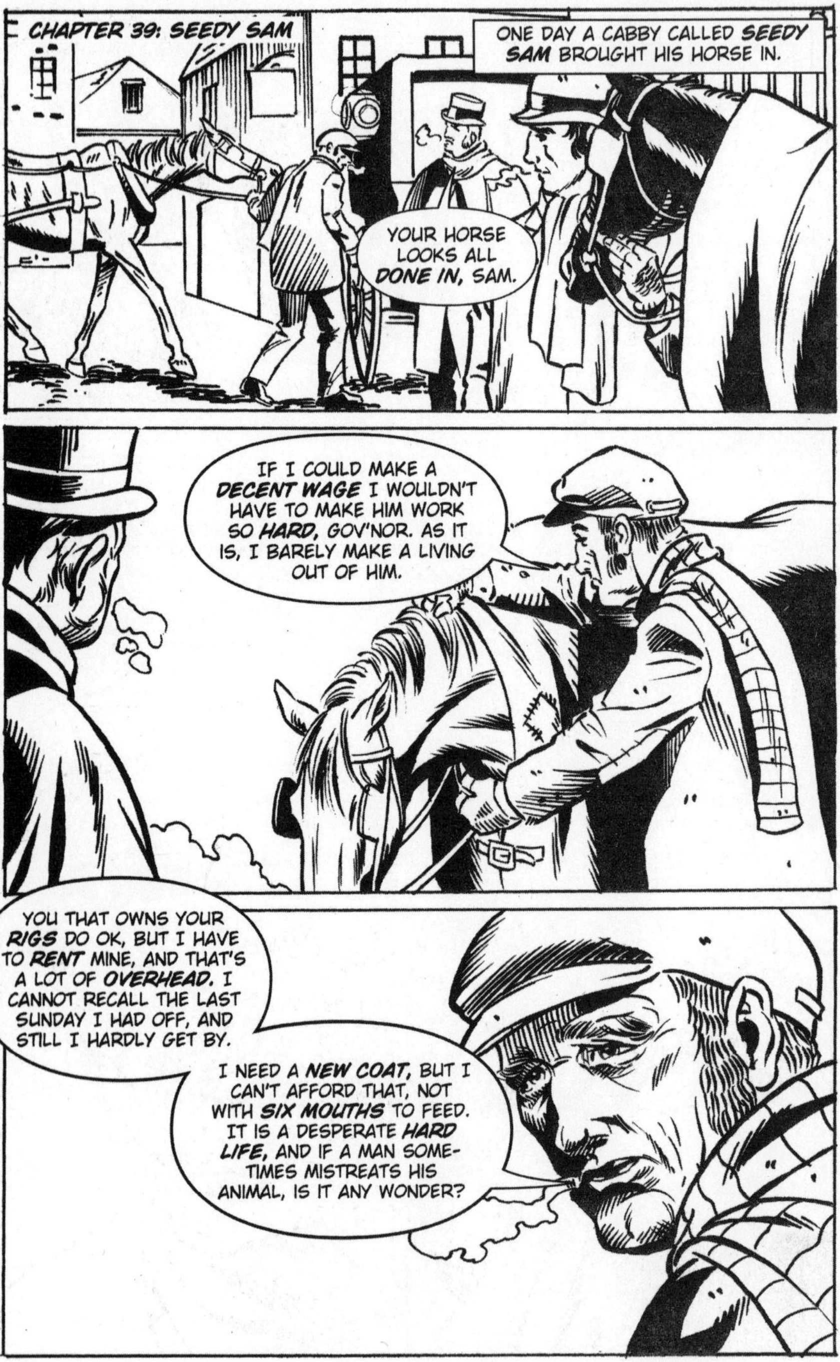
CHAPTER 39: SEEDY SAM
ONE DAY A CABBY CALLED SEEDY SAM BROUGHT HIS HORSE IN.
YOUR HORSE LOOKS ALL DONE IN, SAM.
IF I COULD MAKE A DECENT WAGE I WOULDN'T HAVE TO MAKE HIM WORK SO HARD, GOV'NOR. AS IT IS, I BARELY MAKE A LIVING OUT OF HIM.
YOU THAT OWNS YOUR RIGS DO OK, BUT I HAVE TO RENT MINE, AND THAT'S A LOT OF OVERHEAD. I CANNOT RECALL THE LAST SUNDAY I HAD OFF, AND STILL I HARDLY GET BY.
I NEED A NEW COAT, BUT I CAN'T AFFORD THAT, NOT WITH SIX MOUTHS TO FEED. IT IS A DESPERATE HARD LIFE, AND IF A MAN SOMETIMES MISTREATS HIS ANIMAL, IS IT ANY WONDER?

EVERY WORD IS *TRUE*, SAM, YOU'LL GET NO ARGUMENT FROM ME. ALL I ASK IS THAT YOU GIVE YOUR HORSE A *KIND WORD* NOW AND THEN, IT'S AMAZING WHAT THEY *UNDERSTAND*.

I'LL SURELY *THINK* ON IT, GOV'NOR. <KAFF KAFF!>

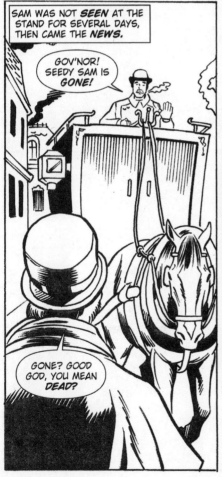

SAM WAS NOT *SEEN* AT THE STAND FOR SEVERAL DAYS, THEN CAME THE *NEWS*.

GOV'NOR! SEEDY SAM IS *GONE!*

GONE? GOOD GOD, YOU MEAN *DEAD?*

AYE, HE TOOK A *FEVER* AND WENT QUICK. HIS *LAST WORDS* WERE, "I NEVER HAD A SUNDAY'S REST!"

LORD HA' *MERCY* ON US, BOYS, THIS IS A *WARNING* TO US ALL!

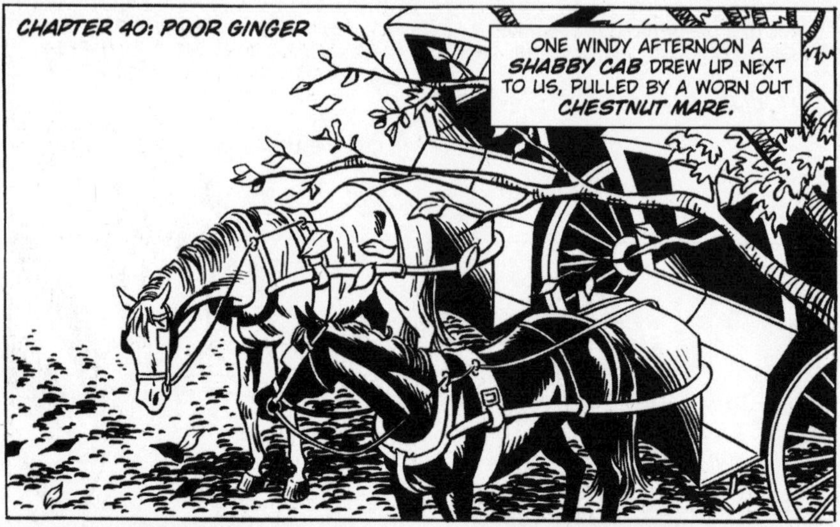
CHAPTER 40: POOR GINGER
ONE WINDY AFTERNOON A SHABBY CAB DREW UP NEXT TO US, PULLED BY A WORN OUT CHESTNUT MARE.

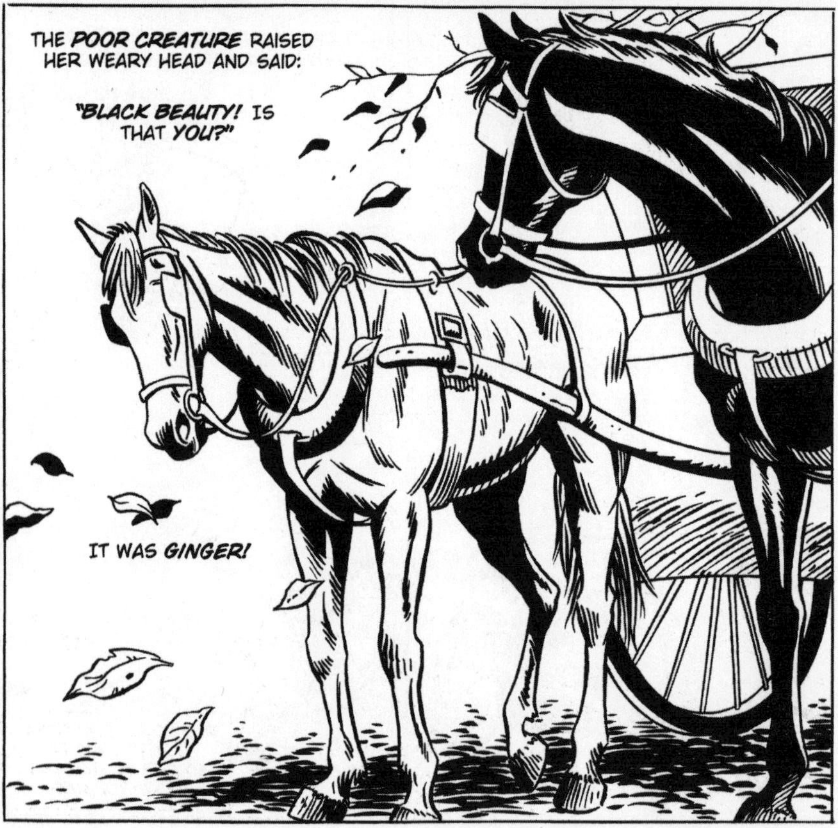
THE POOR CREATURE RAISED HER WEARY HEAD AND SAID:
"BLACK BEAUTY! IS THAT YOU?"
IT WAS GINGER!

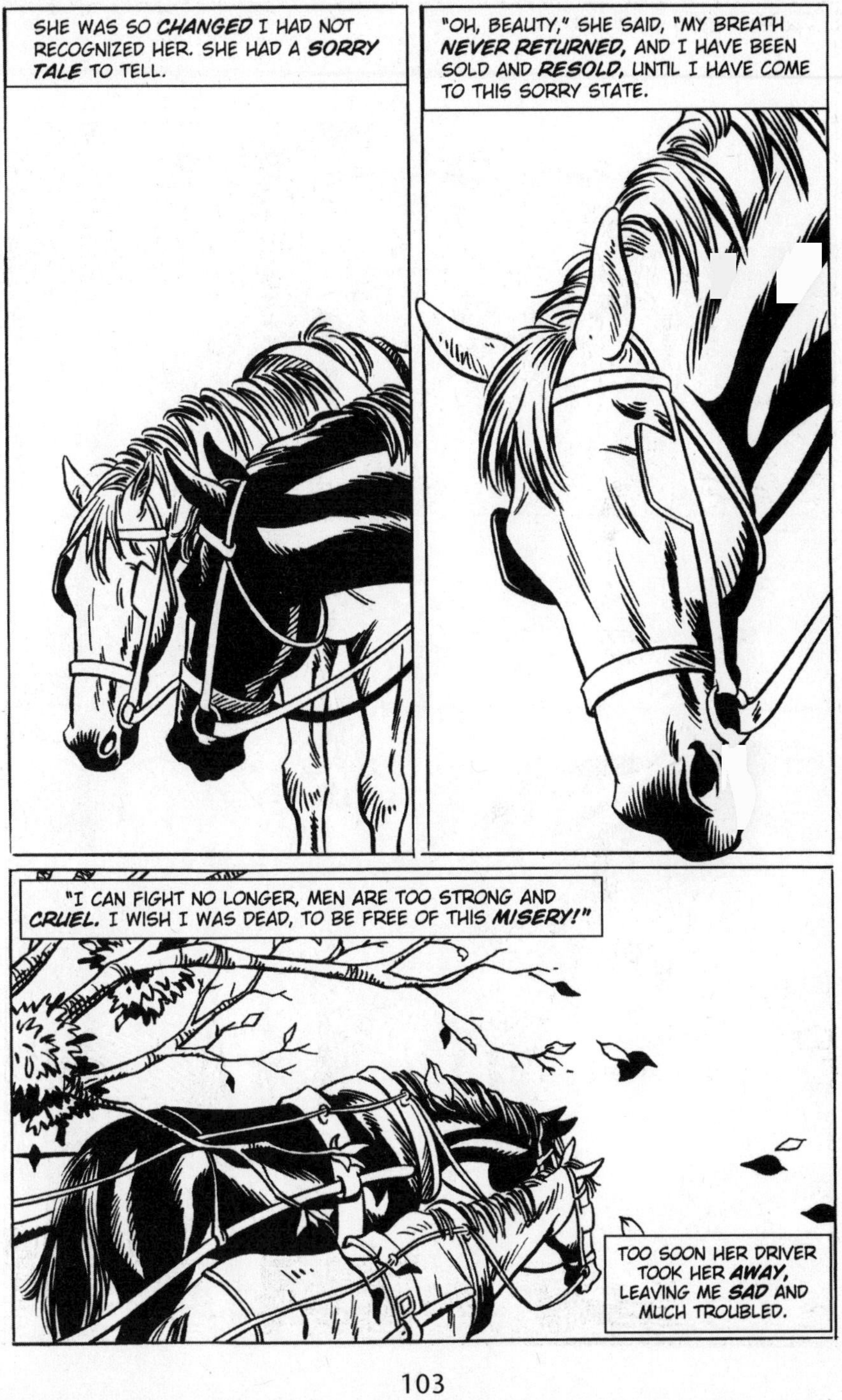
SHE WAS SO CHANGED I HAD NOT RECOGNIZED HER. SHE HAD A SORRY TALE TO TELL.
"OH, BEAUTY," SHE SAID, "MY BREATH NEVER RETURNED, AND I HAVE BEEN SOLD AND RESOLD, UNTIL I HAVE COME TO THIS SORRY STATE.
"I CAN FIGHT NO LONGER, MEN ARE TOO STRONG AND CRUEL. I WISH I WAS DEAD, TO BE FREE OF THIS MISERY!"
TOO SOON HER DRIVER TOOK HER AWAY, LEAVING ME SAD AND MUCH TROUBLED.

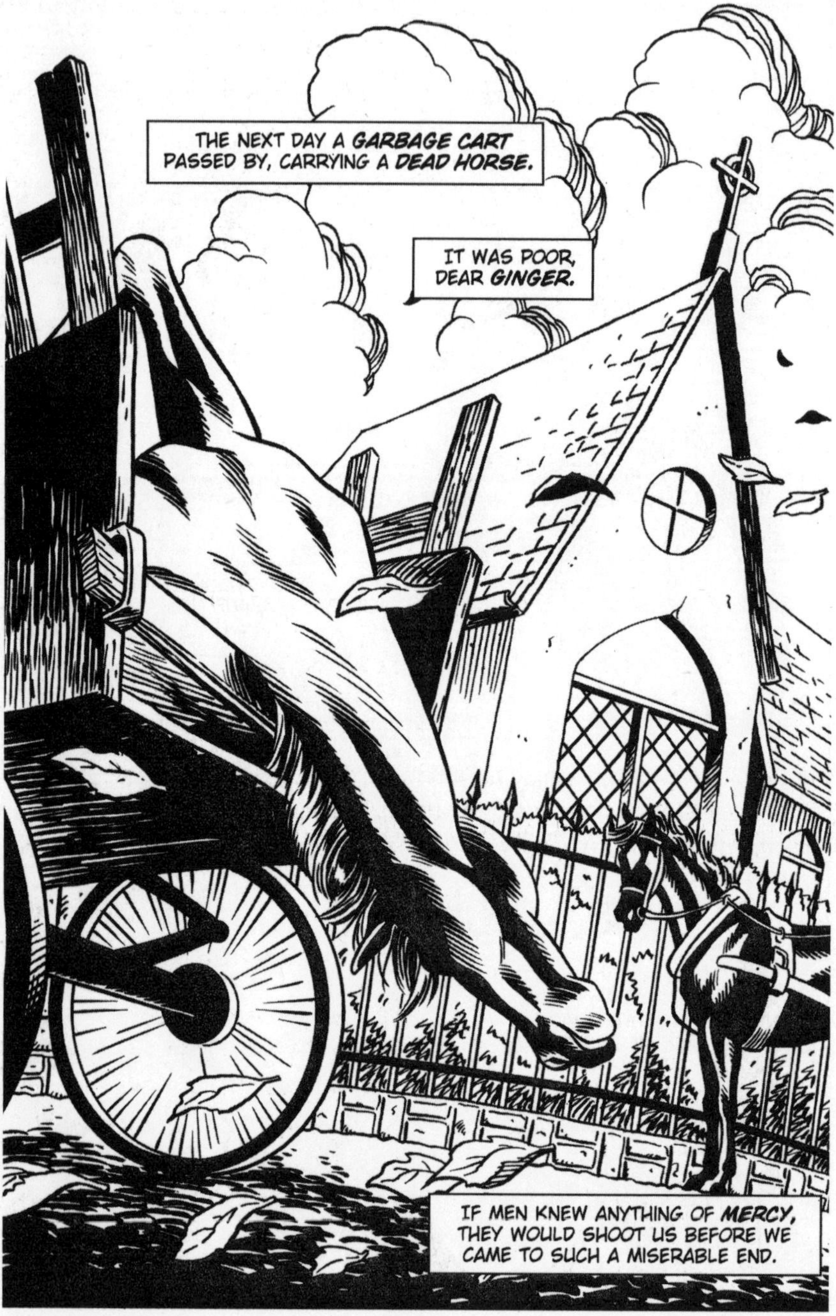
THE NEXT DAY A GARBAGE CART PASSED BY, CARRYING A DEAD HORSE.
IT WAS POOR, DEAR GINGER.
IF MEN KNEW ANYTHING OF MERCY, THEY WOULD SHOOT US BEFORE WE CAME TO SUCH A MISERABLE END.

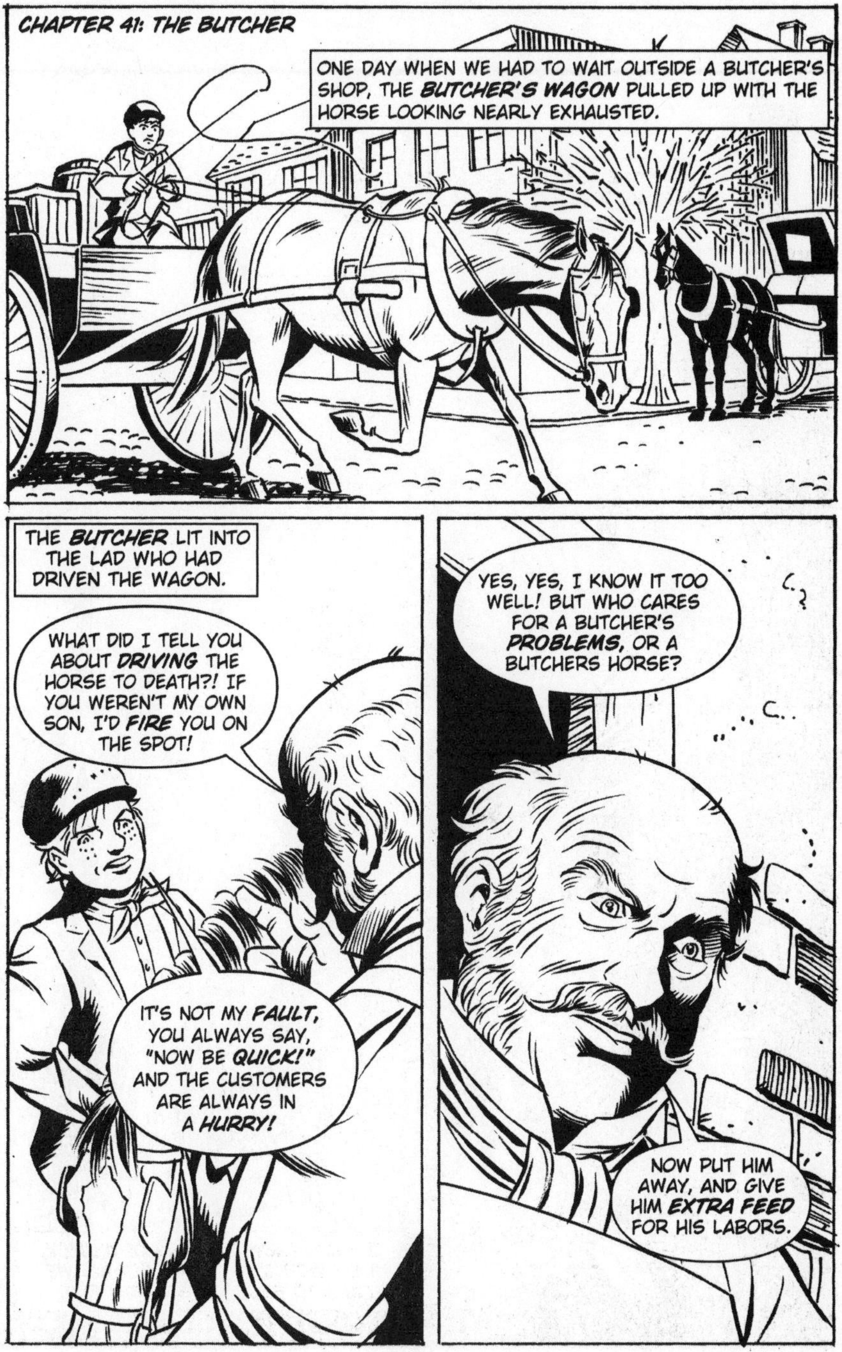
CHAPTER 41: THE BUTCHER
ONE DAY WHEN WE HAD TO WAIT OUTSIDE A BUTCHER'S SHOP, THE BUTCHER'S WAGON PULLED UP WITH THE HORSE LOOKING NEARLY EXHAUSTED.
THE BUTCHER LIT INTO THE LAD WHO HAD DRIVEN THE WAGON.
WHAT DID I TELL YOU ABOUT DRIVING THE HORSE TO DEATH?! IF YOU WEREN'T MY OWN SON, I'D FIRE YOU ON THE SPOT!
IT'S NOT MY FAULT, YOU ALWAYS SAY, "NOW BE QUICK!" AND THE CUSTOMERS ARE ALWAYS IN A HURRY!
YES, YES, I KNOW IT TOO WELL! BUT WHO CARES FOR A BUTCHER'S PROBLEMS, OR A BUTCHERS HORSE?
NOW PUT HIM AWAY, AND GIVE HIM EXTRA FEED FOR HIS LABORS.

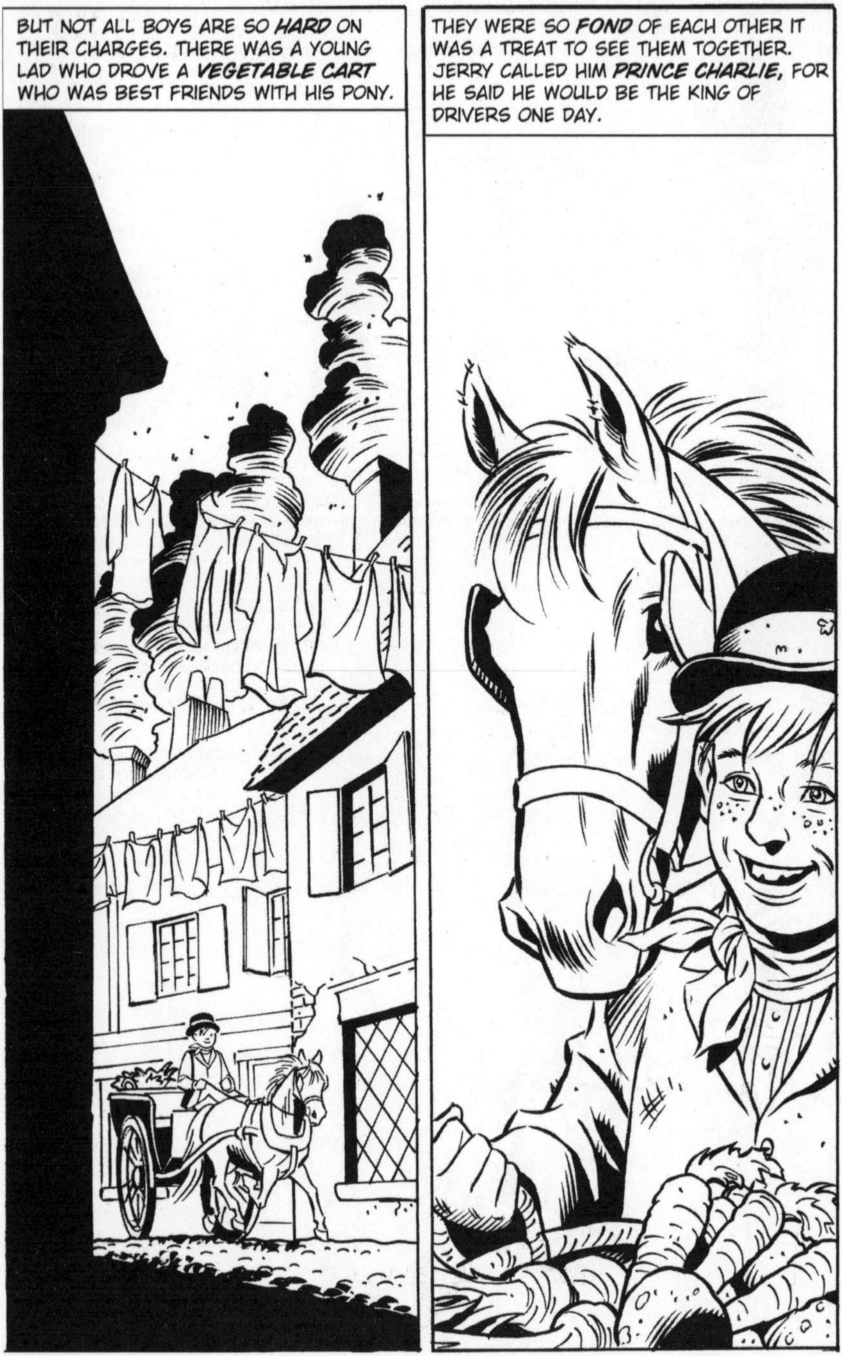
BUT NOT ALL BOYS ARE SO HARD ON THEIR CHARGES. THERE WAS A YOUNG LAD WHO DROVE A VEGETABLE CART WHO WAS BEST FRIENDS WITH HIS PONY.
THEY WERE SO FOND OF EACH OTHER IT WAS A TREAT TO SEE THEM TOGETHER. JERRY CALLED HIM PRINCE CHARLIE, FOR HE SAID HE WOULD BE THE KING OF DRIVERS ONE DAY.

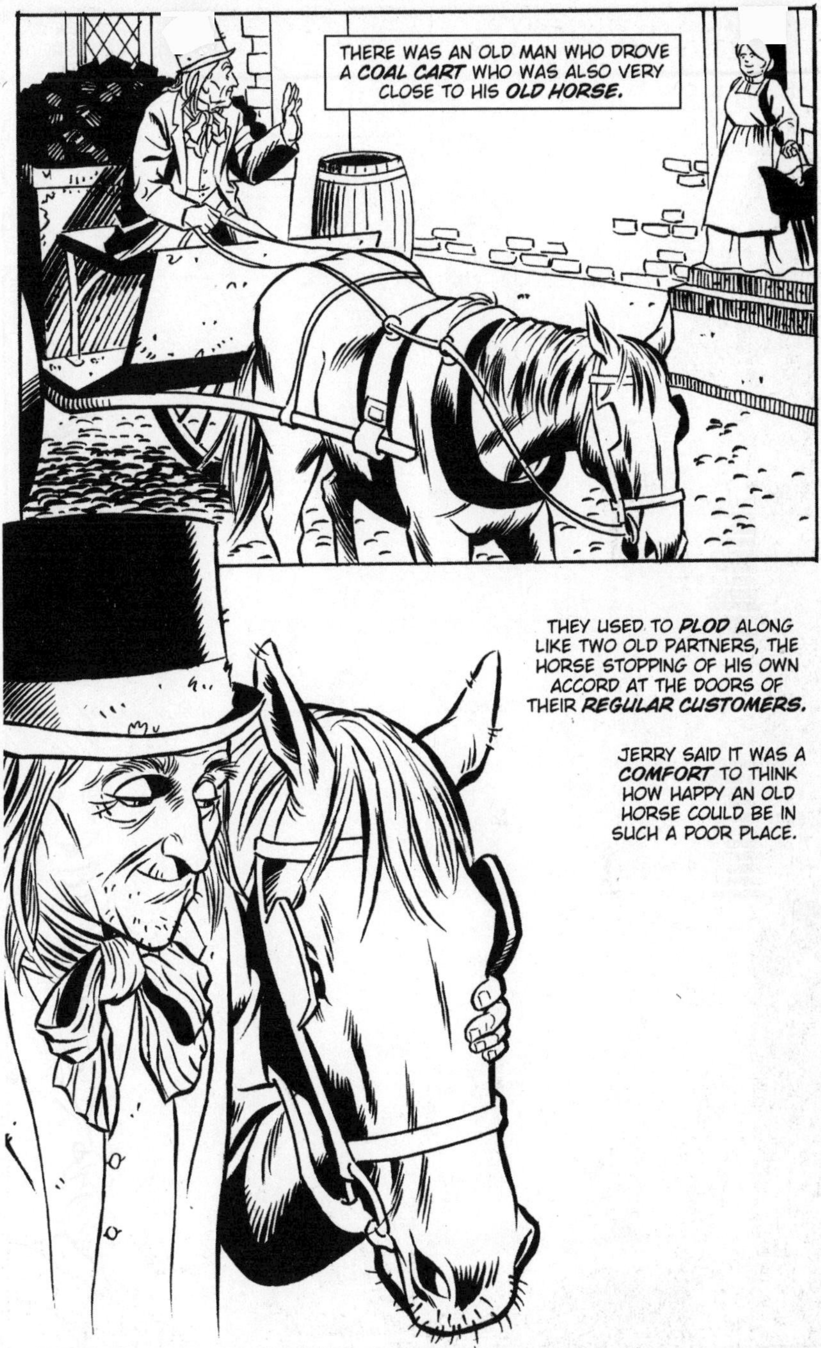
THERE WAS AN OLD MAN WHO DROVE A COAL CART WHO WAS ALSO VERY CLOSE TO HIS OLD HORSE.
THEY USED TO PLOD ALONG LIKE TWO OLD PARTNERS, THE HORSE STOPPING OF HIS OWN ACCORD AT THE DOORS OF THEIR REGULAR CUSTOMERS.
JERRY SAID IT WAS A COMFORT TO THINK HOW HAPPY AN OLD HORSE COULD BE IN SUCH A POOR PLACE.

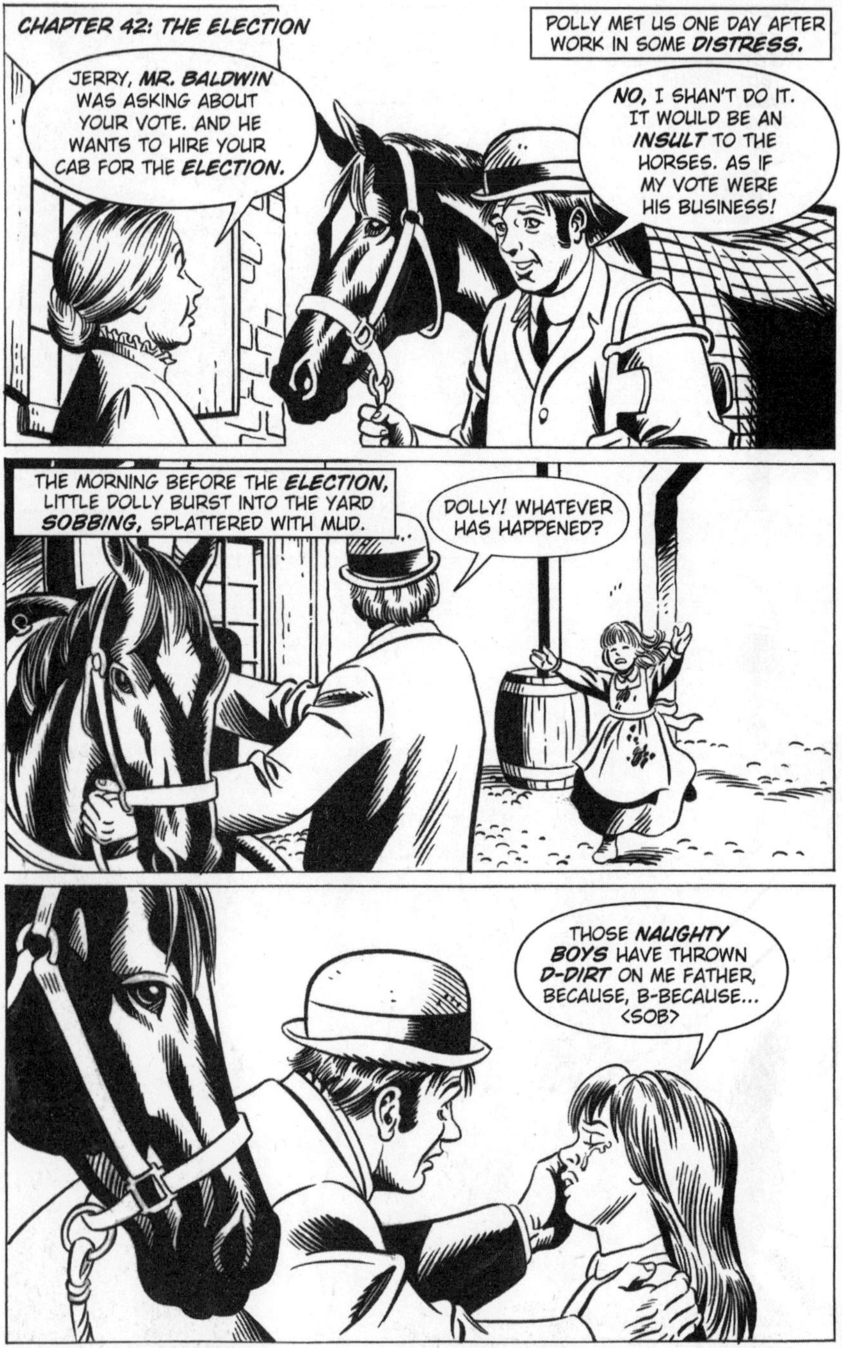
CHAPTER 42: THE ELECTION
POLLY MET US ONE DAY AFTER WORK IN SOME DISTRESS.
JERRY, MR. BALDWIN WAS ASKING ABOUT YOUR VOTE. AND HE WANTS TO HIRE YOUR CAB FOR THE ELECTION.
NO, I SHAN'T DO IT. IT WOULD BE AN INSULT TO THE HORSES. AS IF MY VOTE WERE HIS BUSINESS!
THE MORNING BEFORE THE ELECTION, LITTLE DOLLY BURST INTO THE YARD SOBBING, SPLATTERED WITH MUD.
DOLLY! WHATEVER HAS HAPPENED?
THOSE NAUGHTY BOYS HAVE THROWN D-DIRT ON ME FATHER, BECAUSE, B-BECAUSE... <SOB>

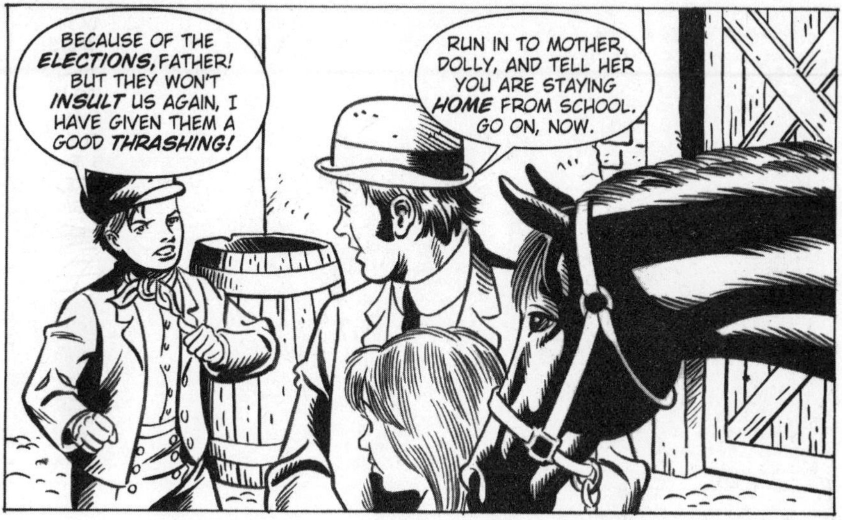
BECAUSE OF THE ELECTIONS, FATHER! BUT THEY WON'T INSULT US AGAIN, I HAVE GIVEN THEM A GOOD THRASHING!
RUN IN TO MOTHER, DOLLY, AND TELL HER YOU ARE STAYING HOME FROM SCHOOL. GO ON, NOW.

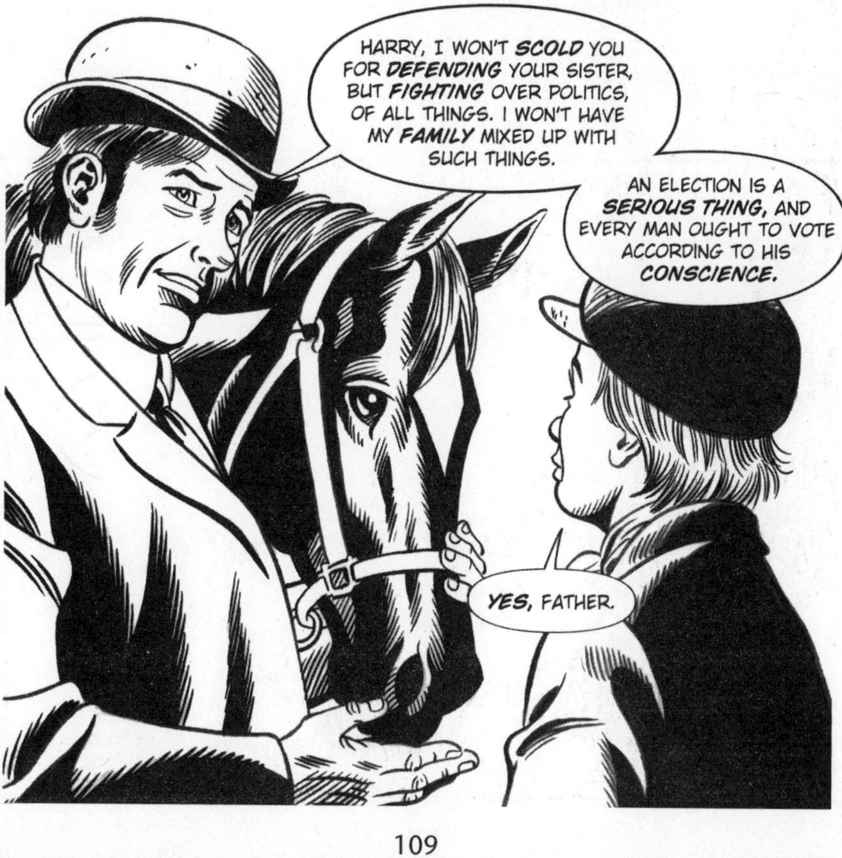
HARRY, I WON'T SCOLD YOU FOR DEFENDING YOUR SISTER, BUT FIGHTING OVER POLITICS, OF ALL THINGS. I WON'T HAVE MY FAMILY MIXED UP WITH SUCH THINGS.
AN ELECTION IS A SERIOUS THING, AND EVERY MAN OUGHT TO VOTE ACCORDING TO HIS CONSCIENCE.
YES, FATHER.

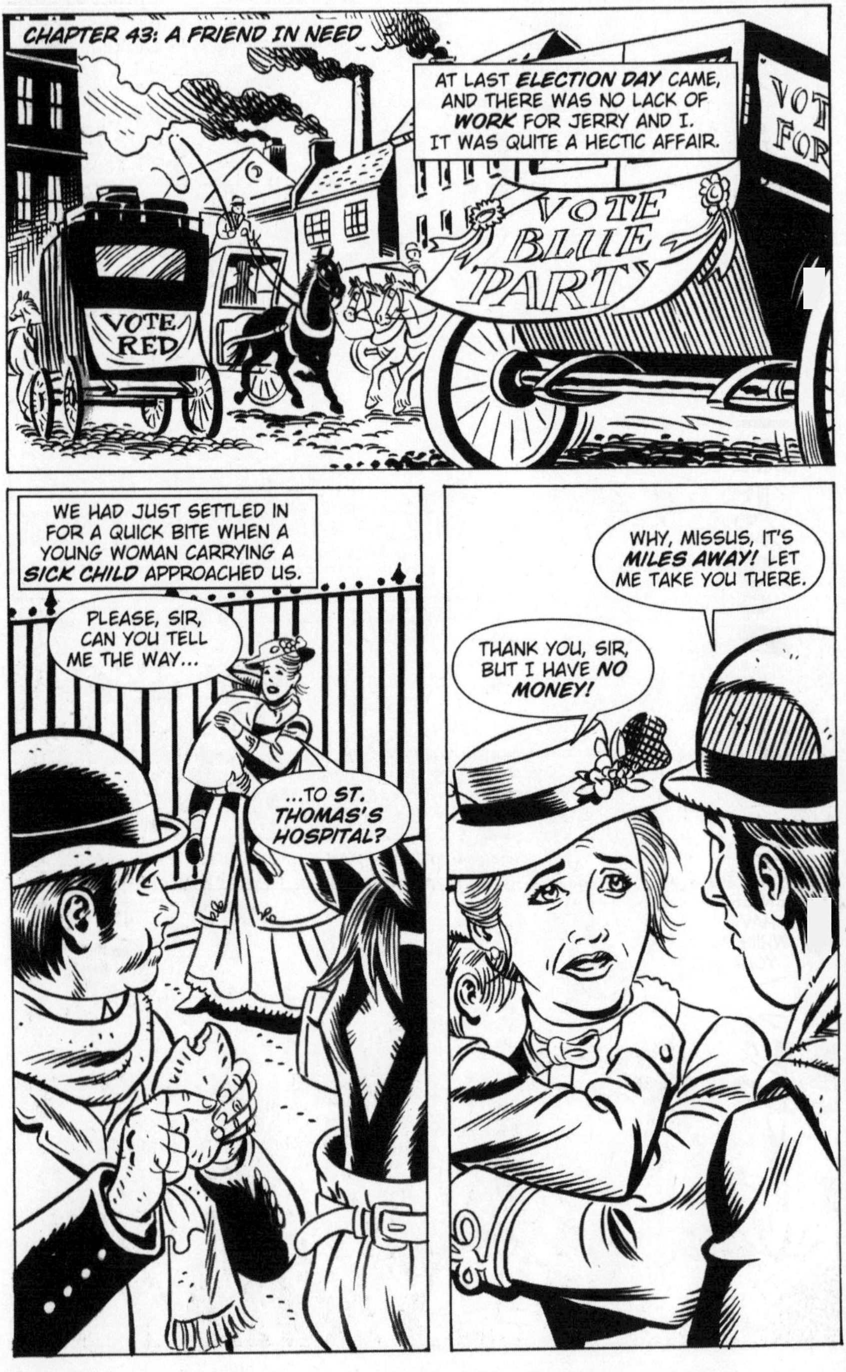
CHAPTER 43: A FRIEND IN NEED
AT LAST ELECTION DAY CAME, AND THERE WAS NO LACK OF WORK FOR JERRY AND I. IT WAS QUITE A HECTIC AFFAIR.
VOTE FOR
VOTE BLUE PARTY
VOTE RED
WE HAD JUST SETTLED IN FOR A QUICK BITE WHEN A YOUNG WOMAN CARRYING A SICK CHILD APPROACHED US.
PLEASE, SIR, CAN YOU TELL ME THE WAY...
...TO ST. THOMAS'S HOSPITAL?
WHY, MISSUS, IT'S MILES AWAY! LET ME TAKE YOU THERE.
THANK YOU, SIR, BUT I HAVE NO MONEY!

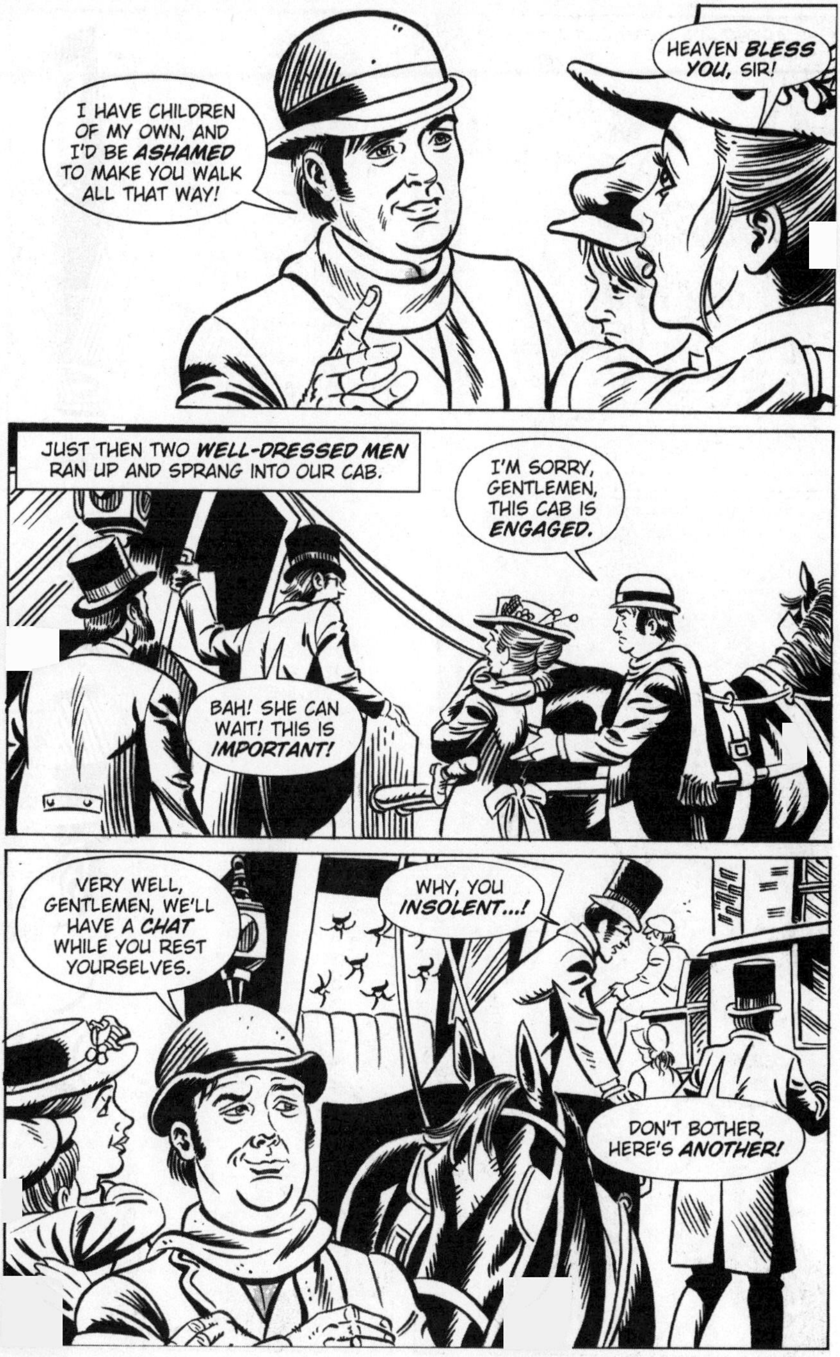
I HAVE CHILDREN OF MY OWN, AND I'D BE ASHAMED TO MAKE YOU WALK ALL THAT WAY!
HEAVEN BLESS YOU, SIR!
JUST THEN TWO WELL-DRESSED MEN RAN UP AND SPRANG INTO OUR CAB.
I'M SORRY, GENTLEMEN, THIS CAB IS ENGAGED.
BAH! SHE CAN WAIT! THIS IS IMPORTANT!
VERY WELL, GENTLEMEN, WE'LL HAVE A CHAT WHILE YOU REST YOURSELVES.
WHY, YOU INSOLENT...!
DON'T BOTHER, HERE'S ANOTHER!

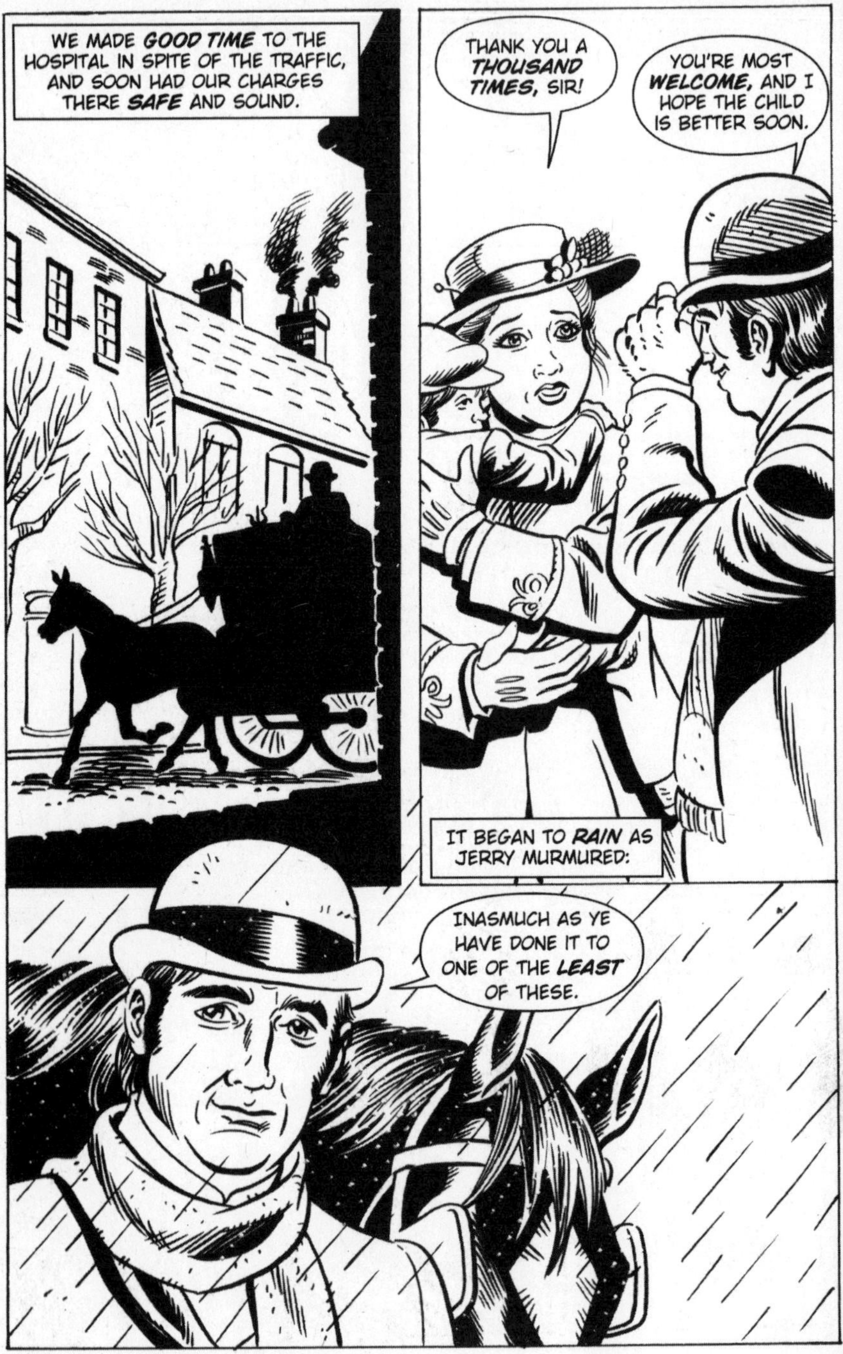
WE MADE GOOD TIME TO THE HOSPITAL IN SPITE OF THE TRAFFIC, AND SOON HAD OUR CHARGES THERE SAFE AND SOUND.
THANK YOU A THOUSAND TIMES, SIR!
YOU'RE MOST WELCOME, AND I HOPE THE CHILD IS BETTER SOON.
IT BEGAN TO RAIN AS JERRY MURMURED:
INASMUCH AS YE HAVE DONE IT TO ONE OF THE LEAST OF THESE.

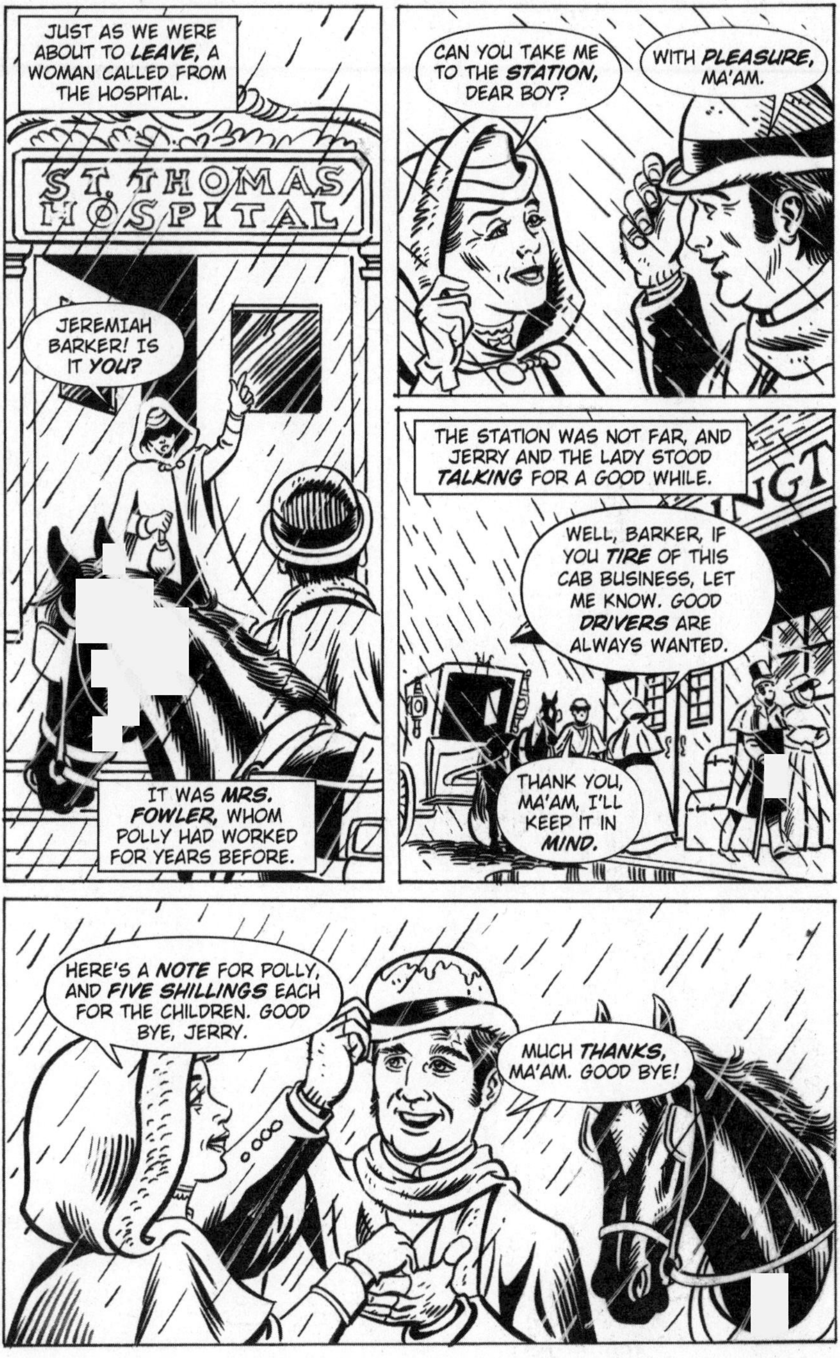
JUST AS WE WERE ABOUT TO LEAVE, A WOMAN CALLED FROM THE HOSPITAL.
ST. THOMAS HOSPITAL
JEREMIAH BARKER! IS IT YOU?
IT WAS MRS. FOWLER, WHOM POLLY HAD WORKED FOR YEARS BEFORE.
CAN YOU TAKE ME TO THE STATION, DEAR BOY?
WITH PLEASURE, MA'AM.
THE STATION WAS NOT FAR, AND JERRY AND THE LADY STOOD TALKING FOR A GOOD WHILE.
WELL, BARKER, IF YOU TIRE OF THIS CAB BUSINESS, LET ME KNOW. GOOD DRIVERS ARE ALWAYS WANTED.
THANK YOU, MA'AM, I'LL KEEP IT IN MIND.
HERE'S A NOTE FOR POLLY, AND FIVE SHILLINGS EACH FOR THE CHILDREN. GOOD BYE, JERRY.
MUCH THANKS, MA'AM. GOOD BYE!

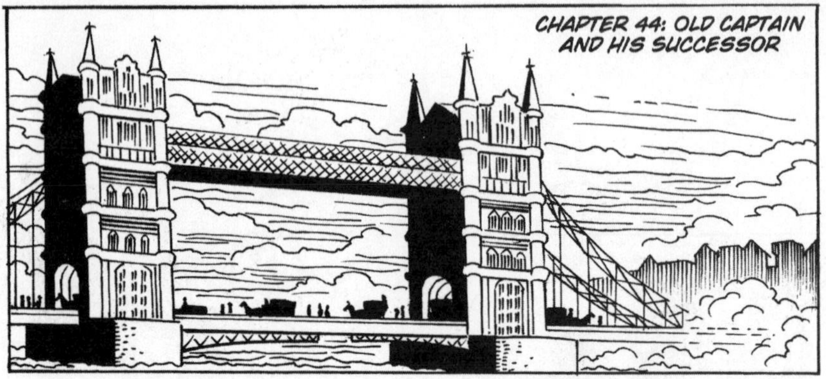
CHAPTER 44: OLD CAPTAIN AND HIS SUCCESSOR

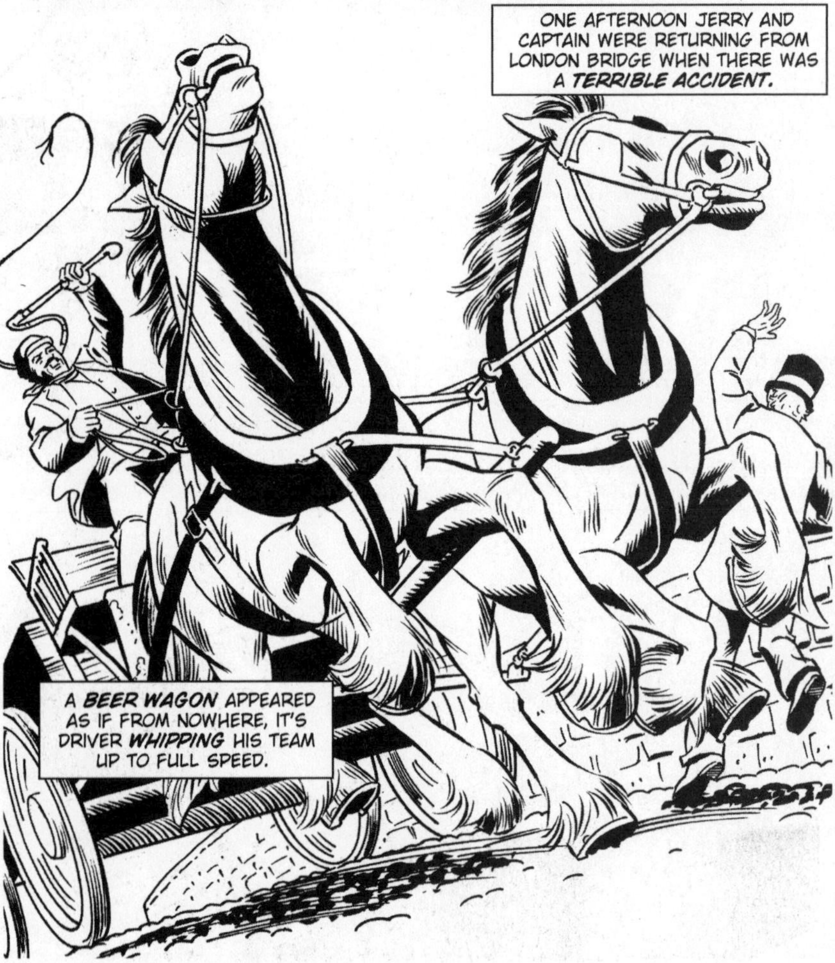
ONE AFTERNOON JERRY AND CAPTAIN WERE RETURNING FROM LONDON BRIDGE WHEN THERE WAS A TERRIBLE ACCIDENT.
A BEER WAGON APPEARED AS IF FROM NOWHERE, IT'S DRIVER WHIPPING HIS TEAM UP TO FULL SPEED.

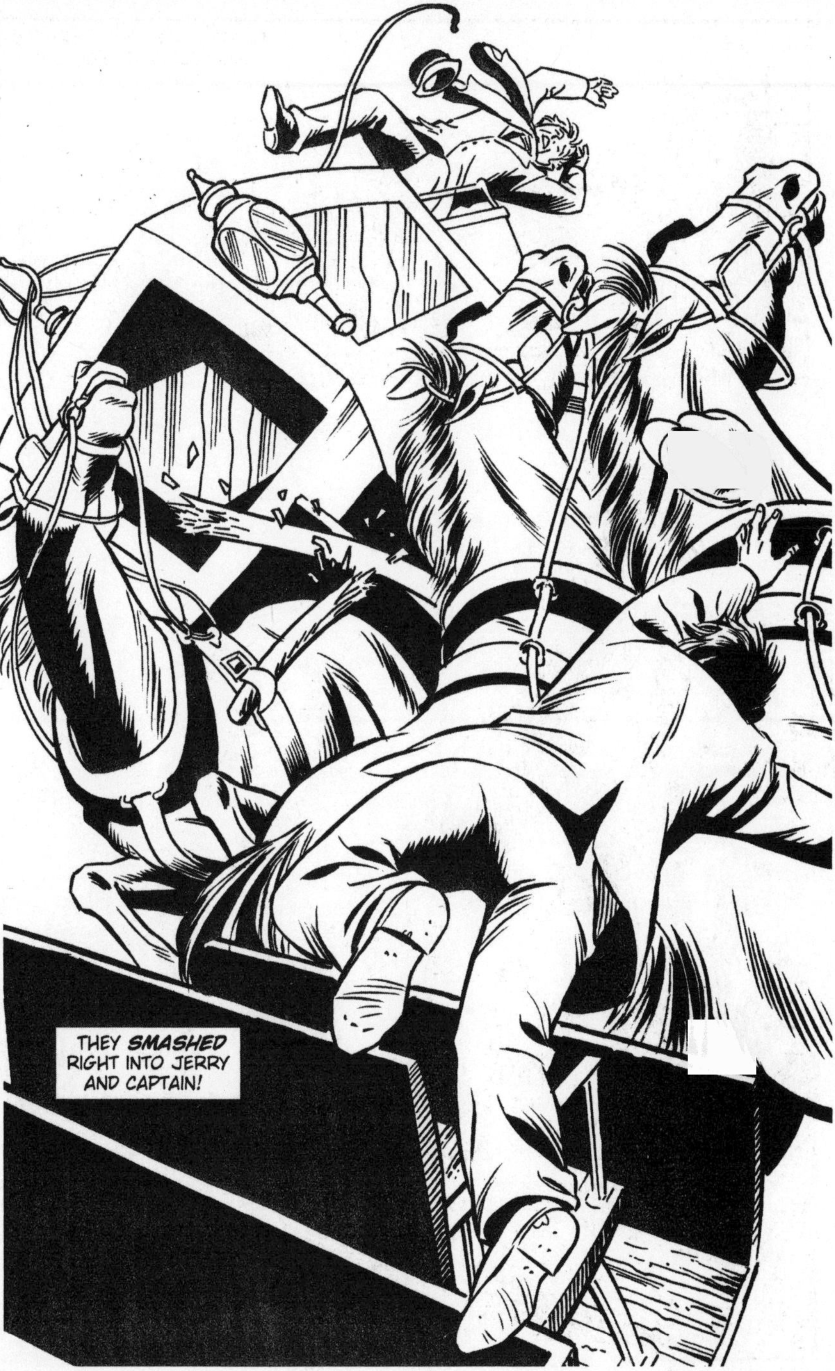
THEY *SMASHED* RIGHT INTO JERRY AND CAPTAIN!

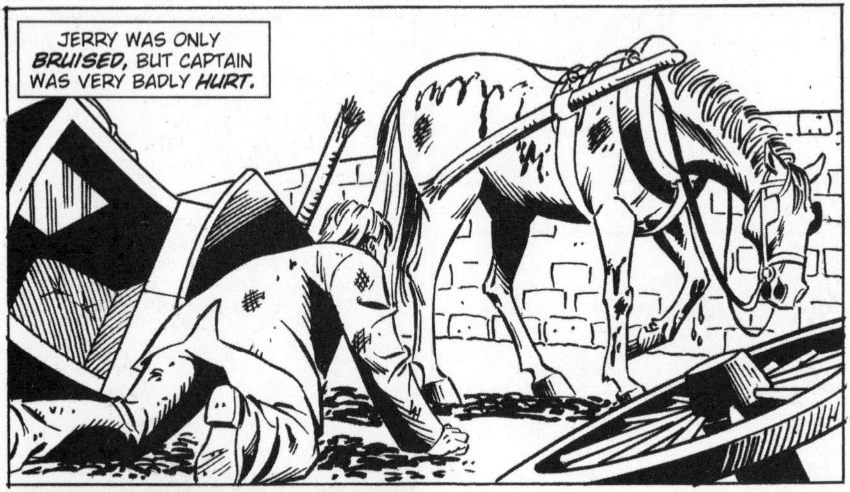
JERRY WAS ONLY BRUISED, BUT CAPTAIN WAS VERY BADLY HURT.

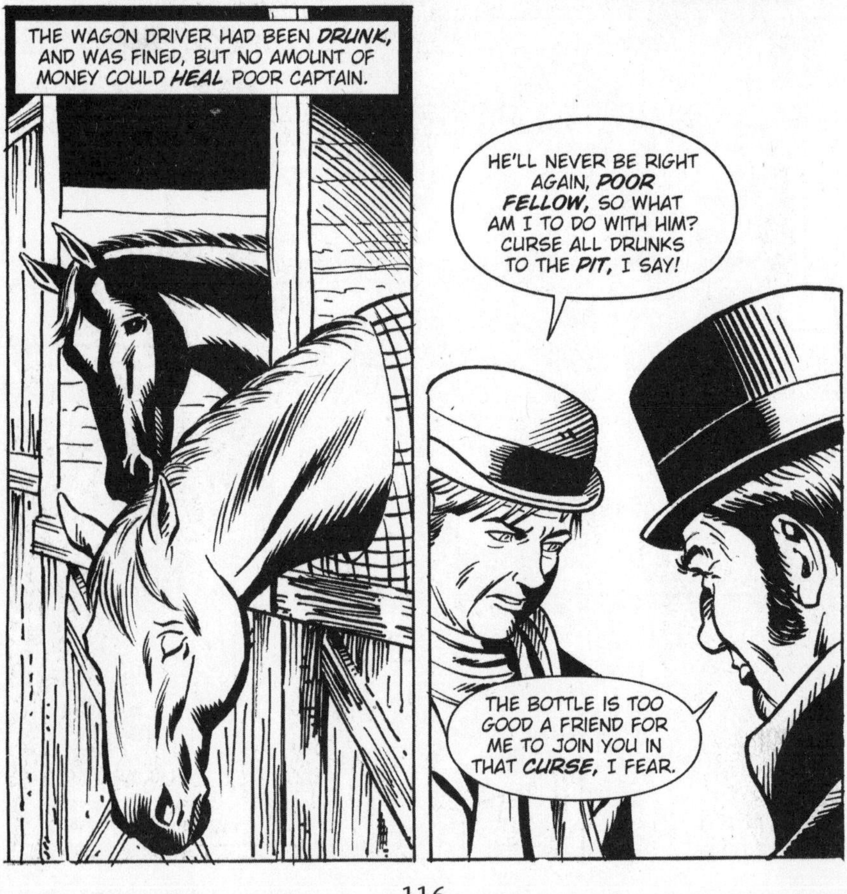
THE WAGON DRIVER HAD BEEN DRUNK, AND WAS FINED, BUT NO AMOUNT OF MONEY COULD HEAL POOR CAPTAIN.
HE'LL NEVER BE RIGHT AGAIN, POOR FELLOW, SO WHAT AM I TO DO WITH HIM? CURSE ALL DRUNKS TO THE PIT, I SAY!
THE BOTTLE IS TOO GOOD A FRIEND FOR ME TO JOIN YOU IN THAT CURSE, I FEAR.

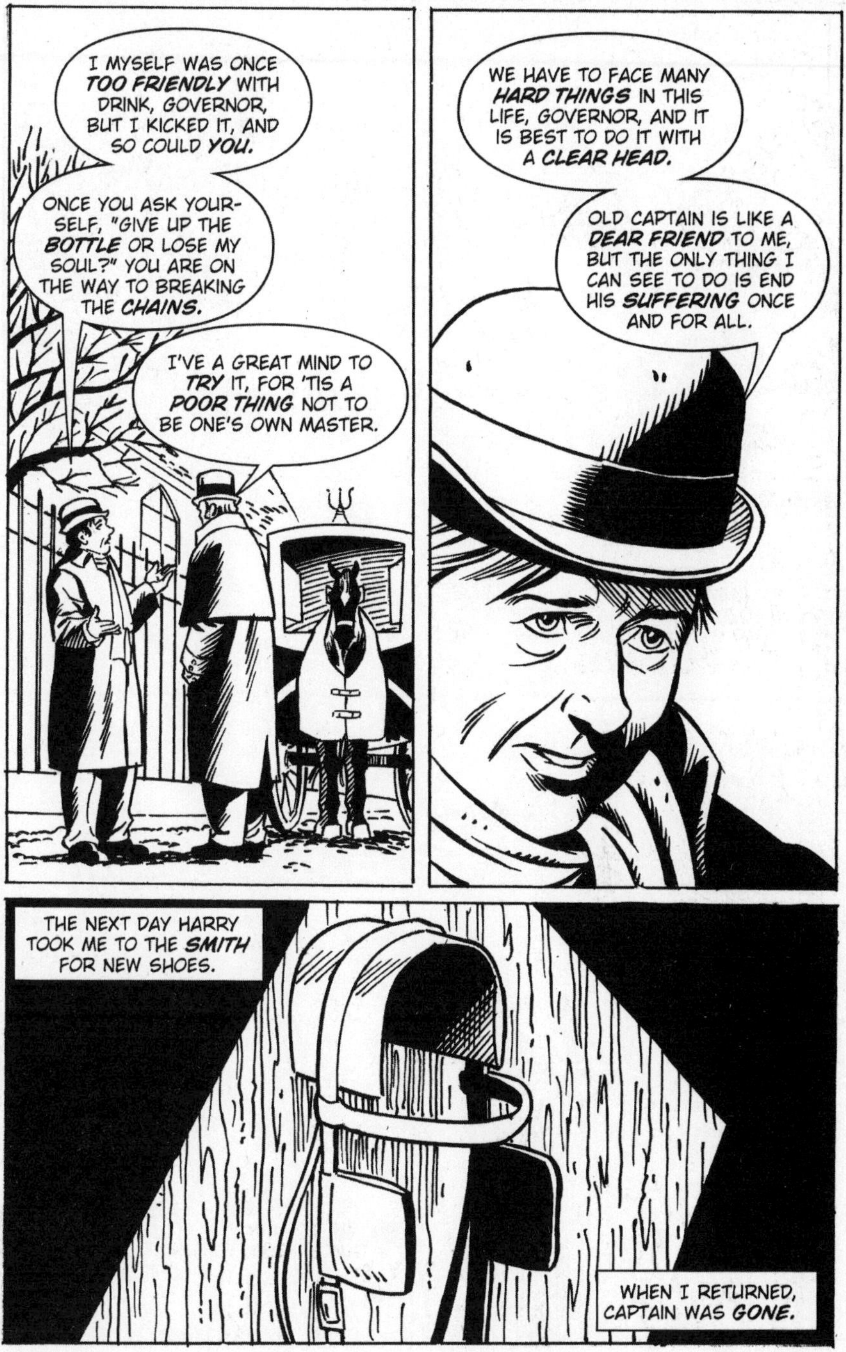

I MYSELF WAS ONCE TOO FRIENDLY WITH DRINK, GOVERNOR, BUT I KICKED IT, AND SO COULD YOU.
ONCE YOU ASK YOURSELF, "GIVE UP THE BOTTLE OR LOSE MY SOUL?" YOU ARE ON THE WAY TO BREAKING THE CHAINS.
I'VE A GREAT MIND TO TRY IT, FOR 'TIS A POOR THING NOT TO BE ONE'S OWN MASTER.
WE HAVE TO FACE MANY HARD THINGS IN THIS LIFE, GOVERNOR, AND IT IS BEST TO DO IT WITH A CLEAR HEAD.
OLD CAPTAIN IS LIKE A DEAR FRIEND TO ME, BUT THE ONLY THING I CAN SEE TO DO IS END HIS SUFFERING ONCE AND FOR ALL.
THE NEXT DAY HARRY TOOK ME TO THE SMITH FOR NEW SHOES.
WHEN I RETURNED, CAPTAIN WAS GONE.

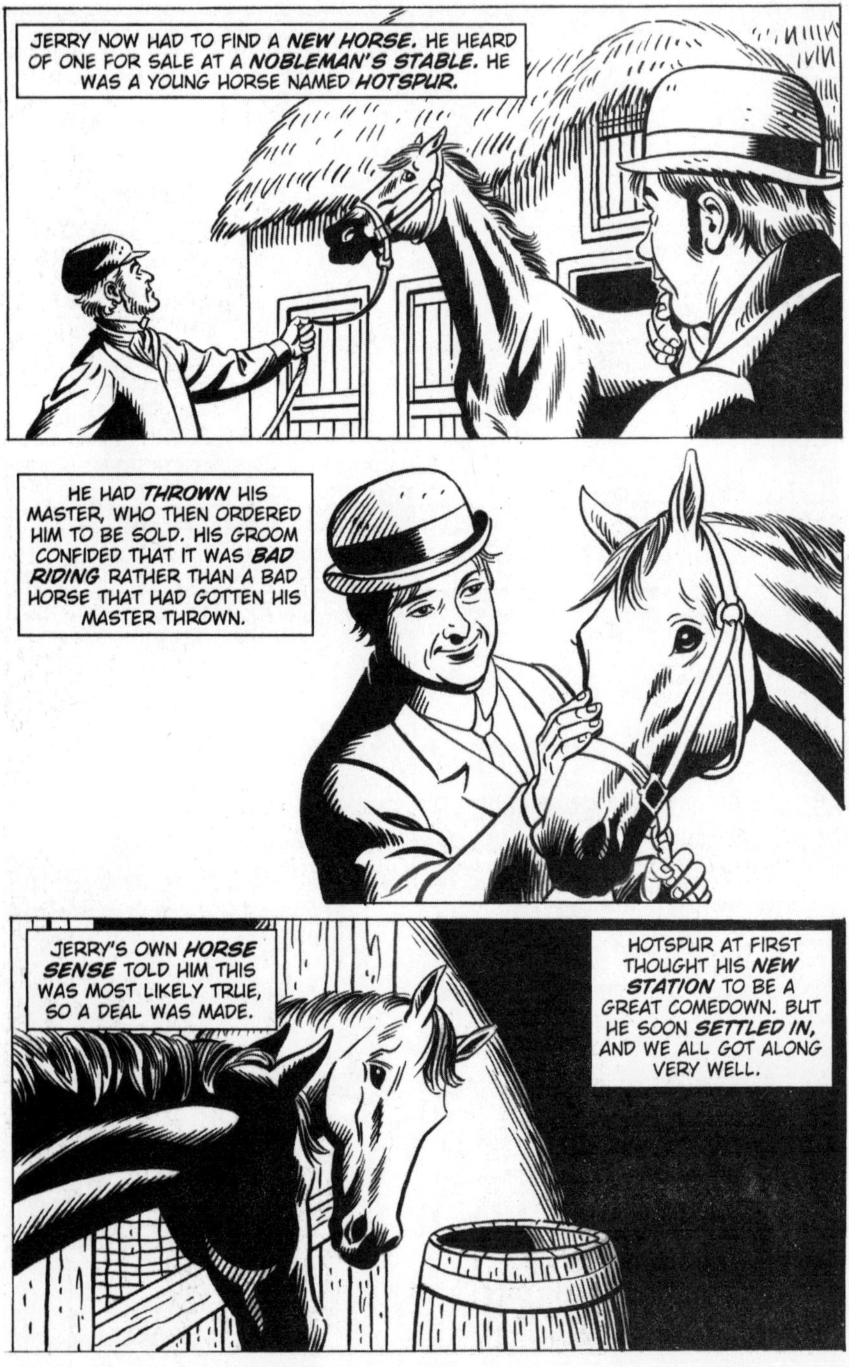
JERRY NOW HAD TO FIND A NEW HORSE. HE HEARD OF ONE FOR SALE AT A NOBLEMAN'S STABLE. HE WAS A YOUNG HORSE NAMED HOTSPUR.
HE HAD THROWN HIS MASTER, WHO THEN ORDERED HIM TO BE SOLD. HIS GROOM CONFIDED THAT IT WAS BAD RIDING RATHER THAN A BAD HORSE THAT HAD GOTTEN HIS MASTER THROWN.
JERRY'S OWN HORSE SENSE TOLD HIM THIS WAS MOST LIKELY TRUE, SO A DEAL WAS MADE.
HOTSPUR AT FIRST THOUGHT HIS NEW STATION TO BE A GREAT COMEDOWN. BUT HE SOON SETTLED IN, AND WE ALL GOT ALONG VERY WELL.

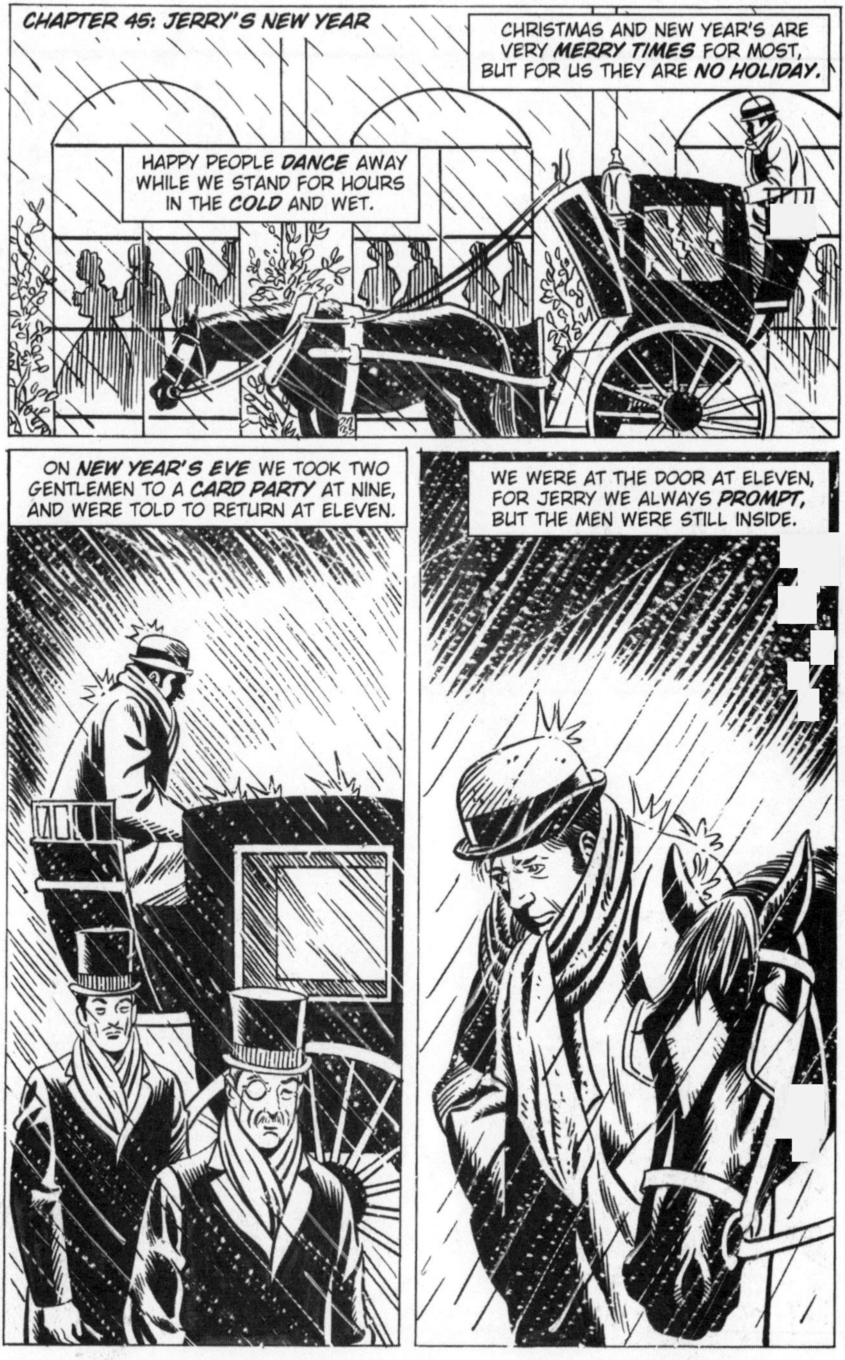
CHAPTER 45: JERRY'S NEW YEAR
CHRISTMAS AND NEW YEAR'S ARE VERY MERRY TIMES FOR MOST, BUT FOR US THEY ARE NO HOLIDAY.
HAPPY PEOPLE DANCE AWAY WHILE WE STAND FOR HOURS IN THE COLD AND WET.
ON NEW YEAR'S EVE WE TOOK TWO GENTLEMEN TO A CARD PARTY AT NINE, AND WERE TOLD TO RETURN AT ELEVEN.
WE WERE AT THE DOOR AT ELEVEN, FOR JERRY WE ALWAYS PROMPT, BUT THE MEN WERE STILL INSIDE.

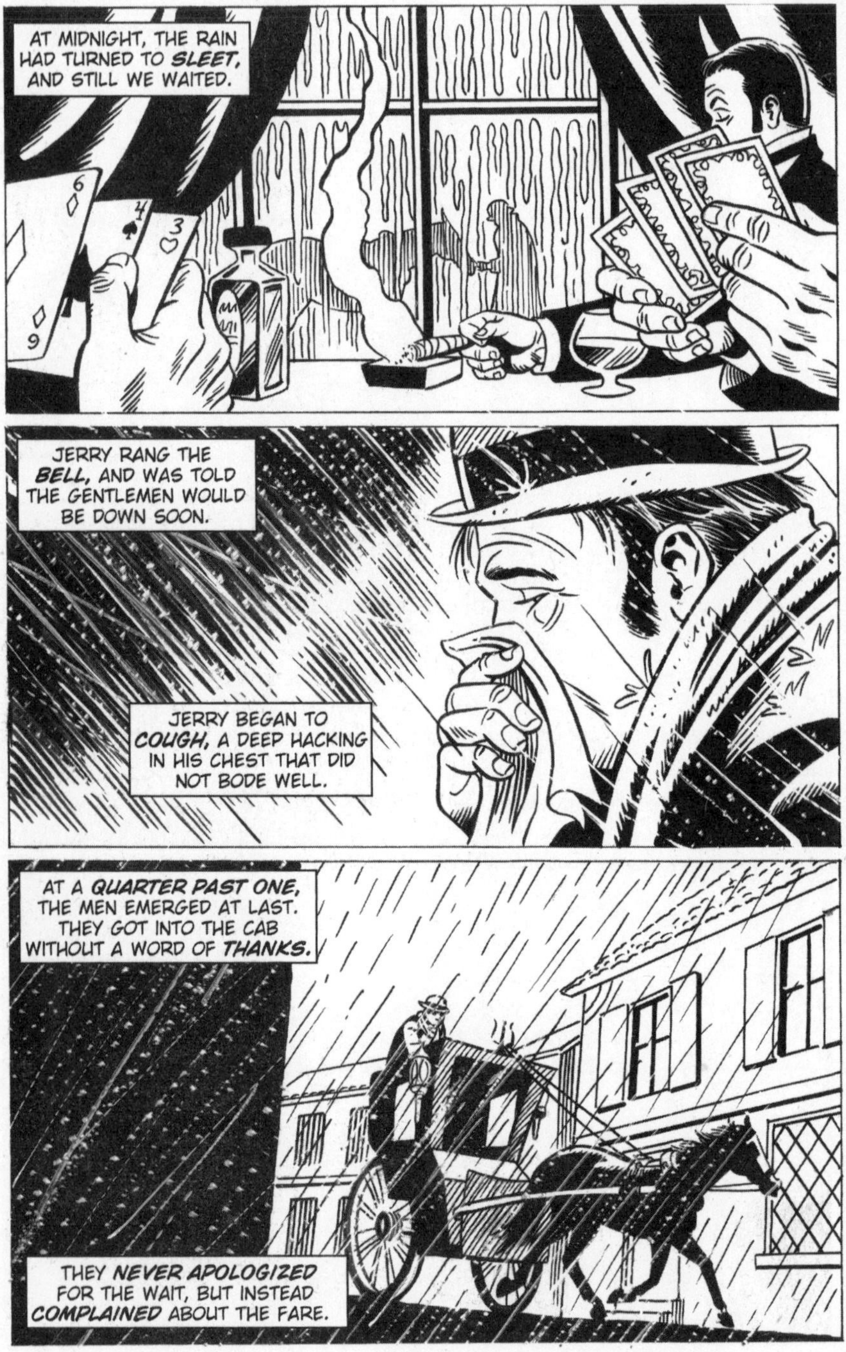
AT MIDNIGHT, THE RAIN HAD TURNED TO SLEET, AND STILL WE WAITED.
JERRY RANG THE BELL, AND WAS TOLD THE GENTLEMEN WOULD BE DOWN SOON.
JERRY BEGAN TO COUGH, A DEEP HACKING IN HIS CHEST THAT DID NOT BODE WELL.
AT A QUARTER PAST ONE, THE MEN EMERGED AT LAST. THEY GOT INTO THE CAB WITHOUT A WORD OF THANKS.
THEY NEVER APOLOGIZED FOR THE WAIT, BUT INSTEAD COMPLAINED ABOUT THE FARE.

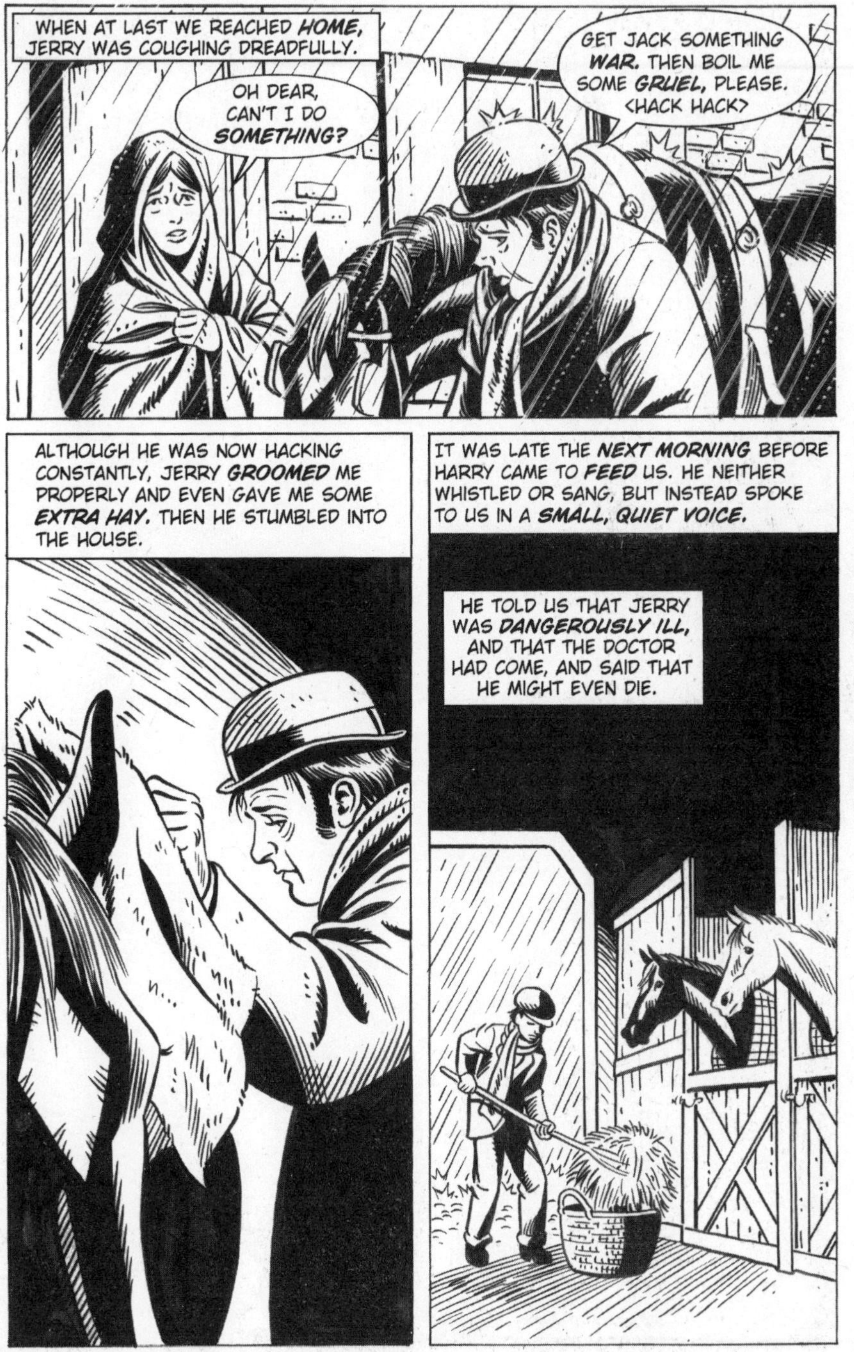
WHEN AT LAST WE REACHED HOME, JERRY WAS COUGHING DREADFULLY.
OH DEAR, CAN'T I DO SOMETHING?
GET JACK SOMETHING WAR. THEN BOIL ME SOME GRUEL, PLEASE. <HACK HACK>
ALTHOUGH HE WAS NOW HACKING CONSTANTLY, JERRY GROOMED ME PROPERLY AND EVEN GAVE ME SOME EXTRA HAY. THEN HE STUMBLED INTO THE HOUSE.
IT WAS LATE THE NEXT MORNING BEFORE HARRY CAME TO FEED US. HE NEITHER WHISTLED OR SANG, BUT INSTEAD SPOKE TO US IN A SMALL, QUIET VOICE.
HE TOLD US THAT JERRY WAS DANGEROUSLY ILL, AND THAT THE DOCTOR HAD COME, AND SAID THAT HE MIGHT EVEN DIE.

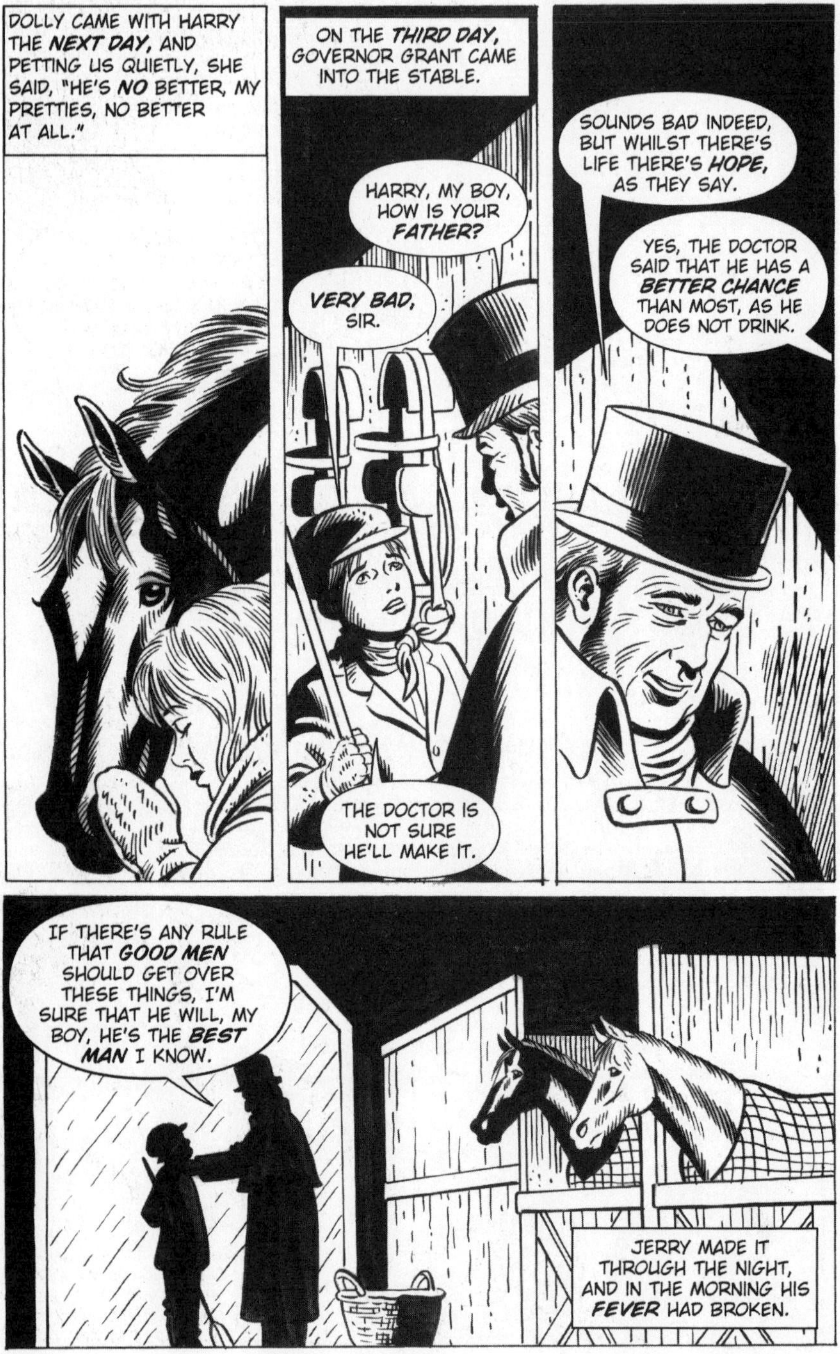
DOLLY CAME WITH HARRY THE NEXT DAY, AND PETTING US QUIETLY, SHE SAID, "HE'S NO BETTER, MY PRETTIES, NO BETTER AT ALL."
ON THE THIRD DAY, GOVERNOR GRANT CAME INTO THE STABLE.
HARRY, MY BOY, HOW IS YOUR FATHER?
VERY BAD, SIR.
THE DOCTOR IS NOT SURE HE'LL MAKE IT.
SOUNDS BAD INDEED, BUT WHILST THERE'S LIFE THERE'S HOPE, AS THEY SAY.
YES, THE DOCTOR SAID THAT HE HAS A BETTER CHANCE THAN MOST, AS HE DOES NOT DRINK.
IF THERE'S ANY RULE THAT GOOD MEN SHOULD GET OVER THESE THINGS, I'M SURE THAT HE WILL, MY BOY, HE'S THE BEST MAN I KNOW.
JERRY MADE IT THROUGH THE NIGHT, AND IN THE MORNING HIS FEVER HAD BROKEN.

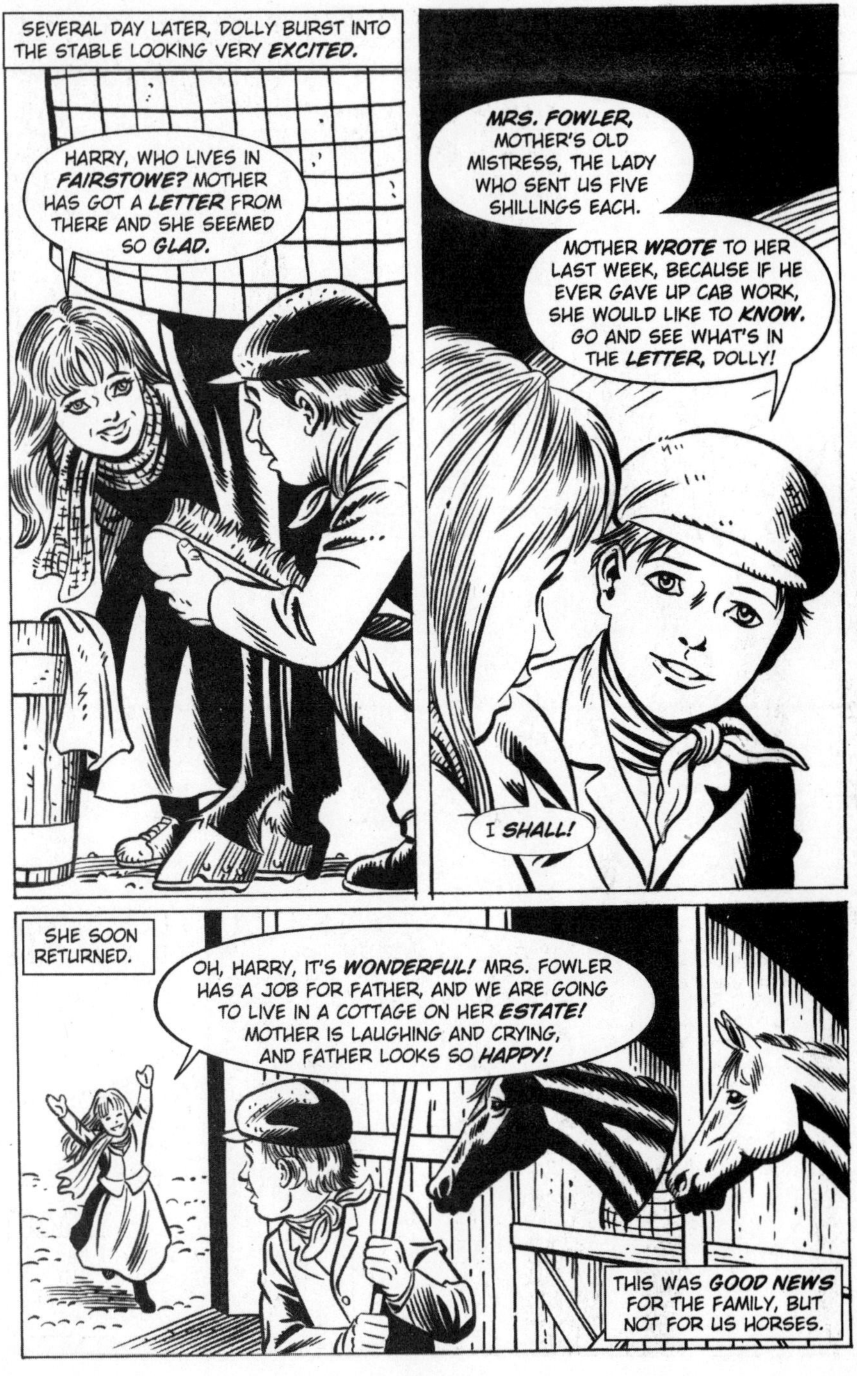
SEVERAL DAY LATER, DOLLY BURST INTO THE STABLE LOOKING VERY EXCITED.
HARRY, WHO LIVES IN FAIRSTOWE? MOTHER HAS GOT A LETTER FROM THERE AND SHE SEEMED SO GLAD.
MRS. FOWLER, MOTHER'S OLD MISTRESS, THE LADY WHO SENT US FIVE SHILLINGS EACH.
MOTHER WROTE TO HER LAST WEEK, BECAUSE IF HE EVER GAVE UP CAB WORK, SHE WOULD LIKE TO KNOW. GO AND SEE WHAT'S IN THE LETTER, DOLLY!
I SHALL!
SHE SOON RETURNED.
OH, HARRY, IT'S WONDERFUL! MRS. FOWLER HAS A JOB FOR FATHER, AND WE ARE GOING TO LIVE IN A COTTAGE ON HER ESTATE! MOTHER IS LAUGHING AND CRYING, AND FATHER LOOKS SO HAPPY!
THIS WAS GOOD NEWS FOR THE FAMILY, BUT NOT FOR US HORSES.

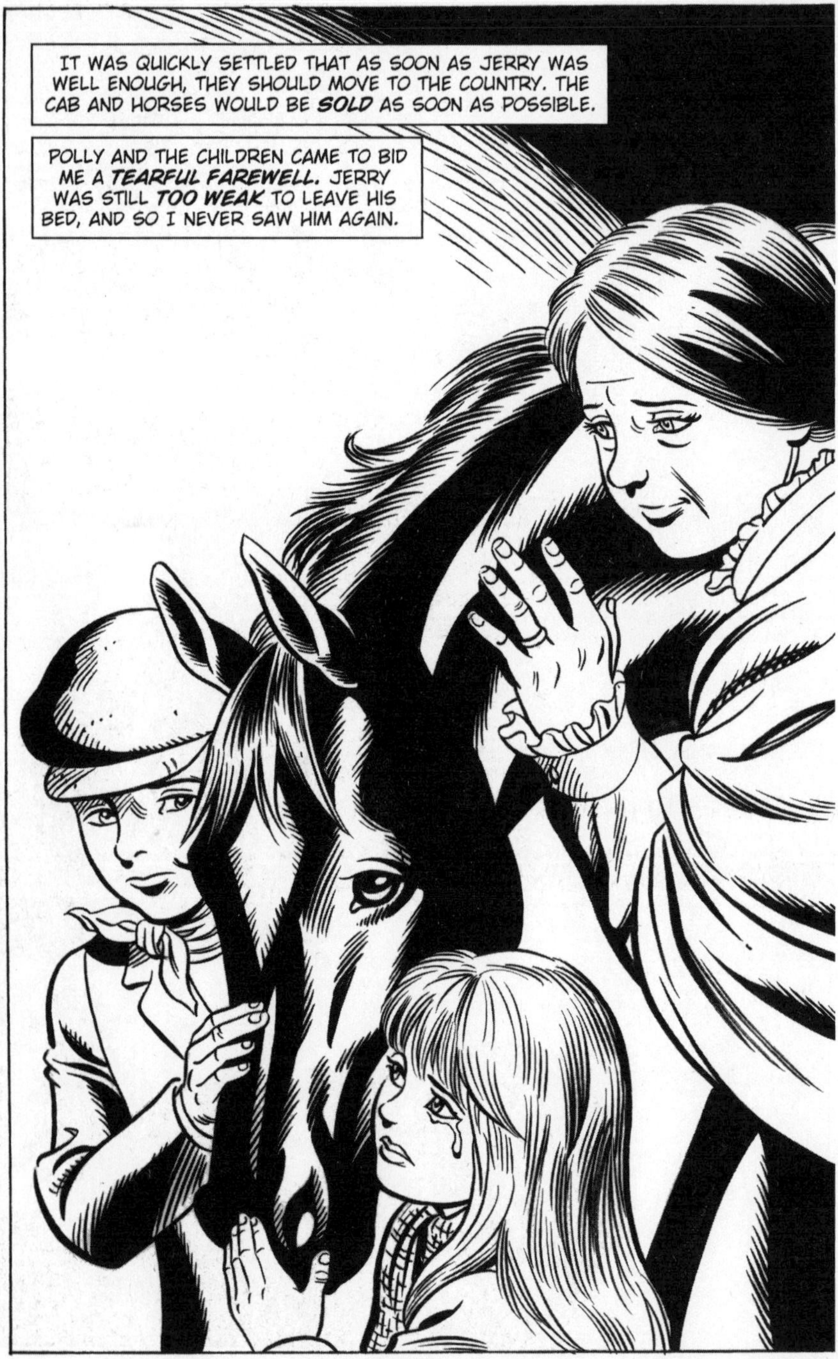
IT WAS QUICKLY SETTLED THAT AS SOON AS JERRY WAS WELL ENOUGH, THEY SHOULD MOVE TO THE COUNTRY. THE CAB AND HORSES WOULD BE SOLD AS SOON AS POSSIBLE.
POLLY AND THE CHILDREN CAME TO BID ME A TEARFUL FAREWELL. JERRY WAS STILL TOO WEAK TO LEAVE HIS BED, AND SO I NEVER SAW HIM AGAIN.

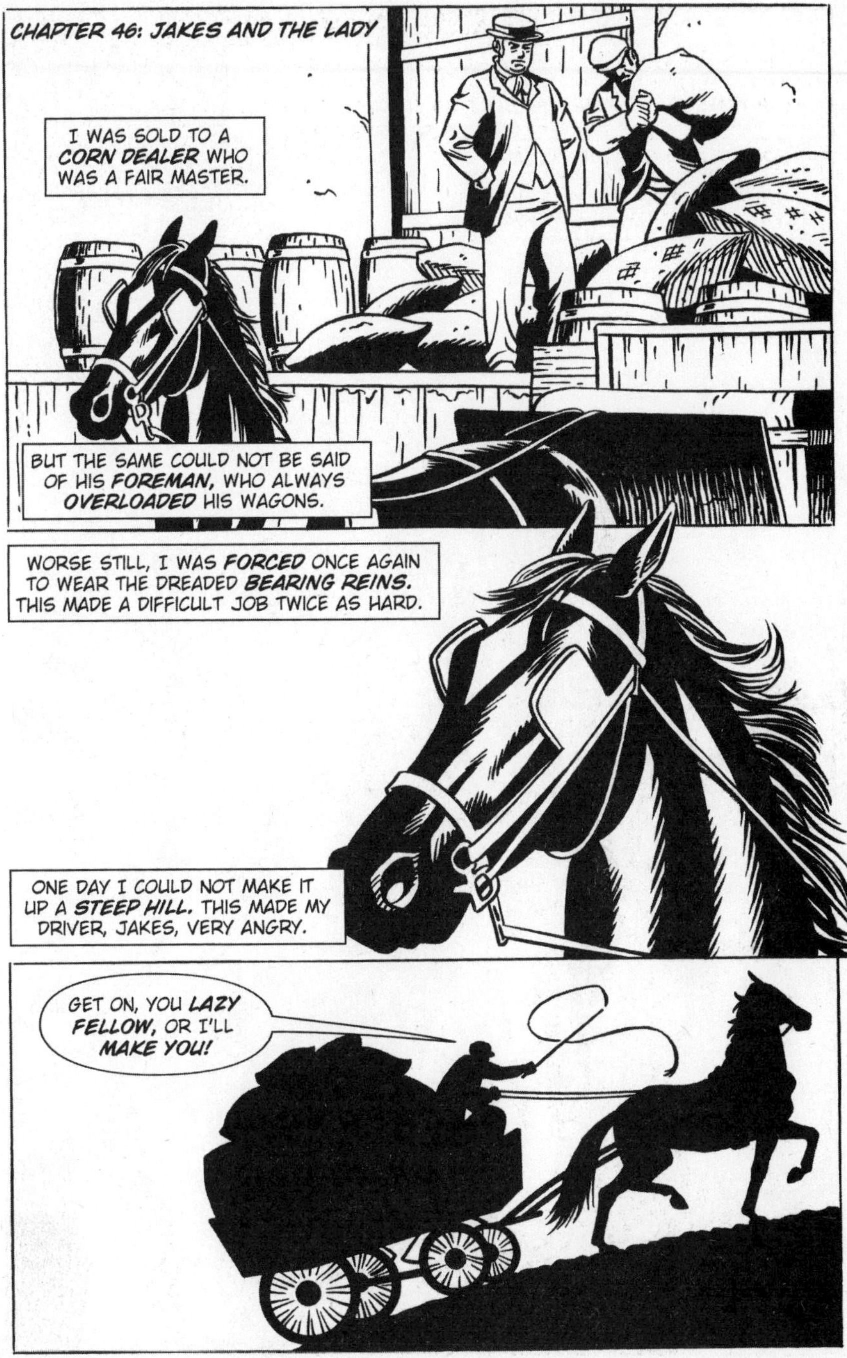
CHAPTER 46: JAKES AND THE LADY
I WAS SOLD TO A CORN DEALER WHO WAS A FAIR MASTER.
BUT THE SAME COULD NOT BE SAID OF HIS FOREMAN, WHO ALWAYS OVERLOADED HIS WAGONS.
WORSE STILL, I WAS FORCED ONCE AGAIN TO WEAR THE DREADED BEARING REINS. THIS MADE A DIFFICULT JOB TWICE AS HARD.
ONE DAY I COULD NOT MAKE IT UP A STEEP HILL. THIS MADE MY DRIVER, JAKES, VERY ANGRY.
GET ON, YOU LAZY FELLOW, OR I'LL MAKE YOU!

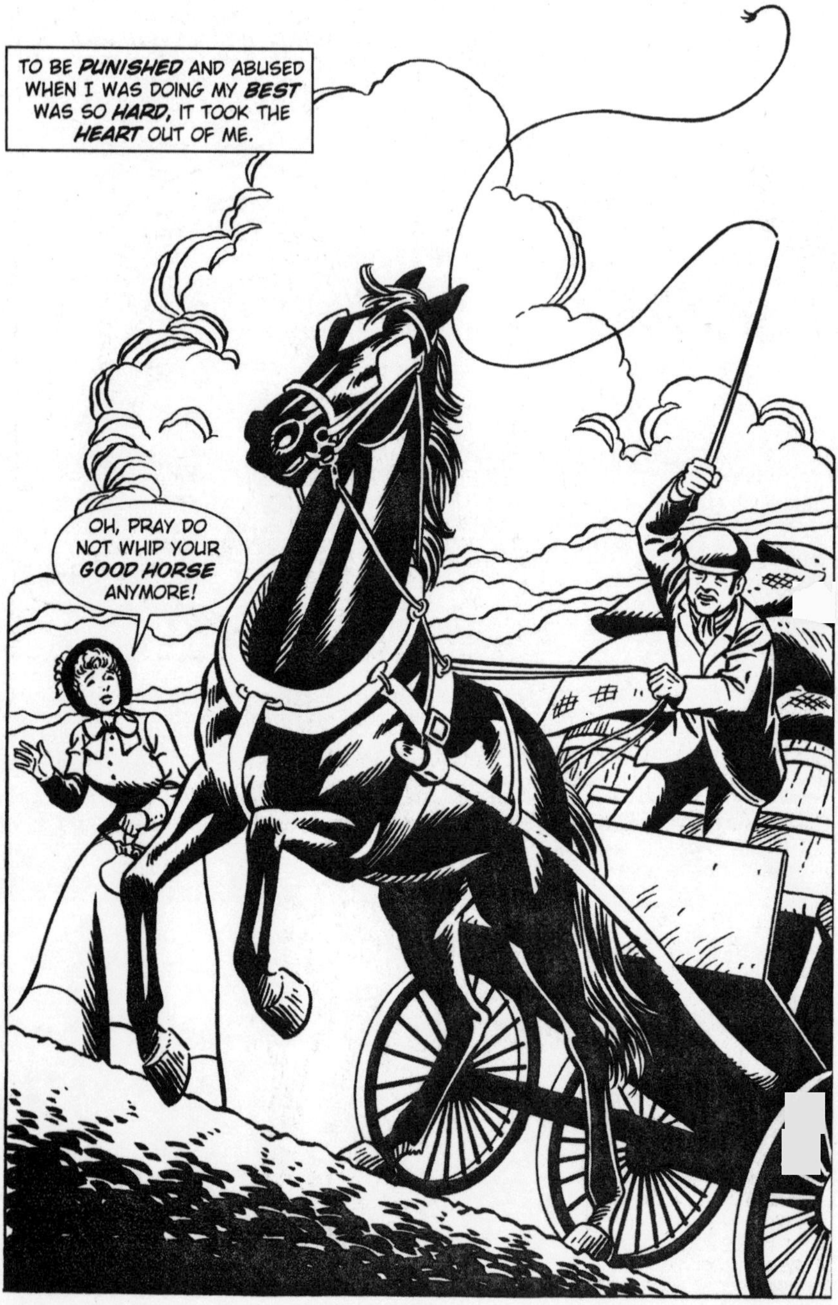
TO BE PUNISHED AND ABUSED WHEN I WAS DOING MY BEST WAS SO HARD, IT TOOK THE HEART OUT OF ME.
OH, PRAY DO NOT WHIP YOUR GOOD HORSE ANYMORE!

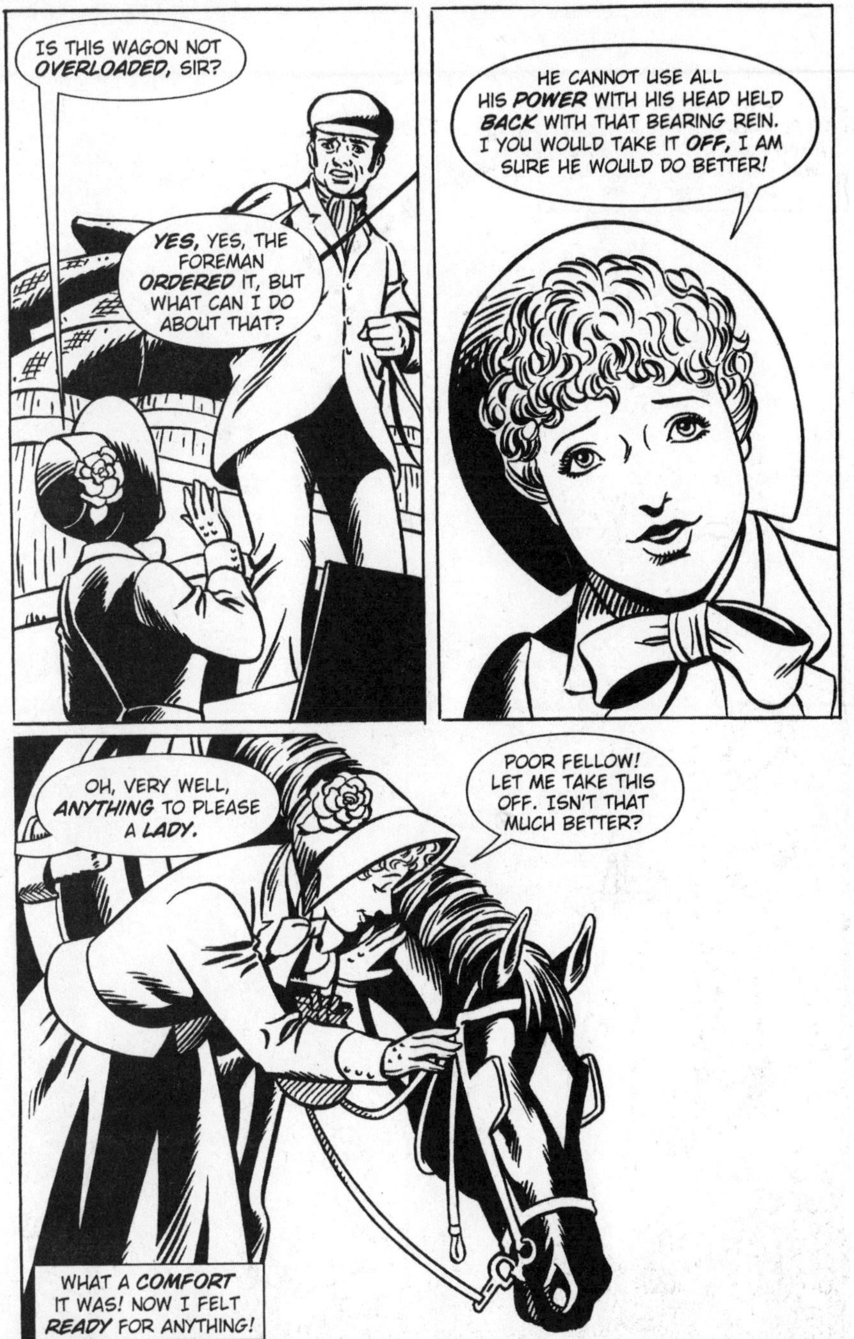
IS THIS WAGON NOT OVERLOADED, SIR?
YES, YES, THE FOREMAN ORDERED IT, BUT WHAT CAN I DO ABOUT THAT?
HE CANNOT USE ALL HIS POWER WITH HIS HEAD HELD BACK WITH THAT BEARING REIN. I YOU WOULD TAKE IT OFF, I AM SURE HE WOULD DO BETTER!
OH, VERY WELL, ANYTHING TO PLEASE A LADY.
POOR FELLOW! LET ME TAKE THIS OFF. ISN'T THAT MUCH BETTER?
WHAT A COMFORT IT WAS! NOW I FELT READY FOR ANYTHING!

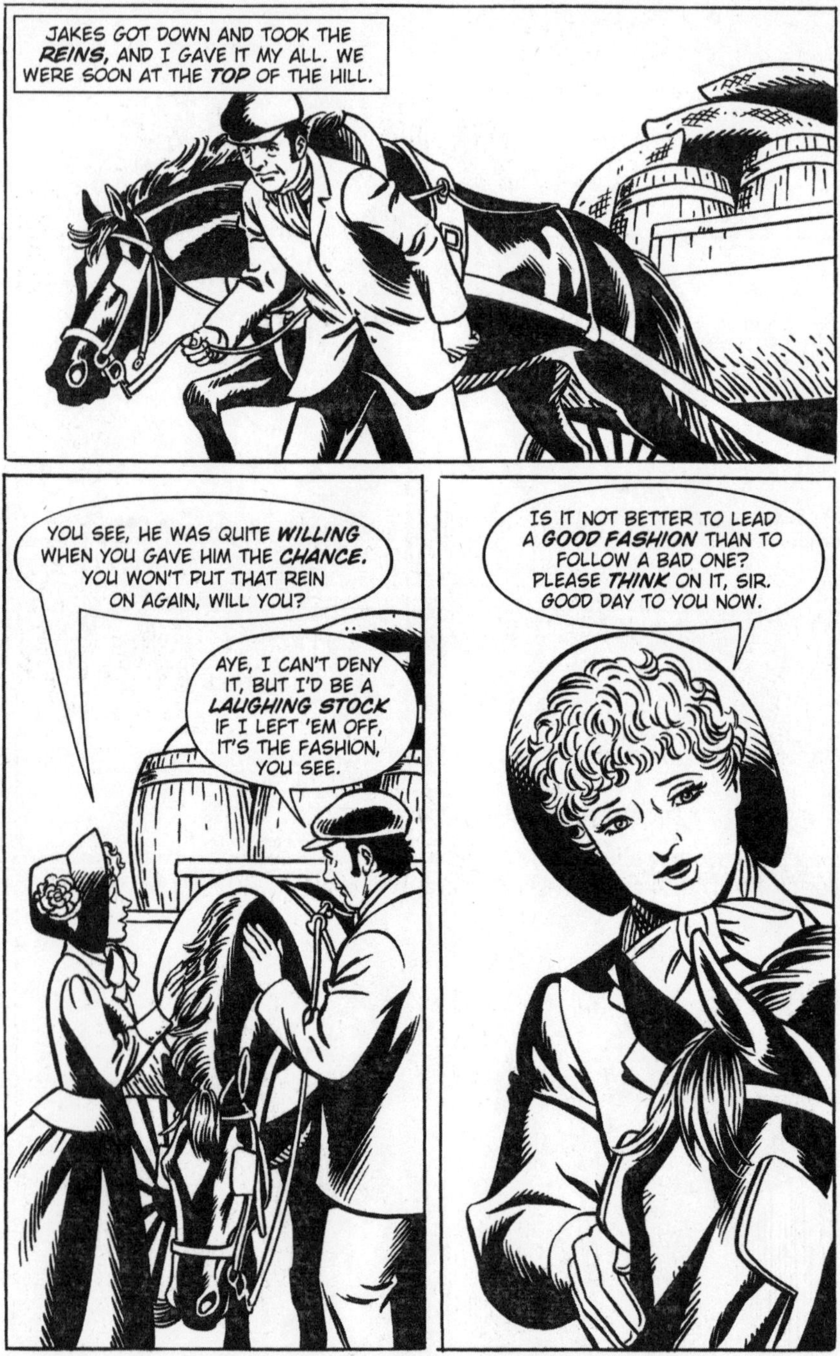
JAKES GOT DOWN AND TOOK THE REINS, AND I GAVE IT MY ALL. WE WERE SOON AT THE TOP OF THE HILL.
YOU SEE, HE WAS QUITE WILLING WHEN YOU GAVE HIM THE CHANCE. YOU WON'T PUT THAT REIN ON AGAIN, WILL YOU?
AYE, I CAN'T DENY IT, BUT I'D BE A LAUGHING STOCK IF I LEFT 'EM OFF, IT'S THE FASHION, YOU SEE.
IS IT NOT BETTER TO LEAD A GOOD FASHION THAN TO FOLLOW A BAD ONE? PLEASE THINK ON IT, SIR. GOOD DAY TO YOU NOW.

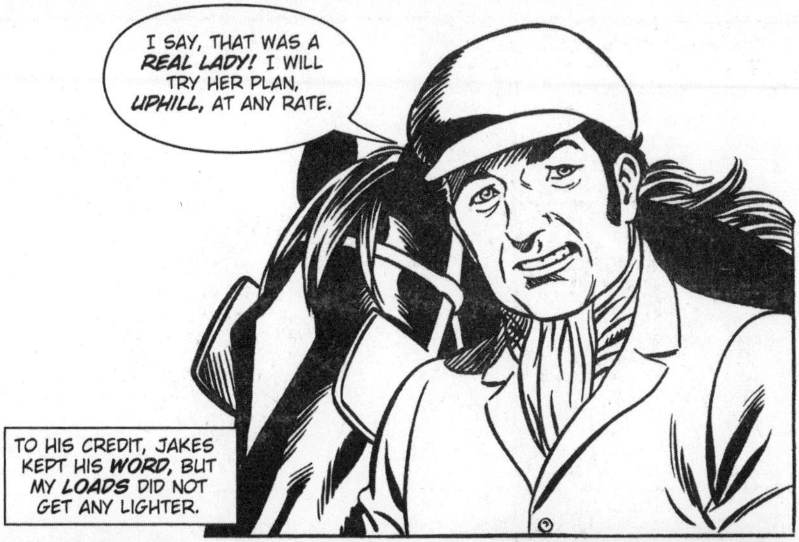
I SAY, THAT WAS A REAL LADY! I WILL TRY HER PLAN, UPHILL, AT ANY RATE.
TO HIS CREDIT, JAKES KEPT HIS WORD, BUT MY LOADS DID NOT GET ANY LIGHTER.

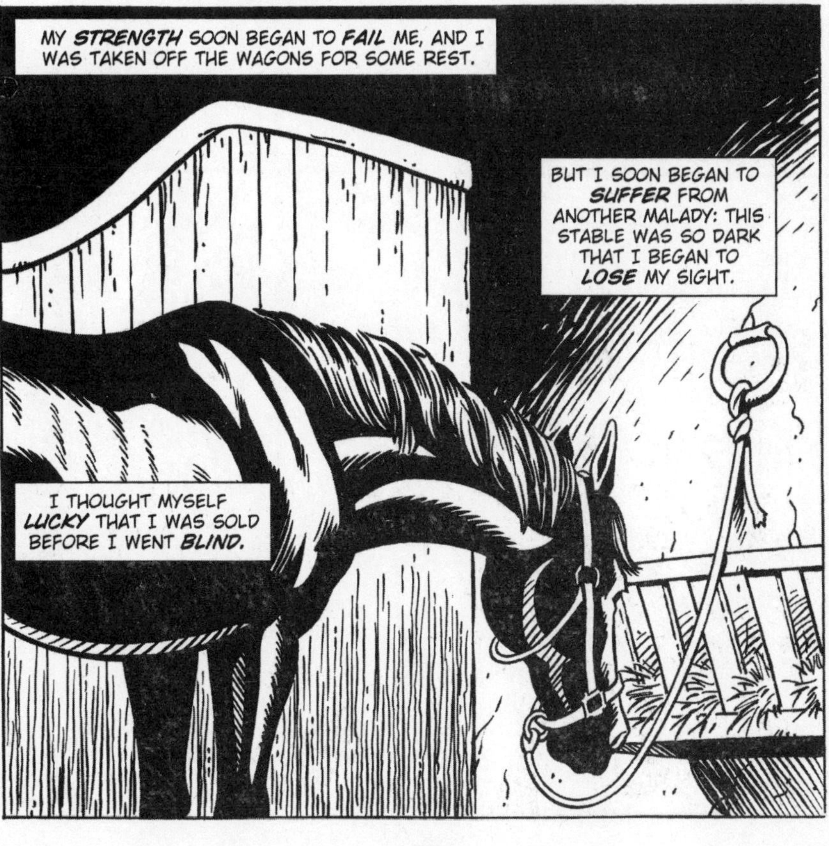
MY STRENGTH SOON BEGAN TO FAIL ME, AND I WAS TAKEN OFF THE WAGONS FOR SOME REST.
BUT I SOON BEGAN TO SUFFER FROM ANOTHER MALADY: THIS STABLE WAS SO DARK THAT I BEGAN TO LOSE MY SIGHT.
I THOUGHT MYSELF LUCKY THAT I WAS SOLD BEFORE I WENT BLIND.

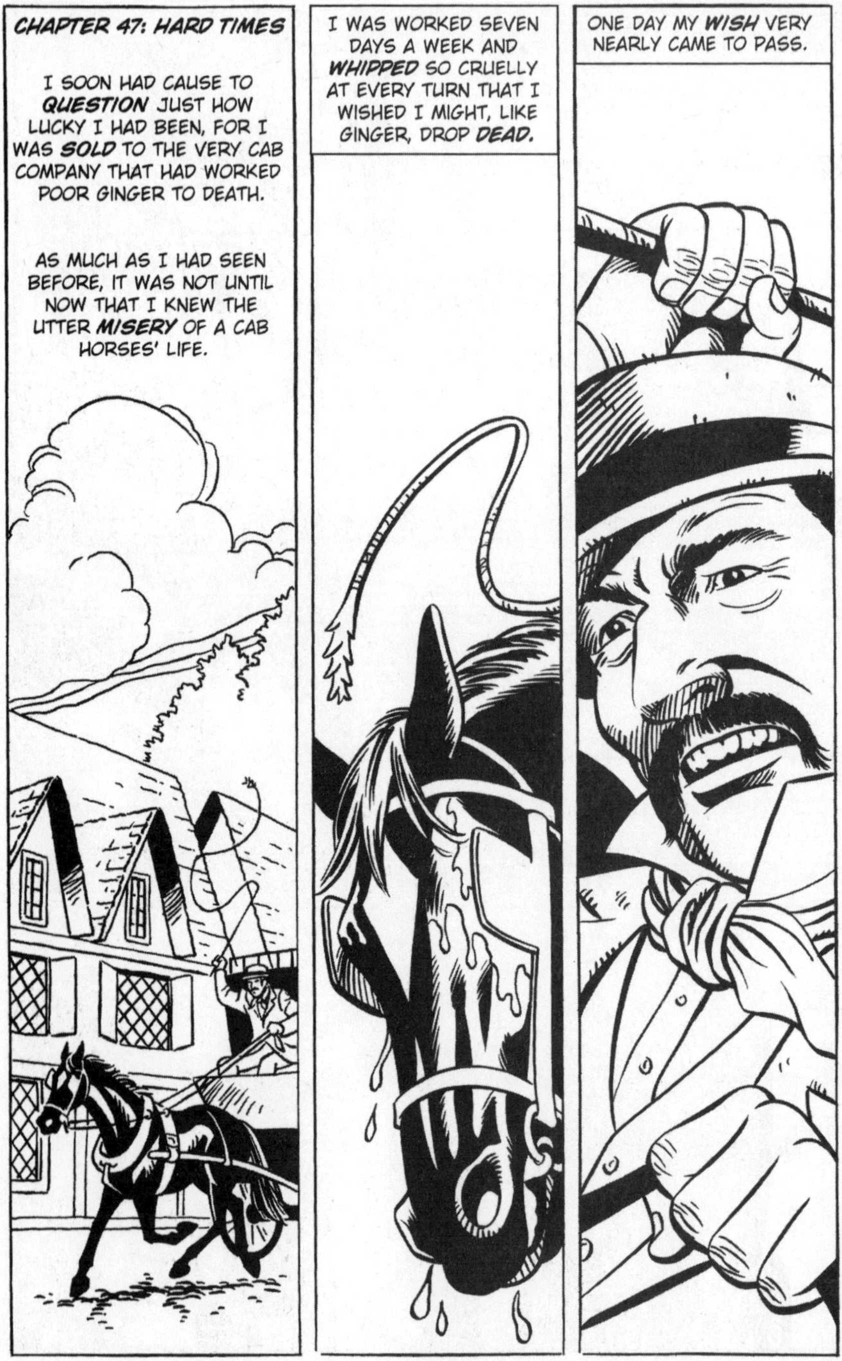
CHAPTER 47: HARD TIMES
I SOON HAD CAUSE TO QUESTION JUST HOW LUCKY I HAD BEEN, FOR I WAS SOLD TO THE VERY CAB COMPANY THAT HAD WORKED POOR GINGER TO DEATH.
AS MUCH AS I HAD SEEN BEFORE, IT WAS NOT UNTIL NOW THAT I KNEW THE UTTER MISERY OF A CAB HORSES' LIFE.
I WAS WORKED SEVEN DAYS A WEEK AND WHIPPED SO CRUELLY AT EVERY TURN THAT I WISHED I MIGHT, LIKE GINGER, DROP DEAD.
ONE DAY MY WISH VERY NEARLY CAME TO PASS.

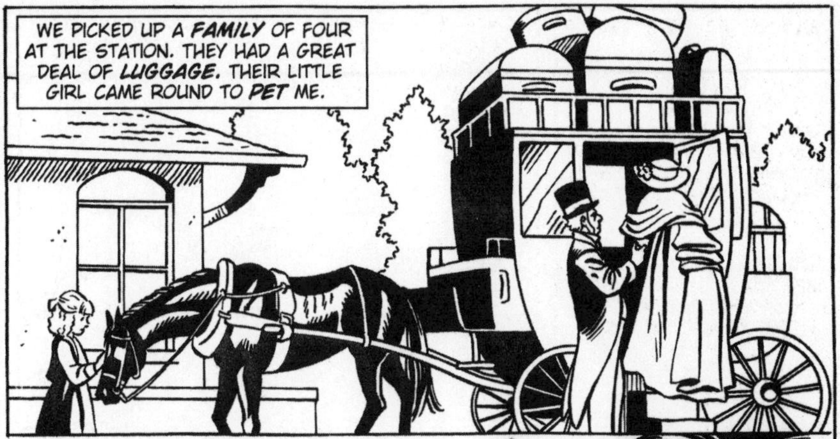
WE PICKED UP A *FAMILY* OF FOUR AT THE STATION. THEY HAD A GREAT DEAL OF *LUGGAGE.* THEIR LITTLE GIRL CAME ROUND TO *PET* ME.

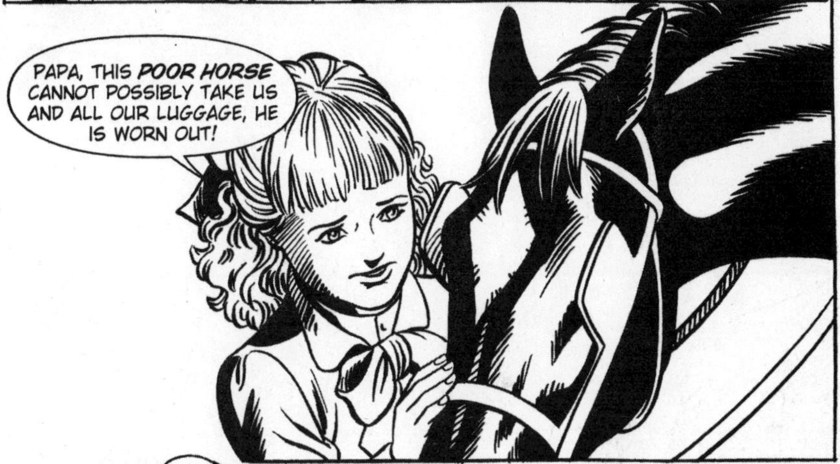
PAPA, THIS *POOR HORSE* CANNOT POSSIBLY TAKE US AND ALL OUR LUGGAGE, HE IS WORN OUT!

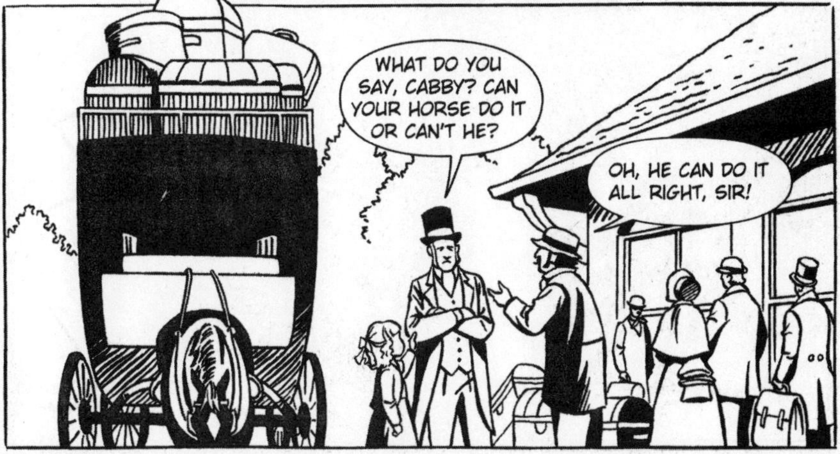
WHAT DO YOU SAY, CABBY? CAN YOUR HORSE DO IT OR CAN'T HE?
OH, HE CAN DO IT ALL RIGHT, SIR!

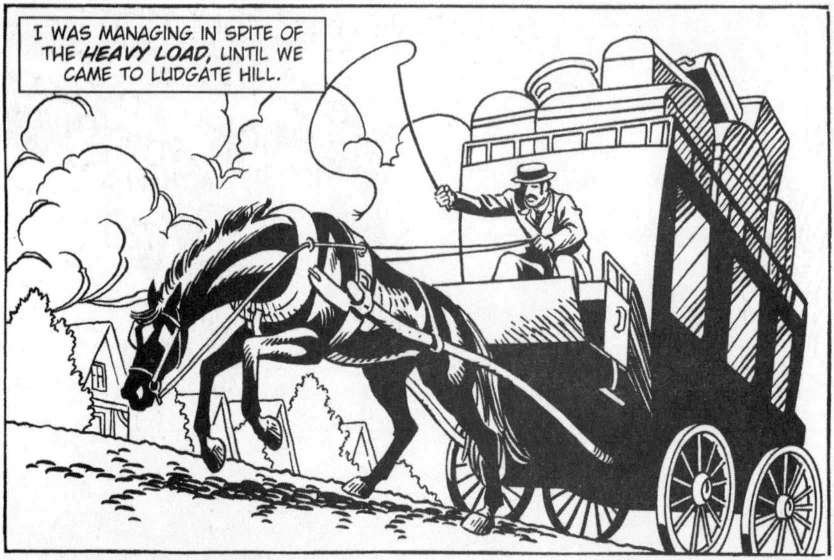
I WAS MANAGING IN SPITE OF THE HEAVY LOAD, UNTIL WE CAME TO LUDGATE HILL.

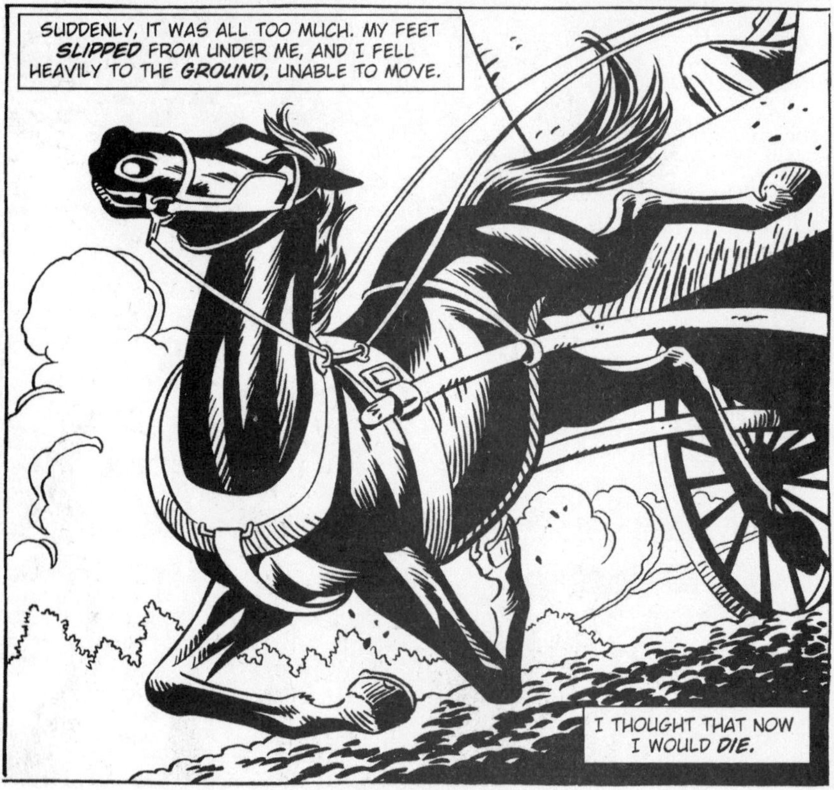
SUDDENLY, IT WAS ALL TOO MUCH. MY FEET SLIPPED FROM UNDER ME, AND I FELL HEAVILY TO THE GROUND, UNABLE TO MOVE.
I THOUGHT THAT NOW I WOULD DIE.

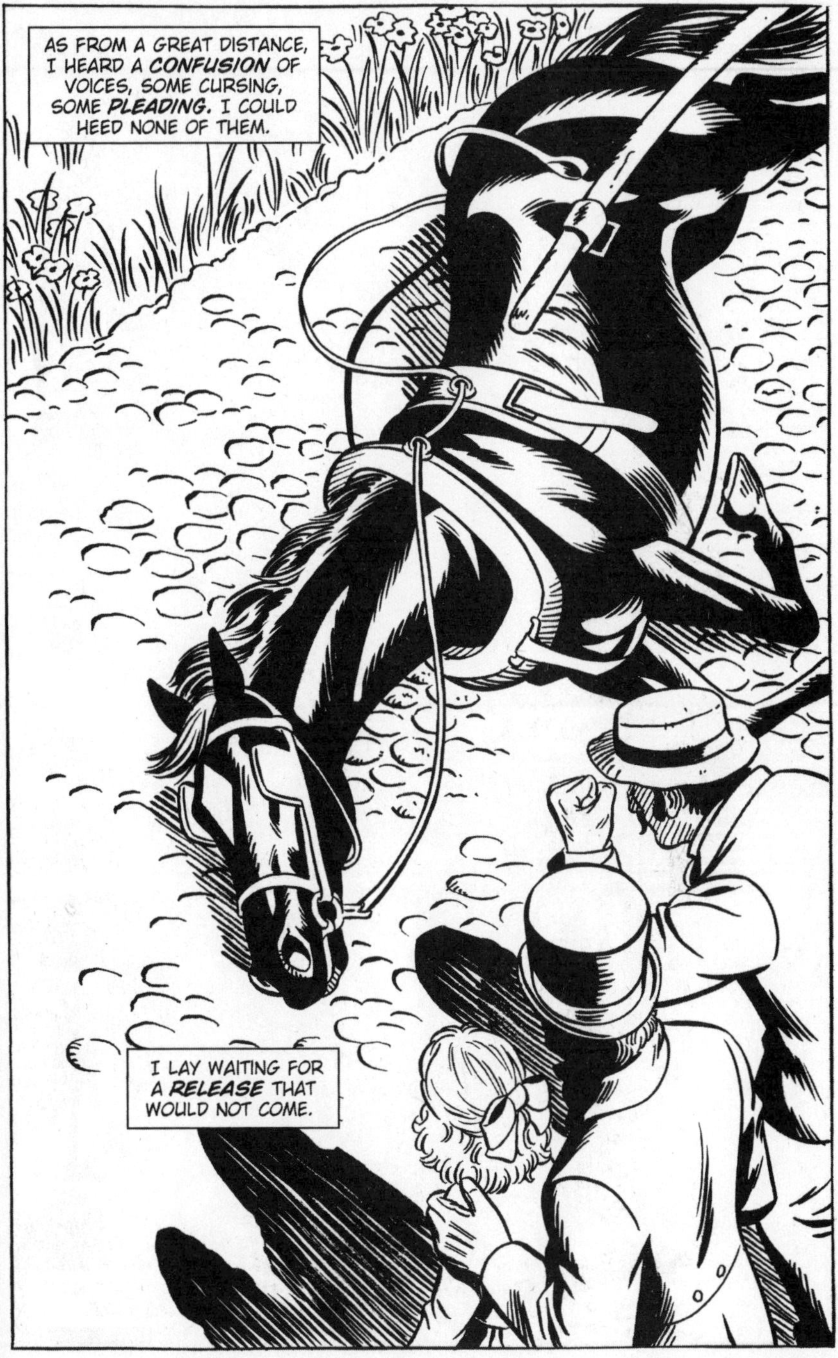
AS FROM A GREAT DISTANCE, I HEARD A CONFUSION OF VOICES, SOME CURSING, SOME PLEADING. I COULD HEED NONE OF THEM.
I LAY WAITING FOR A RELEASE THAT WOULD NOT COME.

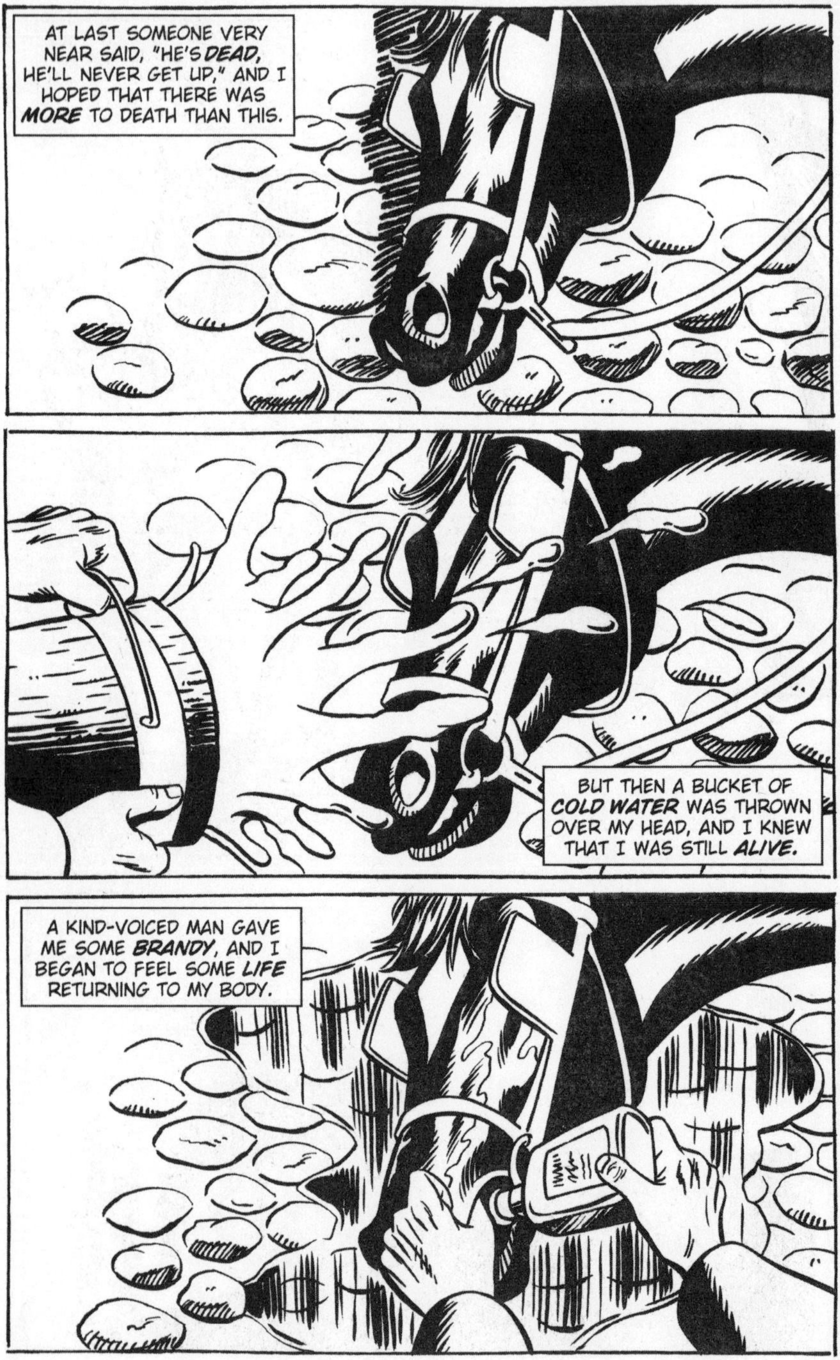
AT LAST SOMEONE VERY NEAR SAID, "HE'S DEAD, HE'LL NEVER GET UP," AND I HOPED THAT THERE WAS MORE TO DEATH THAN THIS.
BUT THEN A BUCKET OF COLD WATER WAS THROWN OVER MY HEAD, AND I KNEW THAT I WAS STILL ALIVE.
A KIND-VOICED MAN GAVE ME SOME BRANDY, AND I BEGAN TO FEEL SOME LIFE RETURNING TO MY BODY.

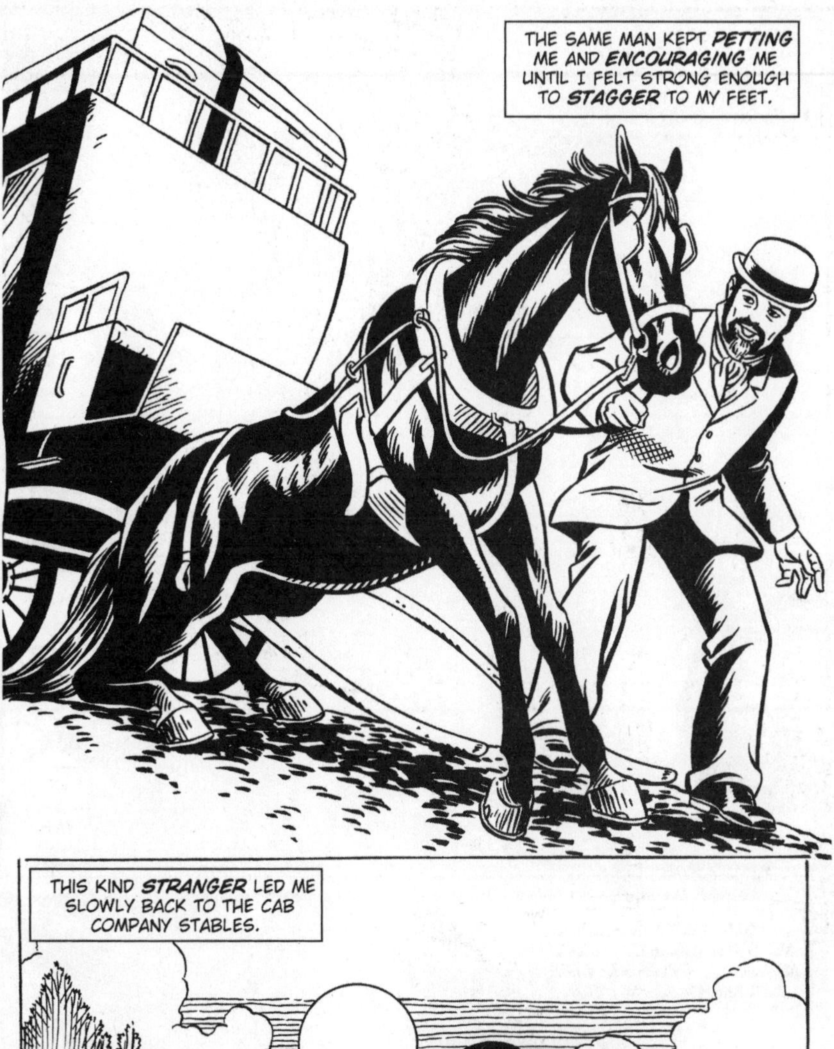
THE SAME MAN KEPT PETTING ME AND ENCOURAGING ME UNTIL I FELT STRONG ENOUGH TO STAGGER TO MY FEET.

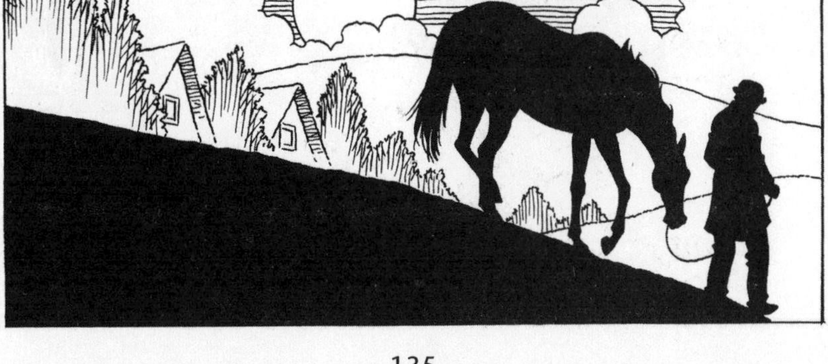
THIS KIND STRANGER LED ME SLOWLY BACK TO THE CAB COMPANY STABLES.

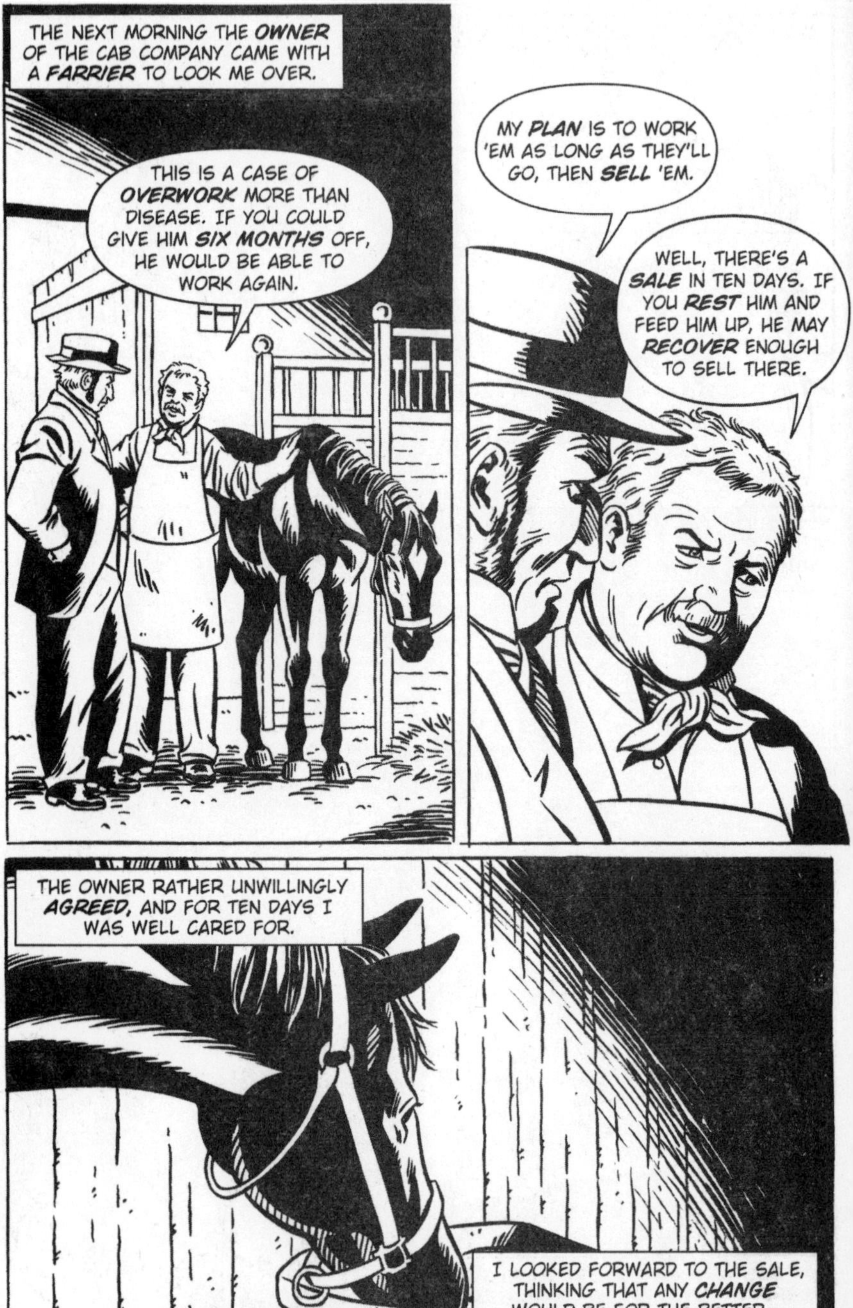
THE NEXT MORNING THE OWNER OF THE CAB COMPANY CAME WITH A FARRIER TO LOOK ME OVER.
THIS IS A CASE OF OVERWORK MORE THAN DISEASE. IF YOU COULD GIVE HIM SIX MONTHS OFF, HE WOULD BE ABLE TO WORK AGAIN.
MY PLAN IS TO WORK 'EM AS LONG AS THEY'LL GO, THEN SELL 'EM.
WELL, THERE'S A SALE IN TEN DAYS. IF YOU REST HIM AND FEED HIM UP, HE MAY RECOVER ENOUGH TO SELL THERE.
THE OWNER RATHER UNWILLINGLY AGREED, AND FOR TEN DAYS I WAS WELL CARED FOR.
I LOOKED FORWARD TO THE SALE, THINKING THAT ANY CHANGE WOULD BE FOR THE BETTER.

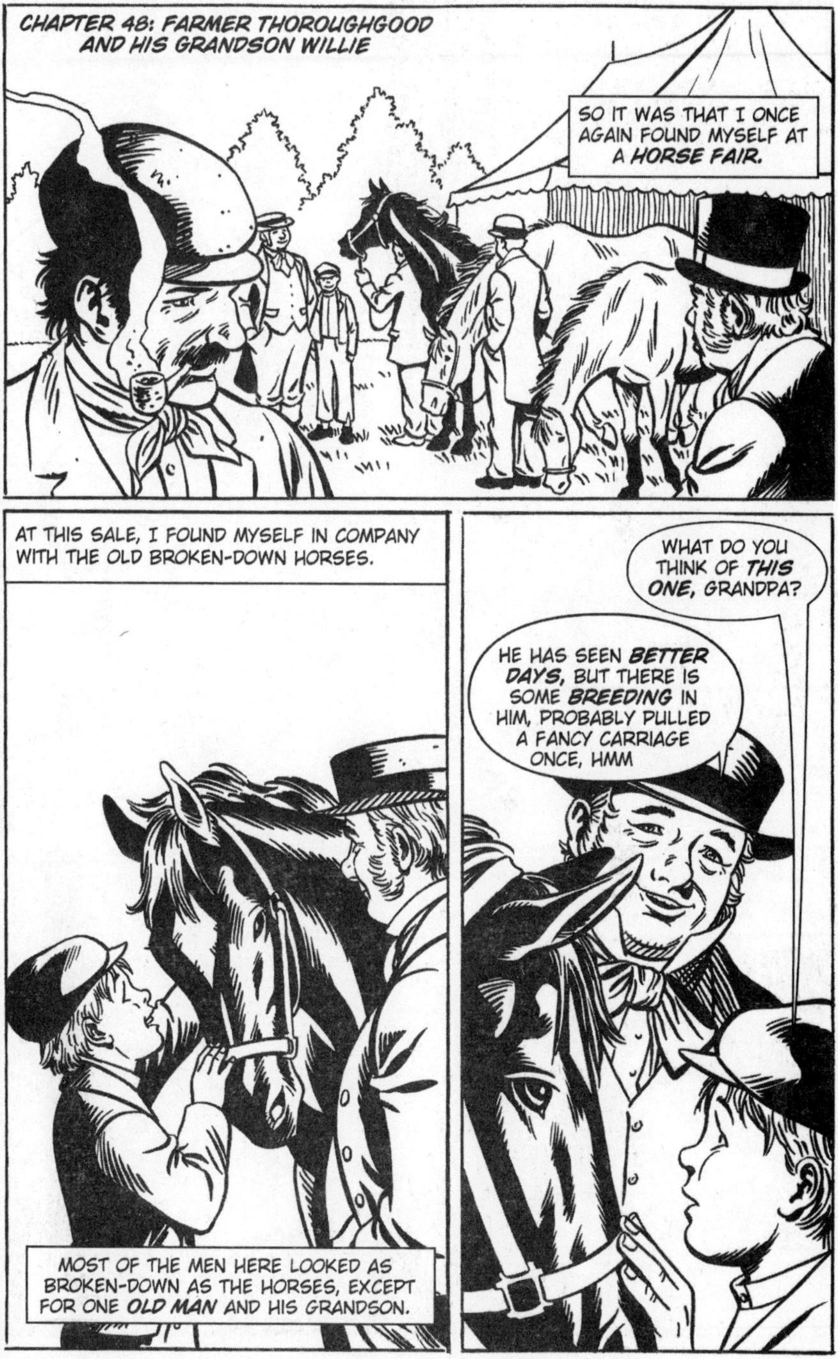
CHAPTER 48: FARMER THOROUGHGOOD AND HIS GRANDSON WILLIE
SO IT WAS THAT I ONCE AGAIN FOUND MYSELF AT A HORSE FAIR.
AT THIS SALE, I FOUND MYSELF IN COMPANY WITH THE OLD BROKEN-DOWN HORSES.
MOST OF THE MEN HERE LOOKED AS BROKEN-DOWN AS THE HORSES, EXCEPT FOR ONE OLD MAN AND HIS GRANDSON.
WHAT DO YOU THINK OF THIS ONE, GRANDPA?
HE HAS SEEN BETTER DAYS, BUT THERE IS SOME BREEDING IN HIM, PROBABLY PULLED A FANCY CARRIAGE ONCE, HMM

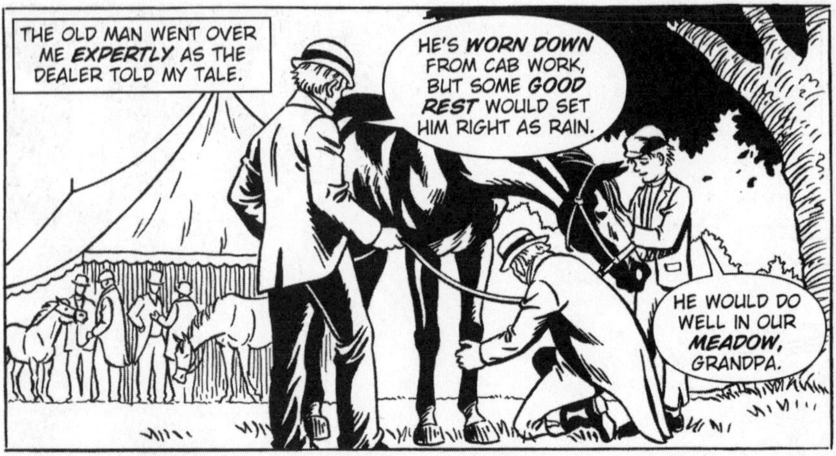
THE OLD MAN WENT OVER ME EXPERTLY AS THE DEALER TOLD MY TALE.
HE'S WORN DOWN FROM CAB WORK, BUT SOME GOOD REST WOULD SET HIM RIGHT AS RAIN.
HE WOULD DO WELL IN OUR MEADOW, GRANDPA.

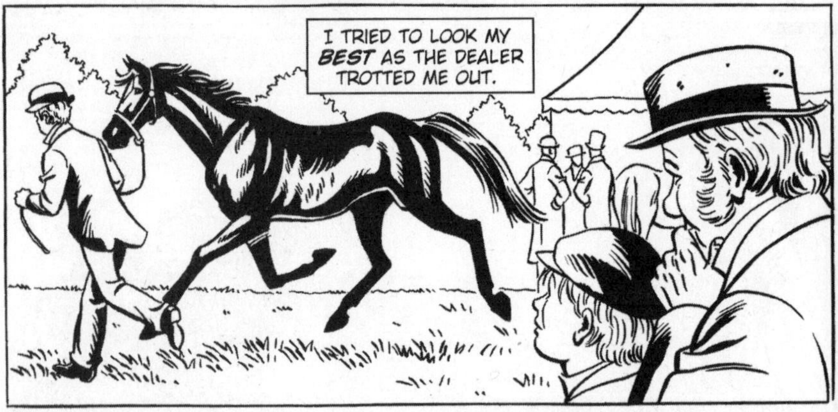
I TRIED TO LOOK MY BEST AS THE DEALER TROTTED ME OUT.

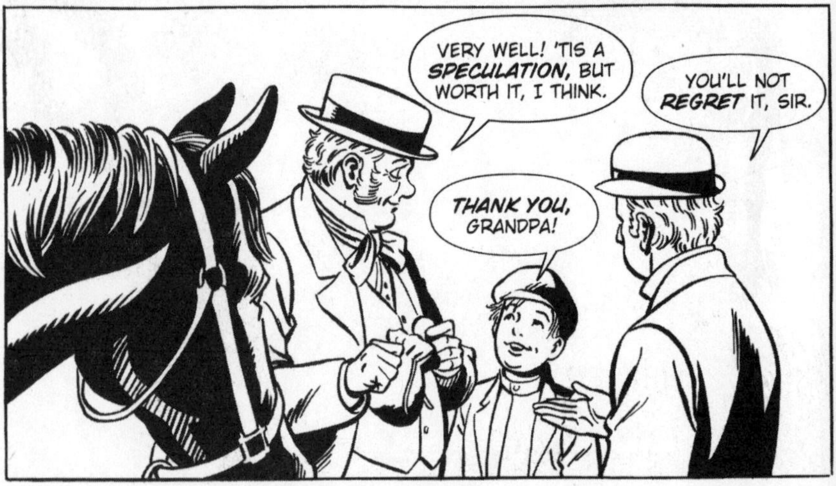
VERY WELL! 'TIS A SPECULATION, BUT WORTH IT, I THINK.
YOU'LL NOT REGRET IT, SIR.
THANK YOU, GRANDPA!

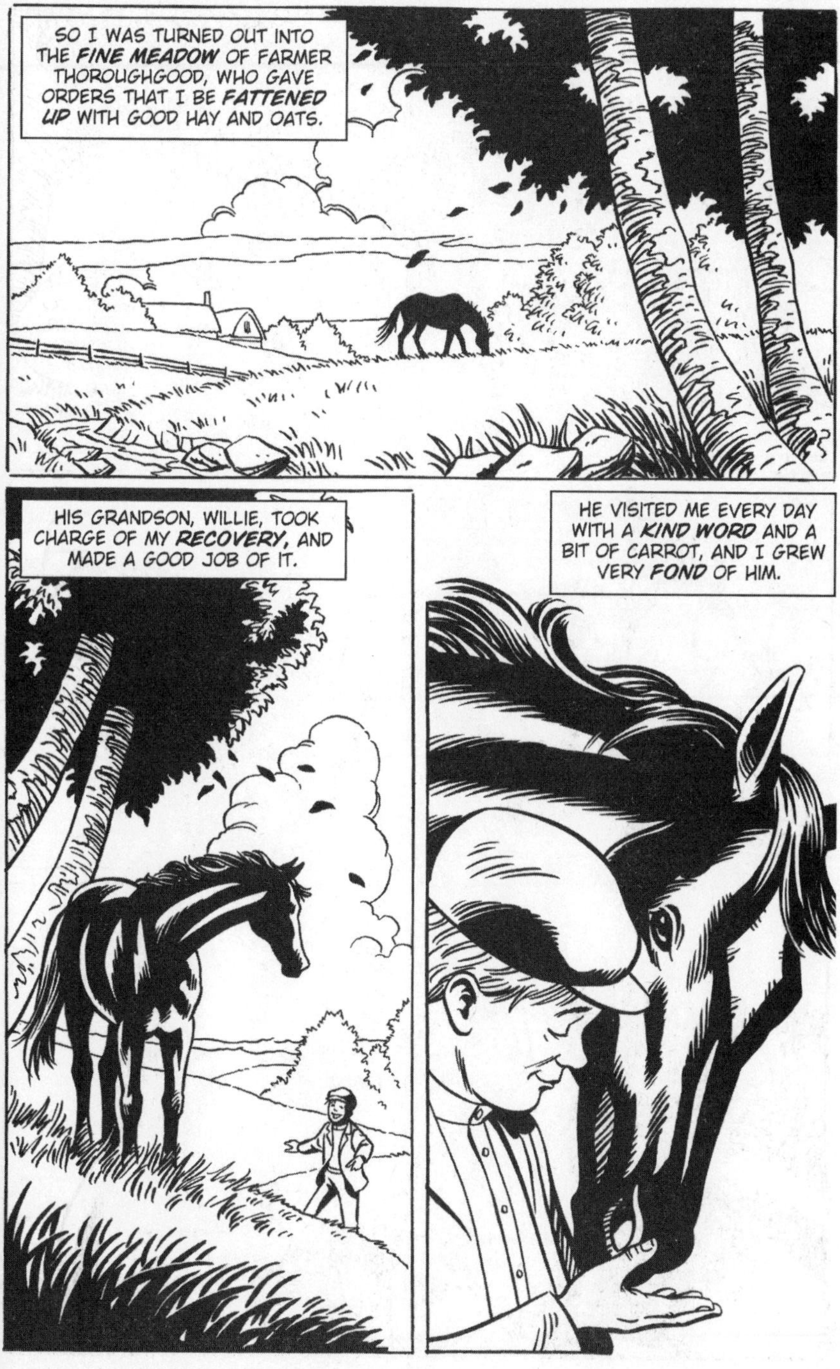
SO I WAS TURNED OUT INTO THE FINE MEADOW OF FARMER THOROUGHGOOD, WHO GAVE ORDERS THAT I BE FATTENED UP WITH GOOD HAY AND OATS.
HIS GRANDSON, WILLIE, TOOK CHARGE OF MY RECOVERY, AND MADE A GOOD JOB OF IT.
HE VISITED ME EVERY DAY WITH A KIND WORD AND A BIT OF CARROT, AND I GREW VERY FOND OF HIM.

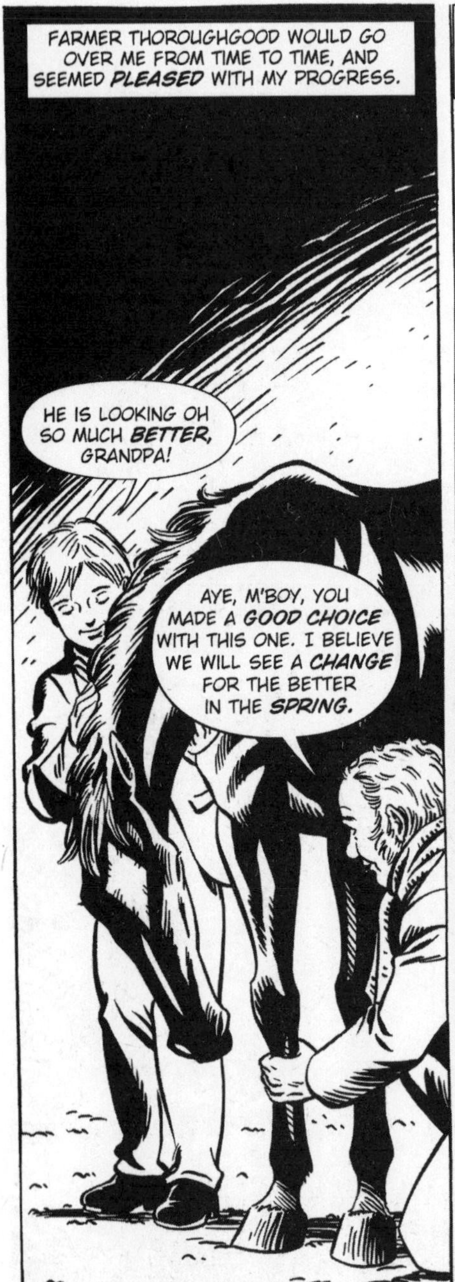
FARMER THOROUGHGOOD WOULD GO OVER ME FROM TIME TO TIME, AND SEEMED PLEASED WITH MY PROGRESS.
HE IS LOOKING OH SO MUCH BETTER, GRANDPA!
AYE, M'BOY, YOU MADE A GOOD CHOICE WITH THIS ONE. I BELIEVE WE WILL SEE A CHANGE FOR THE BETTER IN THE SPRING.

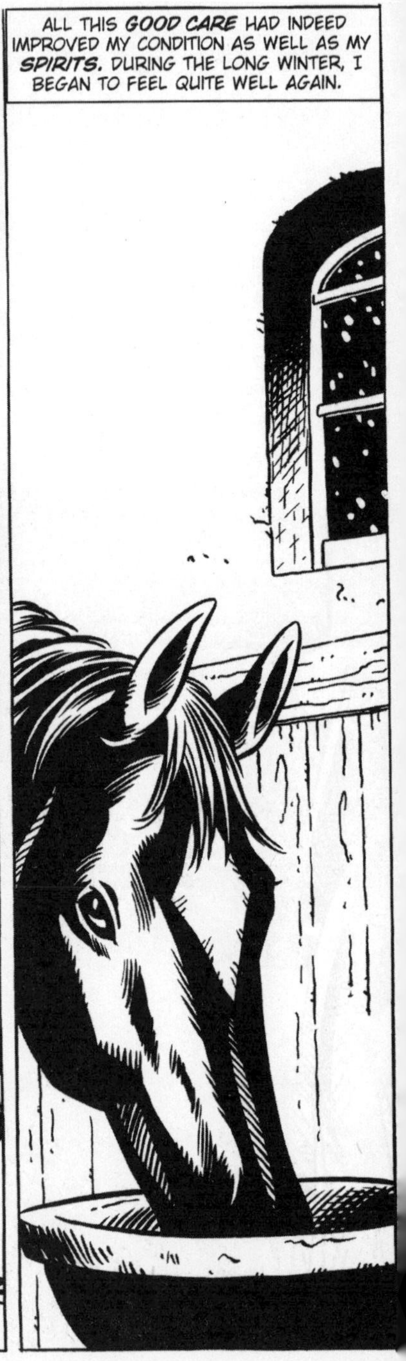
ALL THIS GOOD CARE HAD INDEED IMPROVED MY CONDITION AS WELL AS MY SPIRITS. DURING THE LONG WINTER, I BEGAN TO FEEL QUITE WELL AGAIN.

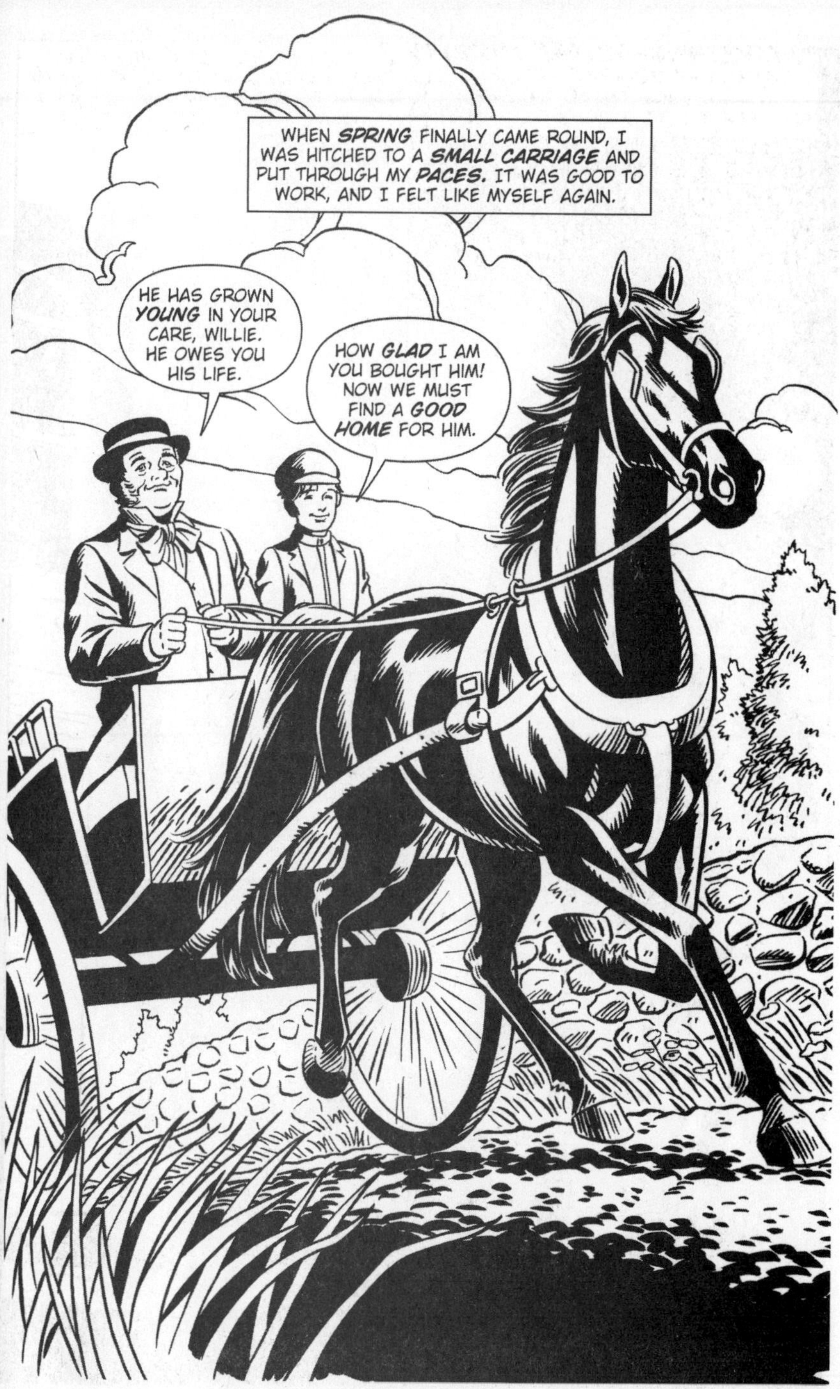
WHEN SPRING FINALLY CAME ROUND, I WAS HITCHED TO A SMALL CARRIAGE AND PUT THROUGH MY PACES. IT WAS GOOD TO WORK, AND I FELT LIKE MYSELF AGAIN.
HE HAS GROWN YOUNG IN YOUR CARE, WILLIE. HE OWES YOU HIS LIFE.
HOW GLAD I AM YOU BOUGHT HIM! NOW WE MUST FIND A GOOD HOME FOR HIM.

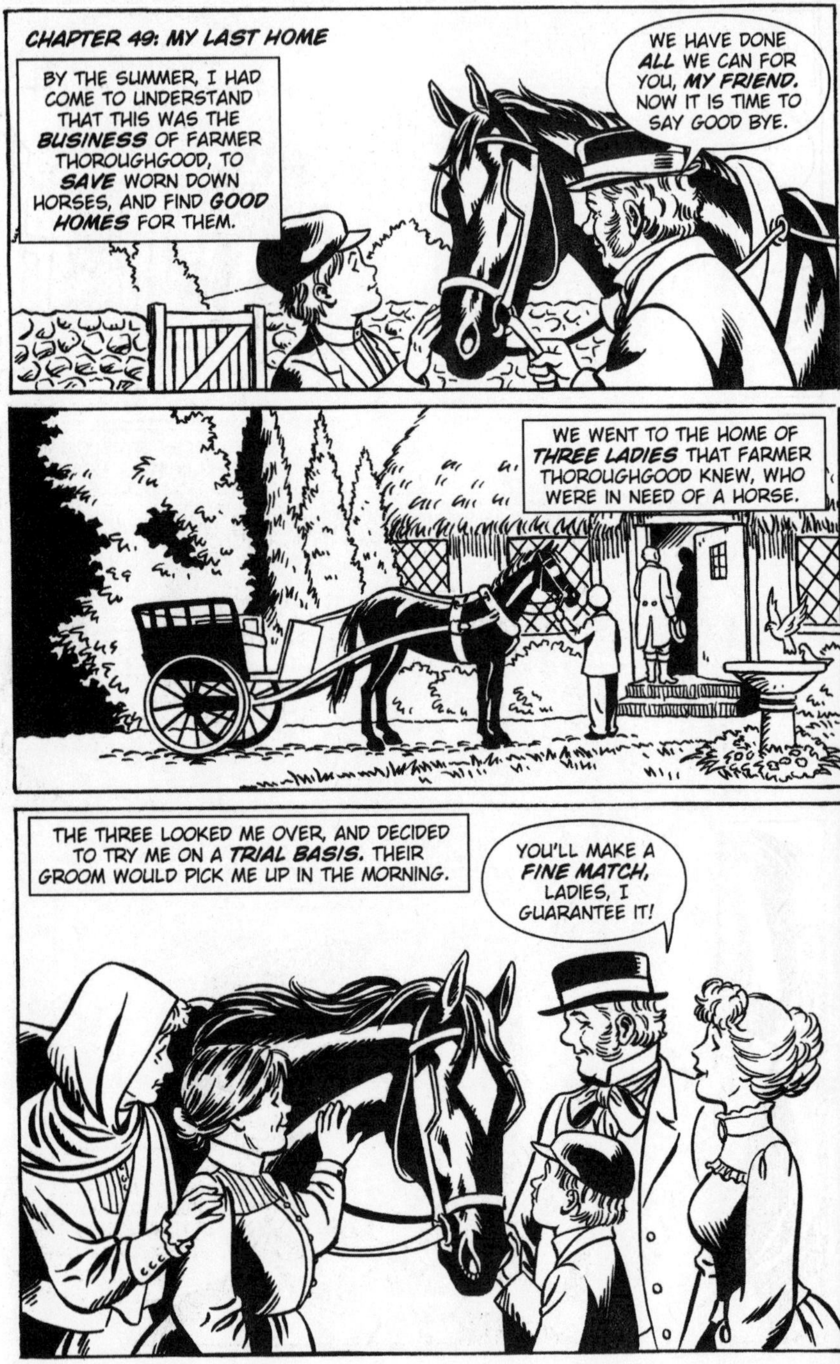

CHAPTER 49: MY LAST HOME
BY THE SUMMER, I HAD COME TO UNDERSTAND THAT THIS WAS THE BUSINESS OF FARMER THOROUGHGOOD, TO SAVE WORN DOWN HORSES, AND FIND GOOD HOMES FOR THEM.
WE HAVE DONE ALL WE CAN FOR YOU, MY FRIEND. NOW IT IS TIME TO SAY GOOD BYE.
WE WENT TO THE HOME OF THREE LADIES THAT FARMER THOROUGHGOOD KNEW, WHO WERE IN NEED OF A HORSE.
THE THREE LOOKED ME OVER, AND DECIDED TO TRY ME ON A TRIAL BASIS. THEIR GROOM WOULD PICK ME UP IN THE MORNING.
YOU'LL MAKE A FINE MATCH, LADIES, I GUARANTEE IT!

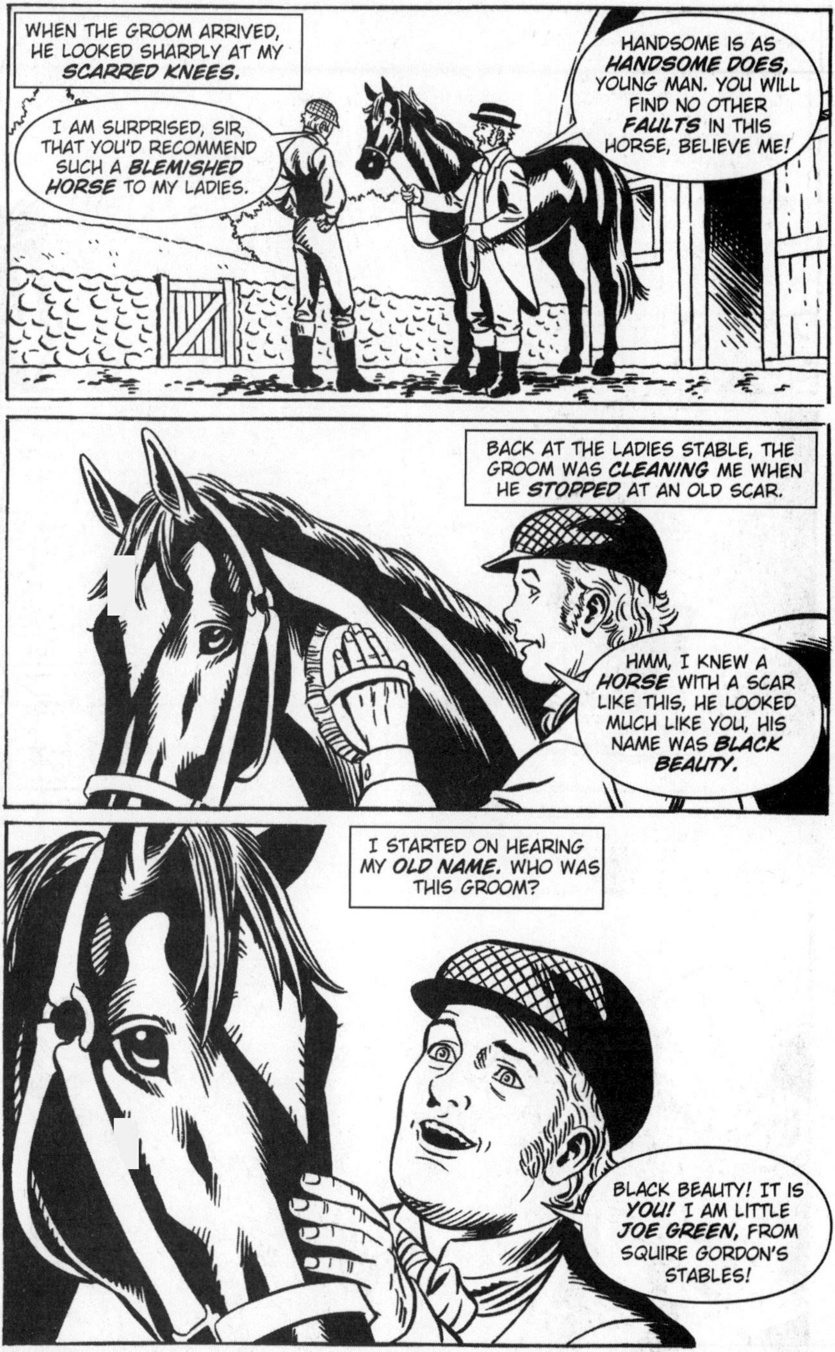

WHEN THE GROOM ARRIVED, HE LOOKED SHARPLY AT MY SCARRED KNEES.
I AM SURPRISED, SIR, THAT YOU'D RECOMMEND SUCH A BLEMISHED HORSE TO MY LADIES.
HANDSOME IS AS HANDSOME DOES, YOUNG MAN. YOU WILL FIND NO OTHER FAULTS IN THIS HORSE, BELIEVE ME!
BACK AT THE LADIES STABLE, THE GROOM WAS CLEANING ME WHEN HE STOPPED AT AN OLD SCAR.
HMM, I KNEW A HORSE WITH A SCAR LIKE THIS, HE LOOKED MUCH LIKE YOU, HIS NAME WAS BLACK BEAUTY.
I STARTED ON HEARING MY OLD NAME. WHO WAS THIS GROOM?
BLACK BEAUTY! IT IS YOU! I AM LITTLE JOE GREEN, FROM SQUIRE GORDON'S STABLES!

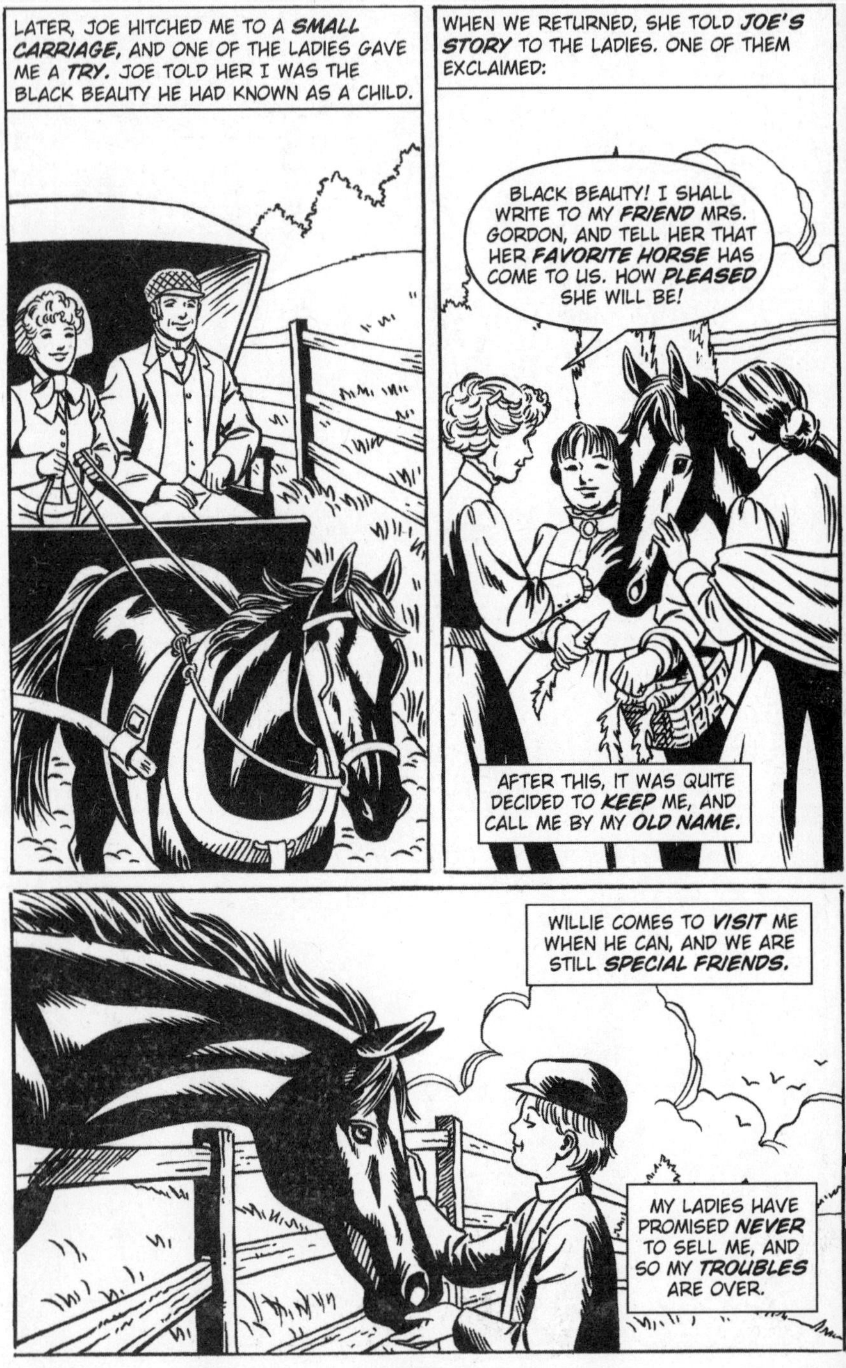
LATER, JOE HITCHED ME TO A SMALL CARRIAGE, AND ONE OF THE LADIES GAVE ME A TRY. JOE TOLD HER I WAS THE BLACK BEAUTY HE HAD KNOWN AS A CHILD.
WHEN WE RETURNED, SHE TOLD JOE'S STORY TO THE LADIES. ONE OF THEM EXCLAIMED:
BLACK BEAUTY! I SHALL WRITE TO MY FRIEND MRS. GORDON, AND TELL HER THAT HER FAVORITE HORSE HAS COME TO US. HOW PLEASED SHE WILL BE!
AFTER THIS, IT WAS QUITE DECIDED TO KEEP ME, AND CALL ME BY MY OLD NAME.
WILLIE COMES TO VISIT ME WHEN HE CAN, AND WE ARE STILL SPECIAL FRIENDS.
MY LADIES HAVE PROMISED NEVER TO SELL ME, AND SO MY TROUBLES ARE OVER.

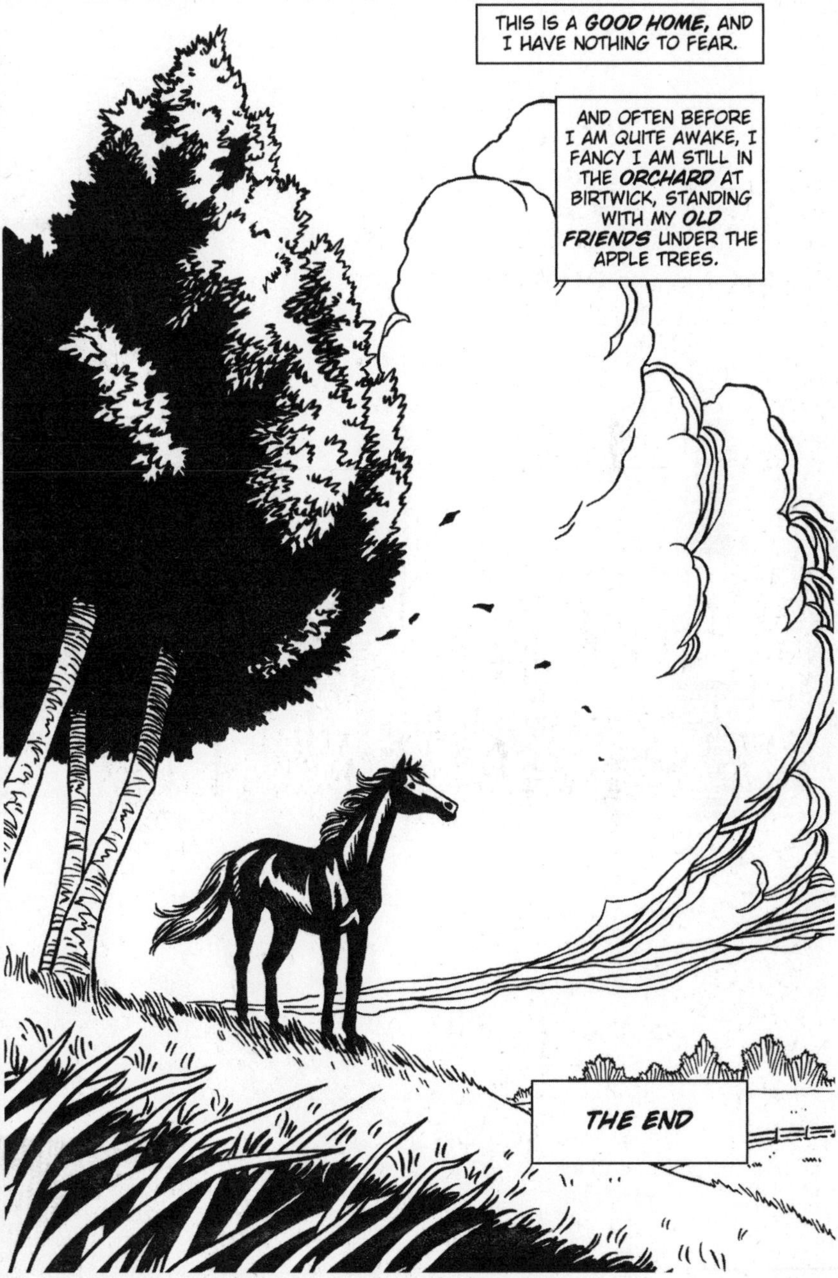
THIS IS A **GOOD HOME,** AND I HAVE NOTHING TO FEAR.
AND OFTEN BEFORE I AM QUITE AWAKE, I FANCY I AM STILL IN THE **ORCHARD** AT BIRTWICK, STANDING WITH MY **OLD FRIENDS** UNDER THE APPLE TREES.
THE END

The Making of ANNA SEWELL'S BLACK BEAUTY

"I couldn't believe I was going to have the chance to illustrate a book that I had loved since I was a child."
—June Brigman

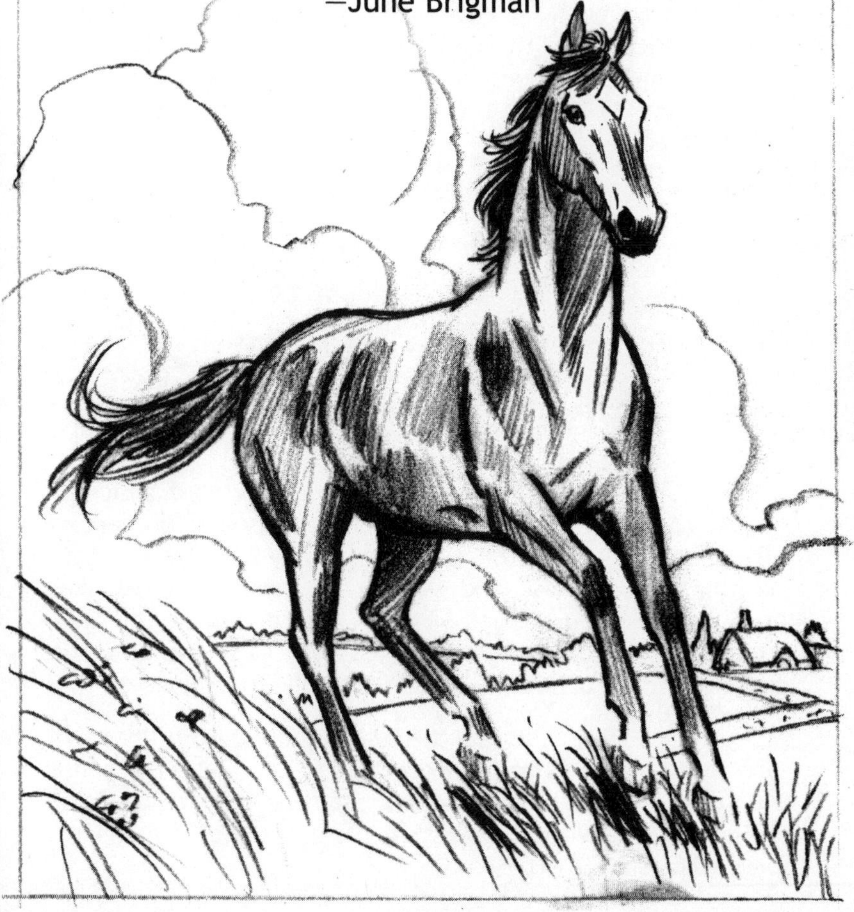

June Brigman talks about creating her graphic novel adaptation of

ANNA SEWELL'S

BLACK BEAUTY

I think drawing horses is easy for me because of my first-hand contact with them. It's always easier to draw something if you've had hands-on contact with it and since I've had experience with horses for so many years they are a very familiar subject to me.

To break down the story of *Black Beauty* into art, I first read a chapter, then I tried to figure out what the main point of the chapter was. Finally I had to somehow fit it into three pages of art, because there are forty-nine chapters in the book!

With the text, my husband Roy, who also inks my pencil art, looks at what I've drawn, reads the chapter, then condenses the writing in a way that keeps the meaning and feel of the original.

In comics, dialogue is typically presented in word balloons. Regular narration is put into captions enclosed in borders or left "open" without borders. Black Beauuty narrates his story from his point of view, and we thought that the horses' dialogue would feel wrong in balloons. After discussing this with our editors, we decided that the best way to go was with the caption form using quotation marks to indicate dialogue.

Doing *Black Beauty* feels like the culmination of everything I've done in my career. I get to draw horses. It's black-and-white illustration which I learned how to produce in my comic book career. And it's also following in the footsteps of my hero, horse artist Sam Savitt.

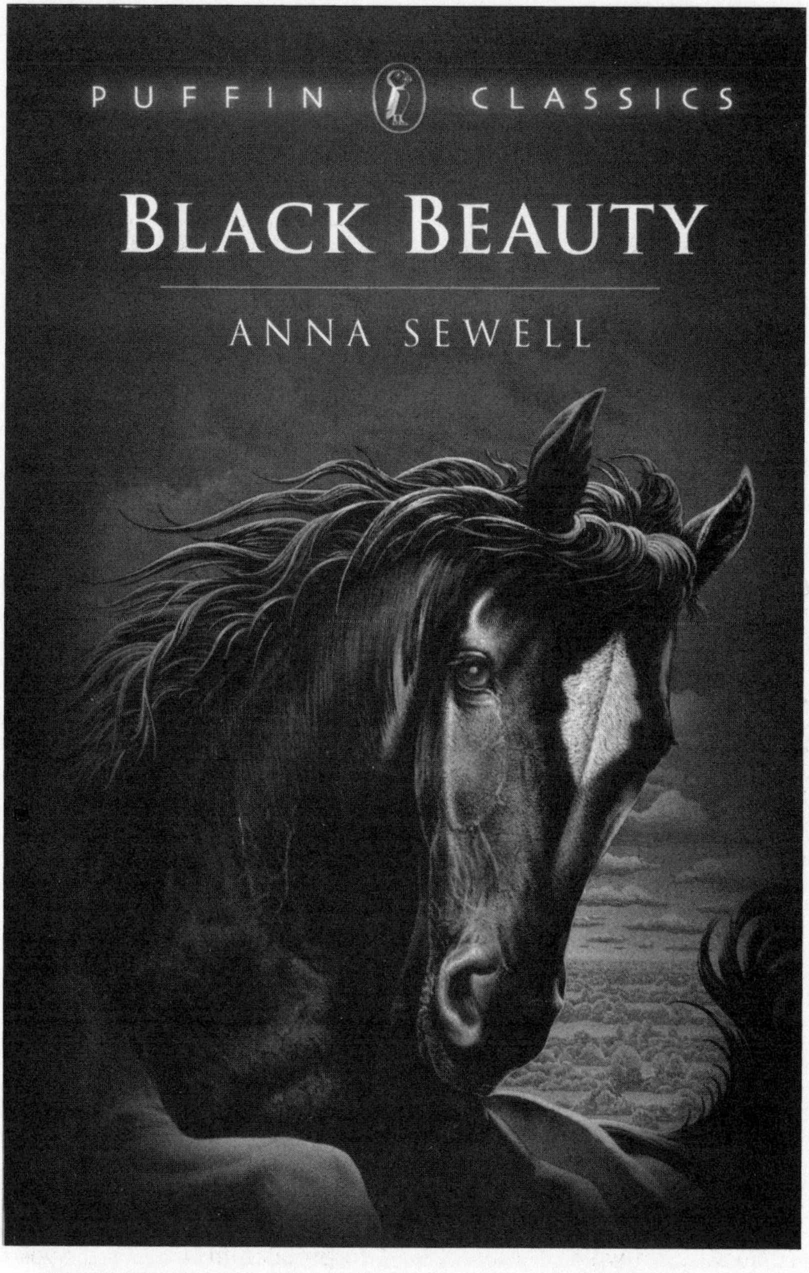
PUFFIN CLASSICS
BLACK BEAUTY
ANNA SEWELL

The Puffin Classics edition that was used as reference for this grahic novel adaptation.

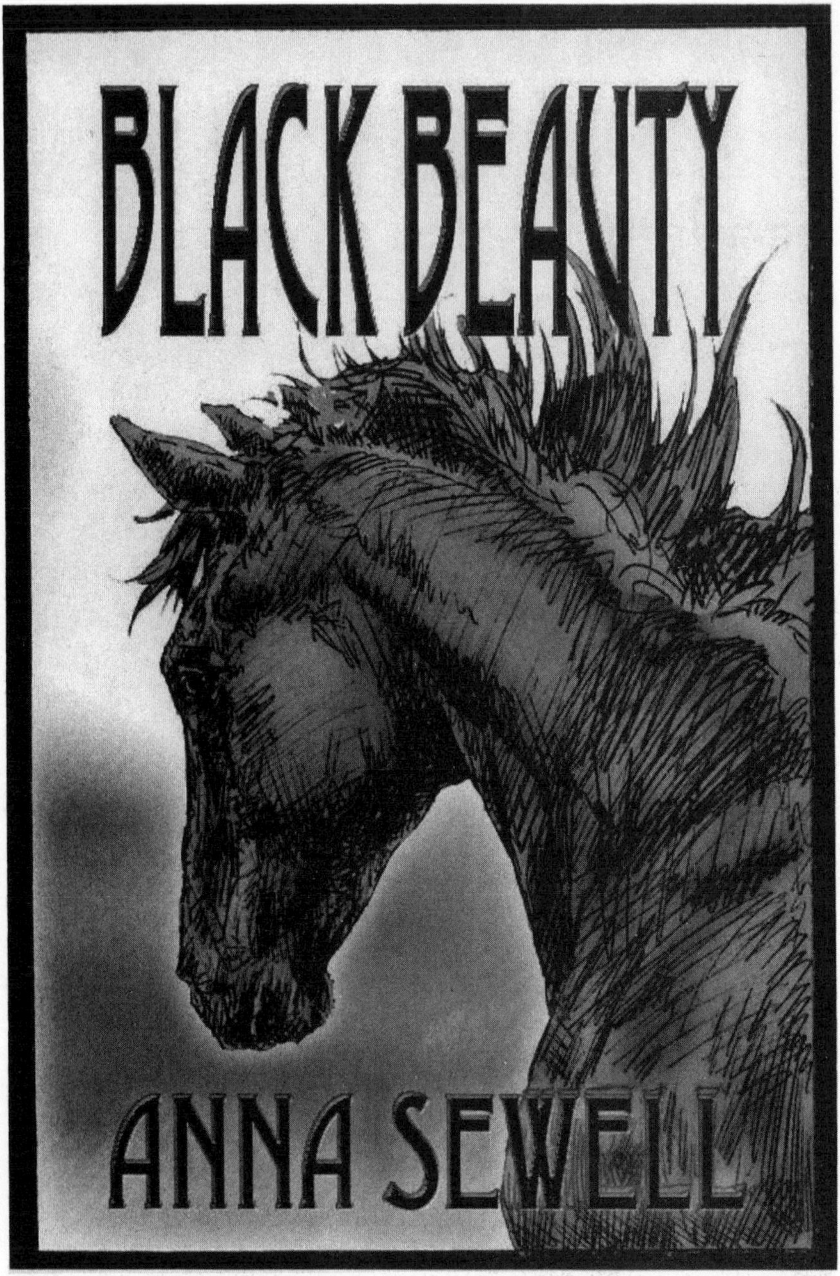
BLACK BEAUTY
ANNA SEWELL

Two of artist Bob Larkin's first concepts for the cover.

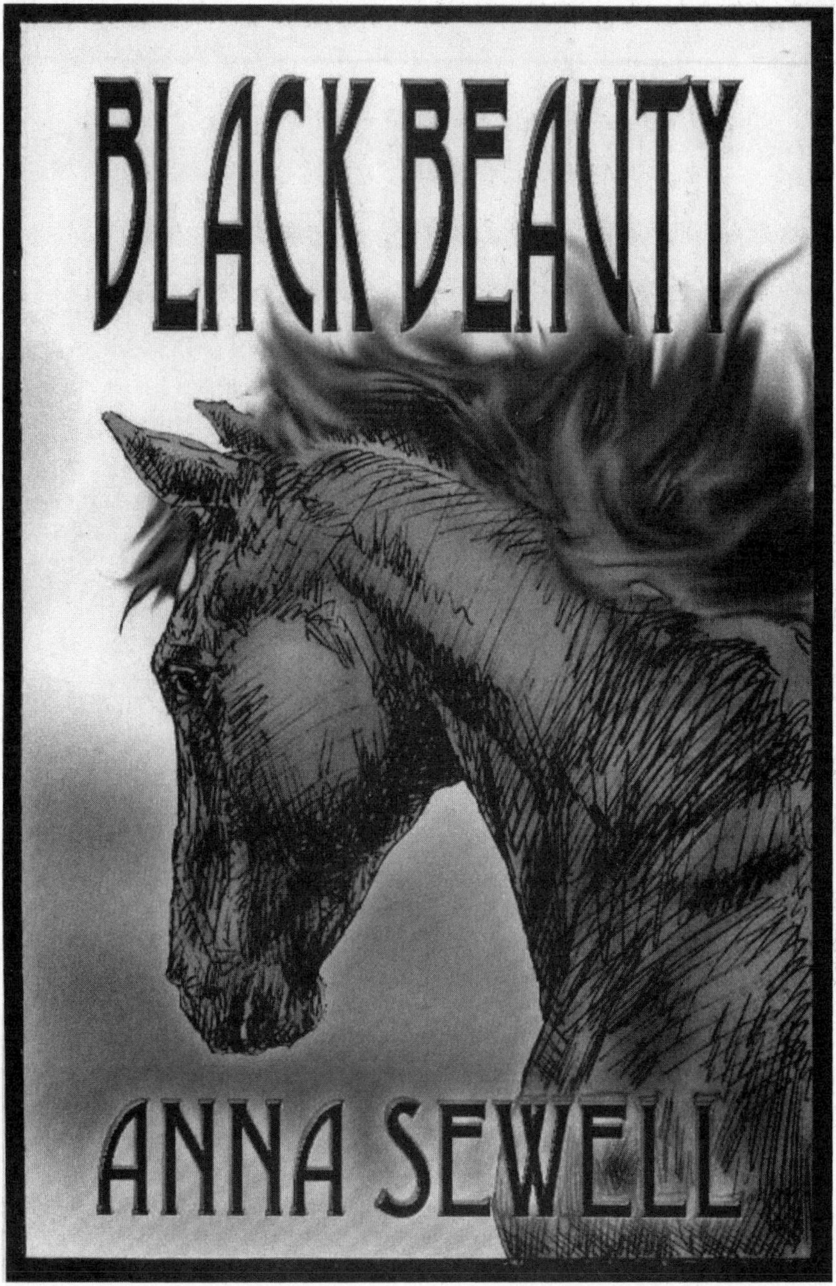
BLACK BEAUTY
ANNA SEWELL

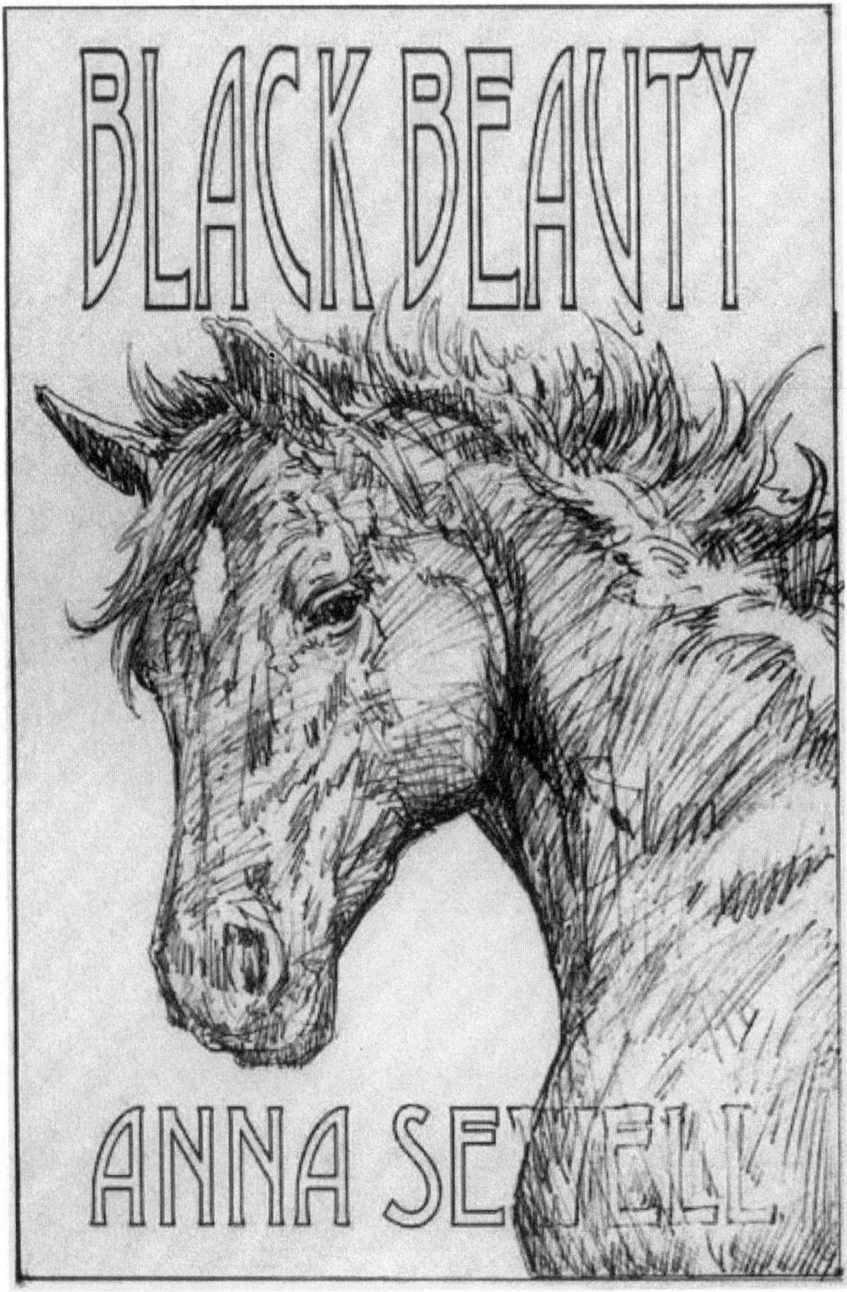
BLACK BEAUTY
ANNA SEWELL

Bob's second set of covers incorporating changes from the editors.

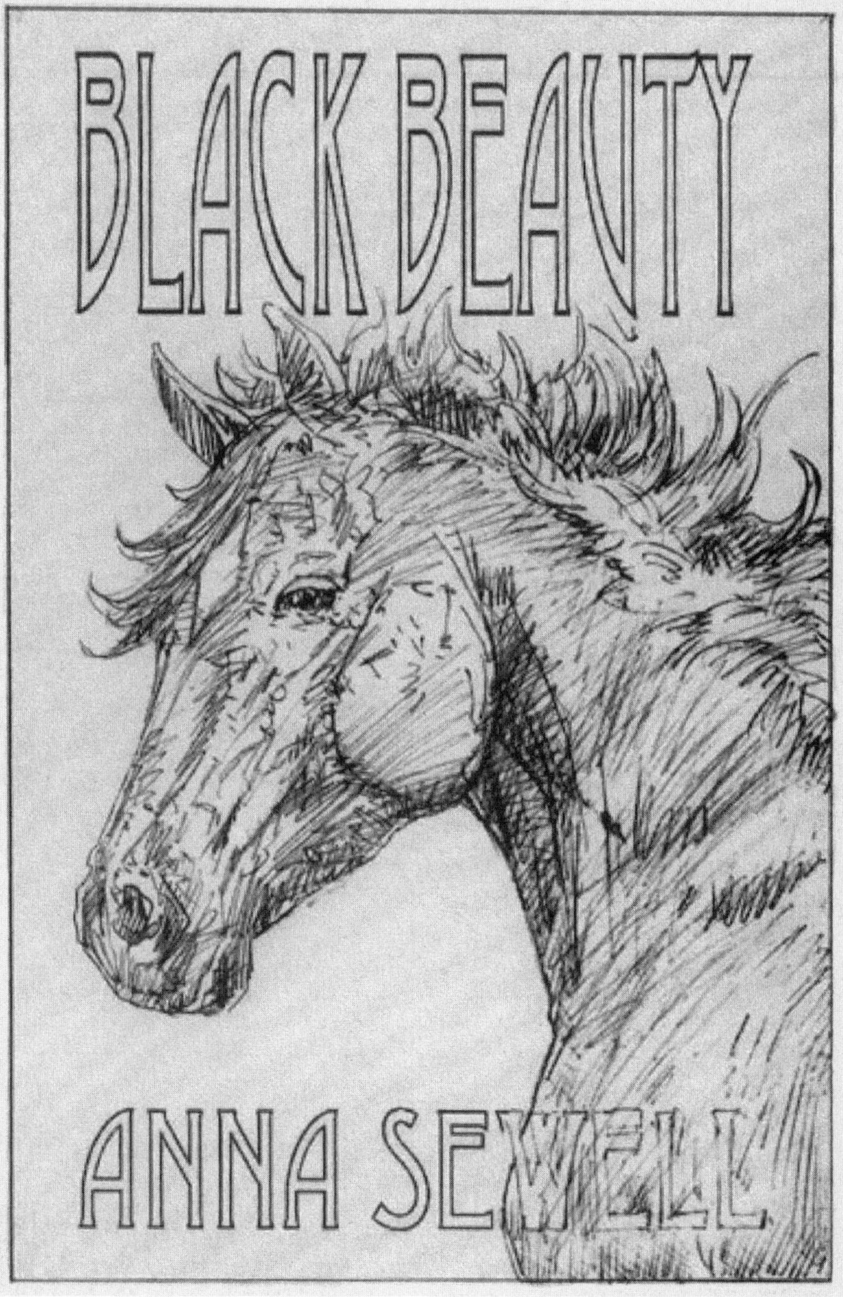
BLACK BEAUTY
ANNA SEWELL

HOW JUNE AND ROY WORK

Traditionally, two different artists, a penciler and an inker, create comics artwork. The penciler is an artist who does all the work with pencils. The inker then finishes the artwork applying India ink with brushes and pens over the pencil art.

June Brigman and Roy Richardson are a married artist team that have collaborated on many stories over the years. June draws with a No. 2 Ticonderoga pencil on Strathmore No. 500 Bristol board. Roy inks her pencils with a No. 102 Hunt crowquill pen and a Rafael No. 2 red sable watercolor brush using Universal India Ink.

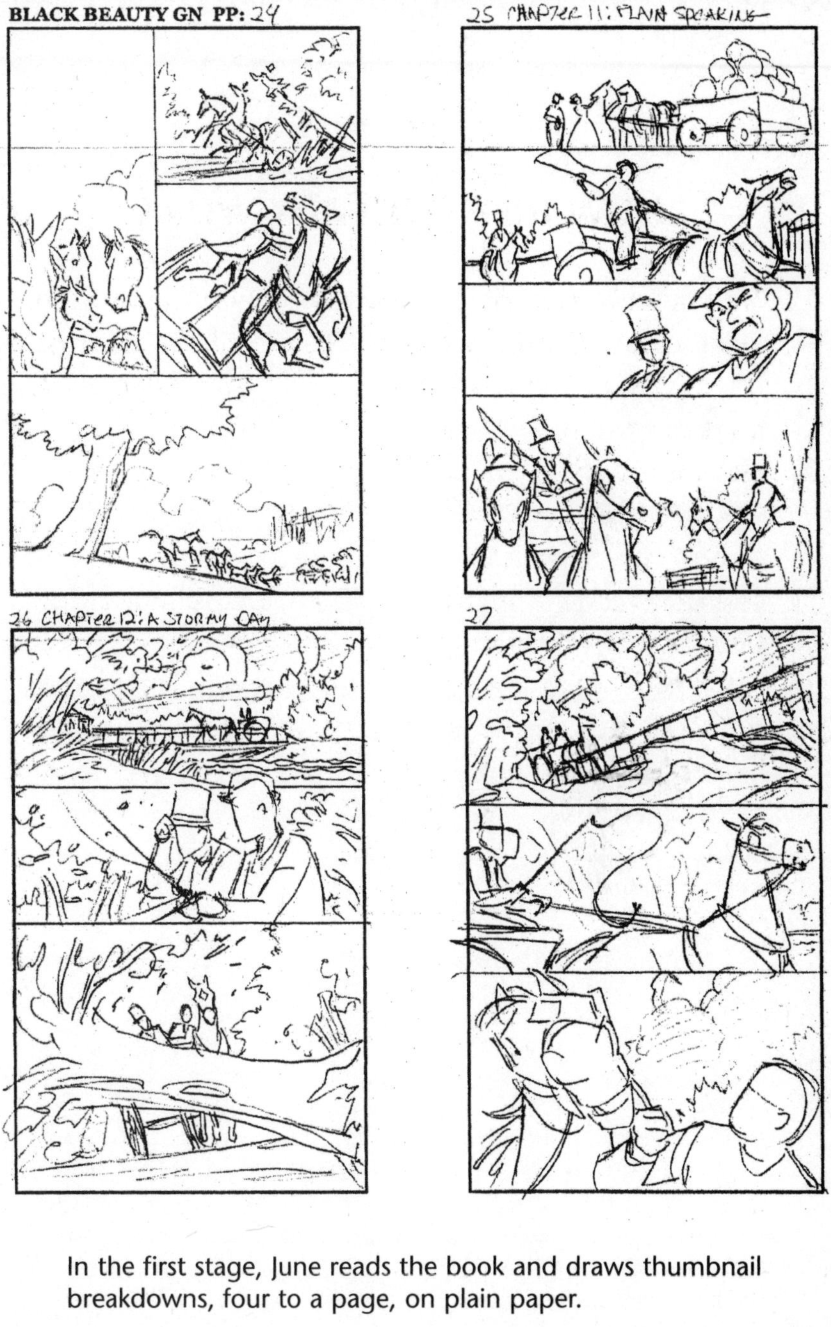
BLACK BEAUTY GN PP: 24
25 CHAPTER 11: PLAIN SPEAKING
26 CHAPTER 12: A STORMY DAY
27

In the first stage, June reads the book and draws thumbnail breakdowns, four to a page, on plain paper.

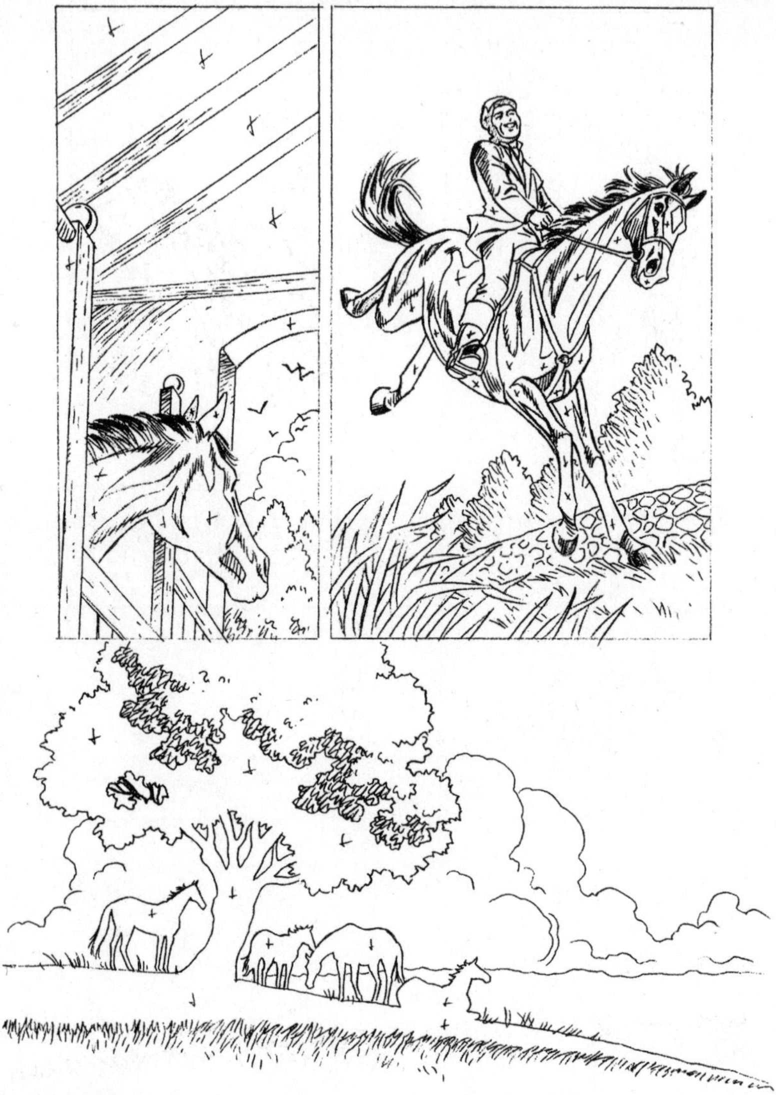

Next, June blows up each thumbnail on her computer to working size, and prints it out. Using an illuminated drawing table called a lightbox, traces the layout onto a sheet of Bristol, where she completes the finished drawing. June is surrounded with reference material to make sure she gets the time period just right. The small "x" marks are an instruction to the inker to fill the entire area with India ink.

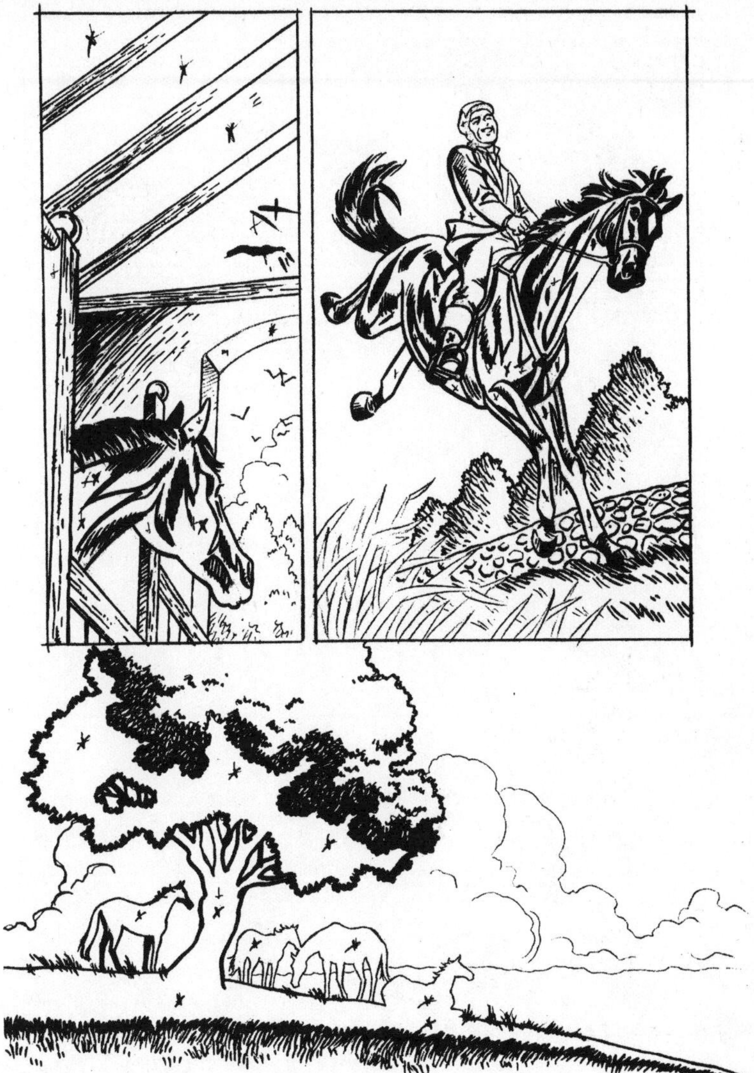

Here is a partially inked page. Note that approximately half of the areas marked with an "x" are now filled in. Roy inks several pages at a time, shuffling from one page to the next to give the ink a chance to dry, and to avoid smears. When he's finished, both Roy and June check the pages to make sure the details are correct.

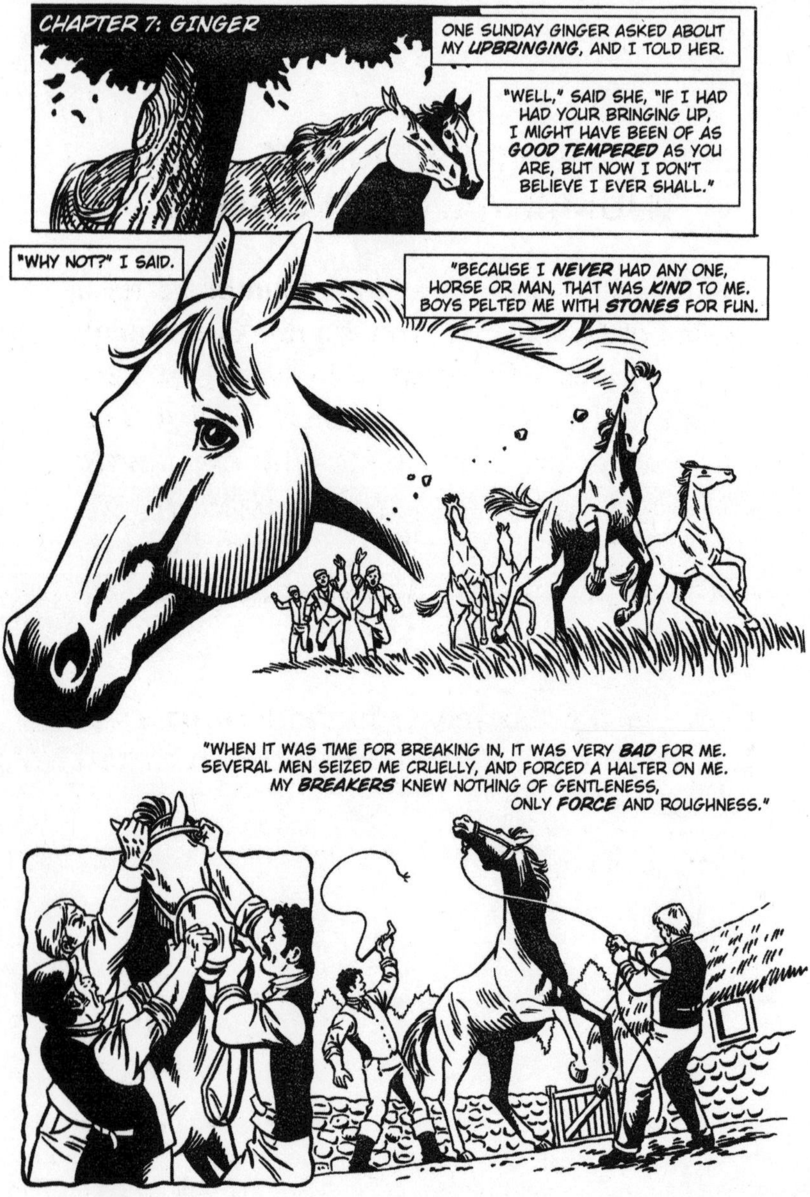
CHAPTER 7: GINGER
ONE SUNDAY GINGER ASKED ABOUT MY UPBRINGING, AND I TOLD HER.
"WELL," SAID SHE, "IF I HAD HAD YOUR BRINGING UP, I MIGHT HAVE BEEN OF AS GOOD TEMPERED AS YOU ARE, BUT NOW I DON'T BELIEVE I EVER SHALL."
"WHY NOT?" I SAID.
"BECAUSE I NEVER HAD ANY ONE, HORSE OR MAN, THAT WAS KIND TO ME. BOYS PELTED ME WITH STONES FOR FUN.
"WHEN IT WAS TIME FOR BREAKING IN, IT WAS VERY BAD FOR ME. SEVERAL MEN SEIZED ME CRUELLY, AND FORCED A HALTER ON ME. MY BREAKERS KNEW NOTHING OF GENTLENESS, ONLY FORCE AND ROUGHNESS."

A finished page showing the art with captions prior to final editing.

JUNE BRIGMAN'S
THUMBNAIL BREAKDOWNS

The following pages are June's thumbnails for a section of *Black Beauty*. This is a rare opportunity to see an artist's first draft of a story. These illustrations are known as "thumbnail breakdowns" because they are much smaller than the finished art. The purpose of this art is to establish both the pacing and the action. From this, the artist will then develop the finished art, making any necessary revisions along the way.

Compare the thumbnails to the final pages to find the differences. Note the spaces left for text balloons and captions.

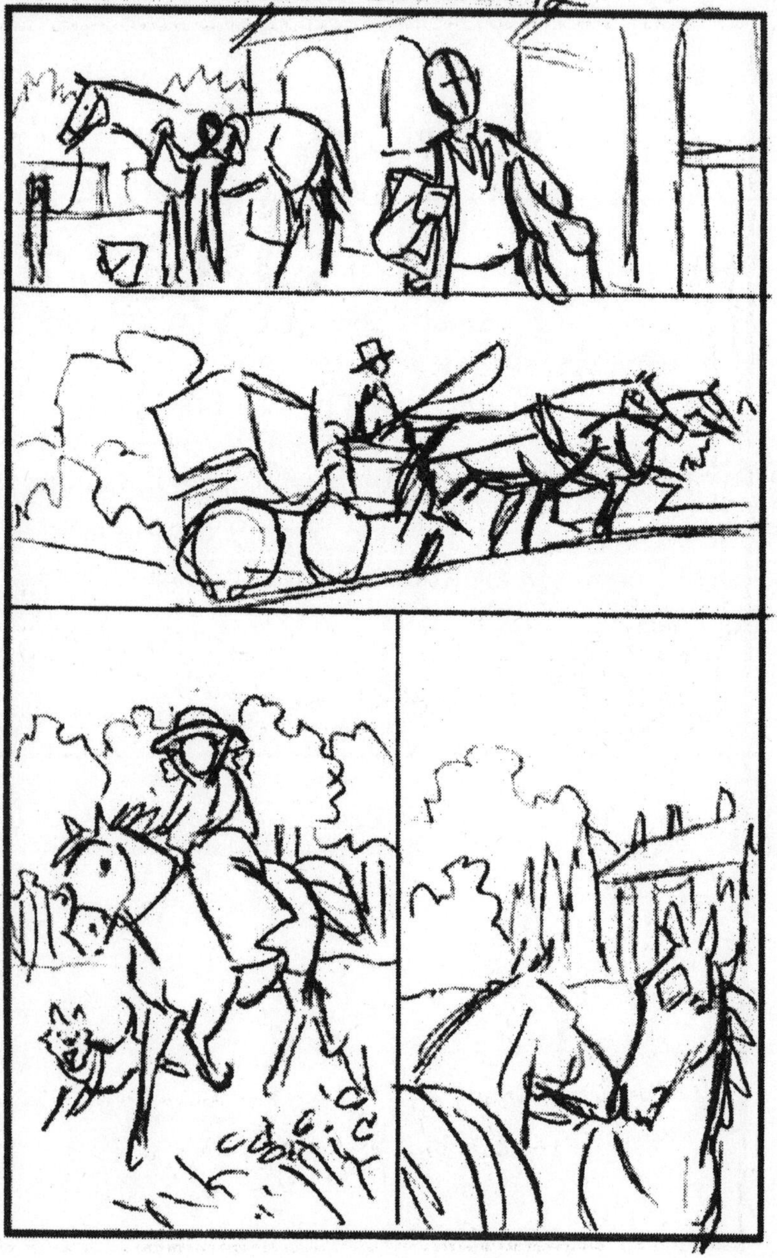

13 CHAPTER 6: LIBERTY

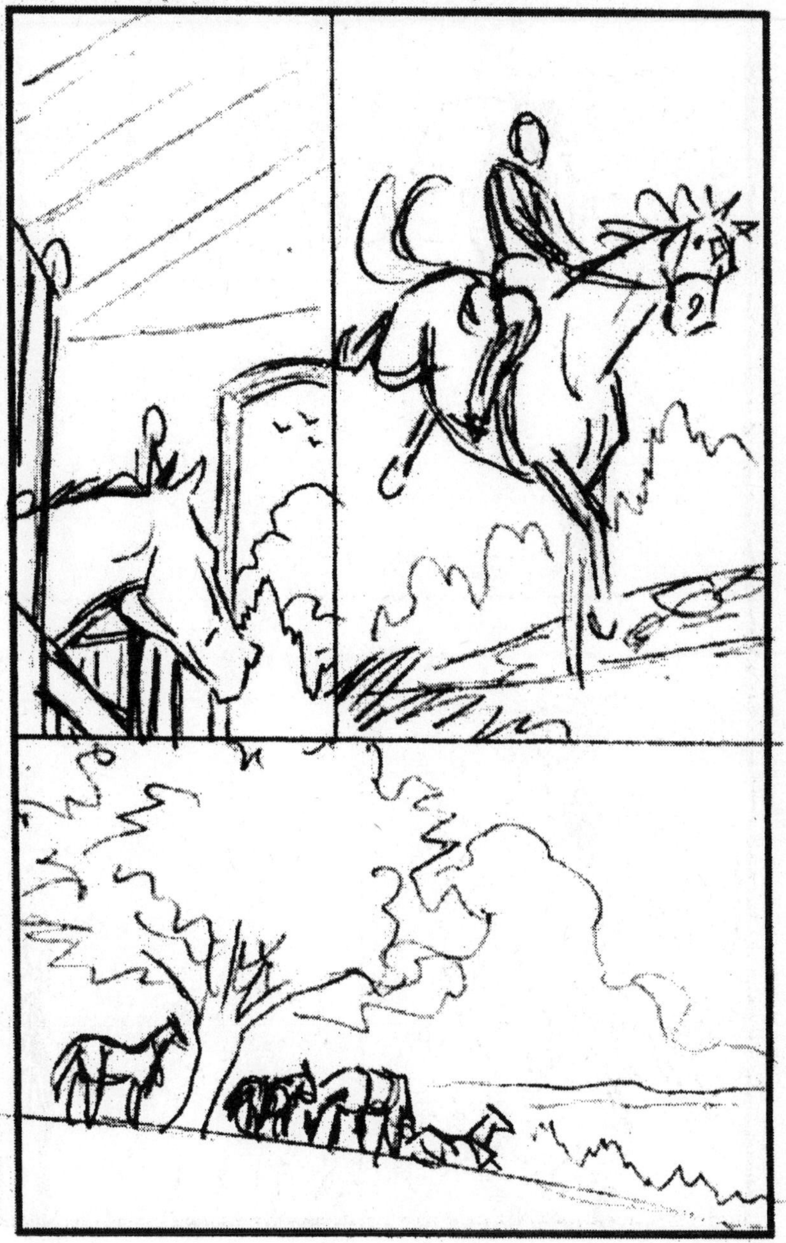

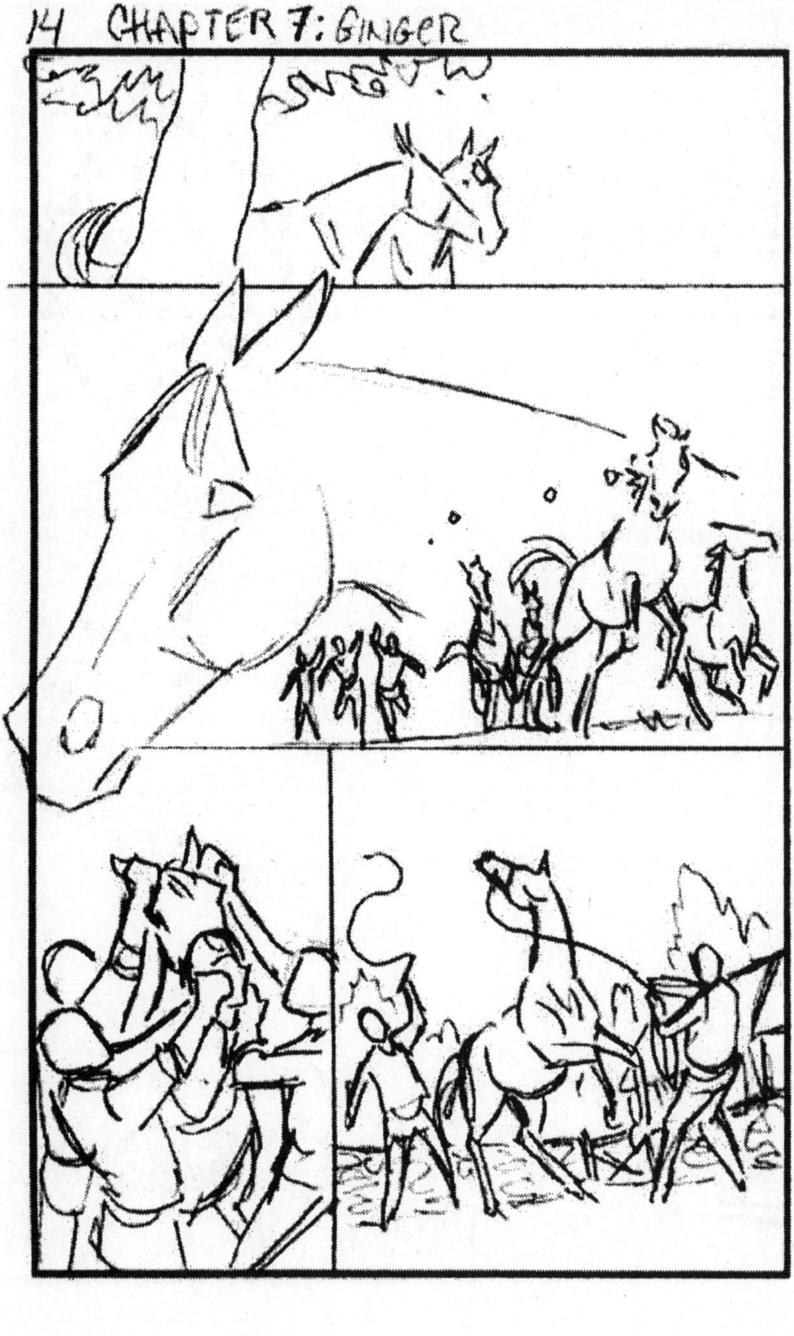
14 CHAPTER 7: GINGER

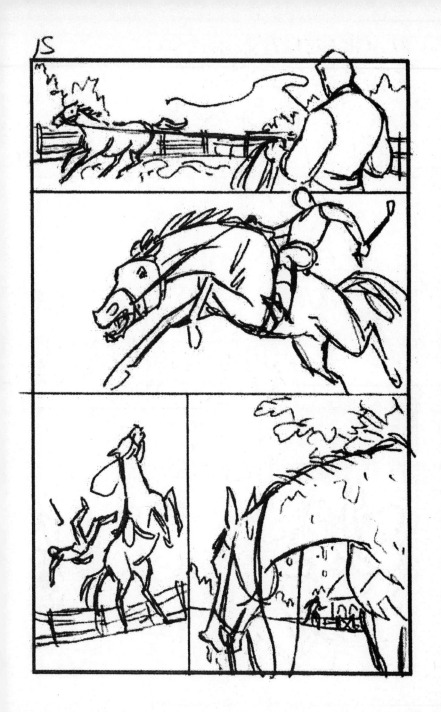

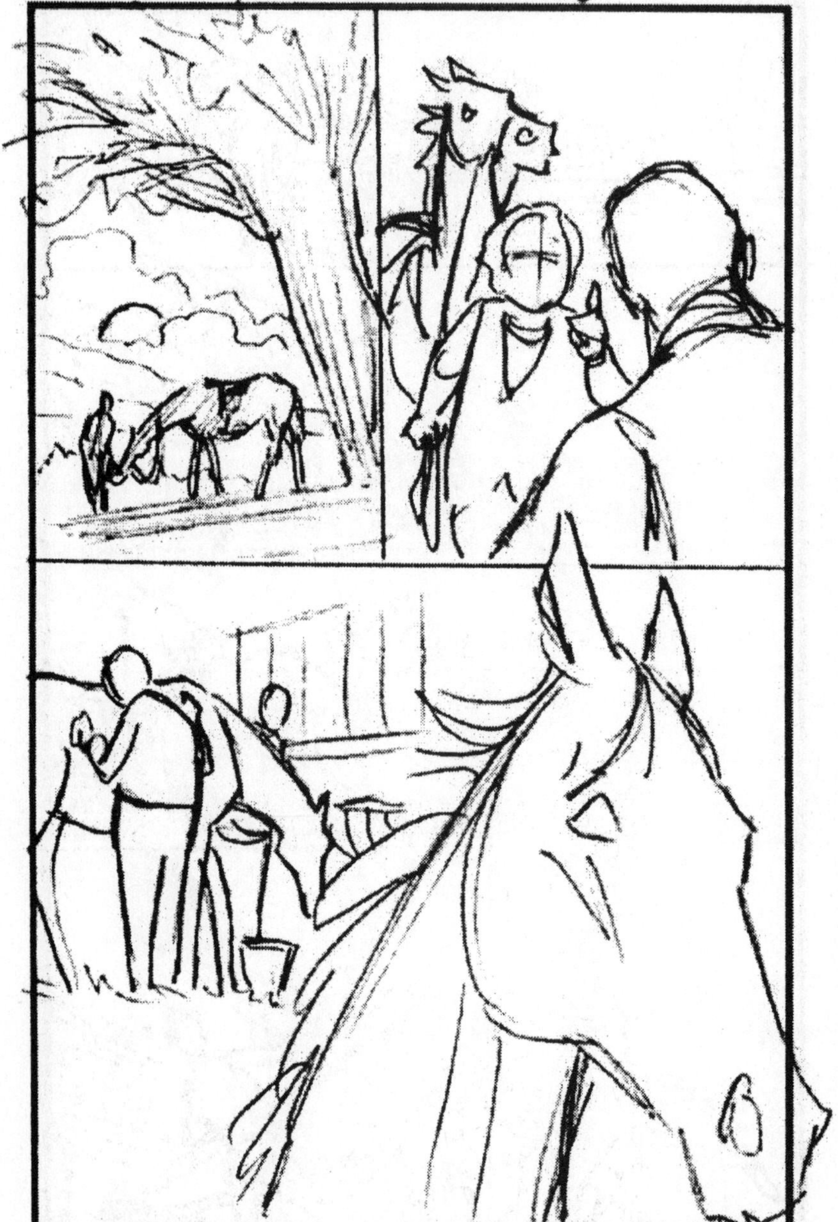

17 CHAPTER 8: GINGER'S STORY CONT.

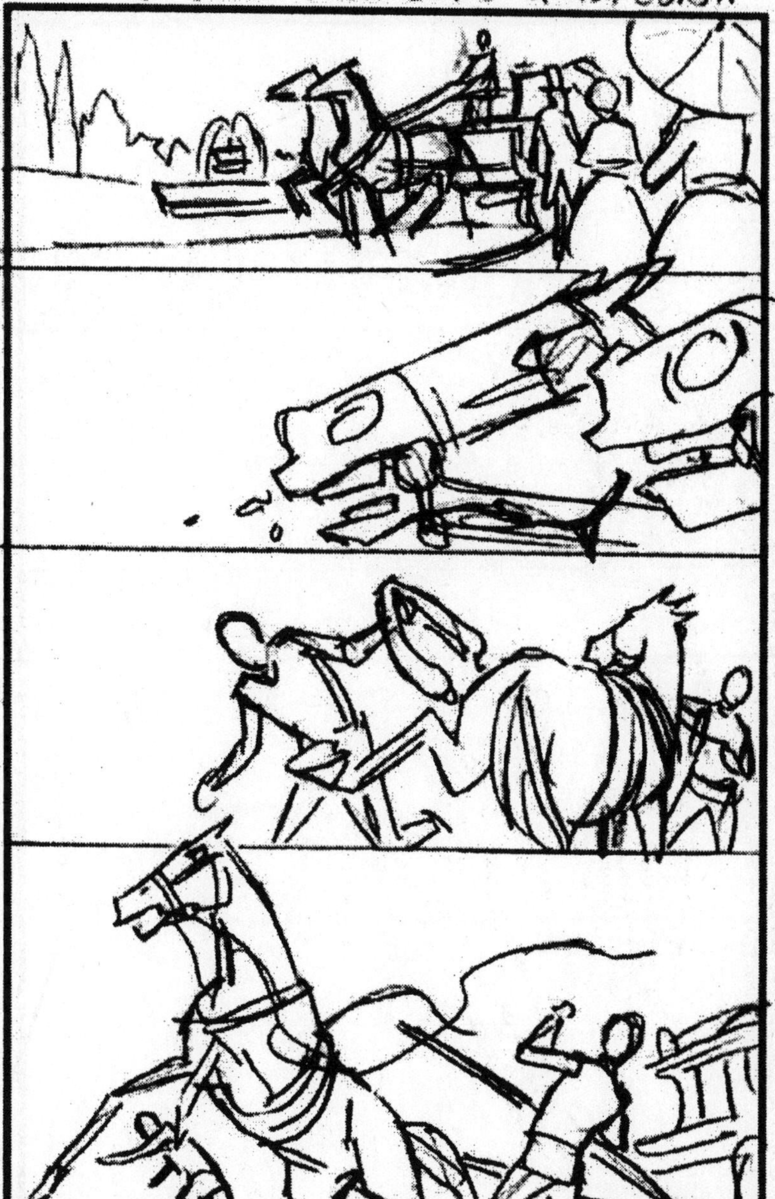

18

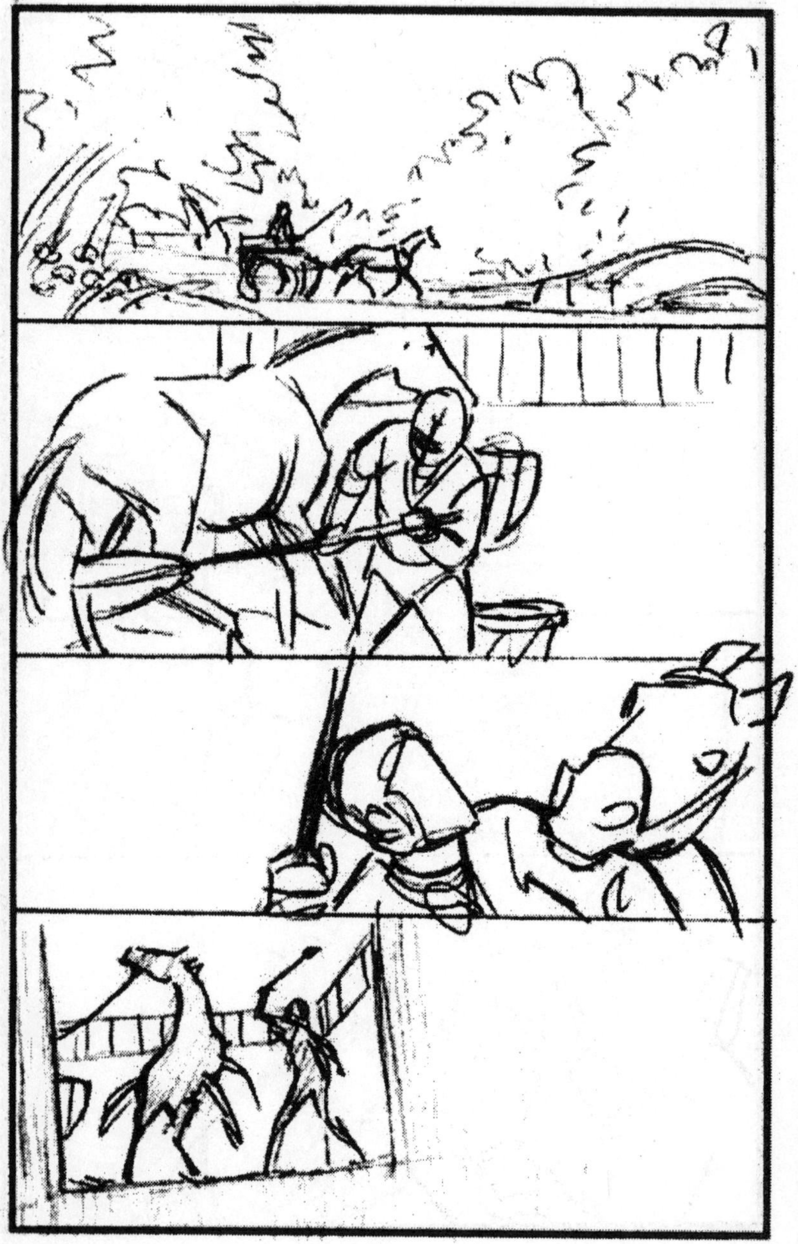

19

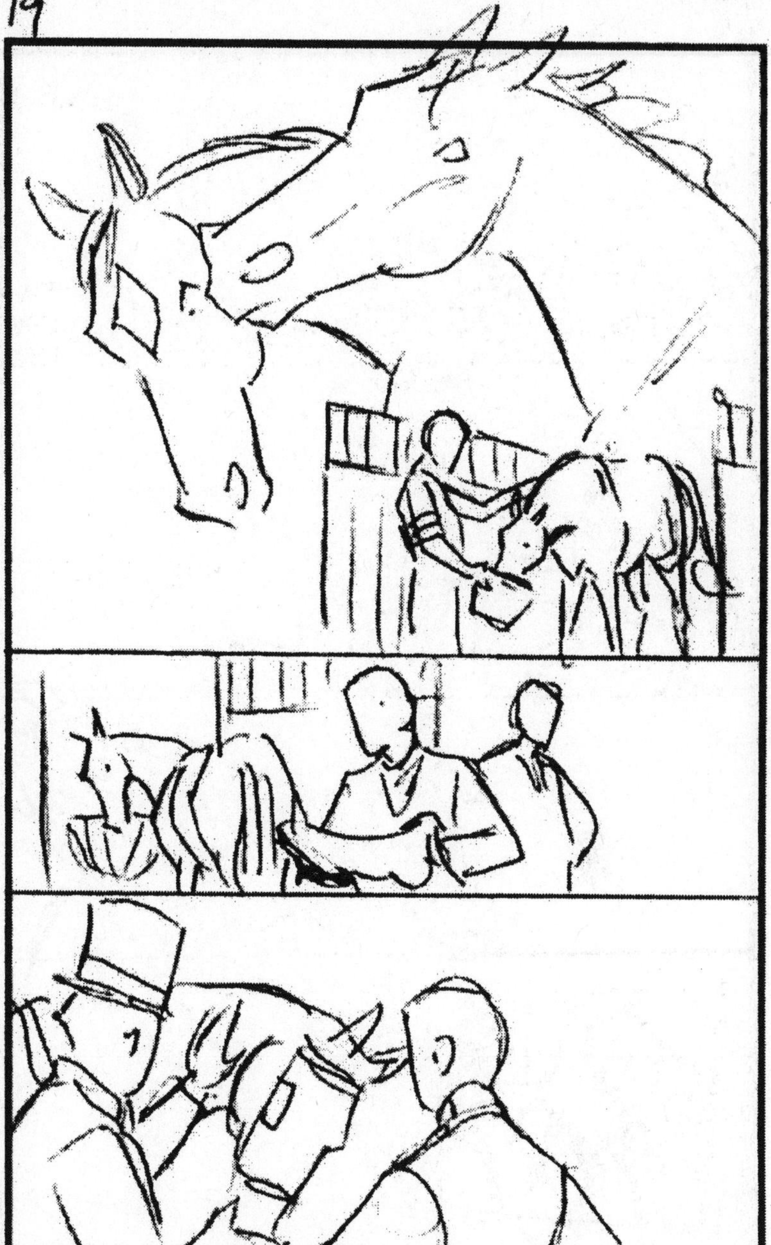

CHAPTER 9: MERRYLEGS

BLACK BEAUTY GN PP: 20

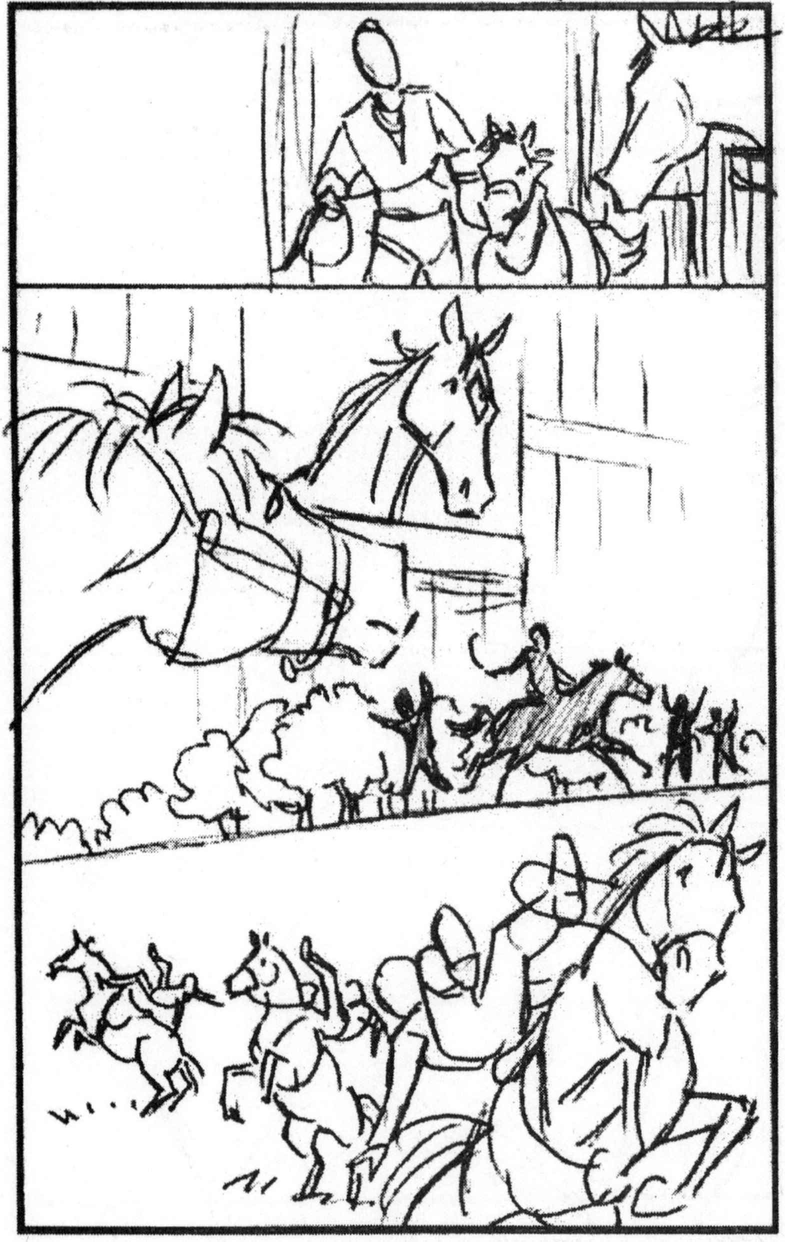

21

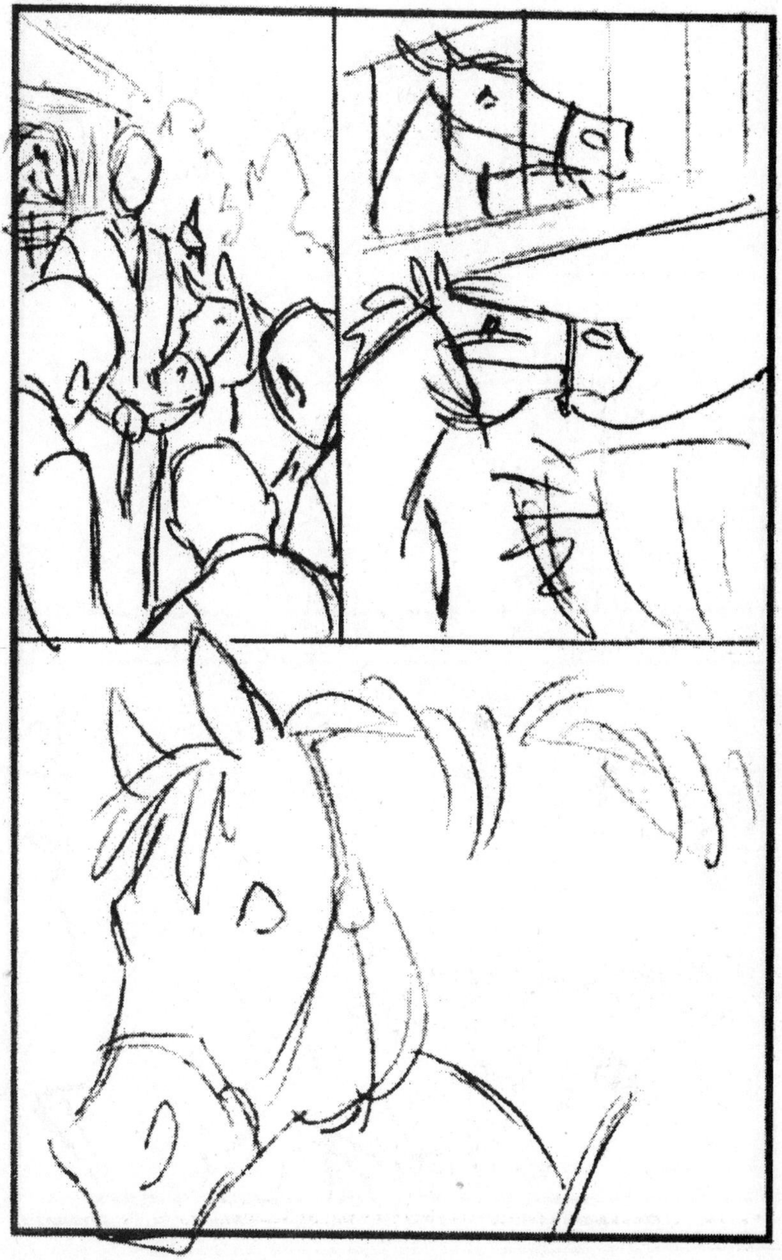

22 CHAPTER 10: A TALK IN THE ORCHARD

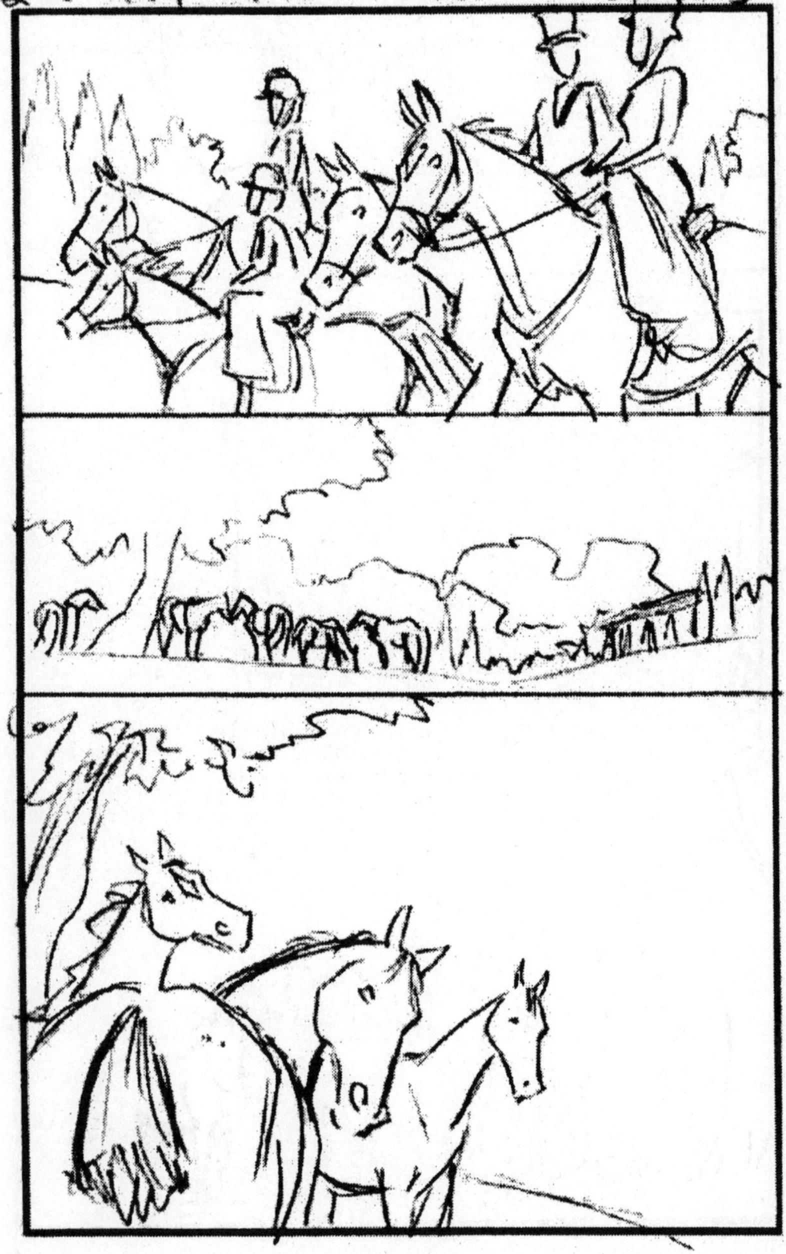

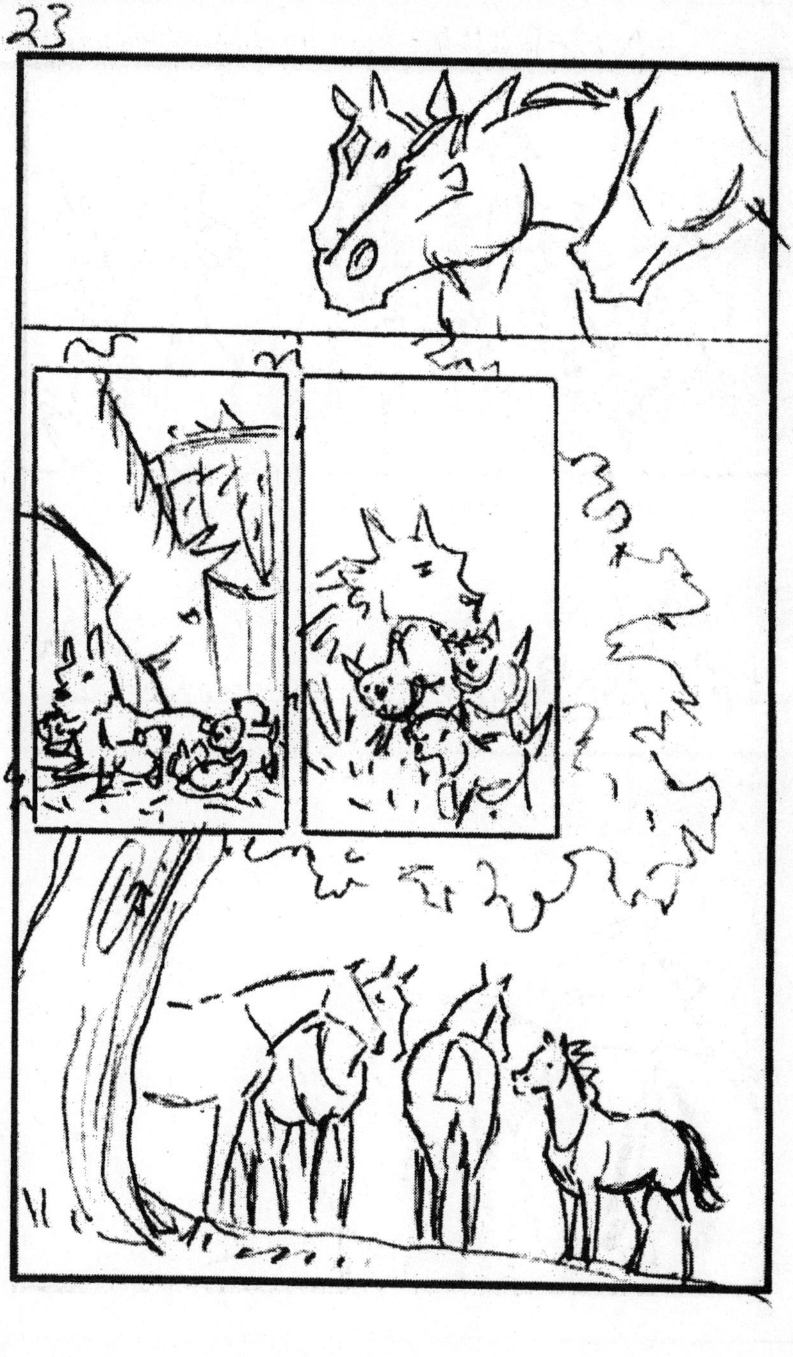
23

BLACK BEAUTY
GALLERY

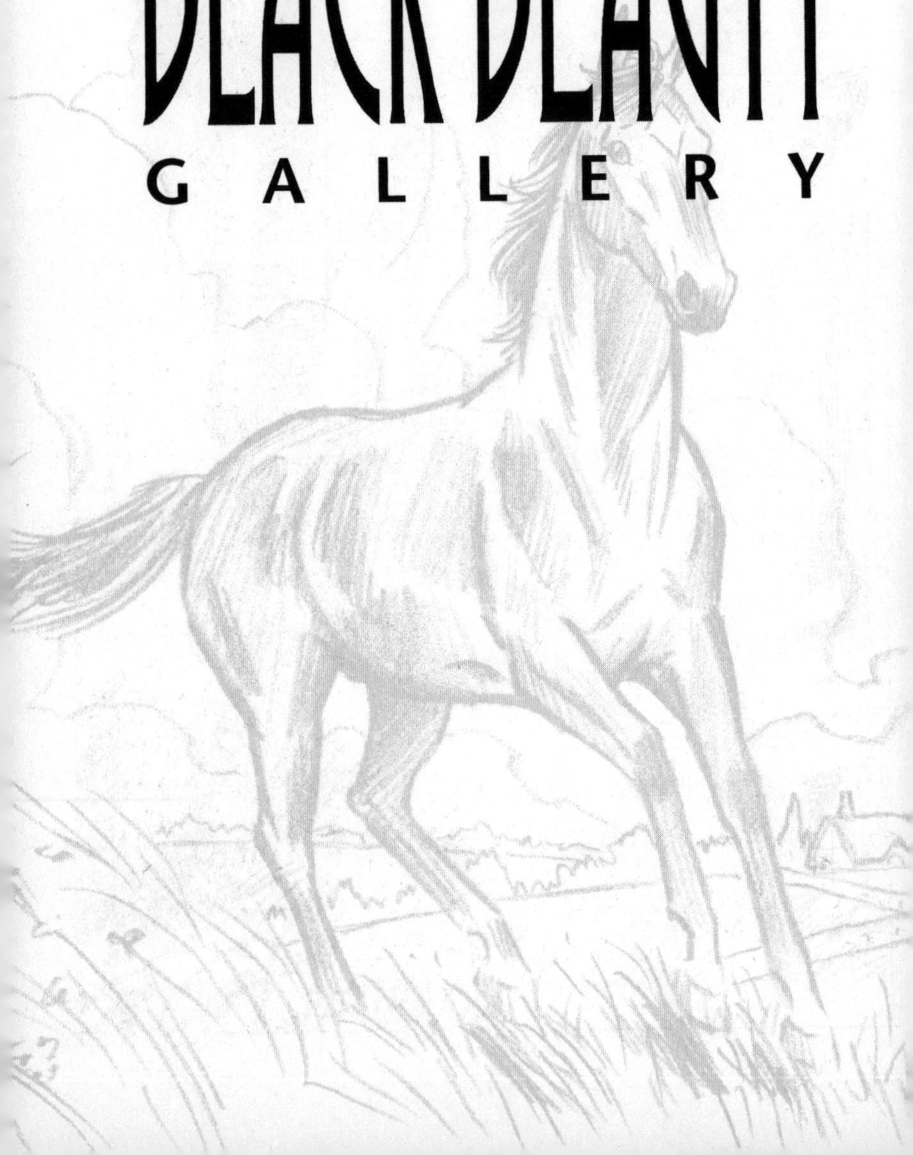

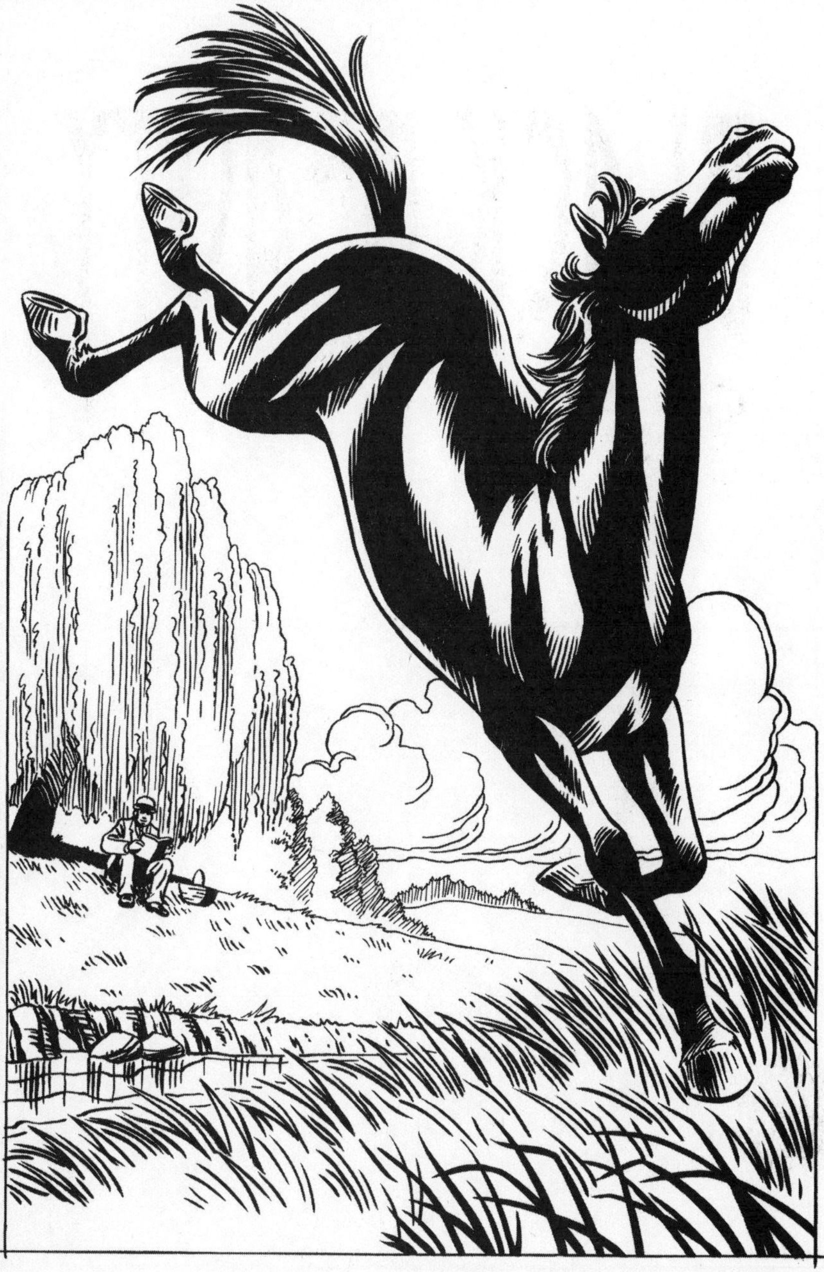

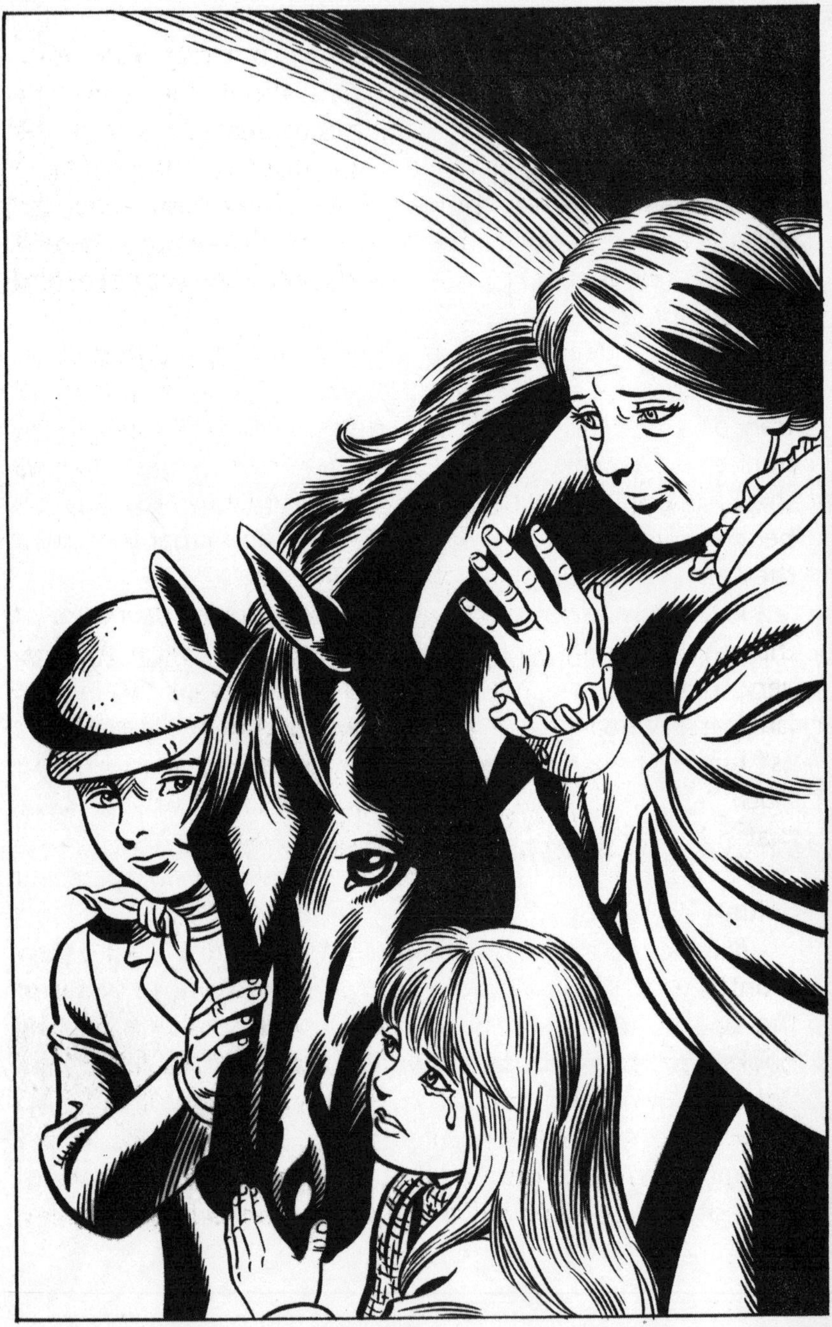

ANNA SEWELL (1820-78) was born in Great Yarmouth, Norfolk, England. When she was about fourteen, she sprained her ankle. Either the injury was treated badly, or she suffered from a degenerative bone disease, because Anna could never again walk properly. Out of her misfortune, the world—and especially the animal world—would benefit through a book that would forever change the way mankind treated animals.

In Anna's days, before the invention of the automobile, horses and one's own two feet were the main means of transport. Lacking the use of her feet, Anna relied heavily on horses to pull her around in a cart or trap. She grew to love them even more than she was naturally inclined to, and she became utterly appalled at the careless and cruel treatment they received at the hands of their owners.

In 1871, when Anna was fifty-one, a doctor pronounced that she had only eighteen months to live. While she was very weak, she was determined to write a book "to induce kindness, sympathy and an understanding treatment of horses" before she died. Five years later, she was still working on *Black Beauty*, her only book. By this time, she was so weak that not only could she not get out of bed, she could write only a few lines at a time. Her mother copied Anna's penciled writing.

Black Beauty was published in 1877. Anna died a few months after its publication, so she did not live to know of the book's huge success. Initially, it was sold not only by booksellers, but also distributed by campaigners for animal rights. It was instrumental in changing people's attitudes towards horses, and domestic animals in general. At Anna's funeral, her mother ordered that the uncomfortable bearing-reins should be removed from all the horses in the funeral train.

JUNE BRIGMAN, and her husband **ROY RICHARDSON**, have had a long career in the comic book field. June created the Power Pack series for Marvel Comics, the first to feature children as superheroes. June and Roy then went on to work for DC Comics on *Supergirl* and for Dark Horse Comics on the *Star Wars* comic series. They have done children's illustrations for the Bantam Doubleday Dell book *Choose Your Own Adventure*, the comic strip "Where In The World Is Carmen Sandiego?"™ for National Geographic *World* magazine, as well as *Star Wars* trading cards for Topps. June also was an artist on *Princess Diana: Once Upon A Dream*, the illustrated biography of the Princess of Wales. June and Roy currently draw the nationally syndicated comic strip *Brenda Starr* (uclick.com). They live in White Plains, New York.